WANT MORE FROM YOUR STORIES?

Sign up for a free no-spam newsletter and free short stories, exclusive secret chapters, and sneak peeks at books before they're published . . . all for free.

Details at the end of this book.

TO MARIA L.

Ever since I can remember, I've thought you were one of the kindest, most genuine people I've ever met. Basically, you set the standard for being the military wife I always dreamed of being.

You were the one responsible for hooking me on Indelible Grace music. You invited me into your home and entrusted me with your precious children, and you brought me the most practical wedding gift in the history of man. (And yes, the hubby does borrow the tools from time to time, just as you predicted.) But most of all, you've remained faithful to God through thick and thin.

Basically, I still want to be like you when I grow up. Thank you for remaining such a true friend all these years.

MY LITTLE ROCK AIRMAN

MY AIR FORCE FAIRY TALE BOOK #1

BRITTANY FICHTER

HOUSTON, WE ARE A GO

JESSIE

"Miss Nickleby, if I don't clean my room, will the tornado come gobble my house up like a cookie?" Nia stared up at me as she hugged her scrawny little legs to her chest.

"Like a cookie?" I echoed.

"Yeah." The little girl nodded. "My mom says a tornado came through my room because I didn't clean it up."

"My mom says the same thing!" the boy behind her piped. Several other students nodded.

"Oh, I see what you mean." I closed the book, using my thumb as a bookmark. "No, honey. That's just an expression. Real tornadoes don't happen in people's rooms. They're far too big. Remember," I wriggled my eyebrows at my kindergarteners and opened the book to point at one of the pictures inside, "tornadoes can't think. They're just bunches of water, heat, and wind all bundled together. So they can't punish you for not cleaning your rooms."

"My cat likes to hide under my bed when I don't clean my room," Elsie announced.

"My dog's name is Carlton," one of the boys called, which, of course, led to a chorus of pet-related declarations.

"I don't like dogs."

"But dogs are the best."

"I have a cat. But I want a dinosaur instead!"

I sighed and looked back down at the picture book. Well, halfway through was better than yesterday, when the class had lasted two whole pages before breaking into incomprehensible, random babble. But before I could bemoan the rocky ending of my last science unit, I realized four of the faces that should have been staring up at me weren't there at all. Having one of these boys missing at all spelled trouble. Missing four of them was incomprehensible. Especially on the last day of school.

I had just stood to look in earnest when I spotted them behind the miniature bookshelf in the math corner.

"Everyone, please go back to your tables and color the pictures I left for you on our weather unit. Blue shirts first." As soon as the children were more or less engaged, I approached the four boys standing in the corner, who were still giggling to themselves.

"May I ask what you're all doing?"

They all whipped around, looking terrified and then sheepish in turn.

"Well?" I pressed.

Finally, D'ante answered, though he stared at the ground the entire time.

"We put sand from the sandbox in our pants."

This should have been a shock. But, to my dismay, I realized it wasn't. "So..." I pinched the bridge of my nose. "Would you like to explain to me *why* you put sand in your pants?" *On the last day of school?* I wanted to add.

Joshua was crying by now, and D'ante at least had the sense to look embarrassed, but Alexander and Jose were still snickering at each other. And sure enough, below each of them sat a huge pile of sand all over the carpet I had just vacuumed. Twice.

"Jose said he could fit more in his underwear than any of us." Alexander grinned. "So we decided to see if he was right."

"One, two, three! Eyes on me!"

I looked up to see Madison waltz into the room, and I silently blessed my friend as the children chanted back, "One, two! Eyes on you!"

"Start putting away your centers and stand at your tables. When I call your shirt color, come sit down on your spot on the carpet." Madison called, shooing a few wandering kindergarteners back to their tables. "Show me how fast you can do it! Go! And you four." She came to stand beside me, crossing her arms and giving the four boys the stink-eye. "You'll be in first grade next year, and then I'll have you in my classroom." She leaned down and glowered at Jose and Alexander, who were still poking one another and giggling. They stopped, however, when she was inches away, giving them her most withering look. "And if you do something like this again, I'll have your parents here so fast you won't know what happened. Understand?"

Three of the boys nodded, but Jose piped, "My dad's deployed. You can't call him!"

Madison gave him her most evil grin, and I nearly laughed as he took a step back. "Just watch me," she whispered.

His smile disappeared, and his eyes grew to the size of sand dollars.

Madison turned to the others. "Now go back to your tables until I call you."

"You," I said as the boys scampered off, "are a lifesaver."

"What's wrong with you?" Madison hissed. "You don't do centers on the last day of school!"

"But—"

"Honey, this may be your first rodeo, but believe me, the last day of school is not for learning. It's for the kids to junk out on movies while you clean your little heart out so you can check out of your classroom as fast as possible." Madison grabbed the broom and dustpan from the corner and began to sweep as though she swept an entire bin of sand off the carpet every day. But then, she'd been teaching for longer than me, so she probably had.

"They've watched movies twice this week," I protested weakly. "I didn't want to give them a third one."

"If you want to keep them busy, have them throw away markers that don't work, or have contests to see who can find the most glue stick caps. But good grief! Don't give them anything that they can twist into a weapon to use against you." She looked up at the children, half of whom were under or on top of the tables.

"All right," I called, "I want the red shirts to go to the carpet."

"What movies do you have?"

I went to my desk and grabbed three DVDs I'd picked up at the library. Madison cringed when I held them out.

"Really?" She shook her head. "They didn't have a single cartoon?"

"Weather was our last science unit." I sniffed. "It's not going to kill them to have their lessons reinforced."

"So you picked tornadoes."

"Hey, these things are dangerous."

Madison rolled her eyes, but I was undeterred.

"You might not realize that because you've lived here all your life. But for us newbs…" I poked my friend with the DVD case, "these are the best safety videos for kids that I've ever seen."

"You've lived here since high school. You're not a newb."

"I don't watch tornadoes from my porch with a glass of sweet tea. I'm hiding in the basement. With all the sane people."

Madison paused then grinned. "You're right. You're a newb." She went back to sweeping, and I turned on the movie then jumped into stuffing piles of paper into the kids' take-home folders.

Once the children were all, more or less, seated on the carpet and watching the movie, Madison finished sweeping then helped me take posters off the walls and stack the chairs in record time. Finally, I was able to step back and breathe a sigh of relief. All but one of the bulletin boards were clear of everything, even their background cloth, and the crayon trays were finally empty. Cleaning the classroom might actually get done.

"Do you think I could leave this up over the summer?" I stared up at my beautiful butcher paper castle, the one that stretched from the floor to the ceiling with little windows all over it to showcase student artwork. Its pink and blues were a bit faded, but I still thought the nine-foot "monstrosity" (as Sam Newman called it) was pretty.

"I wouldn't." Madison grimaced at it. "If they decide to change your classroom mid-summer, you'll have to beat whoever gets the room back next to take it down. And believe me, you're not going to be in a hurry to end your summer break that way."

I sighed a little, but she was right. So with a heavy heart, I took the last piece of my first year of teaching off the wall.

We were struggling to move the broken overhead cart as the bell signaled the final fifteen minutes of the day.

"Where are your kids?" I asked as we shoved the cart into the corner.

"DeBaux's got them in her room watching a movie. I thought you might need help, and she volunteered to take them. Hey, before I go,"

Madison glanced back at the clock, "there's someone I want you to meet." Her blue eyes danced.

"So that's what this was about." I put my hands on my hips. "I told you, I'm not going on any more of your double dates."

The bell rang again, and Madison's grin just grew. She arched one perfectly shaped eyebrow. "Don't think you're being saved by the bell. I'll swing by to finish this conversation after my kids are all gone."

I waved dismissively at my friend, but after she left, I didn't have time to mull. There were backpacks to hand out, dozens of stacks of papers, art projects, and supplies to send home, and a final goodbye to say to my kinderbabies before seeing them again next fall.

That part was harder than I'd expected it to be. My eyes stung as I smiled at each of my students as they gave me goodbye hugs. Even Jose, who had seemed to think it his sole purpose to make me gray at the ripe old age of twenty-three, cried and clung to my legs, his mother trying desperately to pull him off. I knelt in front of him and he threw himself into my arms, and I rubbed the little boy's back as he sobbed into my shoulder.

"I don't want to go, Miss Nickleby!" he wailed.

"Hey, now," I said, sharing a knowing look with his mother, "Doesn't your dad come home this—"

But his mother vehemently began to shake her head, and I let the words die on my tongue. With them, my heart fell.

Jose's mother leaned down and whispered in my ear. "My husband's deployment was extended."

Again? I mouthed, to which Jose's mother only nodded.

I sighed and forced a smile as I pulled back to gaze at the miserable little guy. "You'll have a great summer." I tapped his nose. "I'll bet you won't even want to come back to school next fall."

Jose kept sniffling, but the tears at least stopped. "My dad is sending me a new video game in the mail. Mom says I can play it when I finish my reading in the mornings."

"Well, there you go." I gave him one last hug and watched them go.

A slow clap sounded behind me. "Well, congratulations."

I turned and laughed when Sam Newman emerged from his classroom, which was to my right.

"So," he said, his hazel eyes bright, "you survived your first year. Congratulations."

"Thanks." I grinned back. "They gave me a run for my money, but..." I looked around. "I kind of can't believe it's already over."

He snorted. "Just wait until you have five years under your belt."

"Not even you have five years." I knelt to stack the homework bins in the entryway of my classroom.

"I have enough years to know summer is best celebrated with a drink and other teachers."

I laughed. "So you can commiserate before launching into more discussions about your students?"

He nodded. "Naturally." Then he leaned forward, his sandy blond hair falling slightly over his eyes. "If I did, could I count you in?"

"We're done!"

We both looked up to see Madison launch herself out of her own room straight toward me, two stainless steel thermoses in hand. "Who wants to share some juice?"

"That's juice?" I asked, studying the stainless steel thermoses.

Sam took one and opened one of the thermos lids to sniff it. Then his eyes got big. "Madison, is this what I think it—"

"Sh!" Madison elbowed him. "It's got fruit in it. Ergo, juice."

"And a little bit of something else for on the way down," Sam muttered under his breath.

"Actually," I nodded back at the little figure huddled in front of a computer in the corner. "I've still got one left. And I'm going to disinfect the mat while I wait for her mom."

"Well, your loss." Sam shrugged dramatically before winking and walking down the hall. The hall was mostly clear of parents and students by now, so I waved Madison inside as I got down on my hands and knees with the Lysol wipes on the foam mat.

"Isn't she always here late?" Madison snatched a pretzel from my secret stash.

"Her mom works over in North Little Rock." I pitched my voice lower. "She has a hard time getting up here on time to pick her up."

"Well, I hope her teacher next year is as patient as you are. Oh, but the reason I came over!" Madison's eyes lit up again. "A week from Thursday! Donny's Bar! Seven o'clock!!"

"Madison, I'm not sure I want another one of your dates."

"But Jessie! He's a captain!" She pouted. "And Jason was nice!"

"He was."

"So were Matthias and Jackson!"

"They were." I scrubbed at a stubborn spot. "But every single one was the one thing I told you I'm not interested in dating."

"Oh, come on!" Madison sat in the middle of my desk, right on the clipboard I'd been trying to find. "Jessie, you live in Jacksonville, Arkansas. You teach at the school just off Little Rock *Air Force Base*. Who around here *isn't* on active duty? You never know who might turn out to be that Prince Charming you're always dreaming about."

"Prince Charming had a horse, not a cargo plane."

"You're right. Because a huge flying machine capable of killing bad guys is such a turn-off when compared to a horse."

I stuck my tongue out. "You're not changing my mind."

"What's not to like?" Madison began counting on her fingers. "They've got steady jobs. They have health insurance." She paused. "Hey, those are two of the items on your rule list." She began to count on her fingers. "They've all had some sort of background check. Clean-shaven. Have basic practical life skills. Girl, if you could kick that first rule, your dating sea would be *so* much wider."

"We have health insurance through the school district."

"They work out for a living, and they wear uniforms. Very attractive ones at that." Madison put her hands on her hips. "I dare you to find something not ideal about at least dating an airman."

"Um, two things." I heaved a stack of books into a box. "Called deployment and moving."

Madison groaned dramatically. "Going on one date with an airman doesn't mean you're tied to him for the rest of your life."

I gave my friend a knowing smile. "You also forget that I don't date for fun."

"Don't you want a man of some sort eventually?"

"Of course I do. But I want to find someone to settle down with. Down being the keyword. Not up and moving every two or three years." I held up a hand as Madison began to protest. "And as much as I love you, these one-time dates at the karaoke bar aren't showing much potential."

"What about Sam?" Madison jerked her chin back at the door then grinned. "He digs you."

"He does not!" I hissed, but I was laughing, too. "And keep your voice down! I don't want things to get weird next year if I have to teach next to him again! Besides, I'm hopefully not going to have time for lots of dating in the near future."

"Oh, come on. He stops over here all the time."

"He needed a stapler."

"And tape. And a ruler. The guy's been teaching for four years. There's no way he's *that* forgetful."

I paused. Unfortunately, Madison was making sense. I hadn't thought much about it before, but Sam did stop by my room a lot. Still, I shook my head.

"If he wants to ask me out, he'll have to do it the old fashioned way."

"What? By bringing your father a goat?"

I gave her a look, and she snickered.

"He's going to have to actually ask me out. None of this hinting business. Besides, I've got bigger fish to fry." I stopped packing and pulled an envelope out of my desk drawer. Handing it to my friend, I tried to keep the triumphant smile off my face.

Madison took the letter out and scanned its contents, her face lighting up. "You got into grad school?"

I nodded happily. "Now all I have to do is save a little more, and I'll be ready to go!"

"This is awesome!" Madison paused. "But you're sure you want to do more school? Aren't you still paying off your first round?"

I took a deep breath. "I paid off my degree a month ago, actually. And I've given it a lot of thought. I want to study speech therapy. Here, want some?" I grabbed a bag of goldfish crackers off my filing cabinet and held it out. After Madison had taken some, I went over to the little girl playing on the computer and set a napkin down beside her. "Do you want some goldfish, Jade?"

Jade immediately shook her head, her eyes glued to the matching game on the screen. But then she seemed to reconsider and glanced at the bag again.

"That's what I thought." I chuckled as I poured a little pile of crackers on the napkin.

"I'm here! I'm here! And I'm so sorry I'm late!"

I looked up to see Jade's mother come flying through the door. Her graying blond hair stuck out from her hair twist in several places, and her work slacks were wrinkled.

"It started raining on my way over, and traffic got all backed up on the sixty-seven."

"I'll talk to you later," Madison called, sliding off my desk and heading for the door. "But don't think I've forgotten about Thursday!" she called back with an evil grin before disappearing through the door.

I held back the smart retort I wanted to call after her and instead straightened and smiled at Jade's mother.

"Hi, Mrs. Allen."

"Congratulations on finishing your first year." Mrs. Allen looked around the room. "It sure looks different in here."

"We have to take everything down so the janitors can give everything a final cleaning for the summer. Here, let me get you her things." I turned and tapped the little girl on the shoulder. "Come on, Jade. Get your backpack, please."

"No." Jade hunched closer to the screen.

I was about to correct her when Mrs. Allen touched my shoulder. "Actually," she said in a low voice, "I'd like to talk to you about something first if you don't mind."

"Of course." I indicated to my semi-circle kidney table then immediately regretted it when I remembered that it was the proper height for kindergarteners. But Mrs. Allen sat without complaining and folded her hands in her lap.

"As you know, my husband and I have our own company," she began, playing with the zipper on her Louis Vuitton bag. "This will be our first summer without year-round preschool, and we're not sure what to do with her."

I frowned. "I thought her nanny was taking care of her over the summer."

"Oh, she was going to, but she got married unexpectedly and moved two days later. It was a shock for all of us."

"I can only guess." I looked back at Jade. "What are you going to do?"

"Actually, and I hope this isn't too bold," Mrs. Allen said slowly, "my husband and I were hoping you could help us."

I couldn't keep the surprise from my voice. "Me?"

Mrs. Allen nodded. "My son, Derrick, just moved back here, and he's living with us right now so he can help with her in his time off. But he works night shift currently, so we need someone to care for her and take her to her therapies during the day while he gets caught up on rest."

"I'm honored," I said, racking my brain for reasons to accept or deny. "But if you don't mind me asking, why me?"

"Most people, even at special nanny services like the one we use, don't understand Down Syndrome. Jade loves you, and you're familiar with her. It would take a new nanny several weeks to adjust even if she understood Jade's basic needs. And you wouldn't have to worry about needing time to get ready for school when next year comes around again. We would give you whatever professional days off that you needed." Mrs. Allen began to dig in her purse. She pulled out a blue envelope and handed it to me. "We would pay you, of course. That would be your salary per week. And if it isn't enough, we could always work something out."

When I realized Mrs. Allen meant for me to open the envelope, I did so. And when I read the amount on the check, I nearly fell off my chair.

"This is per week?" I gaped.

"If it's not enough—"

"Oh, it's not that!" I tore my eyes from the check to look back at Mrs. Allen. "I'm just...surprised. In a good way." I grinned. "Thank you for the opportunity. I would love to stay with Jade this summer."

Mrs. Allen fairly glowed as she stood. "I was hoping you'd say that. Here's our address." She handed me a business card then paused. "But you being with her all summer...that's not going to cause you trouble with your boss or anything, is it?"

I shrugged. "I'll double-check, but a lot of teachers tutor over the summer. So this should be fine."

"Could you come on...let's see. It's May twenty-seventh today, so two days from now would be the twenty-ninth. How about Thursday the twenty-ninth? Maybe around nine? I'll be taking that day off, so I can show you around the house and get her therapy information all sorted out."

"I'll be there." I stood as well and shook Mrs. Allen's hand. "And thank you again...so much." I couldn't help beaming. "I really needed this."

Mrs. Allen smiled. "So did we." She checked her watch. "Come on, Jade. It's time to go."

Jade just clicked away on the mouse, not giving her mother a hint of a glance.

"I found a new geology website," I explained as I grabbed a pen and sticky note pad and began to scribble on it.

"Oh." She rolled her eyes. "That explains it."

I peeled the note off and went to kneel by Jade's side. "Hey, kiddo. It's time to go home now."

Jade shook her head, her eyes still glued to the screen.

I waved the sticky note. "I have the website written here for your mom so you can go home and play on it there. But you have to get off the computer first."

Jade turned slowly to look at me. Then she squinted at the sticky note. I had to smother a grin.

"Here." I held it out toward her mother. "I'll give it to your mom as soon as you turn the computer off. I promise."

Jade stared at me for a long time then the sticky note. For a moment, I wasn't sure if she would take the bait, but eventually, she let out a dramatic sigh and did as we asked.

As soon as Mrs. Allen and Jade had collected all of Jade's things and were gone, I bounded over to Madison's classroom, where Madison was wiping down tables.

"Guess what?" I waved the check in the air. "Grad school is a go!"

2

A LITTLE LONGER

DERRICK

"There. That should do it." I put my tool down and slowly eased myself out of the cramped space. My hands were covered in hydraulics fluid, as was my shirt. It was a good thing I'd bought another pack of sand shirts the week before. This one was a goner.

"All done in there?" Hernandez called.

"Yeah." I grabbed my tools, making sure I'd gotten all the extra screws, and made my way down the plane. "She should be good to go."

Hernandez looked at his clipboard. "Wow. We actually finished early. That means tomorrow we can—"

Before he could finish, another man's voice sounded from inside the office.

"Who's that?" I asked, signing Hernandez's clipboard.

"Sergeant Barnes." Hernandez gave me a sly look. "You got a date for the ball yet?"

"I asked my fiancée, but I don't think she can come. She's coming tomorrow, though, for the awards dinner." My heart jumped a little. Not because I was getting an award, as I'd been back in Arkansas and in my new squadron less than a month. But showing Amy off would be the highlight of the weekend. Well, that and just having Amy in the same state. Why she'd made me wait until the end of May to do so I still couldn't understand.

I went to put my tools away. "Why?"

"So you're the new guy."

We both turned to see a man coming toward us from the office. His footsteps were heavy but unusually quick for someone wearing steel-toed boots, and his dark eyes were sharp. I got the feeling that this guy didn't miss much.

"Sergeant." Hernandez stepped forward and shook hands with the man. "Yeah, this is the new guy, Allen."

I stepped forward to shake the man's hand as well. "Derrick Allen, sir."

"When did you get here, Allen?" Sergeant Barnes asked.

"About three weeks ago."

The man nodded. His dark, curly hair was mostly black, but gray was beginning to creep up from his temples and neck. He looked to be in his early forties. "Sorry it took me so long to welcome you. I was on leave with my family in Texas for a few weeks to celebrate my nephew's graduation." He took out his wallet and removed a picture and held it out to me. He was in the picture, as were a handsome woman about his age and a young woman who looked to be in her early to mid-twenties.

"Isn't she pretty?" He pointed with his thumb to the young woman.

I nodded. "She is."

"She's my daughter." He pulled the picture back and looked at it fondly before returning it to his wallet. "Say, it's what, almost June? The ball's in September. Do you have a date yet?"

I glanced at Hernandez, who looked like he was trying not to laugh. "Um, I have a fiancée. I'm hoping she can come." What was the man thinking? Was he really trying to hook me up with his daughter five seconds after meeting me?

But I didn't ask, and Sergeant Barnes only smiled a little and said, "huh," before putting the wallet back in his pocket. "Well, it's good to meet you, Allen. I expect good things."

"What was that about?" I asked when the sergeant was out of earshot.

Hernandez laughed. "I was trying to warn you. Barnes is retiring soon, and he's determined to see his poor daughter attached to one of us before he does."

"But I'm engaged," I said, thinking again of the sergeant's little smirk.

"He's convinced that he'll either see your girl at some event or she's made up." Hernandez hung his clipboard up and shrugged. "He's not completely nuts, though. A lot of guys have made up girls just to get him off their back." He chuckled again, shaking his head. "Which is weird. Because he's a good NCO. Best I've ever had, aside from his obsession with finding his daughter a husband."

"Hernandez."

We both jumped as Barnes came toward us again, and Hernandez was about as red as a cherry. Thankfully, the sergeant didn't seem like he'd overheard.

"I wanted to ask you about this report you left for me last week."

As they went over the report, I washed my hands and grabbed my stuff from my locker. Then I pulled my phone out. Through the window in the locker room, I could see that the sun was just peeking over the eastern horizon. It was seven, which meant it was five in Colorado. But Amy would be up. She always got up to run the track at the gym before going in to work. I decided to call.

"Hey, stranger," I said when she picked up.

"Hello, yourself." She yawned. "What are you up to this early?"

"You're up earlier than I am." I smiled. "I just got off work, and I'm headed home."

"Going home sounds fantastic. I'm on my way to the gym." She yawned again. "As much as I love hearing from you, I haven't had any coffee yet. What's up?"

"What do you mean? Can't I call my fiancée?"

She laughed. "Derrick Allen, you never call before eight in the morning. Not if you can help it, at least."

I smiled and nodded as I leaned against my locker. "Fine. I have a question. And I know you already said no, but I need you to check your schedule and see if anything's changed."

"Huh. All right. Let me pull into a parking spot first." I waited a minute and then heard her clicking through her phone. "What day are we talking about?"

"First week of August. The military ball." I paused. "Can you come?"

Amy sighed. That was never promising. "Derrick, I told you, I'm traveling that day for the firm. I would cancel, but we've been planning this for months." She paused. "I'm really sorry. I wish I could be there."

I bit back the pathetic pleading that I really wanted to employ and took a deep breath instead. "I get it. I just wanted to make sure. I'd love to have you there ." My mind flashed back to the last ball she'd attended with me. She was dazzling. Dark hair piled up on her head, the sapphires in her earrings bringing out the blue in her eyes. The dark green dress she'd worn had been a tad on the revealing side for a military function, but she'd worn it so well no one had said anything.

"I know, babe. I just can't blow this account," she said. I could hear her closing her car door as she did.

"Okay. Well," I paused, "I guess we can talk about it when you get here on Friday."

"Oh, that reminds me!" She cried. "I nearly forgot."

"What? That doesn't sound good." I tried to laugh.

She groaned. "Look, babe. I meant to tell you last night, but it totally slipped my mind. My boss has to have emergency knee surgery, and I have to take his place in a case." She paused. "Tomorrow."

"Oh." I swallowed. "So…I take it this means you can't come to the ceremony then." I could feel Barnes and Hernandez staring at me, and I suddenly had the desire to melt into a puddle.

"I'm so sorry." She huffed, and I could just see her running her hand through her hair. "I really had planned on coming."

I cleared my throat. "No, um. I get it. I…I guess we'll talk later then?"

"Yeah."

"Okay." I took a deep breath. "Love you."

Hernandez and Barnes were still watching me when I hung up and turned around. "Well." I forced a smile. "I guess you'll have to wait just a little longer to see her."

"Uh-huh." Hernandez nodded, but Barnes smiled slightly. Gathering what remained of my dignity, I straightened my shoulders and went out to my truck.

It wasn't that bad, really. I'd only moved back three weeks ago. I couldn't expect her to drop everything and visit me constantly. Not when she had just landed the job of her dreams. Of course, I'd known it would be hard to keep a relationship living in different states, but as we were engaged, I'd figured it wouldn't be too long before we were together again. And yet, four months after proposing, we were apart. Still waiting.

I pulled in front of my parents' house. After locking the truck, I let myself into the backyard and into the little casita on the other side of the oversized swimming pool. As I unlaced my boots and tossed them into the corner, my phone buzzed. It was Amy.

"Hey." Why did I sound like a pouty little kid?

"Look," she said. "I'll go through my schedule again and see if—"

"Derrick? Are you in there?"

I looked up to see my mom banging on the sliding glass door. I huffed as I went to open it. "Hold on, Amy. What is it, Mom?"

"Oh good, you're home. I wanted to tell you to get cleaned up and presentable."

"Mom, can this wait? I'm talking to—"

"Jade's teacher is coming over for a a rundown of Jade's summer appointments. She'll be here within the hour."

I scrunched my eyes shut. "Look, I gotta go, Amy. I'm sorry."

"Don't be. I need to get on the elliptical. But Derrick?"

"Yes?"

"I'll try. I can't guarantee anything, but I'll try."

Even though she wasn't there to see it, I grinned. "Thanks, Amy." Maybe I would get to pull that green dress out on the dance floor again after all.

3

INTERROGATION CAMP

JESSIE

I pulled up the driveway and let out a whistle. I'd known Jade's family made decent money, but I hadn't expected anything like this. Perhaps I should have, though, based on the salary they were offering me.

I might as well have been pulling up in front of a castle. The three-story brick building was set on a corner lot with an emerald green yard twice the size of the other houses on the block. Red and white brick contrasted nicely with a spotless cream-colored garage door. Matching cream-colored trim decorated the rest of the house's windows and rooflines. I was suddenly quite aware of my old blue Camry's dents and scratches as I gazed at the sleek white Lexus beside mine. The only car that looked remotely close to mine on the street was a beat up red pickup parked on the corner. Who did that belong to?

Not that it mattered. I was here to get a job that would pay for my master's degree. And though I felt two hundred miles from home, rather than just fifteen minutes, I was here now. Besides, they had been the ones to offer me the job after all. So I took a deep breath, straightened my skirt, and smoothed my blouse before ringing the doorbell.

The door opened, but instead of Mrs. Allen, I found myself face to face with a young man. His eye shape I recognized immediately, for they were the same as Jade's. He had blue eyes, though, instead of her brown. A piercing ice blue with streaks of gold shooting out from the iris. His hair was shaved close to the sides of his head and a little longer on top, a cut my military students referred to as a high and tight. He had an angular face, clean-shaven, with prominent high cheekbones and a perfectly straight nose, and I quickly realized that he was possibly one of the most attractive men I had ever seen.

He was also in camouflage pants and a sand-colored shirt. I wanted to sigh. So close.

"Can I help you?" His voice was clear and his words crisp.

"Yes." I cleared my throat. "I'm here to speak with Mrs. Allen about taking care of Jade this summer." I hesitated when he didn't open the door any wider or offer to let me in. "I'm Jade's teacher. She said to come on the twenty-ninth…" My words hung in the air like icicles as I waited for him to respond.

"I see," he finally said, giving me a long look up and down, but it wasn't the kind of appraising looks Madison sought when she dragged me around her favorite flashy bars. Rather, from the hardening of his expression, he looked as though he wasn't about to let me in it all. But he finally did hold the door open and step to the side. "Have a seat on the couch please."

"Is Mrs. Allen here?" I looked around and tried to hide my awe. If it were possible, the interior of the house was even more luxurious than the exterior. The walls had been painted a relaxing shade of blue-gray, and the intricate crown molding above was white, as was everything else. White carpet, white couches, white throw pillows, even a white knitted blanket was draped across the couch. If the young man hadn't let me inside, I would've wondered if I was even at Jade's house at all. It didn't appear to be the kind of place a six-year-old could possibly occupy. Nothing was out of place, and there weren't any stains, not even below the knob on the door. I sat on the couch where the man had indicated. Surely now he would go get Mrs. Allen.

I knew from our intervention meetings at school that Jade had at least three private therapists that she saw throughout the week during the school year, and with summer here, there was a good chance she would have even more starting soon. I had brought a pen and notebook in case I needed to create a schedule with all of Jade's therapy locations and times. I pulled it out to prepare myself. But instead of calling for Mrs. Allen, he simply sat in the armchair across from me and leaned forward, elbows on his knees, studying me unabashedly.

I tried not to squirm under the scrutiny of his gaze. "You must be

Jade's brother," I said, immediately hating the way my voice wavered. What had Mrs. Allen said his name was?

"I am." He continued to stare at me then sat back. "So how many children with disabilities have you taught over the years?"

I laughed nervously. "Well, privacy laws would prohibit me from telling you exactly who has what in terms of special needs, but I can say my time working with your sister has been one of my favorite parts of teaching this year."

"And how long have you been teaching?"

I struggled to keep my smile in place. "This was my first year." Well, this was certainly not going the way I'd expected it to. Why was he grilling me like a confirmed terrorist? Annoyance began to take the place of the attraction which had first struck me upon seeing him. Who cared if he was good-looking? He was really starting to get on my nerves. I tried again. Maybe I could distract him until Mrs. Allen arrived.

"Your mother says you just moved back. Where did you live before this?"

"Colorado." He didn't even blink. "What kind of background checks does the school district require?"

"Um…" I tried to sift through my memory to all the paperwork I'd filled out the year before. "Fingerprinting. Federal checks. Stuff like that." Distraction. I needed more distraction. "What do your parents do? I don't think your mother ever mentioned it."

He snorted. "They own their own construction company."

Was that a bad thing? "Oh," I tried to smile. "So that's how your dad got the time off. That must be nice for them to be in charge of their own schedules.""

"They can take time off whenever they want. They just choose not to. Now what about accreditation? Do you have any higher level accreditation for teaching children with special needs?"

"I'm a general education teacher." I squeezed the handles of my bag. "Jade is in a general education class because she's capable of learning in that environment. But I have had training for teaching children with special needs, yes." Two whole classes. But again, he didn't need to know that.

"So how many of your college classes covered teaching children with Down Syndrome?"

I sat taller. "I'm not sure what you're trying to get at, but I can assure you I'm perfectly aware of Jade's needs. I can also assure you that she's a very intelligent little girl. She actually completes much of her work along with her peers."

Instead of relaxing, though, his frown only deepened. "I understand that, but—"

"Derrick!"

I turned to see Mrs. Allen coming down the stairs. Thank goodness.

"I said I wanted you to meet her, not interrogate her. Now quit grilling our guest, and go do something constructive." She paused at the foot of the stairs and frowned. "Have you eaten yet?"

"No." He rubbed his eyes with the palms of his hands then stood and stretched. As he stretched, I couldn't help noticing the definition of his biceps. Not that I cared, of course. Derrick Allen might be nice to look at, but he had pushed nearly every button I had. He was in the military, too. Off-limits for sure.

"Well," Mrs. Allen said, shooing him away from the couch, "go find something to eat and then get some sleep. I'll take it from here." She gave him a good-natured shove when he didn't move, and pointed at the entrance of what looked like a kitchen at the far end of the room. Then she took his seat and rolled her eyes with a smile. "You'll have to forgive Derrick. He cares a lot about his sister. In fact, she's the reason he moved back."

"I thought airmen didn't get to pick where they go." I let myself lean back into the couch a bit now that he was in the other room. When I glanced at the open door, though, I could see him leaning against the wall as he munched on a bowl of cereal. He wasn't even bothering to hide his eavesdropping.

"Oh, they usually don't. But he knew someone who knew someone and was somehow able to get back here." She threw up her hands. "I'm not sure of all the details. We're just grateful to have him here for as long as he can stay. That's not why you're here, though." She pulled a piece of paper from a folder she was holding and handed it to me. "She's with her father right now at physical therapy. He and I both took a few days off to help while we switched caregivers, but she'll be all yours next Monday. Now, if you look here," she pointed to the spread-sheet, "we'll need you at the house around seven in the morning. You'll get her breakfast and help her get dressed and ready for the day.

Therapy always starts at nine, so you'll need to hurry her more on the days therapy is farther away."

I continued to smile and nod the best I could as Mrs. Allen went on, but I couldn't silently help wondering if I was getting in over my head.

"Physical therapy is on Mondays and Thursdays. Speech and occupational therapy are on Tuesdays and Wednesdays, and horse-play Fridays. Horse-play is nearly an hour away, so you'll need to make sure you build in enough time to get there." Mrs. Allen pointed to the address labeled in pink on the color-coordinated spreadsheet she'd given me. "Mr. Allen and I will give you a preloaded Visa card with enough money to pay for the gas as well as lunch since you won't be able to return home in time to eat most days."

As she went on to explain that speech and occupational therapy were across town from one another, I began to pray that my car would last through all the extra miles. That, and that I could learn to ignore the eyes I felt studying me from the kitchen.

"Naps are at two, and her piano teacher will be here by four on Thursdays. We should be home around four as well, but she needs to be ready so our arrival doesn't distract her. And of course," Mrs. Allen smiled, "we're hoping that you'll be able to prepare her for first grade in your free time as well." Her eyes flicked from the schedule to me. "Do you have any questions?"

I wanted to ask when this poor child got any time to be a kid, but that was sure to go over poorly with my new employers. So instead, I grinned and tucked the paper into my bag. "No, I think this is quite eno—"

"I still don't see why I can't just take her myself." Derrick walked out of the kitchen, with his cereal bowl.

"Because you have to sleep sometime," Mrs. Allen said as she also handed me a stack of brightly colored papers. The sticky note on the top said *Therapy Resources.* Oh, goody. More homework.

"What year is your car?" He was peeking through the blinds at the driveway.

"Um…it's eight years old. Why?"

He looked at his mother. "My truck has more safety features."

"Fine then, son." Mrs. Allen threw up her hands and stood with a huff. "Have it your way. You want to run yourself ragged? Drive them around. Be their chauffeur."

"Fine then. I will." He raised his chin.

She crossed her arms and glared up at him. "But Miss Nickleby is starting next Monday. And that's final."

I looked back and forth between them. "So," I stood slowly, "am I still—"

He gave me a sardonic grin. "Guess you and I will be spending the summer together."

I could only stare back. Fantastic.

4

PLAYING HERO

DERRICK

As soon as Jessie Nickleby was gone, I followed my mom back into the kitchen.

"I still don't understand why you need to hire someone else to take care of her." I crossed my arms and leaned back against the table. "That's what I moved back here for."

"And we're so happy you did," Mom said with her usual infuriating condescension. "And now you and Miss Nickleby can make Jade's life even better this summer together."

"I mean it, Mom. I had to pull a lot of strings to get here. I didn't risk my career to play babysitter for an hour a day. I came to be a part of Jade's—"

"Derrick." Mom put her hands on her hips and took a deep breath. "I'm glad you want to be a part of Jade's life. But the fact of the matter is that as long as you're off playing hero, you're going to leave sooner or later."

I gritted my teeth and did my best to ignore the jab at my career. That was another argument for another day. Or for every day, as soon as my dad got home from work.

"And," Mom continued, gathering up the apples she'd just taken from the crisper, "I can't have her completely dependent on you as long as you're going to be moving one day. And even if you weren't in the military, do you have a degree in elementary education?"

"I was in college," I mumbled, studying the apple I'd swiped. "Doesn't that count?"

"So you took college-level education methods courses then?"

"She's going from kindergarten to first grade. How many summer courses does one have to take to play chauffeur?"

"Don't get smart with me." She began to chop the apples and put them in a mixing bowl. "You like to have fun. You always have."

"I got salutatorian."

"And you could have been valedictorian if you'd tried harder. And you would have finished college."

"What's your point, Mom?"

"My point," she said, wiping her hands off on a towel, "is that you always learned easily, even if you didn't study. But Jade learns differently from you. She has to try a lot harder. Now you don't see that because every chance you get, you've got her at the zoo or the ice cream parlor or whatever new shiny thing has caught your eye."

"Because learning can come from more than a book." I took a bite of my apple and immediately cringed. Why did my mother insist on buying green? No matter how many times I tried them, they were always bad. "Especially," I spat the bite into the trash and put the apple back on the cutting board, "if book learning is hard. And geez, Mom. You schedule every waking moment of her entire life. If I don't sneak her out of your color-coordinated prison every now and then, she'll never have time to just be a kid!"

"Prison!" My mom let out a laugh. "If you want to call her life skill therapies prisons, then go ahead. Look, I don't know why this is such a big deal to you. The state's done a better background check than we ever could."

"That." I pointed. "That is exactly what I'm talking about. You want to know why I moved back here? Why I'm being cautious? Because you're not."

She put down the knife. "That's not fair."

"Well, it wasn't fair when you hired that nincompoop last spring and Jade was the one who paid the price."

"Derrick Allen." My mother's eyes darkened. "That is enough. What happened was not your father's fault or mine."

I rubbed my eyes. More sleep was required for these conversations. I turned and headed back to the casita to change.

"Where are you going?" She sounded peeved, but I didn't turn.

"I'm going to go on a run."

"Don't you need to sleep?" she called after me as I stalked out of the kitchen.

"I'm not tired."

My body begged to differ. As soon as I shut the casita door, my arms screamed at me to lie down. In our search for a missing tool the night before, I'd moved boxes that were probably only meant for two or more people to carry. But I wanted to go home, so I'd moved them anyway, and now everything hurt. My mind, however, was far too wired to rest. I would have to clear my head. Then maybe I would be able to sleep.

I changed into basketball shorts and my favorite, beat-up hockey t-shirt and headed outside, pausing only to put my earbuds in and turn them up as loud as they would go. Then I set off.

I didn't particularly enjoy running in my parents' neighborhood with its perfect brick houses and perfectly manicured yards and copious supply of expensive cars. People waved in response whenever I passed, but everyone, including me, seemed to sense that I fit into this neighborhood about as well as my truck. Pretty much the same way I'd fit in at Harvard.

I turned a corner and nearly ran into another runner, this one a young woman. Her hair was nearly the same shades of gold and brown as Jessica Nickleby's, and I immediately felt a twinge of guilt. Could I have been nicer to her? Most definitely. After all, it wasn't her fault my parents had asked for help. And in all honesty, they could have done much worse. A certified teacher would have the basic federal back-ground checks and fingerprints and all that, so at least she wasn't likely to be a serial killer.

She was also exceptionally pretty. I'd been genuinely surprised when she showed up on my parents' front step, so much so that I nearly forgot how to respond when I'd opened the door. She was petite, a little on the short side, her hair in messy, large curls that reached just to her shoulders. When Mom had told me about Jade's teacher, I'd envisioned a matronly woman with too many cats, writing up worksheets for a hobby, rather than a young woman with vibrant green eyes.

Amy. I should call Amy to get my head sorted out. My recent

schedule change that had me working nights instead of days was still messing with my ability to think straight, and my fiancée was a good voice of objectivity. I appreciated that about her, her ability to see things without emotion coloring her judgment. I came to a stop at a little neighborhood park and collapsed on a bench beneath a large tree.

The phone rang six times then went to voicemail. Sighing, I pushed myself off the bench and starting running again.

5

WE'D HOPED

JESSIE

"Hey, Mom! Dad! I'm home!" I hung my purse and keys up on a peg just inside the door. Then I paused and inhaled deeply before heading for the kitchen. "It smells good in here."

"Thanks. It's a new candle scent I thought I'd try." My mom picked up the little pink candle and examined it as I walked in. "It's supposed to be sweet pea, but I think it's more like peach." She brushed a piece of caramel-colored hair away from her eyes. "Where have you been? I thought you were done in your classroom yesterday. I have a whole list of errands we need to run, and I'm going to need your help with planning the church bake sale. Oh, and I forgot. Dr. Neilson wants me to come in again next week."

I froze. "Why?"

"Oh, don't look like that. It's just something about bloodwork. Nothing to worry about. I just needed to know if you wanted to come along."

"Sure thing." I forced myself to smile, as though this didn't shake me to the core. "And I'm all done at school." I helped myself to a pitcher of lemonade from the fridge then drank in small, measured sips, trying to come up with how to word what I was about to tell my mother. But there was no way around it. This wasn't going to thrill them no matter how I put it. Finally, I put the cup down and stared at it. "You know the little girl I told you about at school?" I asked slowly. "The one with

Down Syndrome." If I played the sympathy card first, maybe my parents wouldn't mind so much.

"Jade? We ran into them at the grocery store once, didn't we?"

"That's her."

"She's a cutie. What about her?"

"Her parents," I said slowly, tracing shapes in the quartz countertop, "have asked me to care for her this summer."

My mom looked up from the dishes she was scrubbing. "They want you to tutor?"

"Well, yes." I swallowed. "They also want me to drive her to her therapies. Starting Monday, I'll be there between seven and four every weekday. But you don't have to worry," I hastened to add. "The brother is there, so I should still be able to go with you to your doctor appointments, and anything you need—"

"It's not my doctor appointments I worry about. Jessie. It sounds like they want you to be her nanny."

"It's more of a tutor." But as soon as the words left my mouth, I knew Mom was right.

"Weren't they between nannies when we ran into them last April as well?"

"It's hard to find people who understand Jade's needs." I opened the fridge and studied its contents like a math test. "I know her, though, and now that I'm on summer break, it only makes sense to help her. And they're paying me enough to pay for the rest of my master's degree." I took a deep breath. "Why? Do you think I shouldn't?"

"It's not that I don't want you to help her. Or to finance your degree." She grabbed a knife and began chopping pecans. "It's more..." She set the knife down and shook her head. "I don't—"

"If this is about your doctor's appointments, like I said, I can still drive you to all of them," I said in a rush. "Jade's brother won't mind at all, I'm sure. And—"

"Jessie, I can drive myself just fine. I'm fifty-four, not dead." My mom reached out and took my hand. Her mouth was set in a line, and her forehead puckered slightly.

Oh no. Here came the dreaded *It's just.*

"It's just," my mother said softly, "you work yourself so hard all the time. Your father and I were kind of hoping you could just have a summer to enjoy yourself."

"I enjoy being with Jade."

"I don't doubt that. But you nearly worked yourself to death to get your bachelor's degree. And your license. And last year, you spent the entire summer setting up your classroom." My mom shrugged. "We were hoping to have some time together where you could just let down." Her voice softened slightly. "We were even looking into some vacation destinations we thought you might enjoy."

My heart fell. I should have expected something like this, especially after finding the Busch Gardens brochure in my father's office.

"Maybe...maybe we can still take a fun vacation together." I forced a little chuckle. "Jade's older brother doesn't even want me to watch her. Maybe I can grant his wish for a few weeks with you guys."

"Oh? To what does he object?" My mother's eyebrows went up. "And why do you care? He's what, ten or something?"

I nearly laughed. My mom might want time with me, but she was also competitive. And she would find the thought of some boy insulting her daughter highly offensive.

"He doesn't think one year of teaching is enough to know how to meet Jade's needs." I rolled my eyes. "Stupid stuff."

"She only spends all day with you and an aid." Mom shook her head. "But you didn't say, how old is he?"

"I don't know. Mid-twenties?" I briefly pictured his face. He definitely wasn't some recruit fresh out of high school. His features and his build were too solid for that. But I couldn't remember seeing any strong lines around his eyes or mouth. And he seemed far too serious to be very young. Still, there had been an unusual light to his eyes that was hard to shake off. It was nearly enough to distract me from the fact that he was military. And a jerk.

Mom started laughing.

"What is it?"

"You're blushing!"

"I am not!" But even as she protested, I felt my cheeks heat.

My mom leaned forward on her elbows and placed her chin on her hands. "So tell me more about this brother." Her brown eyes sparkled, disappointment about my job with Jade seemingly forgotten.

"I told you, he doesn't even like me!" I swiped a handful of quinoa chips from the counter. "Besides. He's Air Force."

"You and your rules." My mom scoffed and washed her hands. "You know, it wouldn't kill you to go on a date now and then. As in, one by yourself. Not just tagging along with your friends. That's another thing your father and I—"

"I'm going to my room now." I skipped out of the kitchen into the hallway.

"Oh! Before you go," my mother called after her, "Madison wanted me to remind you of your date next week."

"I'm not going. I told her that."

"No, she said this one's different. Donny's Bar on Thursday. Something about a teacher get-together."

I sighed. "Thanks." This was going to be a long summer.

6

GOT TO GIVE

DERRICK

"What are you doing still in bed?"

I nearly fell out of bed as my mom threw the casita door open and it banged against the wall several inches from my head. As if that weren't bad enough, she went to the windows and raised all the shutters before turning and clapping at me, like that would move me along faster.

"It's my day off." I rolled over and buried my face in my sheet. "Why would I be up?"

"Get your clothes on! She just parked, and she'll ring the bell any minute!"

"I'm pretty sure she's seen someone in sweatpants and a t-shirt before." I pulled the pillow over my head.

"Derrick." My mother glared at me as she threw my dirty uniforms into my laundry bin, "I want this one to at least last the summer. And your show the other day was far from gracious. The least you can do is greet her nicely this time, and I want you dressed, shaved, respectable, and respectful." She wagged a french tipped nail at me. "Get ahold of that sarcasm, and maybe she'll want to stay for more than a week. Then you can sleep in as long as you like. In fact, I hope you do."

I nearly retorted that perhaps my parents' nanny problem was more their fault than mine, but I knew better. She would just find a way to scold and lecture twice as much as usual before she left for work. If I was patient for another minute or so, she would be back in the main house, scolding Jade or Dad, and I would be free to do as I pleased. Which might include going back to bed so I could have five more minutes of sleep before the glorified babysitter arrived.

Sure enough, thirty seconds later, through the open sliding glass door, I heard the doorbell ring, and my mother left to answer it. She sounded as bubbly and vivacious as a teenager.

Every time my parents got Jade a new nanny, I made it my job to do as much research on the new candidate as I could. In Colorado, that had meant snooping online to look for possible criminal records the nanny agency might have missed. Now that I was in Arkansas, I could do it in person. And this time, I planned to have a little fun, too.

I went to the mirror and glanced at my reflection. My chin and cheeks were already covered in dark stubble. My hair was too short to be messy, but I could at least make sure my teeth were unbrushed when I joined the family. Yep. This would work.

"Morning, everyone!" I called as I let myself in through the back door, stretched, and gave a big yawn. Jessie watched me from where she still stood in the entryway with wide eyes, and my mother's mouth fell open before snapping shut, her eyes dark with indignation. But she couldn't thoroughly chide me in front of company the way I knew she wanted to, so I gave her my biggest grin and joined them. Then I smiled at Jessie. "Glad to see your car made it here this morning in one piece."

"Derrick!" my mother snapped. I ignored her, though. I was watching Jessie clutch her tote bag closer to her chest, her eyes flashing. Wow, this girl was wound tight, like a spring ready to snap from too much pressure.

"Yes, thank you," she said through a strained smile.

My mom looked at the ground and shook her head. "Jade is in the kitchen waiting for breakfast. I have another schedule on the fridge in case you need it. After she eats, her clothes are laid out on her bed for therapy. She has snacks in her lunch box, which is here by the door." She indicated to a blue lunch box on the floor. "There are sub sandwiches in the refrigerator. I got extra last night when I went to fetch dinner."

"Thank you." Jessie's smile became more genuine. Until she turned and looked at me again. "And will you be joining us today?"

I folded my arms. "I wouldn't miss it for the world."

"Terrific." She took her bag and went to the kitchen. I nearly laughed as she dropped her bag on the floor with a thud, closed her eyes, and leaned back against the counter where she must have thought I couldn't see her.

"Derrick!" my mother hissed. "What are you doing?"

"Bye, Mom." I bent down and kissed her on the top of her head. Then I headed for the kitchen, suddenly glad she'd gotten me up. I could hear her still muttering to herself, but she needed to leave for work, and she wouldn't risk being late for any reason. Even me. I'd learned that lesson long ago.

Jessie was in the kitchen with Jade, searching, I assumed, for bowls. I folded my arms across my chest and leaned back against the tabled as I watched. Mom had showered all sorts of praise upon this woman when I'd expressed doubts about her abilities. But was she really as good as Mom was convinced?

Good with Jade or not, she seemed well-organized at least. And prepared. Instead of wearing pencil skirts and ridiculous high heels like the last woman my parents had hired, her clothes were practical. A faded turquoise blouse unbuttoned over a white tank top and a pair of khaki corduroys with sneakers. Her large blond-brown ringlets which had dangled down to her shoulders last time were pulled up on top of her head, and though she didn't wear much makeup, there was just enough to make her green eyes pop.

"Which cereal is yours, Jade?" Jessie opened the cabinet door, a rainbow of cereal boxes inside.

Jade briefly glanced at her from the table and then went back to studying her book.

"Jade, honey. Tell me which cereal is yours."

Jade ignored her.

I considered intervening. But Jessie would probably resent that. She seemed the type who wanted to do things her own way. Also, I wanted to see if she really did know as much about Jade as she touted.

To my surprise, instead of pestering Jade or getting angry at her, she went and knelt at her side.

"Hey, Jade," she said in a soft voice. "I know you're used to seeing me at school. But school is over now, and I'm going to be here instead. And I want to know what you like to do in the morning, but I can't do that unless you help me learn how."

Jade didn't look at her, but I could see her wheels turning as she stared out at the window. "Why?" she finally said.

Jessie smiled. "Because I missed you so much I wanted to see you here, too, instead of waiting all summer for you to come back to school."

Jade slowly turned to look at her, and Jessie's smile grew. It was a sweet smile, nothing like the pinched grimace she'd given me. "Now," she said, "Can you tell me which cereal is yours?"

I had to hand it to her. She was better than I'd expected, particularly for a first-year teacher. But as Jade slowly pointed at the green box, and Jessie immediately found a bowl and began to pour, I nearly grinned again. This was the part where I knew I should probably tell Jessie that Jade was going to erupt in less than half a minute. But no. I could play this in my favor after all.

Sure enough, the moment Jessie put the spoon in front of her, Jade scowled at the bowl and pushed it back. Crossing her arms in front of her, she leaned back and mashed her lips together.

"Jade," Jessie leaned down again, "you told me this was the one you wanted. What's wrong?"

But Jade just made another face at the bowl. "No!"

And it all went downhill from there until Jade was screaming, and Jessie looked like she was getting a headache.

"Jade, I don't understand—"

"No! No cereal! No!"

I had planned to let the fit play itself out, for no other reason than to show Miss Teacher that I was indeed more necessary than my mother said. But when the kicking began, I went to the spice rack and pulled down the cinnamon. Before using it, though, I made sure to catch Jessie's gaze and hold it as I sprinkled it all over the cereal, stopping only when Jade quit screaming.

Once her cereal was covered in cinnamon, Jade began to eat as if nothing unpleasant had happened, and I moved in to pour myself a bowl as well. I grinned at Jessie as I spread cinnamon over my own cereal.

"Really?" Her voice was tight and pitched a bit higher than before. "We have to leave in twenty minutes, and you couldn't have done that sooner?"

I stuffed a spoonful of green cereal into my mouth and shrugged. "I wanted to see how you handled stress."

Her green eyes narrowed. "The day I'm supposed to find her therapy center, you decided it would be a good time for that?"

"Pretty much." I swallowed. "But don't get all bent out of shape. I've already moved her car seat to my truck. She just needs to get dressed and brush her teeth and hair, and she'll be ready to go."

"So you're driving us."

"Obviously." I shoveled another mound of cereal into my mouth.

"Don't you have somewhere you need to be?"

"I had last night off, so I got ten hours of sleep." I stretched. "I feel fantastic."

If looks could kill, I'd be on death's doorstep by now. She glared at me for so long I was sure she might pop a vein. But instead of retaliating, she finally closed her eyes and sucked in a deep breath through her nose. Then she turned to Jade, who was focused on her food.

"Jade, I'm going upstairs to find your clothes. I'll be back in a few minutes. Please try to focus on eating." And without a single glance at me, she whirled around and marched out, after which Jade paused and looked up at me, her eyes bright.

"Nickleby mad."

"Yeah, she sure is. But she's right. We need to go soon. Eat your food so you can go see Miss Gina."

Jessie returned a few minutes later with Jade's clothes in hand. As soon as Jade was done eating, Jessie had her dressed so fast that even I was impressed. Then Jessie grabbed their bags and practically dragged Jade out the door. She reached my truck and stopped before picking Jade up and turning to the vehicle. I smiled as she tried to pull the handle with the hand under Jade's legs. It didn't work.

"She can walk, you know." I sauntered over to them.

Jessica turned to glare at me. "We're in a bit of a hurry if you haven't noticed. Her lesson starts in—"

"I'm aware of when her lesson starts. Now let me put her in and go get settled in the front seat."

Jessie's jaw dropped, and from the way her eyes burned, I wondered briefly if fire might come out as well. "I am perfectly capable of strapping her in!"

"But this is my car." I took Jade from her arms. "And I'm used to her car seat. It's a five-point harness, you know."

She stared at me like I had a third arm growing out of my head. "They're all five-point harnesses. They don't even make anything else anymore."

I had to give it to her. She was dedicated. And the way she stuck her chin out when she got mad was actually kind of cute. Still, I opened the back door and plopped Jade inside. "No offense, Miss Nickleby, but you spend what, six hours with her a day? In a single room?"

"Seven and a half, actually. Your point?"

I shrugged. "The classroom's great, and I'm sure you've done a fine job with her there. But this is real life, and no offense, I don't think they trained you for dealing with the parts of Jade's life that happen in the real world."

She stared at me for a long moment before she finally crossed her arms and whirled around. "Fine. You know what? Fine." She stomped over to the truck's passenger seat and slammed the door shut so hard the truck rocked.

Maybe there was hope. Jessie Nickleby had looked more than a little determined the first time I'd met her, but maybe I had misjudged her. Maybe she'd give up and leave us be after all. The thought made my heart a little lighter.

≈

When I was done buckling my sister into her car seat, I joined Jessie in the front. She glowered out the window, which was fine by me. I would turn up the radio and talk to Jade as if Jessie weren't even there.

"Hey, Jade," I called into the backseat. "You wanna hear the eighties rock or seventies classics?"

"Eighties."

"Okay." I found the Bon Jovi album on my phone then pulled out of the drive. The day was unusually cool for early summer, and despite my frustration with the nanny situation, the spring-like air made my muscles relax, and I breathed just a little easier. Oak and hickory trees waved at us from on each side of the highway as we hopped on and headed north.

Just as I was beginning to enjoy myself, however, the steel guitar disappeared. I looked over to see Jessie pulling the jack out of my phone and putting it into hers instead.

"Hey, since when is it okay to mess with the driver's music?" I reached for her phone, but she yanked it back.

"Since he kidnapped me. Now watch the road." A smug little smile crossed her face as she tapped her phone screen and the sound of violins filled the cab.

"Oh no. What is that?"

"Your mother asked me to prepare her for school," Jessie said, her smile only growing smugger by the second.

"So you're turning her into a classical violinist?" It was my turn to glare.

"Studies show that children who listen regularly to classical music can better focus than their peers."

I shook my head.

"It also," she continued, "significantly lowers anxiety and reduces physical tension." She flipped me a wicked, flirty smile. "Does Bon Jovi do that?"

"Jade?" I glanced in the rearview mirror, far less amused with the situation than I'd been five minutes earlier. "Do you want Bon Jovi or classical?"

"Classical." Jade didn't even bother looking away from the window.

"Traitor," I muttered under my breath.

Jessie snickered, and I gripped my steering wheel harder, praying that God would give me strength for the days when I had to do this after working a full shift. Because I got the feeling the week wouldn't be getting any better.

To put it mildly, the rest of the week didn't get any better. Every time I thought I'd won the upper hand, she came back with some below-the-belt blow. I got back at her for the music intrusion by giving Jade a whole bag of gummy worms right before Jessie came over the next day, which meant Jessie arrived to find my sister somewhat akin to a pinball...a pinball she had to get ready for speech therapy.

That was fun to watch until Jade crashed into my mother's side table and broke a vase. Even less fun was explaining the incident to my mother.

Wednesday, Jessie struck back with a shiny new CD of Jade's favorite learning songs, including, "The Cow Says Moo, Moo, Moo, Moo, Moo", "The Green Cat Likes P-I-N-K", and "The Shape Shark Song". By the end of the ride, I was an inch away from pleading for Jessie to go back to Beethoven.

Thursday, at least, was a win in my book. I made sure to slip Jade her iPad, which was supposed to be off-limits until the end of the day, right after my mother left. By the time Jessie arrived, Jade was glued to the screen, and there was an atomic level meltdown that occurred as Jessie fought to separate the child from her game to take her to therapy.

But even with this win, I was forced to admit that I was exhausted by the time Jessie left on Thursday night. As soon as my mom got home, I excused myself and dragged my sorry butt to the casita, where I flopped onto my bed to squeeze in six hours of sleep before I had to dress and leave for work. Thanks to my determination not to leave Jade alone with Jessie, I was going straight from a full work shift to a day with my sister and her bull-headed teacher. That left me time to sleep between four and ten every evening before I got up and started all over again.

As I dozed off, I came to the conclusion that something was going to have to give. And I had the awful feeling that it just might be me after all.

7

WHY I DON'T

JESSIE

Thursday evening, after Mrs. Allen had relieved me of Jade, I climbed into my car and leaned my head against the steering wheel. One more day and this horrible week would be over. How was I going to make it through the summer? Full-time nannying, because if I was honest, that's what I was really doing, was hard enough without having to be on my guard every second for Derrick's next attack.

My phone buzzed, and I answered without looking at the name.

"Hello?"

"Jessie! Please tell me you got my text."

"Hi, Madison." I put the phone on speaker and pulled out of the drive. "What's up?"

"I know you didn't want to go on that double date, so I canceled."

"And I thanked you for that." I rubbed my eyes. "Several times." So why was she bringing it up now?

"You're going to like this so much better. Sam set up a night out at Donny's for the staff for whoever—"

"I know. My mom told me."

"Then why don't you sound excited? Or respond to my texts?"

"I'm sorry, Madison. It's not that. I'm just more exhausted than I can even begin to—"

Madison sighed. "Jessie, Sam told me not to tell, but I'm going to anyway. He set this night up for you when he realized you'd never been to any of the extracurricular staff functions."

Despite my exhaustion, my heart jumped a tiny bit. "Sam set this up?"

"Yes. What did you think it was? Some sort of trick to get you on another date?"

I laughed. "All right, fine. You've got me. I'm in." Maybe I did need a night out, something that would distract me from the annoying owner of the red truck I could see in my rearview mirror.

There was a pause.

"Wait…fine?"

I nodded, still glaring at the red truck in my rearview mirror. "I'll be there."

"Wow. That was easier than I thought."

"You were right. Sam was right. I need a distraction."

"Great!" Madison squealed. "Meet me at—"

"Let me guess. Donny's Bar at seven." As if there was anywhere else to go in Jacksonville.

"Actually, it's six-thirty. But yes. You're the best, Jessie."

If that were true and I were the best, I'd have gotten rid of a certain pesky older brother by now.

"See you then," I said before hanging up. Two weeks before, spending the evening with loads of people after a full day of working would have been detestable. But if they were able to take my mind off the airman I wanted to strangle, my coworkers were welcome to try.

It only occurred to me that I probably should have dressed up a little more as I got out of my car and saw Madison coming out of the bar to meet me. The once-over she gave me wasn't happy.

"You're late. And what are you wearing?"

"It's only six-thirty-five. And this was all I had ready at the last minute."

She huffed. "Well, you'll have to do."

"I thought this was a staff thing. Why do you care what I wear?" I wrinkled my nose at her as she dragged me inside.

Instead of paying heed, her pursed lips turned up into a magical unicorn smile as she dragged me inside.

"Hey, where is everyone?" I couldn't see anyone I recognized at the bar. But before I could investigate, she was turning us toward a corner booth where two guys were sitting.

"I might have asked you to come a little early," she said in a low voice.

"Wait, what? Why?"

"Since I found something to start this evening off even better." She grinned.

"Madison, the only reason I came was because you said Sam—"

"We'll see Sam and the others soon enough. But first I want you to meet someone."

I stopped. "Madison—"

"Please, Jessie?" She stopped walking and clutched my arm. "I met him last week, and I really have a good feeling about this one. Like...a really good feeling."

"And how long have you known him exactly?"

"I told you. I met him last week, and he texted today to say he was bringing a friend, so I said I'd bring one, too."

"Why?" I pulled my arm out of her grasp.

"Seriously, Jessie." She squeezed my hand. "I really need a wingman. I haven't met a guy like Adam in a long time. Not since Bryce."

I glared. Everything in me rebelled. But as Bryce had been the last decent boyfriend Madison had held in her string of beaus, for my own sake, I capitulated. "You have until seven, when everyone else gets here. Then I'm done."

"Thank you!" She squealed and hopped up and down before taking a deep breath and leading me the rest of the way to the booth.

"Gentlemen," she beamed, "this is Jessie. Jessie, this is Adam." She pointed to the blond one with brown eyes and a crooked smile. "And that's Tanner." Tanner's eyes were hazel, and he had a dimple on his left cheek. His hair was the reddest red I'd ever seen. Though they wore civilian clothes (or civies, as my students referred to them), their hair was a dead giveaway, shaved close everywhere but the very top, which had a near square look to the cut. About two-thirds of my boys sported the high and tight as well.

Casting one more longing look back at the bar, I took my seat and groaned on the inside. Leave it to Madison to go to a staff party and find dates. But why I was surprised, I couldn't say.

"Are you a teacher, too?" Adam asked as Madison slid into the booth beside him…a little too close for someone she'd met only last week, in my opinion, but no one asked me.

"I am." I gave him my best tired smile. "Madison's room is next door to mine."

"So you teach first grade, too?" Tanner turned to face me better.

"I will be. We're moving up with our classes this year." I picked up the menu. Why did I think this was a good idea? I was exhausted, and hanging out with strangers was sure to exhaust me further. I should have just gone home. Twenty minutes. I was giving her twenty minutes of this charade, then I was fleeing to the safety of the bar.

"You must like kids then," Tanner said.

I chuckled. "My life would be rather miserable if I didn't."

He leaned forward slightly, his eyes glued to mine. "Do you want any of your own one day?"

I blinked up at him over my menu. "Excuse me?"

"How many do you want?"

"Lives?" I laughed weakly.

"Kids." He folded his hands like one of my old college professors, the one who had liked to make us do mock interviews during our freshman year. "How many kids do you want to have?"

"I…" I looked at Madison, but she looked as though she were stuck between smothering a laugh and blushing profusely.

She was dead. I was going to kill her and write my name in her blood.

When I didn't answer immediately as I was plotting her demise, he tried again. "I just wanted to know if you—"

"Actually," Adam, the blond one, gave his friend a not-so-subtle kick beneath the table, "before we get too far in, would anyone like a drink? My treat."

I wasn't a drinker in general, but this time, I didn't hesitate to order a glass of wine. If Tanner's studious gaze, which still hadn't abated despite his friend's kick, was any sign of the evening to come, I was going to need it.

"Jessie," Madison said, a little too loudly, "is going to be starting her master's degree soon. So she's spending the summer earning a little extra money."

"What are you doing?" Adam asked, casually draping an arm around Madison's shoulders.

"Tutoring." I smiled, taking a sip of my wine. Okay, that was a slight understatement. A big understatement. But I was too tired to explain to the world that I was here to escape. "What are your AFSEs?"

"Ah, so you speak Air Force lingo?" Adam looked impressed.

I laughed. "I've learned enough from my students to make basic conversation and order dinner."

"That's impressive." Tanner was studying me with that intense tilt of his head again. "Military terms are often confusing to civilians."

"So what do you two do?" I took another quick sip of my wine.

"We're security forces." Tanner sat taller in his seat, his chin lifting slightly and his eyes brightening.

I finished off my glass and stared at it morosely.

"Jessie?" Madison said with a nervous laugh, "do you need to—"

"Get some water?" I hopped off the bench. "Yes. Yes, I do." Without waiting to hear her answer, I grabbed her hand and dragged her over to the water station.

"Maddie, are you nuts?" I whisper yelled.

"What?" She played with her purse's zipper.

"They're Security Forces! One little slip here, and we're going to get traffic tickets any time we even think of driving on base."

Madison rolled her eyes. "How often do you actually drive on base?"

"That's not the point. The point is that you have set me up with someone who is very interested in…in procreation. With me, I might add!"

Madison avoided my gaze. "He's in the military." She shrugged. "They move a lot. He's probably trying to find someone before they send him away again." Then she smirked. "You complained that Sam Newman wasn't forward enough. This guy meets your scruples and raises them."

"This," I gave her my best glower, "is why I don't date airmen."

"Would you get your water?" She scowled back. "They're waiting on us."

"You've got five minutes left," I muttered as I indignantly filled my water cup from the clear jug with lemon slices floating in it. After the wine, the water tasted as sour as the look I hoped I was giving Madison.

Under Madison's direction, I pasted a smile on my face, and we returned to our table. Thankfully, Tanner didn't seem as intent on putting his arm around me as Adam was to Madison. But Madison wasn't complaining, and neither was I.

"So, Adam," I said, purposefully ignoring the look Tanner was giving me again. "What kind of car do you drive?" A stupid question, but it didn't involve me or Tanner, and would hopefully get Adam talking.

"I've restored a 1965 Ford Mustang." He sat up straighter with a gleam in his eye that I hoped promised lots of talk about something other than me and my future progeny.

He opened his mouth, but before he could launch into car brags, Tanner said, "I just bought a new car."

"Oh," Madison said politely. "What kind?"

"A fifteen-seater van."

Madison and I stared at him, and out of the corner of my eye, I saw Adam rub his eyes with the slightest shake of his head.

"That's...a lot," I said. "You don't have any kids yet do you?" Please say no.

"No. But...well, you know, car seats take up a lot of space."

Madison, who had been taking a swig of her beer, snorted and just barely missed covering her date in spit. She wiped her mouth on the back of her hand. "Just how many car seats do you plan on having in there at once?"

"Many, I hope." He gave me another sideways glance.

Thankfully, however, I was saved from having to respond when Adam turned the conversation away from me and to his crazy ex-girlfriend.

"You know," Madison laughed. "Jessie has her own way of getting back at people who make her angry."

Adam snickered. "Hopefully, not by sticking fish in people's curtain rods. I still can't get the smell out of my apartment."

"Jessie," Madison's eyes gleamed wickedly, "writes letters."

"Letters?" Tanner echoed, his steak halfway to his mouth.

I rolled my eyes and grinned. "I don't actually send them."

"No, and it's a good thing you don't." Madison put her beer down.

"You should have seen the one I caught her writing to me the day I tried to play a practical joke on her."

"You ruined my school planner!" I laughed. "I'd just filled it out, too! And you wouldn't have seen it at all if you hadn't been poking around my desk."

"If you think this cute little thing couldn't hurt a fly," Madison waved her hand at me, "you'd be sorely mistaken. You wouldn't believe the verbal lashing she can write out. My eyes hurt for a week."

"Man." Adam rubbed his chin. "I can't remember the last time I wrote or sent a real letter."

"I filled out that card to register to vote," Tanner said. "Does that count?" He turned back to me. "You know, if you married someone in the military, you could keep voting here since it's your state of residence." He sat straighter. "Have you ever considered it?"

"Considered what?" I squeaked.

"Marrying someone in the military?"

8

WHAT-IFS

JESSIE

Before I had to choose between decking this guy and figuring out how to escape, a deep, deliciously familiar voice spoke from behind me.

"Jessie, I didn't see you get in."

We all turned to see Sam standing beside our table. Instead of his usual button-up shirt and khaki slacks, he was wearing jeans and a blue polo shirt. Casual looked good on him, and it took all my effort not to start singing a song in his honor.

"Hey, everyone." I turned to the rest of the table. "This is Sam, one of the other teachers from our school." I stood and grabbed my purse. "Thanks so much for keeping me company while I waited for this guy. I'll see you around, all right? And thanks for the wine, Adam."

I put my arm through Sam's and whirled us around to march off in the opposite direction. I wasn't fast enough to miss the look of devastation on Tanner's face, but I made sure he wouldn't be able to get in a final word as we left.

"You were waiting for me?" Sam laughed softly.

"I was waiting for the first person who could drag me away from the train wreck." I let go of Sam and sank onto a bar stool. To my relief, I was safely surrounded by at least six more teachers by that time. "Where does she find these guys?"

"At bars, apparently."

I laughed ruefully and shook my head. "Either way, thank you. I really needed to escape."

"He sounded fantastic. You should get his number."

I rubbed my face. "Not just him. Everything this week has been a disaster."

"Hold that thought." He flagged down the bartender. "What do you want?"

I gave the bartender a sheepish grin. "Shirley Temple?"

Sam watched me for a second before chuckling. "Do you make those?" he asked. The bartender looked less than thrilled but nodded.

"Great." Sam grinned. "And put it on my tab. Now." He turned back to me. "You were saying?"

So I told him about my first week with Jade. Or rather, her brother. It felt good to get it all out. I'd told my parents some, but if I shared too many details, I knew they'd just want me to quit. Telling Sam felt like letting out a breath after holding it underwater for too long.

"You should have seen how intense he was when he was interrogating me that first day." I played with my straw. "Grilled me about my certifications and time spent teaching kids with special needs and background checks. You'd have thought he was in the FBI instead of the Air Force."

"So that explains it."

"What?"

He took a swig of his beer. "He's Air Force. No wonder you don't like him."

"That is not why I don't like him."

"You won't date them."

"This guy doesn't want to date me. He wants me out of his life. And I could say the same thing for him."

Sam tilted his head and leaned back. "So why are you doing this then?"

I shrugged. "I really do love Jade. And you should see what they're paying me."

His eyebrows went up. "That much?"

I leaned in. "Let's just say that they're going to be paying for the rest of my master's."

His eyes nearly popped. "That much?"

"See the draw?"

"Okay. Wow. So if that's the case, then here's my proposition." He cleared his throat. "You finish the summer with Jade and the egomaniac in uniform."

"That's what I'd planned to do."

He held up a finger. "I'm not finished. But instead of enduring it alone, how about I check in on you to make sure you're still alive every now and then."

I snorted. "So when I don't answer and you find my body, it won't be too decomposed to show in an open-faced casket?"

"Hey, you've got this." He smiled and nudged my shoulder, and I felt little butterflies flutter around at the bottom of my stomach. "You've wanted this master's degree since college, right?"

"Right."

"So go get it. And don't let this guy stop you. When he starts being a dolt, just text me, and I'll remind you of how awesome it's going to feel when you graduate."

I looked up to find him staring into my eyes with nearly the same intensity Tanner had held. But this time, I didn't mind so much.

"Fine," I said. "But you owe me another Shirley Temple."

He laughed, and I smiled, glad I'd come after all.

∼

We talked for an hour. There was a sinking feeling, though, that I couldn't stop as it slowly filled my stomach.

It was stupid, really. But Madison's story about the day she ruined my planner kept creeping back into my mind. I felt like that fateful day was bleeding into this one, like the lines in time and space were being blurred.

I was sitting here, enjoying myself with people who weren't my family after being gone all week from my family. And even when I was home, I was studying. The parents I was working so hard to protect had hardly seen me since school got out, and now I was in a bar, sipping my cherry drink like I had all the time in the world.

It was just a memory, I told myself. And I couldn't let memories stop me from ever having fun. The more I fought it, though, the more it haunted me, like the ghost of an evening gone wrong that hadn't happened yet. Eventually, inevitably, the memories won out, and I knew I couldn't force one more smile if my life depended on it. So I excused myself and headed out to the car.

The humidity hit me like a wave the moment I stepped outside. And though it had been bright and cheerful inside, the remnants of all the warm and fuzzy feelings Sam had gifted me disappeared as the sticky Arkansas air descended upon me like a curse. As I fumbled for my keys, I found myself wishing desperately for teleportation. All I wanted to do was go home.

"I thought you were having fun in there." Madison's voice made me jump, and I nearly dropped my keys before taking a deep breath and turning slowly to face her.

"Madison." I put on a practiced *I don't care* look, the one I used a lot with Derrick. "Tanner practically asked if I would have his babies. Of course I didn't try."

Madison pinched the bridge of her nose. "I was talking about Sam, but fine. Tanner was a little enthusiastic."

I arched an eyebrow.

"Okay, really enthusiastic. But..." She shrugged. "At least he wasn't up for casual dating. Isn't that what you're always complaining about? That most men today are too casual about courtship?"

"You know, Madison? I actually wanted a casual night out tonight. For once, I just wanted to leave my house and job and spend some time with other human beings my age. I didn't expect you to pick up random guys and throw them at me. You know how much I hate that." I put my hands on my temples and rubbed them.

She pouted. "You didn't have to leave me like that."

"I endured twenty minutes with that man! If you're really so desperate—"

"All right, I get it. No need to yell." She was quiet for a moment. When she spoke again, her voice was soft.

"Week that bad, huh?"

"Worse." I let my head hang back, and before I knew it, I was telling her everything. But where it had sounded silly and ridiculous back with Sam and the others, I was hit by a sudden flood of melancholy. Sam's planned texts to help me endure the summer had seemed like a good idea back inside, but now that I was out here in the dark, the situation seemed again like it was possibly more than I could handle. "I just can't for the life of me figure out why Derrick is being such a—"

"This is about your mom, isn't it?"

I looked up at the stars.

"And what brought that on?" she asked gently.

I took a long, deep breath. "When you told the planner story, it reminded me that my mom's got an appointment tomorrow."

"With the oncologist?"

I nodded again, not trusting myself to speak.

"Wait...the day I ruined your planner. That was the day—"

"The day she found her second lump." I swallowed hard and stared at the asphalt beneath our feet.

"Aw, Jessie." Madison pulled me into a hug, and I let her. "I wouldn't have brought it up if I'd known..." She pulled back and studied my face. "She's still in remission, though, isn't she?"

"She should be. This is supposed to be just a blood test." I pulled away and fiddled with my unicorn house key. "But it came back once. And I don't..." I sniffed. "I can't do it again. I just can't."

Madison crossed her arms and looked down at her feet, where she traced the white parking space lines with her shoes. "I know this is tough. Believe me, I love your mom. She's impossible not to love."

I gave her a half-smile. It was true.

"But you can't live your life around fear for your mother. Jess, I hate to say it, but you really have no idea how to have fun. You live your life on what-ifs and—What are you doing?"

I unlocked the car and threw my purse into the passenger seat and flashed her a tight smile. "Thanks for inviting me tonight. I know you were trying." But she caught my door before I could shut it.

"I mean, Jessie. You have got to learn to let go sometime."

"Night, Madison." I pulled my door shut and drove home. I had a letter to write.

9

JERK

DERRICK

"You're quiet this morning." I glanced at Jessie as we pulled onto the highway. It was only her fifth day as Jade's nanny, and her ability to stay angry and silent must already be blowing records out of the water.

"Yep." She wrapped her arms around herself and glared at the road.

I passed a sedan and looked at her again. "This wouldn't happen to have to do with the cereal mixup this morning, would it?" Even as I remembered the fiasco that had been this morning, I couldn't help smiling a little. One small step at a time. Maybe when their patron saint of kindergarten failed, my parents would finally listen and leave Jade to me.

But Jessie only set her jaw as she glowered straight ahead.

"Because I can't blame you for not knowing that her second favorite cereal is Fruity O's. That stuff probably doesn't come up much in school discussions." I paused to turn the music down since Jade had fallen asleep in her car seat. "You did a good job of getting the milk out of your hair, though."

No response. I finally shrugged and began to flip through radio stations, but before I found one, Jessie finally spoke.

"She won't eat with forks."

"What?" I turned to look at Jessie.

"She only likes to eat with spoons. She pretends not to know her alphabet, but she can write the whole thing if she's motivated enough, as well as her first and last name and the name of that dog she likes to draw, the pink one with purple whiskers. She's memorized entire books about rocks, and her favorite food is spaghetti."

She was still staring straight ahead, but my face heated uncomfortably when a single tear rolled down her cheek. Great. I'd made her cry.

Driving her crazy had seemed sort of fun thus far, and driving her away had sounded even better. But now, as I played the morning…and the rest of the week back in my head, I had to admit that with each day, I'd grown less annoying and more of a colossal jerk.

But Jessie wasn't done. "She's an introvert," she said, her voice husky as she wiped her cheek on her shoulder. "She likes watching other children, though. Her best friend is Daisy Wilkes, and she wants to be a geologist when she grows up. She doesn't like long conversations, but she can already name more kinds of rocks and minerals than most college students."

Okay, so maybe I had been wrong about her, at least about her not knowing Jade. The woman knew a lot about my sister. I didn't know she had a best friend named Daisy. Heck, I hadn't even been aware she had a best friend at school. Not that that qualified Jessie to look after Jade full-time, but…if I was truthful, this woman seemed like she cared an awful lot about my little sister.

I rubbed a hand down my face and groaned. "Look. I'm not trying to be a jerk—"

"Too late." She crossed her arms.

"You're right. And I'm sorry." I took a deep breath and blew it out slowly, my conscience poking at me. *At least tell her the reason you need to take care of Jade.* But I wasn't going to do that. Because if I did, she'd assure me that she wasn't going to be like the last few nannies, and I'd have to be even ruder and tell her that just wasn't good enough for me. At least, not when it came to Jade. But when I glanced at Jessie again, her face was red and her eyes still shone.

Maybe I could be vague, just so she would know I had a reason. She'd already put up with me all week. She deserved to know something at least.

Vague might work.

"I know I seem overprotective." I slowed as we came to a stop sign. "And it's nothing personal. I swear. I just…" I paused when the light changed to green. This was it. I had to tell her. "Something happened last spring," I said slowly. "I'm not supposed to go into details, but it was actually the reason I moved here."

For the first time since getting in the truck, she peeked at me, her green eyes wide under wet lashes. As if I didn't feel bad enough already. "Is that why you're trying to get me fired?"

Dang, she was smart. Or maybe I was just that obvious. I rubbed my neck. "How about this? Jade likes you, and you obviously do know a lot about her...more than I thought. What if we call it a truce and do this together?"

"You mean," she said slowly, "take care of her together all summer?"

I wasn't about to fold and hand over my sister to be alone with a stranger all summer. But for some reason, I realized in that moment that I did want Jessie Nickleby's trust. Or at least, I wanted her not to think I was really as awful as I'd been carrying on. If she truly was as dedicated to her work as she seemed, she deserved better than that.

"My parents won't dock your pay if that's what you're worried about. They're just happy when their schedule goes without a hitch." I came to another stoplight and gathered the courage to look at her again. "And I promise, I'm really not as much of a jerk as I was this week. At least, I try not to be." I did my best to give her a repentant smile. "Deal?"

She studied me warily for a moment from behind one of her light brown curls, and I couldn't help thinking how she looked a lot like a suspicious little cat. Determined to redeem myself, though, I held her gaze. *Just forgive me and let us move on,* I wanted to say. Anything to make her stop looking at me like I was a Class A villain. Finally, she nodded, and I let myself take a deep breath. This was going to be a long summer.

10

GAMES

JESSIE

I felt as though someone had put me through a wringer by the time we pulled into the gravel lot in front of the equine center. My conversation with Madison from the night before, as well as the feeling of defeat from my mother's newest doctor appointment, were weighing me down like a ton of rocks. If I had to handle one more thing, my brain might actually explode.

And here he was, promising to take a step back. Could I trust him to really do that, though? I wasn't sure. All I knew was that after five whole days, this war had to come to an end. I pulled out my phone.

Remind me again. How much do I want this degree?

Sam's response was lightning fast, and threatened to make me smile.

Jess, you daily have battles of the will with six-year-olds. You can beat this guy. Show him that messing around with Jessie Nickleby is a mistake.

Thanks, I typed back. *I needed that.*

.   .   .

I got a smiley face back. *Anytime.*

But when we got to the center, I didn't have to show him. Because true to his word, Derrick didn't make a fuss when I climbed out of the truck and moved to the backseat to wake Jade up and pull her out of her car seat.

"I'm going inside to sign her in," he called over his shoulder as he headed into the one-story brick building. I nodded and continued unbuckling Jade. Breathing was easier as soon as he was in the building. A storm of emotions was already swirling around in my head faster than I could count them.

After a night of restless sleep as the doctor's voice mail and Madison's words had gone round and round in my head, I had awakened in a mood no better than it had been the night before. Then breakfast had been a royal disaster. Jade's cereal box was empty when I got there, and Derrick hadn't bothered telling me that Jade didn't like the cereal I picked until after I'd poured it out, added milk, and stuck it in front of her. Jade had refused to take a single bite, and when I'd tried bringing a spoonful of it to her lips, she'd thrown the bowl at me. Thankfully, she'd missed, though I'd gotten more than my share of milk in my hair.

Anger and frustration welled up inside me as I recalled the way his blue eyes had laughed while I stood there in shock, milk dripping from my ear. I was also exhausted from arguing with him and fighting with Jade. But if I was honest with myself, I couldn't deny that I also had an inkling of respect for the way he wanted to protect his sister. What had happened to make him so obsessed, and why wasn't he allowed to talk about it?

"I don't want to!" Jade grumbled as I took her hand and we walked toward the building.

"You like horses, don't you?" I gave Jade a smile. "I know you do because you put them on your mommy's Christmas card."

Jade didn't answer, and I smiled to myself. Jade didn't like being wrong. It seemed to run in the family.

We walked into a little reception room that smelled like earth and animals. But the smell wasn't overpowering. Actually, it seemed perfectly fitting, considering we were surrounded by fields of green with horses dotting the pastures.

"Who's this with Jade?" The receptionist peered over the counter at me. The sign in front of her said Mrs. Robinson in big, scripty letters. Her brown eyes moved up and down my figure before a sly smile lit her face. Then she glanced back at Derrick, who was signing a clipboard. "She's sure pretty, whoever she is. Is this your mystery girlfriend?" Then she laughed, as though she'd just told a funny joke. My cheeks heated, but before I could introduce myself, Derrick spoke up.

"That is Jade's new nanny." He kept his eyes on the sign-in sheet. "Amy is still in Colorado."

"Hm-hm." Mrs. Robinson leaned back and flipped through a file from her desk with her long, acrylic nails. "And I'm the next Miss Arkansas."

"Hi, I'm Jessie, Jade's teacher from school." I leaned over to shake Mrs. Robinson's hand before any more assumptions or insinuations could be made.

"Latasha. Nice to meet you." She shook my hand then put her hands on her hips even though she was sitting down. Then she scowled at Derrick. "I already like her better than you."

"She's prettier," Derrick said, still studying the paper.

He thought I was pretty? My face grew hot again. That was uncomfortable for a number of reasons.

But Derrick didn't seem to think anything of it. For some reason, I found this was a bit of a relief and a disappointment. No. Not a disappointment. Just…I was going to ignore him.

Instead, he looked back at Latasha and grinned. "But what about my personal charm?"

She snorted and shook her head. "If you were that charming, you'd have a real girlfriend here with you." She glanced back at Jessie. "Or you'd ask this one. She seems like she could up your worldly game if anyone could."

I wanted to melt into a puddle, but Derrick didn't miss a beat.

"Always a critic." He leaned down and scooped Jade up before she could throw another fit, which looked to be exactly what she wanted to do while we stood in the lobby. "Hey, Geode." He kissed the top of her head. "Let's go back and get ready." And before she could argue, he hoisted her up on his shoulder and moved toward the door. I followed, hoping everyone would forget the conversation that had just taken place.

Ten minutes later, Jade was in her gear and on the horse, and Derrick and I were watching from the sidelines. Derrick kept his eyes on his sister's lesson, and I tried to think of something to say that might erase our recent conversation. He had a girlfriend. Maybe I could get him talking about her.

"So," I shoved my hands into my jean pockets, "you have a girlfriend?"

He grinned. "What, we make peace and now you're hitting on me?"

I gaped at him. "I...No! I don't...I'm making basic conversation!"

"Relax. I'm riling you up on purpose." He stretched and linked his hands behind his head, a cocky grin on his face. "You're just so tightly wound that it's kind of hard not to." He quirked an eyebrow. "Are you going to be this way all summer?"

"I am not tightly wound!" I sputtered. "I'm...I'm professional!" Did the man's ability to annoy know no bounds?

"You're too worried about what the Allen clan is going to think and say." He shook his head. "You're nannying my sister, not applying to be my family's personal nun."

I crossed my arms and pursed my lips. "As far as I can see, there's no pleasing you no matter what I do."

"My fiancée's name is Amy," he said, watching Jade as one of the instructors stopped the horse to adjust her posture. "We met in Colorado, where I was stationed last. She works at a law firm there." He held out his phone, and the lock screen lit up with a picture of a woman with lips so red and skin so white and hair so dark she might as well have been Snow White. She was drop-dead gorgeous. And from the look of her fitted sweater and perfectly pleated mini skirt, she seemed to have the inherent sense of style that I had somehow missed out on.

So he was engaged. Not that it mattered. In fact, I pitied the girl. "Do you get to see her often?" I asked, hoping to keep his attention on Amy and away from me.

He kept his eyes on his sister. "She's pretty busy, but I'm going to try to drive out there when I can. I've got a buddy still at Peterson that I stay with when I go to see her."

"Is Peterson an Air Force base?" I asked.

"It is. It's one of the few bases with C-130's. I worked there as a hydraulics maintainer, same as I do here."

I watched Jade giggle as the horse began to move faster. "What does a hydraulics maintainer do?"

"Brakes. Things that open and close. I make sure the wheels of the plane do what they're supposed to."

"That sounds…hard," was all I could come up with.

He shrugged. "It's not that bad. But it does mean dealing with a lot of hydraulic fluid that doesn't wash out of your uniform." He turned back to me and opened his mouth as if to speak. Then he looked down and promptly shut it.

"What's that?" He nodded down at my feet.

I followed his gaze to my yellow rose backpack. "What? My bag?"

"That book, the one sticking out of the bag. You keep touching it." He reached down into my bag and pulled it out. I thought about yanking it away, then thought better of it. He may be about five-years-old, but I was an adult. "Beauty and the Beast?" He turned the book around in his hand, running his fingers along the gold filigree sprawling across the binding against the dark blue background. "It is Beauty and the Beast."

I smiled and rolled my eyes. "Fine. You caught me. I like fairy tales."

"Actually, I'm impressed." He grinned as he flipped through the blue leather-bound book. "What else?"

"What else what?"

"What about you?" He said. "You can't spend every hour of your day with five-year-olds." He waved the book in the air. "And I can't believe you spend every minute of your day reading this when you're not with my sister or the rest of your students."

I laughed in spite of myself. "No, I don't spend my entire life with five-year-olds or reading Beauty and the Beast."

"So?" He wagged his head back and forth impatiently. "What do you do with your time?"

I played with the sphinx cat keychain on my backpack zipper. "I spend time with my parents. And I study."

"You study. That's seriously what you like to do when you're not teaching or nannying?"

I raised my chin slightly. "I'm applying to get my master's degree at the University of Arkansas. So I use my time to study. What's wrong with that?"

"So…no travel?" He tilted his head toward me and wriggled his eyebrows. "No boyfriends?"

"I don't need a boyfriend right now. I'm busy."

He paused and studied me for a moment. "So tell me, what is it in that book that you like so much? Because based on the movie Jade makes me watch ad nauseam, there is very little in that story about staying at home and studying all the time."

"Belle loves books." I pursed my lips. "And she loves her father."

"But those can't be the only reasons you love it."

"Of course not. I love it for the adventure. The nerd gets her books and goes on a journey while finding true love. It's every bookworm's dream come true."

"Let me get this straight." He picked up my book and held it in the air. "You like to read about adventure. But you don't actually like to have any?"

"I…" I frowned. "I never said that." Why was he muddling everything I said? Taking it and twisting it like a piece of licorice.

"Oh please." He snorted. "You don't like to travel. You don't have time for a boyfriend. Your idea of a good time is studying and working with children who still struggle to take themselves to the bathroom." He gave me a funny look. "And you say you like adventures?"

"Grad school is an adventure!"

He rolled his eyes.

"Well, what do you do that's so adventurous?" I asked defiantly.

He laughed. "Aside from joining the military?" Then his eyes grew brighter, and he leaned slightly toward me, looking very much like an excited little boy. "I mean, why not? You get to travel! Every few years, you go somewhere new." He swept his arm around him, as though all the world were before us, rather than the arena. "Germany. Japan. California. Texas. Colorado. And every time you move, you get a whole new world to explore!" He clasped his hands again and leaned his elbows on his knees. "I'm saving everything I can right now to make sure Amy and I can travel whenever we want wherever we get stationed. It's part of why I joined the Air Force."

"Part of?"

"Well," he gave a half-laugh before tugging his uniform jacket down. "The uniform makes me look tough, you know. I thought that would be a good bullet point on my resume."

I snorted and tried to cover it by taking a sip from my travel mug. "And what does your fiancée think of all that traveling?"

The light in his eyes dimmed a little, and his smile fell. "She's pretty busy. But she says she'll make time after the wedding when things settle down a little."

"What about coming here?" I asked. "Can she visit much?"

He laughed a little and rubbed the back of his neck. "Yeah, well, let's just say there's a reason everyone's teasing me about my imaginary girlfriend."

As annoying as Derrick was, I felt a little guilty. Apparently, his fiancée wasn't as thrilled with travel as he was. Or with him, it might seem. I tried to give him an encouraging smile. "At least you can do video chats with her."

He gave me a tight-lipped smile. "Yeah. We can."

Did they, though? "How—"

"But I'm not worried about me." He sniffed and sat up. "I'm worried that you won't be able to loosen up. Because if you don't, you won't have much fun this summer. And my sister and I will be stuck trying to drag you behind us like a stick in the mud."

I stared at him. For just a moment, I'd come close to seeing something deeper. But now he was back to being everything I'd come to expect of military men. Cocky. Sarcastic. Funny, as much as I hated to admit it. Impudent. The sharp angles of his posture said it all. But he'd thrown up his shields. And because he knew how to take charge, he'd done a fantastic job of directing the conversation as it suited him. But I wasn't about to bow. I knew better than to let him run the game. Because I could play, too.

HOPE

DERRICK

When Jade had about fifteen minutes left in her session, I excused myself and stepped into the hall. It was nearly seven Amy's time, and she would be done with the gym by now and on her way to work. I called her, fully expecting to be sent to voicemail. But to my surprise, she picked up.

"You're quite the early bird lately. Shouldn't you be asleep by now?"

"It's a long story." I scratched my head and peeked through the window in the door at Jessie. "Hey, I was thinking. I know you're busy, but do you think you could make it out here for like a weekend? I could pay for the flight, and my parents have a spare room you could use in the main house."

"Hold on." She paused. "Okay, I'm at a stoplight. What weekend were you thinking?"

My heart leaped as I put the phone on speaker and scrolled through my calendar. "What about two weeks from now?"

"Actually..." She sounded surprised. "I think I'm free that weekend. What did you have in mind?"

I grinned. "Well, Jade has a piano performance that Saturday. My parents are going to be working, so I thought that it might be fun if you could come with the two of us. Then we could take her out for ice cream after and spend a little time together. And I'd like to try a new church out, but I get the feeling that dragging my parents around to shop for one is going to take an act of God."

"Oh." There was a pause on the other end. "And will we have any time for us?"

"Well, I'll obviously take you out after Jade's gone to bed, if that's what you mean." I wanted to kick myself for leaving that part out. Of course, she would want to go out. "There's this great little restaurant in the—"

"Oh, um. My boss is calling me." Amy's voice was oddly tinny. "I've gotta go. I'll...I'll get back to you when I get things more hammered out here schedule-wise."

"But I thought you said that weekend was free." I frowned. "Amy, what's wrong?"

"Look." She sighed. "I'm too tired to talk about this right now. But I'll get back to you, okay?"

I swallowed and forced my voice to sound normal. "Sure. I'll talk to you tonight."

"Bye." And with that, she was gone.

Gathering my dignity, I did my best to appear unruffled as I went out to face Jessie. She was standing up with one shoe resting on the bottom plank of the ring's fence, and she was clapping.

"That was fantastic, Jade!" she called. "I'm so proud of you!" When she noticed me, she turned, and for once, she didn't look at me like she might a sour lemon. Instead, her green eyes were bright. "Jade just tossed a ring on the stick all by herself while the horse was moving."

I went to stand beside her, and this time, my smile didn't feel so forced. "Great job, baby girl!" I called out, clapping along with Jessie.

Jessie was a hard nut to crack, but the way her eyes lit up when she praised my sister gave me hope. Maybe, just maybe, this summer wouldn't be quite so bad after all.

BUY THE BOOK

JESSIE

"Oh, I meant to ask," Madison said as she turned into the warehouse parking lot, "how did your mom's appointment go? It was last Friday, right?"

"It went okay, I guess." I leaned my head back and closed my eyes. "He called today, though, and wants her back tomorrow to repeat a test."

"Well," she said as she pulled into a parking space, "I guess it's not bad to be careful. Less than a week later, though…that's pretty fast."

"No." I groaned. "But I hate going through this stress every time someone loses a sticky note in the office somewhere, and they have to call her in again."

"Got your coupon?" Madison asked as we got out of the car.

"Yep." I shut the door and waved my green coupon in the air. It was like Christmas all bundled up in one little green rectangle of paper. And it was all mine.

"So how much money did you bring?" Madison asked as we made our way toward the warehouse, eyeing the empty canvas bags I'd slung over my arm.

"My credit card."

Her eyes nearly popped. "I can't remember the last time you didn't bring one of those little envelopes with cash in it. You must really need some shopping therapy."

"Books are therapy."

She shrugged. "This is true."

As we neared the door, though, she paused and pulled out her phone. "Sam wants to know if we're still coming to the Back to the BASICS Summit. And if we are, he wants to know if he can just book all our seats together."

I laughed. "How'd he know I was with you?"

"He said he texted you but you weren't answering."

"Oh." I reached into my purse but found only my wallet, makeup, and a granola bar that was Jade's. "I must have forgotten my phone. Tell him sure and sure."

"You know," Madison said, giving me a sideways glance as she texted back, "it's definitely not me he's interested in getting a seat next to."

I rolled my eyes. "Can you please just answer so we can go buy books?"

"Are you telling me you didn't feel something when he stole you away from Tanner the other day?"

My stomach did a stupid little somersault, but I wasn't quite ready to talk about that. At least, not in earnest. "I will be forever grateful for his daring rescue. But he still hasn't actually asked me out yet. So nothing is official as…why are you giving me that look?"

"Your rules are going to get you in trouble one day."

"Books, lady." I clapped impatiently. "I'm here for books."

We approached the door with the green piece of paper that said, Educators' Summer Warehouse Book Sale. A woman with snow-white hair and a t-shirt with a cartoon hog on it greeted us as we walked in.

"Educator passes?"

We both handed her our coupons, and she pointed us at a folding table covered in stacks of thin green canvas bags filled with catalogs. Another woman sat behind it.

"Go over there to Autumn, and she'll get you your warehouse maps and the other goodies that come in the bag."

We thanked her and made our way over to Autumn, where we were each gifted with a green bag and a stack of loose-leaf papers, each promising exciting books for children of all ages.

"Where should we begin?" I gaped up at the warehouse, unable to hide my awe. Ceiling high shelves housed countless stacks of books. Twelve, each double-sided, unless you counted the tables at the front that were also covered in books. Some even had boxes of books. Giant fans blew in air from the entrance, but I started to sweat the moment I stepped inside. But it didn't matter. Because here were thousands of books.

I could die here and be satisfied.

"Let's start with the chapter books since you probably won't need as many of them." Madison laughed as she dragged me down to the shelf farthest away. "Then you won't have to carry so many at first."

Even the novel section was magical. Not that my kindergarteners needed *My Side of the Mountain*, but it was only four dollars. How could I not get it?

"So have you heard from Adam?" I asked. Two weeks had passed since the fateful double date, and I wondered if their cuddly vibe had lasted beyond the restaurant booth.

"He texts sometimes," Madison smiled to herself a little too widely. "Nothing serious, but we have fun. He took me bowling on base the other day." She glanced at me. "Oh, and he apologizes for Tanner. He says the poor guy is desperate to get married and takes it out on every girl he meets, unfortunately."

"You don't say."

Madison shook her head. "Anyhow, I don't care about rehashing Tanner. I want to know about Big Brother." She lifted a heavy book in the air. "Do I need to go down there and thrash someone for you?"

I laughed and picked up a shiny copy of *Caddie Woodlawn*. "We've declared a truce."

"Oh?"

"Well, it was kind of my fault. I was still upset the day after the staff party, and when he started poking at me, I started to cry." Even now, I felt my cheeks flush. Of all the stupid things to cry over.

"Well," Madison twisted her mouth up at the offending *Lord of the Rings* anthology I was holding. "As long as he's leaving you alone."

"I don't know. I used to think it was me, but I'm realizing now that it's someone...or something else he mistrusts. Something happened last spring that has him all in a tizzy. He won't tell me what it is, but it's the reason he doesn't want to ever leave Jade alone."

"Last spring." Madison frowned. "Didn't something happen last spring with Jade? She was all scratched up or something."

I nearly dropped the book I was holding. "That's right! She came in just after Easter Break, covered in scratches! But when I asked her mom, she just handed me a doctor's note and said Jade had fallen in a rosebush." I nearly collided with a pallet full of books. But I couldn't have cared less. "Whatever it was, it shook Jade up pretty badly. She didn't do much work for weeks." Now that I thought about it...she must have started functioning again around the time Derrick came back to live with them.

"The guy sure seems attached to his sister," Madison said. "If he hadn't been such a jerk to you, I'd think it was super attractive." She fixed me with a speculative eye. "You sure talk about him a lot, though."

"I do not."

"You've texted me what he's done five out of the last five days you've worked there."

I rolled my eyes. "I just...I guess he's a conundrum. One day, he'll be just awful and poke fun at everything I say. Then the next day, he takes us out for ice cream and makes sure I have a coffee to go with it. I just can't figure him out."

"You sound a lot more charitable when you talk about him, too," Madison said, her tone just a little too light for my taste.

"I wrote him a letter the day after we made a truce." I smiled smugly at the copy of *Corduroy* I'd just picked up.

Madison turned to me, all laughter gone from her eyes. "Oh, please tell me you didn't send it."

I laughed. "And I thought you were on my side."

"Oh, I am." She hurried to catch up. "But my boyfriend is in security forces, and I'd really like for him not to arrest you for threatening an active duty military member."

"Who's the worrywart now?" I nudged her arm. "And you said you didn't have a boyfriend." Her scathing look made me laugh even harder. "I promise, the letter is safe in my desk. But anyway, I just...I want to understand him and why he's so intent on driving me crazy and himself into the ground for all the sleep he misses because of her. There has to be a reason." He was too...well, too attractive not to have a reason. The guy was brilliant. I'd glanced at one of the study manuals he'd left on the counter the week before, and it boggled my mind that anyone could understand it. And he could be devilishly charming when he wanted to. I had little doubt that he could be doing something that paid a lot more than what he was doing now.

So why was he so determined to keep Jade himself?

"You know," Madison said quietly as I picked up a silver fairy tale anthology, "sometimes you don't have to understand everything. Sometimes you just have to live."

I sighed as I checked the price then put it back. "I know," I said as I lovingly ran my fingers over the silver filigree.

"Why aren't you buying that?" Madison nodded at the book.

"It's too expensive." I made a face. "And I don't really need it. I've got other fairy tales in the unit books we can work on."

"Jessie." Madison huffed as she grabbed the book again and shoved it into my bag. "Buy the book."

"But—"

"Sometimes," she said, daring me to argue with her glare, "you just have to have fun and live a little. What was I trying to tell you last week?"

"I have no idea."

She glared. "Buy the dang book."

13

FUN

JESSIE

My day at the book warehouse sale had been nearly as therapeutic as I'd hoped, and I was decently prepared to face Derrick again after my day off. Letting myself into the house with the key Mrs. Allen had given me, however, still felt strange. It felt weird to walk into someone else's house unannounced. But just as I was about to announce my arrival, I caught the sound of arguing in the kitchen. Not wanting to intrude, I hung back in the entry, hoping it would be over soon.

"...just don't understand why you don't have a wedding date yet. You've been engaged for almost half a year." It was Mrs. Allen.

"I'm aware of that, Mom," Derrick snapped. "But unless my bride sets a date, I can't do a darn thing now, can I?"

"Derrick Allen, you had better not have done something to upset her."

"What business of that is yours?"

"Amy is the one thing in this world that you have done right. She's beautiful and smart and has her head on straight. All the things you need. And if you do something to lose her, so help me, I'm not even sure what I'll do with you."

Ouch. I wasn't a Derrick fan of any sort, but I couldn't imagine my mother talking to me like that. Derrick was talking again, but I decided I'd listened in long enough. I opened the door again and closed it loudly this time.

"Hello?" I called as though just getting in. "I'm here."

The arguing abruptly ended, and Mrs. Allen came out a moment later to greet me, all signs of their argument gone.

"Good morning, Jessie. I'm just about to go, but I left some take-out in the fridge for you from last night. You can have it for lunch if you want."

"Thanks so much." I had to work to keep the smile on my face this time. "I hope you have a great day."

She grabbed her purse and called goodbye to Jade before leaving. After she'd closed and locked the door behind her, I dared a peek at Derrick. He'd followed her out, but now he turned to go back into the kitchen, still muttering under his breath.

We didn't speak much for the rest of the morning. Derrick seemed lost in La-la Land, which would have been fine with me, had I not heard his mother's words that morning. So I did my best to get Jade ready quickly, and I didn't complain at all when he put her in the car and buckled her in himself.

I couldn't keep my mouth shut or my sympathy high, though, once we realized it was the therapy center's first day at their new location. We also learned rather quickly that we didn't know where that was, even with GPS.

"I told you that you should have turned left back at that last light." I shook my head and sipped coffee from my travel mug.

"What?" Derrick asked. "And lose out on our adventure?" He seemed to have forgotten about his mother's jabs and was in finer form than ever.

"Thanks to your little *adventure*, we're going to be three minutes late." I looked at my phone's map in dismay. Jade's therapy center had moved to what they called a "more central" location. But I was really beginning to doubt that moniker.

Derrick came to a stop so fast I shrieked as coffee spilled all over my lap.

"You really are a beast," I muttered as I grabbed a tissue and began to pat my jeans dry.

"I'm okay with that." He grinned unashamedly as the light turned green. "The beast got his girl in the end."

"Lucky for him, he got to change back into a prince. You never had that option to begin with."

"Ouch." He gave me a patronizing look. "No fun today, are we?"

I held his startling blue gaze for a long minute before pulling out my phone again. That's it. I was going in for the kill.

"What are you doing?" he asked after several minutes of silence. I couldn't help being a little thrilled at the suspicious look in his eyes. Good. Served him right.

"You are the third person to accuse me recently of not knowing how to have fun," I said, holding up my phone so he could see. "So the three of us are going to have more fun than you ever imagined."

He squinted at the screen. "What is that?"

"Guess what, Jade?" I gushed, turning around in my seat. "We're going to the diamond mine next week!"

"Yay!" she squealed, nearly dropping the book she'd been looking at.

I turned back to Derrick triumphantly. "A full day of digging for diamonds. Doesn't that sound like an adventure?"

For the first time since I'd met him, he looked truly miffed. "That's your idea of fun?"

"Of course!" I feigned surprise. "Who wouldn't want to go digging in the dirt for a full day?"

"Jessie, I don't know—"

"We mine! We mine!" Jade was singing from the back seat.

I took another sip of my coffee and batted my eyelashes at him. "See?" I asked in a saccharine voice. "Who says I don't know how to have fun?"

14

WHY

JESSIE

M y chance for fun came sooner than I thought. After Jade's therapy, we got back to their house for lunch, and as soon as he'd finished off his triple-decker meatball sandwich, Derrick passed out on his mother's couch. He crashed so hard that by the time I found him he was snoring hard, and a little bead of drool had formed at the corner of his mouth.

Part of me wanted to feel sorry for him. The guy was working all through the night then driving us everywhere we went. I hadn't even been able to convince him to leave me alone with her for more than an hour. He was obviously exhausted, and I would have thought the whole thing ridiculous. Except that after hearing about Jade's incident, whatever it had been, I could see it had shaken him to the core. His weird interrogation at our first meeting was starting to make sense.

But sympathy wasn't going to help me much this afternoon. I'd told him I would need to leave early to take my mom to the doctor to get a blood test done, and he'd been more than happy to take Jade. Now that he was so comfortably unconscious, however, it seemed a shame to wake him. It also made me uncomfortable to leave Jade as the only conscious one in the house, particularly with their ginormous pool in the backyard, even if it did have a gate.

The fact of the matter was that Derrick needed sleep.

I needed to leave.

And he needed to see that I truly could take care of Jade all on my own for one afternoon.

"Jade." I popped my head into the kitchen, where she was playing with her string cheese while she looked at the same picture book she'd had in the truck earlier. "Finish up and get your shoes. We're leaving in just a few minutes."

She looked at me but didn't put down her cheese. "Where?"

"We're going to have a girls' day." I winked. "We might even get a smoothie."

Jade shoved the rest of the cheese in her mouth and trotted out to find her shoes. As she put them on, though, she cast an uneasy glance at her brother.

"Coming?"

I shook my head and put my finger to my lips. "Your brother is really sleepy right now, so we're going to let him sleep while you and I go out and have some girl time."

She nodded and finished putting on her shoes, but the little crease didn't leave her forehead as she grabbed her book and followed me out the door.

I felt like a nefarious kidnapper as I moved her car seat to my car. This was what her parents hired me to do, I reminded myself. Derrick had decided to insert himself into the equation, but he'd never been a vital part, to begin with. For some annoying reason, I couldn't make the guilt go away completely, but it wasn't enough to stop or even slow me. So I settled for leaving a note on the door letting Derrick know where we were going and that we'd be back in three hours.

"All right," I said as I buckled my own seatbelt and turned to back out, "it's a girls' day! We're going to run an errand at the doctor with *my* mommy, then I'm going to get you a smoothie. Are you excited?"

Jade shrugged. She was looking at her book again.

"What flavor do you want? We can get strawberry, vanilla, blueberry, cherry, you name it."

No response.

"Hey, pretty girl." I glanced in the rearview mirror. "What's wrong?"

She shrugged again as she looked out the window. "Nothing."

"Then why won't you talk to me?"

"Thinking."

"Oh." That wasn't the answer I'd been anticipating. But I didn't have time to focus on it because my phone began to buzz. "Hey, Mom," I said, putting it on speaker. "I'm on my way."

"Sounds good. I'll be waiting for you."

Sure enough, my mom was standing outside the house when I pulled up. She hopped in and gave me a kiss.

"Thanks for doing this, but you really didn't have to."

"I want to, Mom." I nodded at the back seat. "We have an extra friend with us today."

"Hi, Jade." My mom turned around to wave, to which Jade gave her a glimpse and then looked back down at her book.

"Why are they having you come back in anyway? You had your test last week."

"Who knows? He said it was nothing serious. They just need to do a little more bloodwork, that's all."

"I don't like them not telling us on the phone." I frowned at the road. "It makes me suspicious."

"Oh, quit worrying so much. I'm sure it'll be fine. If it was that important, he wouldn't have waited long to schedule me."

"Mom, it's been a whole weekend."

"Jessie." My mother groaned. "If you don't stop, I'm going to get out and walk."

"No need," I muttered. "We're here."

My heart fluttered out of rhythm as we pulled into the medical center's parking lot. I hated this place with its clean walls covered in swirling beige and maroon wallpaper. I hated its cheery TV music with its looping tips for healthy living. And I especially hated waiting for almost an hour in the lobby then going back to the little waiting rooms and waiting for yet another half hour before the doctor even showed up.

"Jade," I unzipped her backpack as we waited for my mom to get checked in at the desk, "would you like your coloring book?"

She shook her head, still studying her picture book as though it contained the secrets of the universe.

"What is that?" I peeked at the cover. *LaRissa is The Fairy Princess*. It showed a little girl up on a stage in a princess costume with a spotlight shining down on her from above. She was holding a microphone.

My mom sat down next to me with a clipboard. "It's nice to see you, by the way. I feel like I've barely had a sighting of you in the last few weeks."

"Sorry about that." I grimaced. "Sam gave me a used copy of a textbook I'll need for one of my first classes for the master's program. I've been studying."

"I know." She sat back against the headrest and sighed a little.

"Okay, what does that mean?"

She kept her eyes on the clipboard. "What does what mean?"

"That sigh."

"Oh, nothing. I was just…" She sighed again and put the clipboard down. "Okay, you want to know what's bothering me?"

"I do, or I wouldn't have asked." Though I was kind of regretting that now.

"Honey, if you would just slow down for five minutes and talk to someone now and then, you could have a little fun sometimes instead of studying all the time."

"I talk to people. I went to that teacher's get-together at the bar."

"And how much of that did you spend with Madison and whatever random guy she found for you to sit next to?"

I burst out laughing so loudly a few of the other people in the waiting room sent me glances. "Are we that predictable?"

"What about that cute teacher at your work? I've seen him eyeing you every time we go to any of your staff functions."

Because I wasn't feeling uncool enough already. My mom had to remind me that I took my parents to staff functions because I hadn't been on a real date since college.

"Sam is the one who gave me the textbook. He thinks it's important to get this degree." I smirked slightly. "He got the same master's as I want, and he's working on his doctorate."

"Hun, look." My mom sighed and looked up at the ceiling. "I'm not going to tell you what you have to do. You're twenty-three and too old for that. But…I just want to see you stepping out of your safe space every now and then, that's all."

"Mom, I'm happy with my life. I work hard, but I'm helping people. I'm helping my students. I help you and Dad. Right now, I get to hang out with Jade." I paused to grin at her, but she ignored me, still entranced with her book. "Why are people so obsessed with changing that? I like to be needed. I want to be needed."

Before my mother could respond, the nurse called us back. And to my shock, the doctor was waiting for us when we got there.

"This is five-star service," Mom said as I helped Jade get seated. The nurse immediately began taking my mother's vitals. But I didn't need to worry about that. Because nurses always did that, no matter which doctor you were at.

Right?

The doctor shrugged. "Well, the patient before you canceled, so I thought I'd try to get this done quickly so you can be on your way."

"Were the tests all okay?" I asked, unable to contain myself. Was this it? The beginning of another roller coaster where my father and I watched my mother battle for her life? Should I run out of the room now to have just a few more minutes of blissful ignorance? My hands were slick with sweat, and the room seemed suddenly far too small for my taste.

He gave me a patient smile, his white, bushy mustache moving slightly against his dark skin as he grinned. "Nothing to be alarmed about. It's just that there was a slight irregularity on one of the tests."

"What kind of irregularity?" my mother asked. Her voice sounded far more stable than mine.

"I'm not sure. In fact, I'm confident that it's nothing you need to worry about. I just want to make sure."

The floor beneath me threatened to tilt, but before it got too off-kilter, Jade tugged on my sleeve. I looked down, wanting nothing more than to throw up. But I did my best to smile when I found her big eyes searching mine.

"I want to do this."

I tried to focus on what she was pointing at while keeping an ear open to hear what the doctor was telling my mom.

"Dance?" I asked.

"No." She frowned for a second before pointing to the stage. "This."

Still trying to listen in on the doctor's conversation, it was a moment before what she was saying clicked.

"You want to sing?" I paused. "On stage?"

She nodded enthusiastically. "The Candy Choir."

"Oh." I looked down at the page again, my heart falling. The Candy Choir was a private choir run by a few of the parents of students at our school for girls in the lower elementary grades. Jade was the perfect age, but there were requirements. First, you had to be willing to spend quite a bit of money for matching costumes and such, something I knew wouldn't be a problem for the Allens. Unfortunately, however, the girls were also required to try out for the positions, and to do that, they had to be able to read the lyrics in their little song booklets. And while Jade's memorization skills were actually above the levels of several of her peers, her reading was an area of constant struggle.

"Why don't you ask your mom?" I asked lamely, hoping to shift the responsibility to someone else.

Jade shook her head and closed the book slowly. "Too busy."

For just a moment, I forgot to listen to the doctor, and my heart cracked just a little. But no matter how I poked and prodded, she refused to say anything else about it.

My mom was done soon after that, and we left the doctor quietly. The whole drive, I mentally pleaded for my mom to talk. I needed to hear her voice so badly that it hurt. But she stared out the window for most of the drive, and her expression was unreadable. By the time we got home, I still hadn't thought of anything to say. But when she got out, before she closed the door, she turned to face me.

"Jessie, I know this kind of thing is exactly why you do what you do."

"Mom, you had surgery less than a year ago."

"And," she said with an irritating calm, "I was declared in remission. The surgery was a success."

"But—"

"Hun, if you let my every doctor visit dictate the way you live the rest of your life, I'm going to live the rest of my life feeling like I've let you down."

Her words haunted me as I drove us to the nearest smoothie shop. As we sat inside and Jade inhaled her strawberry vanilla smoothie through an oversized straw, I couldn't remember the last time I'd felt so lost.

This was my life. My decisions. So why couldn't anyone else accept that? Everyone thought I was too rigid, too set in my ways. Well, everyone except Sam. I smiled slightly. That guy got me.

"Hey, let me see that book again." I shook my head as though it would dispel my morbid thoughts. Jade put her book on the table, and

I began to read it to her. When we were done, I watched the way she looked longingly at the girl on the stage. Then I got an idea.

"Jade, do you really want to be in the Candy Choir?" I had no idea whether or not Mrs. Allen would let Jade try out for anything on-stage with a private group. But since they always performed in the school's spring talent show, it just might qualify as a different matter entirely. They practiced in the school cafeteria after school as it was. And I had a feeling I just might know how to make certain arrangements, even if Jade couldn't read. But first, I needed the little girl to be on board as well.

Jade nodded profusely.

"What if," I said slowly, "we started practicing now? They don't have tryouts until several weeks after school starts, which means we could get a lot of practice in. But that's a lot of work. Are you sure you're up for that? I mean, I can't promise anything," I hastened to add. "But we can try."

Jade's eyes sparkled so brightly I had to laugh.

"All right, kiddo. That's what we'll do then. As long as your mom is okay with it, we'll start practicing."

Jade started going on and on about the costume in the book, and a sense of peace settled over me as we planned.

This. This was why I lived the way I did. Because God had given me the chance to change my little corner of the world. Jade. My other students. My parents. Everyone. And if I didn't make my corner better, who would?

My mother, as much as I loved her, would just have to wait to watch me sail off into the sunset with the guy and life she imagined. Because right now, my happily ever after was here.

15

THANK YOU

DERRICK

A fter two long hours in the car...two and a half, if you counted all the bathroom stops we had to make for Jade and Jessie, we finally passed the sign that said *Crater of Diamonds State Park*.

"I still don't think this is a good idea," I muttered.

Jade, who was looking at her torn and beaten copy of *A Geologist's Guide to Minerals*, ignored me completely, but Jessie flashed me a daring grin.

"And why not?"

"I'm serious. Jade wanders sometimes, and you know that. And when she doesn't want to come back, she hides." I tighten my grip on the steering wheel. "A cave...a mine is the last place she needs to be. And I'm still upset at you, by the way, for Tuesday, when you took Jade without asking." I'd been giving her the stink-eye for four days now, but she just wasn't taking the hint.

Jessie just rolled her eyes and twisted around in her seat to face Jade. "Guess what, Geode? It rained last night, which means we have a better chance of finding a diamond this morning." She looked back at me. "And I don't know what all your fuss is about. I returned her safe and sound and with a smoothie. No sugar added. You're welcome."

I bit the inside of my lip. Geode was *my* nickname for my sister. What had possessed Jessie to think she had any right calling my sister by that name? Probably the same thing that had convinced her it was okay to take Jade to some doctor appointment without letting her family know where she was.

Not that it mattered in the grand scheme of things. Half the reason I was even taking us on this stupid danger hunt was to take pictures and prove to my parents what kind of places Jessie was willing to take Jade. And just to spite me at that.

"You need to lighten up." Jessie leaned back and stretched. Her cheeks had a rosy color to them, and she was still wearing that self-satisfied grin. Beneath the white baseball cap with a yellow rose patch sewn onto it, which she swore was to protect her from the sun, she actually would have looked really cute.

If she hadn't been bound and determined to ruin my sister's life. And mine.

"After all," she added, her green eyes flashing, "don't you want a little adventure in your life?"

I ignored her as she giggled to herself, and I focused on turning off the highway to follow the signs.

Had I not been so ticked with Jessie, the day would have been a beautiful one. The trees, which grew thick as carpet in central Arkansas, had thinned a bit and given way to more open fields, complete with white fences and flat green hills dotted with cattle and horses. The trees soon swallowed us up again, though, which Jessie claimed meant we were getting close.

I glanced at her again out of the corner of my eye. What on earth did she need the hat for if we were going to be in a mine?

Jessie struck up some counting song with Jade as we went. She said it was meant to make the time pass faster, it felt as though a year had passed when we finally pulled into the parking lot.

I stepped out and tried to see where the mines might be. But all I could see were trees and a tan, metal-roofed building on the far side of the parking lot. Jessie fussed with Jade about wearing her hat and putting on sunscreen before turning to me and holding up the can.

"All right, your turn."

"I'm not putting on sunscreen for a walk through the parking lot."

"That's fine," she said, "but you'll want it for the mine."

"Who puts sunscreen on in a mine?"

Jessie smirked and pulled my favorite baseball cap from her back-pack. I snatched it out of her hands and put it on.

"Where'd you get that?" If she'd been in my casita, snooping...

"Your mother gave it to me when I told her what we were doing. She also said you probably wouldn't want the sunscreen but to make you wear it anyway."

"Come on, Jade." I scooped Jade up and marched through the parking lot. Jessie followed behind, still wearing that know-it-all grin.

She took the lead as we started up the path toward the building but paused in front of a giant sign with a diamond on it. After shoving me in front of it and taking a forced picture, for which I did not smile, she led us into a lobby with several diamond displays and a small gift shop. Instead of pausing in here, though, she took us out through the other side of the lobby, where a long covered platform spread out on both sides. And I stopped dead in my tracks. There was not a cave to be seen. Just acres of...mud. Lots and lots of mud.

"You have got to be kidding me."

Jessie let her head fall back and laughed a little too hard.

"It's not that funny."

"What did you think *crater* of diamonds meant?" She pulled Jade from my arms, and taking her hand, put her on the ground. But before getting in line at one of the little windows along the side of the building, she tossed me the sunscreen. "You might want to try this after all."

I couldn't remember the last time I'd felt this stupid as Jessie happily bought us tickets and then rented us the "mining" supplies. They looked like the sandbox toys I'd played with as a kid, only these were made of wood and steel mesh.

"These," she told Jade as we made our way out into the field of mud farthest to the right, "are going to help us separate the dirt from the rocks." She got down on her knees and beckoned for Jade to do the same. Then she dug into the dirt and began to sift it through the mesh frames.

"Derrick." Jade looked up at me and pointed at the ground beside her. "Come dig."

Mucking around in a field of dirt wasn't exactly how I'd planned to spend my Saturday. In spite of my annoyance at Jessie, however, it was impossible not to smile at Jade's joy. I'd never seen her so focused as she and Jessie hunched over the mesh frames together.

"Don't my parents pay you for five days a week?" I asked as I obeyed my sister and filled my first frame with dirt. "Because in case you didn't know, it's day six."

Jessie paused in her work and grinned up at me, her eyes sparkling just a bit too much. "This is pro bono," she said, flipping her ponytail out of her face.

My phone buzzed in my pocket, so I let Jessie and Jade enjoy their digging while I answered. I was rewarded with Amy's chirpy greeting.

"I'm sorry I've been so busy this week," she rattled on. I could hear her loading her dishwasher in the background. "We just finished one of our big cases, so I thought I'd give you a call."

"I'm glad you did." I put my hand on my hat and looked around. "You won't believe where I am right now."

"Hopefully not any place I'll have to get you out of."

I laughed. It felt good to laugh with my fiancée again. I hadn't realized how much I missed it until now. "No, Jade's obsessed with rocks, so Jessie thought it would be a good idea to take her diamond mining."

"Oh, I've heard about that! It's actually on my list of things to try."

Really? "If spending a day getting covered in dirt is your idea of a good time, be my guest."

Amy giggled again. "You know you can't blame Jade or even her nanny. This is your fault for being so stubborn. If you weren't so determined to always be with—"

"I know, I know." I huffed. "Hey, have you given any thought to my offer?"

She sighed, and I had to keep myself from visibly cringing. The moment was gone.

"I was wondering..." she said in a small voice. "Is there a weekend that maybe Jade doesn't have some sort of event?"

I frowned. "I don't know. I'd have to ask my mom. Why?"

"I was just hoping that maybe you and I would have a little more time together...alone when I came. That's all."

"Oh." I looked back down at my little sister, who was happily smearing dirt all over a squealing Jessie. "I'd actually kind of wanted you to get to know my family a bit better. I mean, you've only met them once."

She was silent. Several seconds passed by. Finally, I heard her take a deep breath. "You know what? You're right. Just give me some time to find a weekend that would work. Okay?"

I nodded as though she could see me. "Okay. Sure."

"Bye, Derrick."

"Bye. Love you." My chest felt heavy as I put the phone back in my pocket, but I did my best to smile as I rejoined Jade and Jessie. Right now. I would just focus on this moment and worry about the rest of it later. We'd get it all worked out, and someday, Amy would realize how much fun Jade really could be.

"All right, Tiger." I took Jade's spade, which she was using as a paintbrush to dab mud on Jessie's pants whenever Jessie wasn't looking. "Let's dig for some diamonds."

The visit itself actually didn't go so badly. I had the unfortunate fate of getting rather sunburned, and then the worse humiliation of Jessie insisting on spraying me down so I didn't burn further, but other than that, it really was fun. None of us had found any diamonds after the first hour and a half, but the time outdoors and the sound of Jade's laughter seemed to melt the boulder that had been sitting on my chest, and soon, I was just as dirty as the girls were.

Jessie really was a good sport, particularly about the dirt. She had dirt everywhere, thanks to my sister. In her hair, on her face, and one time, I caught Jade trying to put it down her shirt. But none of that seemed to faze her. In fact, none of Jade's obstacles seemed to bother Jessie, as long as I wasn't making them worse.

I really had been horrible to her in the beginning. I had reasons to have my doubts, of course. But the longer I watched her, the more I realized that she loved Jade the way...

Well, the way I wished Amy would.

"Derrick."

I turned to see Jessie holding an arm to her left eye. "I think I've got some dirt around my eye. Can you grab a wet wipe for me out of the backpack?"

I rummaged through Jade's green backpack, the one we brought everywhere she went. It took a moment, but I finally found it in the side pocket. Just as she wiped the corner of her eye, however, we heard a shout from behind us. When we turned to look, we found Jade several rows away, where she stood looking up into the face of a very angry man.

"Give that back!" The man growled down at my sister.

Jade stared up at him, unresponsive until he tried to yank the frame from her hands. Then she shrieked like she was being eaten by a bloody ghost.

"That's mine, you brat!" he bellowed as Jade screamed louder.

Jessie and I were at her side in a flash. I grabbed Jade up in my arms, but before I could get in the man's face, Jessie was already there.

He was probably six feet tall, just an inch or so shorter than myself. And he was no feathery thing. But that didn't seem to bother Jessie in the slightest as she stood on her toes to get inches from his face.

"What is wrong with you?" she snapped. I stood behind her, leveling a dark look at him over her head.

"She stole my tools, that's what."

"I'm sorry." Jessie didn't sound sorry at all. "But she's six. It was just an accident. No need to scare her."

"I rented these, and I'll be—"

I put my free hand over Jade's ear as he let loose a string of profanities.

"...if I let some brat take them so this park can charge me ten times what they're worth."

Jessie snorted. "It didn't occur to you to ask her nicely?"

"Wouldn't have done any good." The man gestured at Jade. "Don't know what you're here for anyhow. Shouldn't let kids like that free unless they're on a leash." He snorted. "In fact, my sister's on the state senate, in case you didn't know. Maybe I'll have her start some sort of action to keep kids like her under control in public places."

"Kids. Like. What?" Jessie enunciated each word slowly.

People were staring now, and a few had started to step forward. The man glanced around as our onlookers began to murmur and several more sent him scathing looks.

"Keep talking like that," Jessie hissed, "and I will have a lawyer so far up your butt that you're not going to need a colonoscopy this year."

"And if you so much as look at my sister the wrong way again," I added in a low voice, "I will make sure you leave this park on a gurney."

The man held my gaze for several seconds before glancing around at the people who were watching. A man in a uniform was making his way out to us.

"Do we have a problem here?" he called.

The man looked back at Jade once more before turning and shaking his head. "No. No problem."

"Come on, Geode." I put my hand on her cheek as she leaned into my shoulder. "Let's go back to our digging."

But Jade wouldn't have it. In fact, she was too scared to be within fifty feet of the man, and we had to move three times before she was willing to start digging again.

The move was worth it, though. Because not fifteen minutes later, Jade found her diamond. She held it up proudly to show me, and my jaw nearly hit the floor as I found myself looking at a shiny brown stone nearly the size of a pea. Jessie gushed all over Jade, too, of course. And as we made our way back to the building to return our equipment and get Jade's stone looked at, she stopped and cupped a hand to her mouth.

"Thanks for making us move," she called to the man who had yelled at Jade. When he'd looked up, Jessie grinned and added, "Without you, she never would have found it."

He sneered. "Found what?"

"Her diamond."

The man watched us walk away, his mouth open, and I paused long enough to level him one last glare.

The diamond was nothing short of 2.7 carats. I swung Jade up onto my shoulders, where she gleefully clutched at her little drawstring bag as we made our way back to the parking lot.

"How about ice cream for our geologist?" I asked, to which she squealed and began to chatter happily, naming at least five different flavors she wanted on her cone.

After we got back into the car, I turned on the ignition. But instead of backing out, I turned to Jessie. Dirt was still smudged beneath her eye. Without thinking, I reached up and wiped it off. "Thank you," I said.

She stared at me, eyes wide. "What for?"

I gave her a sad smile. "You did something for my sister most people wouldn't know the first thing about handling."

"I told you," she said, smiling sadly. "I really do care."

I smiled, too, and for once, it wasn't forced. "I know." Then I put the truck into reverse as a new atmosphere settled over the cab. It was a strange sensation, knowing that we were now a team. Also strange was the sudden awareness that I didn't really want her to leave Jade. Not anymore. Anyone willing to stand up to someone twice their size for the sake of my sister was all right in my book.

"Also," I added, trying to lighten the mood slightly, "my mother will probably want to thank you, too."

"She doesn't need to."

"Oh, not for Jade." I gave her a wry grin. "For keeping me out of jail."

"Well," she studied me before a slow grin spread across her face. "I guess this means you owe me."

I laughed as we pulled out of the parking lot. "I guess it does."

16

PRO BONO

JESSIE

I n the week that followed, I wasn't sure what to expect after my unorthodox bonding moment with Derrick at the diamond mine, and it sat on the back of my mind for the remainder of the weekend. I felt as though I'd seen a color in him that I hadn't even known existed before. He joked about jail, but back in that moment, when I'd caught a glimpse of him staring over my shoulder at the man who had yelled at Jade, I'd known he truly was very likely to put the man out of his misery.

It's funny how a single look can change the way you think about someone. Sure, he'd told me about his passion for his sister, but I hadn't realized until that moment just how deep his devotion ran. And it was impossible not to be touched by that kind of love.

And the moment he wiped the dirt off my face? For some reason, stupid alarm bells went off in my head. And though I knew it meant nothing...it should mean nothing because he had a fiancée, I had to wonder. When was the last time I'd been touched by a man? Except for my relatives, of course. And me grabbing Sam's arm in the bar to pretend he was my boyfriend to escape Tanner didn't count.

The last time I could remember having any sort of physical contact initiated by someone of the opposite sex was in college, when I'd stumbled in a stairwell, and my friend's boyfriend caught my arm so I didn't plunge to my death.

Maybe Madison was right. I did need to get out more.

Sam's text didn't help either. That evening, after I got back from the diamond mine, I noticed his message, which I had missed in the excitement of the day.

So how was the beast today? Do I need to take someone by the horns and toss them around a bit?

The beast was fine. It was me, apparently, who needed a good shakeup.

We didn't kill each other today, I responded. *So that's something.*

I was spared the humiliation of having to figure out how to talk to Derrick the next Monday when he was called away at the last minute for a temporary duty assignment in Mississippi and would be gone the entire week. I found myself relieved at the reprieve and yet, anxious. I'd have to see him again sometime. If only we could just get it over with.

The week was strangely quiet. I took Jade to all her appointments and without the arguing, even had time to slip in a little fun. Mrs. Allen didn't seem particularly interested in the Candy Choir, probably since she was sure Jade wouldn't make the team. But all I needed was the go-ahead, so we chose a song and costume for the tryouts. Everything went as expected, and I came out another week closer to starting my master's degree.

What I didn't expect, however, was a text at nine-fifteen a.m. Saturday morning, a week after our little mining adventure.

Up for more pro bono work?

It took me several seconds to wipe the blur from my eyes as I squinted at the screen. Pro bono? Oh. Derrick. He must have gotten my number from his mother.

. . .

What did you have in mind? I typed back.

Be ready in fifteen. We're on our way to get you.

I stared at the phone for another minute, trying to sort through my foggy brain, when I realized what he'd just said.

Be ready in fifteen.

I half-fell, half-jumped out of bed and riffled through my closet, muttering to myself as I did. He could at least have the decency to tell me what to wear if he was dragging me out of bed on my day off. I glanced in the mirror, but it didn't matter what I saw. There wasn't enough time to shower, so I made do with my favorite white baseball cap and a ponytail. Figuring I'd better be ready for anything, I threw on a pair of jeans and a faded but slightly dressy pink t-shirt before grabbing my socks and sneakers and stumbling through the door.

"You're up early," my mom said as I tore through the kitchen. I grabbed three of the chocolate chip blueberry pancakes she'd stacked on a plate. I wasn't known in my house as a great lover of the morning sun.

"Apparently, I'm going to hang out with Jade and Derrick." I stuffed the pancakes in my mouth, careful not to bite all the way through as I pulled on my socks and shoes.

My mother put her spatula down. "I thought you were only working on the weekdays."

I took the pancakes out of my mouth. "This is pro bono."

My mother narrowed her eyes at me. "Which means you're working for free."

I paused and took the pancakes out of my mouth. "Actually...I think it means we're going to go have fun."

She tilted her head at me, and for a long, rare moment, I had no idea what she was thinking. But to my surprise, she finally shrugged.

"Well, if anyone needs a little fun, it's you. Just…don't let them start using you as a free babysitter. Your time is worth more than that."

I laughed. "I don't think I'm going to have any problem with that."

A car horn honked in the front yard. Grabbing a napkin for my pancakes, I kissed my mom goodbye and dashed out to the front drive.

Sure enough, a red truck sat just in front of the door, the door already open. Letting myself in, I dropped my purse on the floor and shut the door as Derrick gave me a reproving look.

"Pancakes? Really? I thought we'd established the rules for my vessel."

"Your vessel can thank you for waking me up on a Saturday." I took a defiant bite and smiled at him as I chewed.

"I want one!" Jade called from the backseat.

"No," Derrick called over his shoulder. "You already had breakfast. And you." He turned to me, "You can sleep in tomorrow, so stop whining."

"No, I can't. Some of us have responsibilities on Sundays. Like church."

He gave me a funny look. "You go to church?"

Why was that surprising? "Only my entire life." I raised my eyebrows. "And you?"

To my glee, he looked slightly discomfited. "I need to find a new one Jade can be comfortable in."

If I hadn't known Jade's struggles with sitting still, I would have made fun of him. But instead, I focused on my food. "So," I said between bites, "where am I going pro bono?"

"You'll see." Derrick wriggled his eyebrows.

"Well, if I'd known I was getting kidnapped, I would have at least brought another pancake."

"All you need to know," he said as we came to a stoplight, "is that I'm going to prove once and for all that I can be more fun than you."

"You can try." I finished off my first pancake. Once my second was gone, I dove into my purse for gum and lip gloss.

"You don't need makeup where we're going," he said.

I ignored him and pulled down the little mirror on the sun visor. "Some of us need more than fifteen minutes to look presentable."

"You look fine. What's important today," he sat back with a smirk, "is that you understand how deep my fun level goes."

"Um…my fun got that girl a diamond all her own." I snapped the cap back on my lip gloss. "I really doubt you can beat that."

He nodded for a moment before turning to me once more. "Fine then. Put your money where your mouth is."

"Excuse me?"

"Let's make a bet," he said slowly. "This summer, we'll take turns picking new places to take her. And whoever suggests the one she likes best wins."

"What will I win?" I asked.

"Haha, very funny. Winner will get to choose what we do for an entire day."

"That's not so hard."

His grin widened. "And the loser can't complain."

I studied him. He seemed so sure of himself, and honestly, I couldn't fault him for that. If anyone in his family knew what Jade would like, he would be the one to know. But I wasn't in his family. And I hadn't spent the entire first two weeks of school convincing Jade to talk out loud for nothing. Derrick might know her past, but I knew who and what she was now.

"Fine," I said with a shrug. "It's a deal."

He turned the music up. "All right, but be prepared to lose."

I had to work hard to hide my shock when we pulled into a parking slot. I was impressed, as much as I hated to admit it, with his little gem. But I wasn't about to let him know that.

"What is this place?" I asked as he pulled Jade out of her car seat.

"Burns Park," he said, taking the backpack from me and putting it on himself. "My parents used to take me here as a kid. I'm honestly kind of surprised it's still up and running."

I was, too. But that only made it more delightful. The park itself was huge. We'd passed at least two covered picnic spots and two play areas for children of different ages. But smack dab in the middle was a miniature theme park, complete with an old fashioned Merry-Go-Round. There were several of those carnival rides, the kinds that go up and down or just round and round in circles. A small but real train tooted as it made its circled the other rides, and there was one of those really tall slides in the back.

"How have I never heard of this?" I asked as we made our way through the metal railings which had been moved back so the entrance was clear.

"I don't know." He shrugged before giving me a wicked grin. "Maybe you just needed to meet a real Arkansas native."

"Hey!" I called as he scooped Jade up and ran with her to the ticket counter, both of them laughing as he went.

"Fifteen tickets, please," he was telling the teenager behind the window when I caught up.

"I count as a native," I argued as he counted out the bills. "I've been here since I was fifteen. You, however, have been gone for years."

"But, you didn't know about this one, did you?" He winked at me before turning to Jade. "Okay, Geode, which one first?"

She pointed to the ride where the little hot air balloons went up in the air in circles. To my surprise, though, Derrick frowned.

"I don't know, hun. That one's pretty tall, and I can't go on it with you."

"Why?" She pouted.

"I'm too tall. They wouldn't let me on."

I pointed at the height requirement board "She's tall enough. Why not let her go on by herself?"

He turned his frown on me. "I don't know."

"Come here." I took Jade from her brother's rather unwilling arms. Then I set her on the ground and let my hands rest on her shoulders. "Jade's going to be seven soon. Definitely old enough to go on a ride on her own." I smiled down at her. "She has also gone on several trips this year, including our visit to a ski lift to see the mountain scenery. And she never once tried to get out or run away."

His eyes nearly popped. "You took her on a ski lift?" Then he shook his head and rubbed his eyes with the heels of his hands. "It doesn't matter. You were with her on those rides. And there were other children."

"And I think," I said gently, "that she's proved herself to be trustworthy." I looked down. "If we let you go on that one, are you going to try to jump or climb out?" I fixed her with a warning look. "Because if you did, you'd get very hurt."

"No, won't get out." She let out a dramatic huff and rolled her eyes.

"There." I looked back at Derrick. "How about that?"

"I don't know." He looked back up at the ride the way some people look at the edge of the Grand Canyon.

"Look," I said softly so Jade couldn't hear. "You're a great brother. And you take wonderful care of her. But...she's six. She'll be seven soon. You need to let her grow up a little."

"I want to. But she's..."

"She's what?" I leaned back and gave him a knowing look.

"She's...different from other kids her age. And if she gets on that thing—"

"She'll begin to understand that she's capable of living life on her own. But if you keep picking her up and carrying her around, she's never going to learn how to be her own person. I promise you," I leaned forward, willing him to meet me with those startlingly blue eyes. "She's ready."

He drew in a deep breath and covered his eyes with his hands before moving them behind his head.

"Fine," he finally said after a few short paces. "Just...let me walk her up."

I nodded and stepped back as he took her by the hand and led her to the line. Then he bent down and talked to her quietly for a moment before kissing her on the forehead and handing the man a ticket. Once she was seated in the green balloon and buckled in, he gave her one more kiss before heading back to stand with me.

"I promise," I said, trying to give him an encouraging smile. "She'll be fine."

"I know." But his frown deepened.

"Then what's wrong?"

"I just..." He swallowed, his eyes never leaving his sister. "I didn't realize how bad it had gotten until I came back after the...the incident."

I wished desperately that he would tell me what the incident was, but I knew better than to get my hopes too high. So I tried a less direct tactic instead.

"What do you mean?"

"My parents weren't always like they are now." He reached up to touch the brim of his hat.

"Obsessed with color-coordinated schedules?"

"No." He laughed. "No, I mean they…they were present. Don't get me wrong. It's not like they're actually hurting her or neglecting any of her needs. Technically. But—"

"They're always gone," I finished.

He nodded. "Even when they're home."

"I wasn't going to say anything." I paused. "But I think that's partly why I took this job. When your mom told me they were looking for someone to stay with Jade, I knew I'd rather be the one with her than force her to find a new nanny. Again." I watched as the balloons began to slowly revolve. "She's been through at least…two. Three? Since the school year started. And every time she gets a new one, we fall back a step in class and have to make up lost ground. I wasn't trying to usurp you. I promise. I just wanted to give her a little stability in her life."

For the second time in eight days, he gave me that smile, the one without teasing or secrets or challenges in it. And as those blue eyes met mine, I tried to slow the uneven rhythm of my heart.

I turned to look back at Jade and snapped a picture with my phone. "Look at her," I said, hoping my voice sounded even. "She's doing great."

"Yeah," he said. When I glanced back at him, that smile still lingered in his eyes. "She is."

And for the first time since meeting him, I felt completely at home. It was oddly like magic. Last week, standing beside him had made me feel like my body was on high alert. I nearly jumped every time he moved, and by the time I got home every night, I was exhausted from staying stiff as a board. But this…this was nice. There weren't more than six inches between our arms, and for the first time, I couldn't have cared less.

With this revelation came another that was slightly less comfort-able. A dull ache hit my chest as I wished I had someone to stand beside me all the time. Not Derrick. He was engaged, as my subconscious had reminded me earlier. And an airman. But *someone* would be nice.

"Hey," he said, looking at the ground with his hands in his pockets, "do you think…do you think your church might be a good fit for Jade? I really do want to take her to a church with a Sunday school she'd enjoy, but it's hard to know what to try. And I know my parents are going to make a stink about giving up their Sundays, wherever I try to take her."

I smiled. "I happen to know the Sunday school teacher for her grade at my church, and I don't think she could find a better place."

"Cool. Um, could you send me the address and name maybe?"

"Sure." I had to laugh to myself as I texted him the information. I was already spending five days a week with him, and now we were edging up to a regular six. Was I really setting myself up to see him every day of this entire summer?

Something was wrong with me. And much to my horror, I didn't mind.

Jade ended up loving the ride so much she insisted on going on it six more times. After the fourth time, I excused myself to make a call. Madison picked up on the second ring.

"Hey, you. You're up early."

I laughed. "Jade and Derrick dragged me down to Burns Park."

"Well, that's…nice of them?"

I kicked some loose gravel off the path. "Hey, Maddie? I just wanted to let you know that you were right."

"I usually am. But what about?"

"I'm out with Derrick and Jade, and I realized that I think I do really want someone. You know, to have fun. To be with."

Madison screeched. "I knew it! You do like him!"

"I'm not saying that! And I told you, he has a fiancée. And he's in the military, so that's definitely a no go. I only meant that…maybe someone like him. One day. You know, good with kids. Doesn't mind getting a little dirty to have fun with them. I mean, I'm having fun. And I haven't had fun like this in a long time. And so you were right."

"Sam will be happy to hear that," she muttered.

"What? No, don't tell Sam. This is not a group conversation." I might be ready to start seeing someone, but that didn't mean I wanted it announced to the world.

Madison snorted. "Never mind. Hey, I gotta go. I'm about to meet the plumber so he can fix my sink. But Jess?"

"Yeah?"

"If he's that off-limits, you'd better watch yourself for the next six weeks."

I laughed and told her to go see to her plumber. After hanging up, I started the walk back to the ride as Jade started another trip in the balloons.

"What was that about?" Derrick asked.

"Oh, I just remembered something I wanted to tell Madison." I pointed at Jade. "So this is what, her seventh trip around in that thing?"

"Yes. And I've told her I'm getting seasick just watching her. We need to go find something else after this." Then he turned and gave me an ornery look. "What did you have to step away for? Were you talking about boys?"

"I don't date boys," I said, flipping my hair defiantly. "Just men."

"I'll believe that you make time in that schedule for dating when I see it." He made a face at me. "You're almost as bad as my mother when it comes to your schedule."

I gave him a wry smile. Someone else. Definitely someone else.

JADE

DERRICK

I groaned and leaned back on the stairs with my elbows. "Mom, Sunday school starts at nine-thirty. It is now nine twenty-five." Just yesterday, I'd made fun of Jessie for being able to sleep in on Sundays, and now I couldn't seem to drag my family out if my life had depended on it. I might as well have been the one to sleep in.

My mom popped her head out of her room and scowled down the stairs as she fastened an earring on. "You could have given us a little more warning."

"I told you last night."

"Yes! Right as your father and I got in from dinner."

"I'm not the one that made you stay out until eleven. Look, you don't even have to look formal. Just put on a skirt and shirt and let's go."

"You may be twenty-five, but remember who you're talking to and have a little respect," she snapped as she went back into her room.

I rolled my eyes, but as I started to make a retort, my phone buzzed. Relief flooded me when Amy's picture popped up on the screen. Instead of continuing to argue with my mother, I read my fiancée's text.

Hey, I'm trying to narrow down wedding dates. There's a new venue, and everything's going to be booked up soon if we don't get a day picked. Any days that won't work for you?

Finally. I'd been waiting for this text since February. And it was now late June.

Jade's echocardiogram at the beginning of August, I texted back, *and I really want to be there for it. Also, that trip to the Grand Canyon I'm taking her on in October will probably be in the first week before the snow hits.*

There was a longer pause this time. So I added,

But we can get married before that. You could come with us that way.

An even longer pause. Finally, she replied.

Any other Jade events I should be aware of that might be more important than our wedding day?

I stared at my phone for a long moment before hitting the call button.

"Hi."

It wasn't a happy *hi.*

"Hey, what did you mean by that?" I leaned forward and rested my elbows on my knees. "About Jade events."

"Derrick, I think you know what I mean."

"Please enlighten me." I frowned. "Because I really don't."

She sighed. "Look, I didn't want to get into this, but...well, this is the most important day of my life. Our lives. And I just can't believe you're putting other things first. Like trips to the Grand Canyon or echocardio-whatevers."

"It's a checkup to make sure Jade's heart is working properly." I had to work hard to make my voice sound civil. "She had a heart murmur that they picked up when she was younger, and her doctor wants her checked every now and then. I don't think it's really unreasonable for me to want to be there for it."

"Okay, I get that. But it's not like that's the only thing. Every time I want to do something, we have to check with Jade's schedule first. And that's not normal."

"Oh, you want to talk about normal?" I stood and went outside so my family couldn't hear. Sitting on the stairs in the middle of the house wasn't exactly the best place to have an argument with one's fiancée. "What about every time I've tried to ask you about dates for my stuff? I've been asking you about wedding dates for months. But every time I start talking about us getting hitched and you moving down here, you're suddenly booked up at your work until Christmas. I don't know why you're upset about my trip with Jade in October if you're still planning on working there in December."

"Derrick, that's not fair, and you know it."

"Is it? Because last I checked, most couples live in the same state. Or they at least have some sort of plan to do so eventually. But at this point, I don't know if it would even make a difference when we got married. Because you wouldn't be here until next year at the very earliest."

"I have worked very hard to get this job!" I heard a car door slam in the background. "And I think I deserve to benefit at least a little from my efforts before quitting to follow you around and then waiting to get a decent stable job who knows when."

"Amy, you knew I had at least three more years in my contract when you agreed to this. I'm not sure why it's a surprise now."

She scoffed. "Like it matters. You probably wouldn't even notice if I was there or not as long as you were near your sister."

"What is that supposed to mean?"

There was a pause. Finally, she spoke again. "You know what? I'm driving, and it's raining. We'll just pick a date later." The line clicked off.

∾

An hour and a half later, we pulled into a back spot in the church's crowded parking lot.

"If you're so determined to drag us all with you, couldn't you have found a service that was a little later?" My mom got out of the car as though she were seventy instead of forty-nine.

"Once again, nine-thirty is not that early, Mom." I adjusted my tie in the rearview mirror before grabbing my Bible and getting out of the truck. "And it's five after eleven now."

"Your father and I work every day of the week but Sundays." She unlatched Jade from her car seat. "Is it really asking that much to sleep in at least one day?"

"No one makes you work on Saturdays, Mom. Or any day. That's your choice."

"Do they have coffee?" my dad asked as he helped Jade down. "I'll be fine as long as they have coffee."

I took a deep breath and mentally counted to five. "I don't know, Dad. Probably. When I was asking Jessie about her church, a coffee bar wasn't high on my list of priorities."

Once the family was successfully out of the truck and walking toward the building, I had a bit more time to study it. It was a pretty church with red brick walls, topped by a white steeple with a cross and high floor-to-ceiling windows. An awning connected it to an annex that was built similarly, though that one looked a little less churchish, and there was a playground out back.

I usually enjoyed trying new churches whenever I traveled, but I especially needed the distraction today after my conversation with Amy. She had yet to answer any of the five texts I'd sent her. And I would go nuts if I couldn't find something else to think about soon.

"Nickleby here?" Jade asked, tugging on my hand.

"She should be, Geode. She said she had to come early for music practice."

A lady with silver curls greeted us at the door, along with her husband, who was tall and thin with glasses.

"Welcome to Grace Rock Presbyterian Church," the woman said in a thick Louisiana drawl as she shook my hand. "I'm Helen, and this is my husband, Joe." Joe grinned at us and handed us each a bulletin.

"What brings you here today? New in town?" He was looking at my dad, but a glance at my father told me he was too concerned with the thought of coffee to listen.

"Nah," I said, shaking his hand back. "I'm stationed at home for once, and these are my parents and little sister." I paused, sneaking a peek through open doors. "We're actually friends of Jessie Nickleby?"

"Okay," Helen said, nodding at two wooden doors across the lobby. "Well, you just missed her. She's in the sanctuary singing with the worship team. But she'll be out when the service gets over. Her family usually sits up front and on the left."

Of course. "I know we're a bit late." A bit. I had to work not to visibly cringe at the gross understatement. "But is there a Sunday school class for my sister?"

"Well, hi there, sugar." Helen leaned down to Jade's level. "What's your name?"

"Jade." The word was spoken so quietly it was nearly inaudible, and it came with an impressive get-back glare. But Helen didn't seem fazed.

"Unfortunately, Sunday school is already out, but if you want, I can have someone show you the room."

"That's okay. I'm sure Jessie can do that." I glanced back to see another family coming in behind us. "We'll find our way. Thanks again."

Since I usually went to the base chapel alone, it had been a long time since I'd done the walk of shame, squeezing through the already filled pews to the few spots that weren't taken in the back. I had planned to be at the church by nine-thirty. Unfortunately, my family had been next to impossible to rouse from their beds. Now that we were insanely late, most of the rows were packed. Of course, there were the usual spots up front that were free. But I wasn't about to take that risk of being easily seen and overheard with the current company involved. And it wasn't my sister I was worried about.

We did find seats in a back pew on the left side, and I quickly opened Jade's backpack and pulled out fish crackers and her magnetic doodling pad. She settled on the floor with her snacks and toy and looked quite content.

"I don't see why you're suddenly so worried about this," my mother whispered. "You've been home over two months, and not once have you—"

"Mom," I hissed. "Can we do this another time?" Preferably, when the pastor wasn't praying.

My mother pursed her lips, but she did finally sit back and open her bulletin. I opened mine as well, but after perusing the order of worship, my gaze was was drawn up to the front to a familiar face.

Instead of her usual t-shirt and jeans, she was in a knee-length dress that was navy blue with little yellow dots all over it. Her hair, which she usually wore up in a ponytail, was down, and it curled up around her neck and face. She wore a no-nonsense expression as she turned a page on her music stand, but as soon as the music started up, her body visibly relaxed as she scanned the congregation. She made eye contact with several people, smiling a little extra for each one. Then, for just a moment, her eyes met mine.

And as she let the first note fly, I knew I could relax here, too.

～

When the service was over (during which I'd successfully kept myself from checking my phone more than twice), Jessie came bounding over to us and scooped Jade up like she hadn't seen her in a month. Then she greeted my parents.

"Mr. and Mrs. Allen! It's so good to see you here!"

"Nice to see you, too," I said, bumping her shoulder. She laughed, and I couldn't take my eyes from her face. Who was this happy, angelic creature with nothing but smiles and magic unicorns and butterflies for everyone she laid her eyes on? If I'd seen her here first, I would never have known she was as no-nonsense to the point of nearly being neurotic.

"Here," she said, pulling Jade back up the aisle and gesturing for us to follow. "Come meet my parents."

A woman who looked to be in her late forties with short, curly blond hair and a man just slightly older with a small paunch and thick graying hair came out of the second-to-front row to greet us.

"Mom," Jessie said, coming to a stop. "Do you remember Jade's mother?"

"I do." The woman came forward to greet us with a smile. As she got closer, I realized she looked older than I'd first thought. Or maybe it wasn't old. Maybe...frail was the right word. She said hi to Jade and shook my father's hand as well. When her eyes reached me, they widened slightly, and her mouth quirked up at one corner. "And you must be the infamous Derrick."

"Mom!" Jessie whispered, but I just grinned back.

"Guilty as charged."

"So," her father said. "What brings you to Grace Rock?"

"Well," I put my hands on Jade's shoulders. "I've been going to the base chapel since moving back, but Jessie told me about your church, and I thought it was time Jade got a chance to go to Sunday school like I did when I was little."

"They don't have Sunday school at the chapel?" my mother murmured.

"Actually," Jessie came to my rescue. "I was telling Derrick yesterday that the teacher for Jade's class is a special education teacher. I thought she might be a good match for Jade."

"Oh." My father scratched his head. "That was…thoughtful."

"Jessie," I said, hoping to stave off any more awkward conversation as begun by my parents. "Would you mind showing me Jade's Sunday school room? We got here too late to see it."

Jessie glanced back at my parents and seemed to be smothering a smile. "Sure." She took Jade's hand and led us to one of the corner lobby doors. Along the way, she greeted people and introduced me and Jade. Then she continued until she found someone new to say hello to. It took a while, but eventually, we made it out of the sanctuary, back through the lobby, under the covered walkway, and into the annex.

"I'm sorry we were so late," I said as we went. "You'd have thought I was dragging everyone to their deaths."

Jessie laughed. It was a sweet sound, clear and unhindered. "Don't be sorry. You got everyone here, and that's more than I can say for lots of people. Here we are." She opened one of the doors that led to a long hallway. Inside, I found a little room with a miniature table, chairs that barely reached my knees, and lots of cubbies full of toys, as well as a sink and fittingly miniature bathroom.

"This is nice," I said, taking a few steps inside. Something clattered behind me, and I turned to find that Jade had dumped a bag of wooden blocks on the blue speckled tile. "Jade, no, this isn't our—"

"It's fine." Jessie waved me off. "Let her play for a minute." Then she turned those green eyes on me and tilted her head. "I have to say, now that we're away from the parents, why did you decide to bring her?"

I sighed and rubbed my neck. "After we talked yesterday, and you mentioned your church, I started thinking about how my parents used to take me to church. I loved Sunday school, and it just hit me that she's missing all of that." I sat down in one of the tiny chairs. "I think sometimes...I think they just get overwhelmed. I mean with the speech therapy and occupational and physical and equine and—"

"It becomes easy to assume she can't."

For the first time since coming home, her words rang true inside me, like someone had strummed a harp. Which was stupid, considering Jessie was the one who had nearly driven me insane. And yet, for some reason, this was the first time I felt like someone truly understood all the frustration that had been welling up inside of me. And all I could do was nod.

Jessie knelt at Jade's side and began to pick up the blocks. "Help me clean up, kiddo, and then we'll go get something to eat."

"No spinach," Jade said decidedly.

Jessie laughed. "There might be some good food there, but we'll need to go quickly before that's all that's left."

"You have lunch here?" I asked as she closed the room and led us back down the hall.

"We have a potluck on every fifth Sunday of the month," she said as we turned into a larger hall, which was now crowded as everyone moved in the same direction. Then her eyes lit up. "Mrs. Walker!"

A plump elderly lady in a bright blue blouse with a matching bandana turned around. She smiled and waited until we'd caught up. Jessie quickly made introductions. Mrs. Walker, it turned out, would be Jade's Sunday school teacher. And no sooner had we been introduced than she took Jade's hand and leaned down.

"I have to get my cookies from the kitchen still," she said, her blue eyes twinkling. "Want to be my helper?"

I was about to explain that Jade didn't like going with strangers when Jade did the unthinkable and nodded. I watched, open-mouthed, as she let the woman lead her down the hall. Jade didn't even look back.

"Should I be worried?" I asked, only half-joking.

But Jessie laughed. "I told you, she's a special education teacher. She's just got a way with kids. Now come on, let's get something to eat."

After we'd made our way through the line, with me glancing nervously back at Jade about a dozen times, Jessie led us into the fellowship hall. Most of the seats were filled by now, so we sat on the dais at the front of the room where we could see Jade as she sat next to Mrs. Walker.

"Talking to Amy?"

"Huh?" I asked, shoving my phone back in my pocket.

Jessie gave me a knowing smile. "You've checked your phone every thirty seconds since we left the sanctuary. What's up?"

"Meh." I dug into the pile of barbeque chicken on my plate. "I'm just waiting for an answer. She's probably busy."

Jessie nodded, but the curiosity stayed in her eyes. "I see."

Huffing, I picked up a roll and turned it over a few times. I could ask her. When I wasn't torturing her and she wasn't made at me, she was quite capable of being nice and sympathetic. And we were friendly enough now that I doubted she'd tease. Not that Jessie really needed to know all the goings-on between me and my fiancée. But after yesterday, I suddenly wanted someone to talk to. Someone to assure me I wasn't being a crazy, obsessed, stalker-type fiancé. And since she seemed the only one who understood my fears about Jade, maybe she would understand them about this.

"You're a woman," I said slowly.

She snorted, nearly spitting her food out. "Last I checked," she chuckled, wiping her face with a napkin when she'd swallowed.

I laughed, too. "You know what I mean. I just...I'm trying to understand whether or not..."

"Just spit it out, Allen."

Amy would kill me if she knew I'd asked another woman this question. But she wasn't answering mine, so...

"Is it normal for an engaged woman to not pick a wedding date?"

She looked at me for a moment before her big, green eyes widened. And I felt rather sick as understanding filled her face and she looked down at her plate.

"Well," she said, toying with her serving of mac and cheese. "I mean, there are a lot of factors that go into planning a wedding. Venue, work schedules, family schedules, cost, dress, cake, catering..." Her voice trailed off. And she still wasn't looking at me.

"Isn't it normal for most people, though, to have like…a few dates? Or even a month picked out?" I pressed.

She shrugged slightly then sighed. "Every circumstance is different. But I guess that might seem a bit…unusual." Her green eyes flicked up to mine. "Why? What's going on?"

"It's Amy." I dug into a big piece of apple pie, but it seemed a lot less flavorful than it had looked back on the serving table looked. "The weekend I proposed…back in February, she was so excited. She and her mom started making plans three minutes after she said yes. But every time I ask her now, she seems less sure about when she wants it." I shook my head. "I don't know. I just…when I proposed, I thought I'd be getting married. Not in a constant holding pattern." I paused. "And I think it has something to do with Jade."

Jessie was quiet for several minutes, chewing her food slowly as she looked out at the dozens of round tables before us. I followed her gaze to where my parents were sitting with hers. They looked like they were having a good time. My dad was even ignoring his styrofoam cup of coffee.

"How does Amy get along with Jade?"

"What?" I turned to look at Jessie, and this time, she was studying Jade.

"I was just thinking. Who's Jade's legal guardian?"

"I am." I'd made sure of that the day after Jade's incident last spring.

"Then," Jessie said slowly, "there's a good chance you'll be responsible for Jade one day."

A moment passed before I realized what she was alluding to. "You know," I said, "I never really thought about that."

"It could be nothing," she added quickly. "But people with Down Syndrome range all over as far as their abilities and skillsets go when they grow up. Some can live by themselves and function quite well in the world like their neurotypical peers. Others have to stay with care-takers of some sort for their whole lives. I mean, I quite honestly can see Jade one day powering her way through the world like any of her classmates. But to someone who's not familiar with needs like hers…" She shrugged. "It could be scary."

I'd been frustrated and angsty that morning while I'd waited on Amy's reply. But now, I felt a weight on my shoulders that put my misery that morning to shame.

"You don't think that would make her want to call off the wedding, do you?" I heard myself asking.

"I could be totally wrong," Jessie said, holding her fork out at me. "So don't quote me on that. I only bring it up because it's something I'm trained to see a little more than the average Joe."

Stupid. I never should have asked that. Now it would drive me crazy until I talked to Amy myself. Forget texting. We were going to talk soon. Face to face. But until then, I was going to need more distractions than ever.

"What about you?" I forced a smile and turned back to Jessie. "You have everything scheduled out. When's your wedding?"

Jessie stared at me for a moment. Then with a straight face, she stabbed a green bean with her fork and said, "Three years from now on October thirteenth."

I must have looked ridiculous because she began to laugh.

"I'm kidding! Look at your face!"

I shook my head. "I don't know. I wouldn't put it past you." Then I chuckled. "Okay, if the date isn't quite in yet, what about all those things you mentioned? The—the venue and the caterer and the dress and the cake and all that." I was teasing still, but the morbid part of me wondered if every woman but the one I'd proposed to had all this planned out.

"I'm cheap," Jessie said before taking a bite of a chocolate-covered strawberry. "So I'll probably make my own cake with my mom."

"Sensible, as always." I nodded my head.

"The venue's easy. That'll be here." She smiled up at the vaulted ceilings. "I knew I wanted to get married here the day I first set foot inside. And we'll probably just ask people to do a potluck instead of catering."

"And the dress?"

She gave me a sly grin.

"No way." I sat back and laughed. "You already have it picked out, don't you?"

She turned away, but I caught her blush. Then she mumbled something.

"What was that?"

"I said...I might have already bought it?" She grimaced. "Why are you looking at me like that?"

"Because I've never heard of a girl who buys a dress before she's engaged...or has a boyfriend, for that matter." I leaned closer, hoping to make her blush again. For some reason, that was more fun than I would have imagined, the great Jessie Nickleby being embarrassed about...well, anything. "Unless you already have a guy picked out."

"No," she chuckled. "No groom yet." Then she sighed a little. "Just my beautiful dress staring at me from the closet."

"I'm just in awe." I held up my hands. "You have my mom beat hands-down for planning. And the fact that it's a princess dress only makes it better."

"It was an online sale! If I didn't bid on it, someone else would have!" She rolled her eyes. "Not that it matters. I don't have a groom yet." She glanced at my plate. "Hey, are you going to eat that cornbread?"

When my family finally left the church that afternoon, I felt strangely lighter, despite my talk with Amy. Oh, I hadn't forgotten, and I would mull on that later until I went stark raving mad. But for now, as I glanced back at the white and red-brick church, I knew without a doubt that I'd found someone who without a doubt, understood. On many levels. And for just a few moments, I would bask in that glow.

DOUBTS

JESSIE

Madison shook her head at me. "We've only been out of school for a month, and you look like you're about to burst with excitement."

"You know what the best part of these conferences is?" I asked, thanking another vendor as she handed me a book.

"It wouldn't be the free stuff now, would it?" Sam laughed as I slid the book into my canvas bag. It hit the bottom with a satisfying thump.

"Please and thank you." I grinned as we paused at another stall. This one had buckets full of plastic letters covered in foam dots. "And don't make fun of me. You guys have been to these things before. This is my first time."

"Neither of us is as cheap as you are, either." Madison rolled her eyes as I happily snatched a packet of the letters from their sample table.

"Master's degrees are expensive. Ooh! What's that? Let's go over there!"

The Back to the BASICS conference hadn't been cheap. I wouldn't have even bought a ticket if our school hadn't sponsored the whole lower elementary team. But now that I was here, I swore to myself never to miss another conference again. I'd never seen so many free supplies in one place. Besides, as much as I was enjoying Derrick and Jade, (or rather, Jade, as Derrick wasn't really an option) it felt weird to be away from my classroom for so long. Being here felt right.

Derrick had been great about letting me go for a few days, not that I doubted that he'd mind having his sister all to himself. His parting words had been, *You might as well go. I've had to look at your face for the last nine days straight.* I smiled to myself as we stopped at another booth. Things had already been better since the diamond mine. But after our conversation at church last Sunday, I felt like we finally had common ground.

How were they doing today?

"So," Sam said, dragging me from my thoughts. "How's your summer going with Jade?"

"I couldn't be happier. She's doing great. I think I'm going to be able to start her off with a lot of the general curriculum this year." We weren't supposed to talk about students' IEP's (also known as *individualized education plans*), but since our school did a lot of shared time between teachers and classes among grade levels, Sam and Madison were both familiar with Jade's particular needs.

"That's fantastic." He stopped and studied a table's stack of multi-colored letter wheels before shrugging and throwing one into his bag. "I was sure her parents were going to work you to death when you first told me about how they made you nanny for the summer." He glanced at me. "You know, if you wanted some help, I could come over sometime and help tutor her to give you a break. Since I got my math endorsement, I'm dying to try some new techniques that I've learned, and I think she might be the perfect guinea pig."

"That's really sweet of you," I said. "But I think we're good. She's just starting to get the stuff I'm giving her now."

"Well, just so you know, the offer stands." He gave me a warm grin. "Oh, before I forget, what did you think of the book I gave you?"

"I've only just started it, but I think it's fascinating," I said, grateful to be talking about something else. The last thing I needed was for sweet Sam to show up at Jade's house. Derrick would love that.

"You're going to own this degree. And when the partiers," he poked Madison, "rag on you for studying, you can tell them I said that."

I laughed. "Well, thanks."

He glanced over at the food court, where instead of educator booths, food stands had been set up. "I'm going to grab some nachos. Anyone want a pretzel or something?"

"I'm good," I said, and Madison said the same. The moment he was gone, however, she turned to me and arched one perfect eyebrow.

"I told you he likes you."

"He's just being helpful." I intently studied a table covered in building bricks arranged in patterns.

"Girl, he offered to come over and help you by working for free. No teacher just randomly offers to drive to a student that isn't his own and work for free on his summer break."

I hefted my bag to my other shoulder. "I don't know—"

"You want a sure test?" She smirked. "Mention Derrick and just watch. You'll know then what he thinks of you spending every day with a hot guy you're not dating or married to."

"How do you know he's hot?"

"Because of the way you blush when I ask you what he looks like. Here, give me your phone."

I'd been looking up a textbook publishing house on my phone, but Madison snatched it away and pulled up my pictures. I felt my face get hot as she immediately scrolled to and landed on one of the...two dozen? How had I taken that many pictures in just one weekend?

"This him?" She held the phone out.

Meekly, I nodded.

"Now look me in the eye and tell me that this man is not hot."

As I stared at the picture, I knew I wouldn't be able to do that. Because even though I wasn't interested in him...in the slightest, it was impossible to deny. Not when his workout shirt and basketball shorts showed what they did. Because the man might be on the wiry side, but the muscles he did have were sharp and contoured well on his calves and shoulders and neck and his trim waist—

"He's engaged," I blurted out. "It's not like he's hanging out at the house all day for me."

"Mm-hm," Madison said. "You keep telling yourself that."

"But—"

"Look, here's how you test Sam. Just mention Mr. Good Looking here and see what Sam's reaction is. Or better yet, show him the picture." Her eyes gleamed.

"I most certainly will not." I snatched my phone back as Sam walked back up.

"Here. I know you didn't want anything, but I got you ladies each a lemonade and pretzel bites anyway."

"Thanks." I took the snack from him with the sinking feeling that maybe Madison was right. The last thing I wanted to do was hurt Sam. I mean, no, he hadn't asked me out. But he was still a very sweet friend.

"Hey," he said, checking his watch, "the TESOL demonstration is coming up soon in the third classroom. Want to hit that one up?"

Madison and I both agreed, and we made our way toward the presentation, eating and drinking as we went. On the way, Madison decided she had to go to the bathroom, so we waited outside.

"So, how's the beast treating you?" He grinned. "Did he come weeping at your feet, begging you for forgiveness when he saw that you don't actually eat kids?"

I laughed, but it sounded uneasy even to me. "Actually, we've come to more of a compromise. At least, for the moment."

"Oh?"

"Yeah, well…" I swirled my straw around in my drink. "I found out that something…something happened with one of Jade's previous care-givers. So there was a reason for all his crazy interrogation. I mean, yeah, it was still stupid. But…I guess he's just not quite as horrid as I thought he was at first."

Sam nudged my shoulder with his elbow. "You know they have a name for this. It's called Stockholm Syndrome. Spend too much time with someone, and you start to like them, even if they are colossal jerks. And you've got to admit it. He's a colossal jerk."

"He was." I kept my eyes on my straw as it squeaked against the lid. "But he's a little more relaxed now. We're actually kind of…having fun sometimes." I thought back to the weekend and how much fun we'd had at Burns Park.

"Fun." He chuckled. "I'll believe that when I see it. I just think you're too nice for your own good."

"No, really. He's not been that bad lately." I would be the last person on the planet to say Derrick Allen was perfect. But after the last few weeks, it just felt wrong to have someone badmouth him to my face without saying something.

Madison rejoined us and grinned wickedly. "Do you have pictures? To prove all this fun?"

I turned to glare at her, but Sam tilted his head.

"Do you?"

"You don't want to see pictures." I folded my arms.

His eyes widened. "So you do have pictures of him."

I scoffed. "With his sister."

He gave me a wry smile. "Then let's see them."

I gaped at him. "Are you for real right now?"

"I'll believe it when I see it." He held his hand out.

"You can't be serious." Why were men so awful? And why was Madison so evil for that matter? I needed to get a new best friend.

"I am because you're not telling the truth." Sam smirked, the left side of his mouth pulling up slightly higher than his right.

With a huff, I unlocked my phone and handed him the picture Madison had pulled up before.

The smile briefly melted from his face. Then he handed the phone back and checked his watch.

"We'd better go if we're going to make the next session." He grinned again, but it didn't reach his eyes this time. "You ladies coming?"

I rolled my own eyes before following. Madison grabbed my arm and whispered, "Well, if you had any doubts, that should take care of them." She gave me a knowing look and set off to catch up with Sam. And it was all I could do to take my phone back and follow miserably behind.

19

COWARD

DERRICK

I slowed to a jog as my workout music turned into Amy's ringtone. If I was honest, I wasn't sure I wanted to answer it. Because there was no telling what the outcome might be. Jessie had been gone to some warehouse thing all day, which meant I'd had Jade to myself, and I had work in five hours. Did I really want to deal with this right now?

The phone rang again, and I knew better than to ignore it again. Slowly, I came to a stop and answered.

"Hello?" I'd barely been running. Why did I sound so breathless?

"Hey, Derrick."

Well, she sounded…not angry. That was a start.

"Hey." I ran a hand through my sweaty hair. "I wasn't sure when I'd hear from you."

"Yeah. About that. Look, I'm sorry for being so snappish. I was coming down with the stomach flu when I called you but didn't know it until about an hour later. Not that it excuses it, but I just wanted you to know. I wasn't thinking straight."

"I'm sorry you were sick."

"Yeah." There was a long pause. Giving up on my morning run, I sighed and walked over to one of the little ponds just off the trail. "What's up?"

"Oh! Right. I got your gift." She giggled.

"My gift?" I racked my tired brain, trying to remember when I'd sent her a gift.

"The pink chinchilla?" She chuckled again. "You swore you couldn't top the checked fish, but I think you've officially found the ugliest stuffed animal in the entire world."

I chuckled, too, as I remembered. We had an ongoing competition to see who could find the ugliest stuffed animal. The contest dated back to before we were dating. Man, it felt good to laugh with her again.

"Now you can look at it every night before you go to sleep," I said, stretching my calf muscles.

"Oh, no. It's shoved under my bed where I can't see it. That thing gives me the creeps. Its eyes are just...no."

We laughed for a few more minutes, reminiscing about the beginning of our competition, then fell silent once more. I decided to take advantage of the break and try again.

"I was just thinking," I said, taking a deep breath, "I know you're busy. And I know you're trying to finish up all your projects before the wedding. So...what if Jade and I came to visit you instead?"

She sighed. "I don't know. My grandma has relatives staying with her for a while, so you couldn't use her guest room. You'd have to get a hotel, and I don't know if that would be good for your sister—"

"Amy, my sister has Down Syndrome, not a severe immunodeficiency. Hotels are fine. Besides, I've got a buddy of mine who says he'll let us stay with him."

"I...I guess that would work," she said slowly.

Encouraged, I continued. "Anyhow, I was thinking. You said you wanted to visit those caves northwest of where you live. We can all go together, and you and Jade can spend some time getting to know one another?" For some reason, my voice caught in my throat. "I know you don't know her well yet, but she means a lot to me, Amy. And you mean a lot to me. And...I think you'll understand better once you really get to see who she really is. Because she's an amazing little person."

There was a long pause. I bit my lip and wiped the stupid stinging out of the corners of my eyes.

Finally, she let out a little laugh. "When you get an idea, you're about as stubborn as a toddler, you know that?"

"So I've been told."

She laughed again. "But I think maybe that would work."

"That's great!"

"When would you come?"

"I don't know yet." Honestly, I hadn't even thought she'd say yes. "Um, maybe at the end of the summer, just before her school starts up again. I just got here, so I don't really want to ask for time off yet, but this...this will happen."

Some voice inside wondered when I was going to ask about our future wedding date. Amy might have been sick during our previous conversation, but she hadn't been sick all those times she'd dodged my direct questions before. And yet, as we laughed together and she told me about something dumb one of her coworkers had said, I decided that I was just too much of a coward today. And for once, that was okay.

20

DEAL

JESSIE

It was Friday, and moods were high. After two whole days of enduring Sam's looks of concern at the conference, it was good to be back to normal. Well, at least my summer normal. Jade was in a good mood, humming her favorite cartoon's theme song as I sipped my decaf, which I'd filled with three creamers on a whim instead of my usual two. Even Mr. and Mrs. Allen had wished me a sweet farewell as they'd gone off to work.

Derrick was the only one who stumbled in that morning looking bleary-eyed and decently confused.

"What?" I asked him as he stiffly collapsed into the booth that ran around the table and stared at his coffee cup. "Not a morning person today?"

He grunted. "I went to sleep an hour ago."

"You know," I said, winking at Jade as she giggled, "you don't have to be up. Your parents hired me specifically so you could sleep during the day."

"Can't do that." He shook his head, eyes still bored into his mug. "It's my turn for the contest."

"I'm pretty sure whatever you have isn't going to beat her finding a diamond at the diamond mine." I waltzed across the kitchen to get Jade her cup of juice. But as I turned to waltz back, I ran smack into Derrick, who had stood up again. His steaming mug, which he was clutching, sloshed all over my jeans.

"Ow! Ow! Ow!" I shrieked, hopping around, as if that was going to stop my legs from burning.

Derrick, seeming fully awake now, grabbed a towel and ran water over it really fast. Then he made me sit down and threw the wet towel over my legs. Slowly, as the cold water dripped on the floor, the heat began to recede.

"Thank you," I sighed, thankful that when I removed the towel, my legs no longer steamed.

"You okay?" he asked, his blue eyes flicking back and forth between my legs and my face.

I forced a slight laugh. "You know, if you thought I needed a bath, you could have just said so."

"I am so sorry." He stood as if to do something, then just stayed there and shoved his hands into his pockets. "You got any extra clothes?"

"No, I used them when we went mining." I stood and went to the double oven, where I could see most of my reflection in the oven doors. Sure enough, I would need new clothes. My pants were drenched from my thighs to my shins, and my shirt wasn't much better.

"Hey, I know." He ran upstairs. A few minutes later, he came back down holding a shirt and jeans. "I don't know your size or whatever, but these are my mom's old clothes, and they look like they might fit you okay."

I warily eyed the hot pink shirt. The fabric looked like it cost more than all my clothes put together. "And you're sure she won't mind?"

"Nah." He smiled slightly and leaned forward. "Don't tell her I said this, but these are about two sizes too small now. She just won't admit to it, and keeps them all in the back of her closet where she thinks no one will see them."

I twisted my lips. They were very nice, and I'd hate for anything to happen to them. But then, I really, really didn't want to walk around crunchy and smelling like coffee all day.

"All right, I'll try. Thanks." I took the clothes and headed to the bathroom.

Even the bathroom was fancy here. Every surface that wasn't a mirror seemed to be finished with blue glass tiles or white marble. I looked at the clothes again before cringing as I checked the size. They were my size all right. But they were also skinny. Skinny jeans. A very fitted short-sleeved sweater with what looked like real pearls for the buttons. All just...yuck. I hated clingy clothes. They made me feel like a suffocating, overindulged wiener dog, even if they were my size.

The pants went on with more tugging than I would have liked to admit (which was precisely why I avoided skinny jeans like the plague at clothing stores). And thankfully, the shirt wasn't quite as bad as I would have thought. When I finally turned to face myself in the full-length mirror on the door, however, I nearly fell over. It was far, far worse than I'd thought.

After I'd mentally picked myself up off the floor, I texted Madison.

Madison, can I in good conscience wear these out of the bathroom?

Two seconds later, my phone buzzed, and I smiled. That girl might be busy, but she never missed a text.

Why are you in the bathroom? And what am I looking at?

Oh. I quickly snapped a picture and sent it to her, cringing again when the screen showed the image sent. This time, four seconds passed before I got a reply.

Guuuuuuurl. You. Are. Hott. Where did you get those, and why on earth wouldn't you wear them out of the bathroom?

I groaned and rubbed my eyes. Of course, Madison would like them. I should have texted my mom instead. Unfortunately, she was at the dentist and wouldn't be answering her phone for another hour at least.

I spilled coffee on my clothes, and Derrick gave me some of his mom's old ones.

How on earth am I supposed to spend an entire day with him and Jade dressed like this? In public?

I could just imagine her snickering as she replied. *You know, some people are okay with showing their collar bones in public.*

I show my collar bone, I typed back.

Jessie, you look like a teacher even when you're not teaching. You're making a big deal out of nothing. Just wear the stupid thing. Maybe you'll pick up some non-mil guy while you're out. If you do, ask him if he has a brother.

I shook my head at my phone. Adam must have bitten the dust. But my friend's constantly revolving boyfriends were the least of my concerns right now. After a few very long leg stretches and squats and a few sharp tugs in an attempt to loosen the infernal pants, I opened the door and peeked out. All clear.

Unfortunately, the privacy lasted all the way to the middle of the staircase, when Derrick appeared, hauling a rather uncooperative Jade to the front door to put on her shoes. I tried to dart the rest of the way downstairs, but the movement must have caught his attention because he looked up just as I reached the bottom step.

To my horror, his eyes widened, and for a very, very long second, neither he nor I looked away. Finally, he seemed to come to his senses.

"Um..." He shook his head and turned his head down toward Jade. "I'm—"

"I'm going to pack lunch," I said, stepping sideways toward the kitchen.

"Yeah. That sounds like a good idea." He kept his head down as he spoke.

I half-ran into the kitchen. My cheeks burned as I mentally slapped myself for not packing extra clothes. Lunch was packed far too quickly, and all too soon, I had to follow Derrick and Jade to the truck. Only Jade chattered away as we buckled her into her car seat. I stayed busy on my phone as he drove, but two minutes into the drive, Derrick seemed unable to keep it in any more.

"So…" He put his hand on his head and ran it through his hair. "About earlier. I'm really sorry for making it awkward." He laughed nervously. "I guess you just caught me off-guard. I mean, I knew you were too short to be a model, but I never expected you to be so…"

I stared at him. Was he really doing this? Because if he thought it was awkward before—

"So hideous." He shook his head sadly as I gasped. "I mean, I know beauty's in the eye of the beholder, but—"

"You brat!" I reached across the middle console and slapped his arm, relieved laughter bubbling up in my chest.

"Really, though." He gave me a lopsided grin. "I really didn't mean to make you uncomfortable. And I'm really sorry if I did."

"It's fine." I waved a hand at him. Maybe one day, I added in my head, I would find a guy of my own to look at me like that. Because, if I was honest with myself, that look in his eye, that spark of wonder would feel really nice. If only it were mine to keep.

~

Derrick's newest contribution to the Jade contest was the new self-serve yogurt stand at the mall, complete with thirty-six possible toppings. And despite my admonitions, he let her add all the toppings she wanted. The only upside was his face when he had to pay for the mountain of sugar he'd helped her build.

As we ate, though, I knew I was going to have to step up my game. Jade liked geology, but she liked sugar nearly as much. Then again, what six-year-old didn't? I, of all people, knew that. I was going to have to get creative.

"Sergeant Barnes!"

Derrick's exclamation brought me back from my musings, and I turned to find a man in a camouflage uniform standing beside our table. He had the darkest skin I'd ever seen and the whitest smile, and he looked to only be a few inches taller than I was. But from the way he carried himself, I got the feeling he could arm wrestle the tall, skinny guys like Derrick, and he could probably win.

"Derrick." He smiled. "This must be Jade, and this must be…" He raised his eyebrows at me then looked back at Derrick. "Is this…"

"Jessie." I shook his hand and smiled.

"So," he said, turning to Derrick. "I saw you buying your tickets for the ball. Is this lovely lady who you're bringing?"

Derrick's face turned a strange shade of white, and for a brief second, I saw panic in those blue eyes.

I opened my mouth to tell the sergeant that I wasn't Derrick's fiancée, but Derrick spoke first.

"Actually…" he said slowly. Why was his voice so high? "Yes."

My spoon stopped halfway to my mouth as my eyes met his pleading ones. Had he lost his mind?

"Because if that mystery fiancée of yours doesn't work out…" The sergeant gave me a knowing wink. "Mika's available."

"Thanks." Derrick pasted a smile on his face. Even I knew *that* wasn't real. "I really appreciate it. But yeah, Jessie here is coming with me."

Sergeant Barnes looked expectantly at me, and I managed to dredge up a smile that probably looked even less genuine than Derrick's. But we must have convinced him somehow because he clapped Derrick on the back.

"Good for you, Allen. Well, I'll see you next week then." He nodded at me. "Ma'am."

As soon as he was out of hearing, I crossed my arms.

"Would you like to tell me what that was about? And why I'm going to a ball?"

Derrick groaned and put his head on the table. Then he mumbled something.

"I'm sorry, what was that?" It better have been an apology.

"I'm so sorry." He raised his head off the table about three inches to give me the most pathetic, disheveled look I'd ever seen on a man. "I can explain."

"I'd like that."

Derrick sat up and let his head fall back so he was staring at the ceiling. Jade just continued to eat her yogurt, sending us glances every now and then that made it pretty obvious we were both pathetic. After this morning, I was inclined to agree with her.

"Sergeant Barnes is always trying to push his daughter on the newest single airmen."

"Why the newest?"

"Because those who have been there for any length of time know what he's up to and are too stupid to get caught without a date."

"Wait." I frowned. "He can't make you go out with her...can he?"

"No. But no one wants a grudge with Sergeant Barnes." He gave me a wry grin. "He's actually a really nice guy and a really good leader. But every time we have any sort of party or ball or anything formal, he starts trying to hook his daughter up with whoever's available."

Poor thing. "Is she really that undateable?"

Derrick looked at me like I was a moron. "It doesn't matter. She could be Miss Universe. But no one wants to take the chance of being the schmuck who broke his boss's daughter's heart." He shook his head. "The thing is...he's a good guy. Best supervisor I've ever had, and he treats us like people instead of numbers. He even asks about Jade all the time. I just don't want things to get awkward with him and ruin all that."

"So where do I come into all of this? Why can't you just take Amy?"

He huffed and started tapping his empty yogurt cup with his spoon. "I've been begging her to come since I got here. But she's really busy with her work and doesn't think she can make it out that evening." He finally dared a guilty glance up at my face. "I'm going to keep working on her. I'm going to ask her if she could maybe make it if we just do it all in one night. Show up, shmooze a bit, and then leave in time for her to catch her flight back to Colorado."

"That still doesn't answer my question. Where do I fit in all of this?"

He gave me a sheepish grin. "I was hoping maybe you could be like a...a stand-in? Just in case she can't make it after all?"

"Absolutely not. Why'd you even buy the stupid tickets if you don't have to go? And don't tell me you do. Because I know from my students that this ball is optional."

He made a face. "It looks good when the commanders see you at base functions. They take participation to mean you're dedicated." He sighed. "And I bought the tickets back when I thought she could make it. I didn't realize she'd keep saying no. Also...I might or might not be on the planning committee."

I closed my eyes and shook my head. "You know this is the reason men are known for being stubborn to a fault."

"Yeah, I know." He snuck another peek at me. "So you'll go?"

"I told you. Absolutely not."

He studied me for a moment before pulling out his phone. "What do you want?"

"I want you to leave me alone."

"I mean it. What if we made this a business deal? We can even write it out in a contract and sign it if you like. Terms, addendums, all that. You can tell me what you want, and I'll agree to it as your payment in exchange for one and a half hours of standing or sitting beside me, eating the very nice catered dinner they serve, not making faces at me while I talk to my superiors, and then we leave." He held up his hands. "We won't even think about dancing. Literally, all you're going to be is a warm body."

"You mean a bodyguard."

"Yes, one that will protect me from my overenthusiastic, well-intentioned boss so he doesn't stick his daughter on my arm in the absence of my fiancée."

The answer was no. Obviously. And yet...I couldn't help thinking of what a tightwad I'd been since...well, since I'd had my first job. Everything had been scrimped and saved as I prepared to buy my own car. To pay for my own college. Now to pay for my master's degree. It might be nice to make a deal where for an hour and a half, all I had to do was stand there and get a bit out of it in return.

I lifted my chin so he knew I meant business. "I don't have anything to wear."

"I'll buy you a ballgown."

I looked up from my phone, and he rolled his eyes.

"I'm not taking you shopping if that's what you're insinuating. I'll send you with my credit card. If you want, I'll even hook you up with my friend's wife so she can tell you what you need."

"Fine, but I get to keep the dress."

He leaned forward, and so did I. "So you'll do it then?" he asked.

"Only if Amy can't make it."

He stuck his hand out, and I shook it.

"Deal."

21

COLORADO

DERRICK

As soon as we got back from the mall, I left Jade with Jessie and went to my casita. I needed some space to think about what I was going to do. Because if anything was sure in this world, it was that I'd messed up. Majorly. But before I dealt with that, I would need some sleep.

Unfortunately, deep sleep was hard to come by, and my mind was still spinning in useless circles by the time I got to work. Thankfully, we had a lot to do, so it wasn't until I got off the next morning that I realized I still had to deal with everything I'd been avoiding.

I was such an idiot. I tossed my gear into my locker harder than necessary. An idiot of idiots. First for buying those tickets, which were non-refundable. Then for allowing someone...I didn't even remember who, to get me involved with the planning committee. Third, for doing what I knew Amy wouldn't like right after we'd made up. Okay, well, we hadn't really fixed our problem. But at least she was talking to me again. It had been a long four days before she'd broken her silence this time. And she'd only done that because I'd had the foresight enough to send her a stupid stuffed animal before I knew any of this would become an issue.

Before I had any more time to berate myself, my phone rang. My heart rose and fell when I saw Amy's face on the screen.

"Hey, babe." I held the phone up to my ear as I ducked into a back corner of the locker room to get some privacy.

"Hey yourself."

"What's up?" I asked, staving off the inevitable.

"Your mom said you were acting funny last night. She texted and asked me to check on you."

"Of course she did."

"What was that about?"

"Oh, nothing. Well, no. Actually, yeah, there is something." I rubbed my eyes. "Look, I don't know how else to say this, but...is there any way, any feasible way to get you out to the ball?"

"My gosh. Derrick, we've been over this. I can't go. We've got a huge case the week after that—"

"Wait, wait, wait." I put my hand on my forehead. "You said it was that weekend. Not the one after it."

"The judge pushed it back. But I still need that weekend to prepare."

"Then you can come. You just won't."

"Derrick." She let out a long slow breath. "I told you. This is the case that's going to make my career. And I know the ball is important to you, but—"

"Amy." My laugh sounded hysterical. "I don't know how else to tell you this. I need you. I need you here. I need you to marry me. I need you to be my date at a ball. I need you...and you're never here. Ever. Heck, you don't even want me to come visit."

Silence. Then a sob on the other end. I closed my eyes and sat down on the locker room bench. "I know you're busy. And I know you're trying to make a career for yourself. And I support you. I always have. But—"

"You couldn't care less about my career."

"That's not true, and you know it. But you can't keep dodging things, Amy. Sooner or later, we're going to have to figure things out."

"We had them figured out. Until you decided you just had to move back."

And there it was. All my fault again. I might as well be in this relationship with myself.

"I gotta go." I stood. If I didn't get some sleep soon, I was going to pass out on the road. "But we're going to finish this conversation. Soon."

∼

I don't understand, I prayed as I made my way out to my truck, exhaustion temporarily forgotten as frustration built inside me again. It wasn't like I could just up and move back. I'd offered time and time again to fly her out, and my parents had extended the use of their guest room. She still hadn't given me a date for the wedding, and the harder I pushed, the farther she seemed to be from picking one. After my conversation at church with Jessie, I really got the feeling a lot of this had to do with Jade. But what could I do with that?

My phone buzzed again as I climbed into the truck. I pulled it out and glanced at the screen. It was from Hernandez.

Dude, I forgot to ask you, is Barnes right? That your girl's coming to the ball?

I made a face at my phone. *She's just a friend. I'm working on getting my fiancée out still. Why?*

I just thought you should know, he texted back. *You should probably just buy your girl a frequent flyer card.*

I had the sudden urge to throw the phone out the window. Instead, I gritted my teeth and texted back. *Why?*

Because they're moving the squadron picnic up. It's in three weeks instead of six.

Crap. I'd completely forgotten about the squadron picnic.

Taking my keys out of the ignition, I got back out of the truck and slammed the door. Thankfully, Barnes had gotten there early and was already in his office. I knocked on the door frame.

"Sir?"

"Come in." He looked up from the file he was reading. "Allen. What can I do for you?"

"I hate to ask this." I wished it was acceptable to fidget with one's uniform when talking to a superior. But it wasn't. So instead, I did my best to stand still. "But I'm going to need permission to go to Colorado."

Barnes put his paper down. "When?"

I swallowed. "Tomorrow."

22

PAYMENT

DERRICK

The elevator dinged as I reached the sixteenth floor, and as several men in business suits stepped past me to get on as I got off, I suddenly felt underdressed. I checked my phone again for the suite number Amy's mother had given me for her new office. Funny, now that I thought about it, it really wasn't a new office. She'd been here since last spring. I guess she'd just never thought to invite me to see.

Slick black marble floors flecked with gold led the way in intricate patterns to a door made of red wood with a golden plaque that said *Johnson and Marks*. The room inside had several leather couches and chairs, and the walls were decorated with paintings that looked custom.

"Can I help you?" A young man wearing a headset and behind the desk leaned forward.

"Hi." I smiled. "I'm here to see Amy Junder."

He nodded as he typed something into his computer. "And what time is your appointment?"

"I don't have one."

He stopped typing and looked up.

"I'm her fiancée."

Understanding came to his eyes. And was that...pity?

"I see. I'm so sorry, sir, but Amy's with a client right now. Would you mind having a seat? I'll let her know you're here."

"Sure." I sat in one of the leather seats away from the door and tried not to look up as he made the call.

"Miss Junder? A gentleman is here to see you." He paused. "He says he's your fiancé." He nodded. "Yes. Yes, I'll wait for your call then." Finally, he turned back to me and smiled as if I hadn't been able to hear him. "Miss Junder will see you as soon as she's finished with this client."

"Thanks." I pulled out my phone. Hopefully, she'd be done soon. I had a million words I'd rehearsed in the plane and in the car ride over. And now they just needed to be said.

Let me say all the right things, I prayed as I glanced at the dark door beside reception. *I have a really bad feeling about this.* Because whether I wanted to admit it or not, Amy and I were at a crossroads. And something had to give.

∼

Thirty-eight candy games later, the guy behind the desk nodded at me. "Sir? Miss Junder will see you now." As he spoke, the door beside his desk opened, and a beautiful young woman stepped out.

I hadn't seen her in months, but the moment Amy gave that little dimpled smile, the pain from our separation that I'd been burying floated to the surface like cream. But with it, a tightness in my chest, one I'd never felt before in her presence. Back before I'd left, when we were together all the time, I used to think she helped me breathe easier. Now a too-tight rubber band seemed to be all that was holding my chest together.

"Derrick," she said in a soft voice, her blue eyes wide and sparkling. The rubber band seemed to grow tighter when she said my name.

After staring at one another from across the waiting room, she ran a hand through her bangs and laughed a little. When had she gotten bangs? "Um, come inside." My heart fell a little as I followed her through the door and down two halls.

Not that I could expect her to hug and kiss me in the waiting room, I chided myself. She was at work, and if she'd shown up at my work, I wouldn't have been able to give a public display of affection either. At least, not in my uniform. *It's not you, Derrick,* I told myself. *It's just the rules.* And yet, the silence of our walk only served to heighten my anxiety.

She led me into a spacious office with a wide desk the same color as all the red wood on the walls and doors. One of the walls was taken up by floor-to-ceiling bookshelves, and a ficus grew in the corner by the bay window.

I turned in a circle and gave a low whistle. "This is nice." This was weird. Why was this so weird? And why hadn't we hugged yet? I would have tried, but she hadn't even come close enough for me to nab a handshake.

"Thanks." She looked around as well. "I still have a few things I'd like to do, but most of it feels right."

A few things. That didn't sound like I'm-moving-to-another-state language at all.

"So," she said, turning her soft blue eyes on me again. "What are you—"

"Come here, you." I opened my arms, and she came. But even as she leaned against my chest, it felt strangely awkward. Hugging her had never felt awkward before.

"I am here," I said before anything could get any worse, "to kidnap you."

"To kidnap me." She stepped back and smiled. "Usually the victim isn't warned, you know."

"Well," I shrugged, arms still wrapped around her, "I might be aware of just how much makeup my kidnappee requires on average to feel put together."

She laughed. "And why, precisely, am I being kidnapped?"

"Because," I said, pulling back enough to see her reaction, "my squadron's annual summer picnic is coming up. And I really want to show you off." I forced a hard laugh. "My coworkers don't think you exist. They're taking bets." I watched her carefully as I spoke. "I even had to hire a stand-in for the ball in case you couldn't come—"

Her eyes looked like they might fall out of her head. "You did what?"

I held my hands up. "Just so my sergeant would leave me alone and quit pestering me to date his daughter."

"Wow." She shook her head and smiled. "Just...wow." Well. At least she wasn't angry?

I shoved my hands in my pockets and tried not to think about how much she used to like holding my hand. But then, that was before she had her own office and wore fitted pantsuits and had a secretary to take her calls, including the ones from her fiancé. That was before she pulled out of my arms and went to stand across the room and started leaning against her desk with her arms crossed as she looked at me expectantly.

"I know...something's wrong," I blurted. "And I came because we need to figure out what it is."

She picked up a file and stared at the folder. So I crossed the room again and took the file out of her hands before taking them in mine.

"I don't know what I need to do to fix this," I said, willing her to look me in the eye. "But whatever's happened between us, I wish you would just tell me."

Another pause.

"Because I'll do what you want. I'll tell Jessie I don't need her to go to the ball. Heck, I'll hang in the back the whole time so Sergeant Barnes doesn't see me and I can attend without attending. And if you're that busy, I'll fly here as much as possible until our wedding." Inwardly, I cringed at the hole that would put in our honeymoon travel savings. But at this rate, our future travel seemed like a bit of a distant dream anyway. "But I can't," I said, leaning down so we were face-to-face, "fix any of it until you tell me what's wrong. I need to know what happened that makes you want to avoid me at all costs." *What's preventing you from picking a wedding date,* I almost added. But one thing at a time.

No answer.

"Amy—" I groaned.

"It's not what," she said in a small voice. "It's who."

"I'm confused."

When her eyes met mine again, they were no longer soft, like a summer sky. Instead, they were hard and cold.

"You up and left me without even asking me how I felt about it."

I gawked, dumbfounded.

"Just called one day to announce that you had pulled some strings, and you were requesting a transfer back to Arkansas."

"Well, yeah." I nodded. "I didn't think that would be a surprise. You knew the military is a transient lifestyle. I warned you over and over again I could get orders to leave any day."

"But you didn't just *get* orders, did you?" She leaned forward, eyes bright. "You requested them. Geez, Derrick, it's not *that* you moved. It's *why* you moved. It's why you do everything!"

"I don't—"

"Jade, Derrick. It's Jade. Everything in your world revolves around Jade."

I felt like someone had just punched me in the side. "Jade? Jade needs me."

"Your sister has parents, in case you've forgotten. And you have me. Or at least, I thought you did. But after you proposed to me, and you spun me all those wonderful tales of traveling together and adventures and a lifetime of us, then you were gone. And I couldn't seem to buy a minute of your time without your sister being dragged into everything. It's like you can't breathe without her."

My mind flicked back to the conversation with Jessie from the week before, and before I knew it, her words were in my mouth.

"In case you forgot, my sister has Down Syndrome. Yeah, she's doing great now. But you don't understand. People with her condition are prone to health problems. And physical problems."

"That didn't seem to bother you before."

My throat started to swell, and my eyes pricked at the corners, but I forced myself to croak through it anyway. "When I got that call last spring, though, and my parents told me that she—"

"Yes, I know what happened. You've already told me more times than I can count."

"My parents aren't young anymore, Amy. There's a good chance Jade will live with us one day. Because she deserves a good life, and I'm not going to abandon her." How could she not have known all this? How had we not had this conversation before?

"Derrick." Amy stepped forward and squeezed one of my hands. But for the first time, I couldn't return the squeeze. "I'm not saying you have to abandon her. I'm not that cold-hearted. But everyone has to find a happy medium in life. Boundaries, you know?"

"Oh." I took my hand from hers and crossed my arms. "And what kind of happy medium are you suggesting for my baby sister in the case that my parents die?"

"Well," she looked at the picture on the wall behind me, "there's always adult daycare. Or one of those homes—"

An emotion I'd never felt for the woman standing in front of me flamed up in my chest. It felt a lot like the time I'd made that stupid bet in junior high that I could drink a whole bottle of hot sauce by myself.

"So you've been putting me off because my sister has special needs?"

"It's not just because of that. It's because you're obsessed. Gosh, you treat her like...like your daughter!"

"I'm her brother. If I don't look out for her, who will?"

"Your parents, Derrick! The ones who birthed her."

"Are you really this opposed to spending our lives with someone who might need us? Because if you are, then we might as well just skip kids."

"She's not your kid!"

The silence was deafening after her shout died. Amy closed her eyes and muttered something beneath her breath then went to stare out the window.

"We're done," I said quietly as sounds of her quiet sobs filled the air. "Aren't we?"

She didn't turn. "We were done the moment you asked to leave Colorado."

I nodded and ground my teeth. As I turned to open the door, however, I felt a hand on my arm. When I turned, she was holding her ring out, her eyes dripping with mascara and her face red and blotchy.

"Here," she whispered. "Have it back."

I stared at the ring for a long time before shaking my head.

"I had to wait like a client. Consider it payment for your time." Then I left and didn't look back.

23

YOUR FAULT

JESSIE

A nother Saturday with Derrick and Jade. My mom had given me a suspicious look when as I'd left the house, and I knew I deserved it. This was beginning to be a weekly thing.

I looked around as I stepped into the little cafe. I felt more than a little guilty for being here this morning in particular, as my parents had hoped to spend the whole Fourth of July together. But after enduring a whole week of Derrick's strange moods and exceptional silence, his text that morning had set off more than one alarm bell.

I hate to ask this of you, but I need to break something to my parents this morning, and I really need moral support. Could you be at Mugs Cafe by nine?

If he was asking me for moral support, it must be big. At first, I was inclined to say no, as I wanted no part in any drama that involved Mrs. Allen. But my conscience nagged at me when I remembered the way she'd spoken to Derrick that one morning, telling him Amy was the only thing he'd ever gotten right.

Also, he really had been acting funny all week.

So with many apologies and the promise of spending the rest of the day together, I'd set off to join the Allen clan for breakfast.

The little café was busy when I walked in, mostly full of people with headphones, and laptops. But just as I spotted the table where they were sitting, someone caught me by the wrist. I looked up, ready to backhand whoever had grabbed me, just in time to see Derrick. He put his finger to his lips and nodded at the door. Once my heart had slowed, I let him lead me back outside.

"Well, hello to you, too," I said, rubbing my wrist. "Does this mean I'm uninvited to breakfast?"

He laughed, but there was no humor. "Sorry about that. I just wanted to warn you that this meal is going to be…well, awkward."

I would have laughed, too, had he not looked so completely miserable. "What's up?"

"I know this is presumptuous on my part and really stupid, but… would you be okay if I asked you here to help suppress an atomic explosion of sorts?"

"Um, sure?"

"Because I know I'm going to get zero support from my parents. Zilch. At least in this arena." He glanced back at the window. Did he really consider me that much of a friend? Or was he just that hard up for friends? "Also," he continued, giving me a weak grin, "my parents like you. So they'll be less likely to kill me if you're present."

"That's why we're in public, isn't it?" I looked back at the crowded room. "Because you don't want a scene."

He gave me a sheepish grin. "You've met my mother. Can you blame me?"

"Fine. I'll try. But on the off-chance they do kill you," I said, hoping to ease the anxiety evident in the lines on his face, "can I at least call dibs on your truck?"

He stared at me for a moment then let out a laugh. It was good to hear that sound as we went back inside. But neither my joke nor the laughter was able to chase the sudden angst from my stomach as we wound our way through tables and customers to where his family was sitting.

Jade was drinking a milkshake that was red, white, and blue. Mr. Allen was adding creamer to his coffee while Mrs. Allen stuffed enough napkins into Jade's shirt to cover her in the Splash Zone at Sea World.

I slid into the booth beside Jade, and Derrick sat next to me. Wow. Whatever it was, he didn't even want to sit with his folks.

"Mom, Dad," he said, leaning his elbows on the table. "Thanks for meeting me here on a Monday. I know you have work, so I'll try to make this quick."

At the mention of work, I gave him a sharp look. Yeah, it was Monday, but it was also the Fourth of July. I'd even been given the day off. And *they* were still going to work?

"I trust your trip to Colorado went well?" Mrs. Allen added a packet of sweetener to her tea. "You got back late enough last night."

"It was the only flight available." Derrick cringed slightly, and I could only guess he was thinking about the cost of such a flight. "Anyhow, that's what I'm here to tell you about. As of last Saturday..." He glanced at me. "Amy and I are officially done."

"What?" Mrs. Allen spilled her tea on her lap, which made her shriek as she hopped up and down in her seat, trying simultaneously to clean it up and demand answers from Derrick. Mr. Allen tried to help his wife while uttering words under his breath that I prayed Jade didn't hear.

Derrick gave me an exasperated look, and I gave him what I hoped was a sympathetic smile. *I'm sorry*, I mouthed as the waiter arrived with our food while Mrs. Allen fussed about a new cup of tea. Only then did I realize I hadn't gotten to order for myself. Still, somehow, I got the Greek yogurt with fruit that I would have ordered had I been given the choice. Stressed or not, Derrick seemed to know me better than I thought.

"I knew it." Mrs. Allen finally threw the wet napkin on the table and glared at her son. "You have one success in your life, and you manage to blow it up."

I stared at Mrs. Allen as she started covering her bagel with cream cheese with a violent passion. Never in my life had my parents uttered anything like that.

"Mom, that's unfair."

"No. No, what's unfair is a son who goes to three years of college and quits."

"I joined the military."

"You quit." Her hand shook as she continued to smear cream cheese all over what was by now a very battered bagel. "Perhaps I should just save the military the trouble of taking your application for OGF—"

"OTS. It's Officer Training School—"

"Whatever!" She stopped to glare at him before resuming the spreading of her cream cheese. "And I can tell them how you'll just quit. Just like you quit everything."

"I don't quit ev—"

"Track, basketball, karate..." His father began counting on his fingers. "Violin, French."

"You didn't even give me a choice for half of those!" Derrick leaned forward in his seat. "I wouldn't have had to quit if you'd listened to me in the first place and signed me up for soccer and guitar like I wanted."

I made myself busy wiping the milkshake from Jade's face, wishing very much that she and I could excuse ourselves and make a dash for the door. This so wasn't my drama.

"You had the perfect life," Mrs. Allen growled, putting the bagel down but not the knife. "Tell him, Gary. The perfect life."

"I still don't see why you had to join the military." Mr. Allen put up his hands helplessly. "I had you lined up to do consulting with Howard Conway. You would have made more than three times what you're making now."

"Yeah," Derrick said. "In five years. Maybe. If I'd done really well. But you don't understand. I don't want a high-powered...You know what? Forget it. You didn't listen then just like you're not listening now. Heck, you haven't even asked why we broke up. You just assumed it's my fault. As always."

Mrs. Allen sat back. "Because it generally is your fault."

A look crossed Derrick's face that I wouldn't soon forget. For just a second, he was a little boy. And he was hurting. "Excuse me, Jessie. I need to get some air."

I stood and let him pass. He stalked toward the front door. I glanced back at his parents, who were talking in angry whispers—mostly his mother—before grabbing my yogurt and following him.

≈

He was sitting on the edge of the raised flower beds in front of the restaurant when I found him. I sat beside him and said a silent prayer with a lot of pleading for words then started eating my yogurt. I had no idea of what to say now that I was actually here. I could say I was sorry he'd broken it off, but I wasn't. The more I'd heard about Amy and the way she treated Derrick, and more importantly, Jade, the less I liked her. In truth, I was relieved. Derrick may not be my best friend, but that was not the kind of future I wished upon him.

Life had suddenly gotten a whole lot more complicated.

And he was right. His parents hadn't even asked about the reason for their split. All they seemed to care about were Amy's perfections. As if she was out of his league, and he was swinging high. No. Derrick could be awful, but he was also one of the most caring people I'd ever met. All you had to do was see the way he looked at Jade to know that.

"Sorry you had to witness that." Derrick didn't look up from the straw he was twisting in his hands. "I shouldn't have asked you to come."

"No, I'm glad you did."

The look he gave me made me laugh.

"Really," I said. "No one should have to go through anything like..." I nodded back at the window. "Like *that* alone."

He gave me a grim smile. "Thanks. And I mean it. Believe it or not, that would have been a whole lot worse if you hadn't been there." He sighed and looked down at the straw. "At least they'll be gone for the rest of the day, and I can ignore them and all their guilt tripping until tonight."

At that moment, Jade and her parents appeared at the top of the steps holding take-out boxes, and we both sobered up. From the look on Mrs. Allen's face, Derrick wouldn't be allowed to forget this for a long time. What an awful way to spend the Fourth of July.

But then I had an idea.

"Hey, your parents are going to work now, right?" I asked quickly as they made their way down the steps.

"Yeah. Why?"

"Why don't you and Jade come spend today with my family?" I asked. "An airman shouldn't have to spend Independence Day nannying alone."

He gave me a long, thoughtful look, his blue eyes piercing mine before his mouth curved up into a lopsided grin.

"You know what? That actually sounds really nice."

And I would have been lying to myself if I didn't say that the way he looked at me made my heart do strange things.

24

COMPLICATED

JESSIE

We hadn't planned on doing any fireworks, but the moment I called my parents to tell them we were having guests, that changed.

Of course, my mother was a little peeved with me at first for changing our usual tradition, which was to watch School of Rock while eating red, white, and blue popcorn covered in white chocolate with sprinkles. But the moment she heard that my two charges were without parents, in spite of the fact that Derrick was twenty-five, she was rolling out the red carpet. My dad was sent to the store to buy sparklers and snacks, and I was put to work cleaning.

They arrived around five and were promptly stuffed with every kind of snack and grilled meat imaginable. Then as soon as it was dark, my mom and dad took Jade out to the end of the drive to do sparklers. They were like two kids again, laughing and exclaiming as they did silly things for Jade. Derrick and I sat in the folding chairs at the edge of the garage to watch.

"Are you sure you're not worried about my parents doing that with her?" I glanced at him.

But to my surprise, he just shook his head and shrugged. "Nah. They're fine."

"Are you serious?" I sat up.

"What?" He laughed.

"It took me weeks to earn your trust! And you're fine with my parents? Just like that?"

"Well," he took a swig of beer, "they did keep you alive this long. But you don't have any kids, so…"

"I was responsible for your sister for an entire school year! And not just keeping her alive. I had to educate her, too. And twenty-plus other kids at the same time!"

His smile was genuine now. "Look, I can honestly say that your whole family has made it into the circle of trust."

I quirked an eyebrow. "Once you realized I wasn't going to murder your sister in her sleep."

"Once the nannycam proved me right."

My mouth dropped. "You nannycammed me?" I slapped his arm, and he laughed even harder before reaching over and poking my arm.

"What was that for?" I swatted his hand away.

"Just to poke your buttons."

I rolled my eyes but couldn't help smiling as he chuckled to himself just a little too hard. But when the chuckle was gone, that light in his eyes was gone, too.

"Hey." I leaned forward slightly to see him better. "You okay?"

"Yeah, I just…this is what's getting me." He frowned down at his hands. It sounded to me like he'd been having this conversation with himself all day, but I was the first person he had the chance to actually tell.

"I don't even feel that heartbroken. Not like I thought I would. And I guess that makes me feel…guilty? Like, what if we'd gone through with it, and I realized I felt this way after?"

"Well," I said slowly, hoping I didn't sound too trite. "You didn't go through with it, though. Maybe God was…I don't know. Sparing you that heartbreak so you wouldn't have to feel like that when it was all over."

He gave me a pacifying smile, but his eyes didn't meet mine. "That won't matter to them."

"Your parents?"

He nodded.

"You didn't get the chance to tell them. They didn't give you the chance."

He shook his head. "Nothing I do is good enough for them. And I didn't even realize that's not normal until I went to college and started meeting friends with families like yours. I spent a couple holidays away from home, and it dawned on me that some parents are actually proud of their kids."

My heart twisted as he talked. My parents had pushed me, for sure. And there had been a few report cards as a kid where I'd gotten the lecture about using study time wisely. But never in my life had I doubted their satisfaction in my accomplishments. In fact, their confidence was the reason for a number of my undertakings, such as grad school.

"But I kept going," he continued, "until my junior year of college. Dad had an episode with his heart. The doctor said it was from stress… big surprise. And it hit me that my parents weren't getting any younger. Mom was forty-two when Jade was born, and I came to the realization that if something happened to them, I would be completely responsible for Jade."

"I'm curious," I said cautiously. "Your dad said the job would have paid three times what you're making now. Wouldn't that have helped Jade?"

"In five or ten years, maybe. But a lot of young interns in my field were barely able to survive. I didn't know what I'd do if I ended up in charge of a medically delicate kid. And she really was delicate when she was little. She had heart problems and everything for a while. I didn't have insurance, and I wouldn't have been able to take time off with her. And I definitely wouldn't be able to afford daycare. Not the kind she would need."

"So you joined the Air Force." I stared at my popcorn. "That doesn't seem like it would have a whole lot of benefits for her."

"Actually, you'd be surprised." He reached into his pocket and pulled out a pack of gum. "The EFMP is the program that makes sure all military dependents with special needs receive it."

"EFMP?"

"Exceptional Family Member Program. They make sure that my duty stations are only in locations where she can receive the care she needs. It's easier to get referrals for therapies, and they have advocates in case I'm put in a position where her needs wouldn't be met. And our military insurance would cover all her basic medical needs and any special needs her doctors thought she required. Or it's supposed to, anyway."

Guilt crept up my arms and legs as I listened. When I first met Derrick, I'd been sure he'd just joined to feel macho and for all the traveling. When really, it had cost him a lot. At least where his family was concerned.

"You don't have to answer if you don't want to," I said slowly, "But I'm curious."

"Ask away." He pushed the popcorn around in his bowl.

"Everything with Amy and your parents and your moving here... everything seems to go back to last spring." I waited until he met my gaze. "Around the time Jade came to school covered in scratches. She didn't want to talk for weeks." I paused. "She...she didn't fall. Did she?"

"Oh, she fell all right." His face darkened. "But she did a lot more than that, too."

"That thing you can't tell me about, right?"

He leaned back. "Well, you're here and practically family now, so you might as well know." Then he leaned forward. "Jade, don't chase people with sparklers! I'll have to take those away if you don't listen."

Practically family. Did he really mean that?

"My parents," he continued, "don't like to talk about it because it makes them uncomfortable. Actually, it's the reason I fought you so hard when you first got here. You were the first permanent caregiver to come after Jade's little nanny incident."

I nearly interjected that I was a summer tutor, but the way his eyes tightened kept my mouth shut.

"The nanny before you worked out okay for a few weeks. But she got distracted on the phone one day and didn't see Jade slip out." He ran a hand down his face, and when he spoke again, his voice hitched. "She was lost for hours. We had the neighbors and the cops all looking for her. I can't...I can't tell you what it felt like. I was back here visiting from Colorado at the time but was out running an errand when it happened. Those hours, though, not knowing where she was or if someone had taken her or if..." His voice cracked. "If someone was hurting her. It was a worse feeling than I've ever had in my life. And when we did find her, she was covered in bruises and cuts and was pretty shaken up."

"Where was she?" A renegade tear ran down my face as I imagined her lost and crying alone for hours.

"On the golf course behind the house, in one of those big groups of trees. It was a miracle she was there, though, and not in a pond. They're all over the course. She'd somehow squeezed between some of the fence posts in our back yard and made her escape there. She was crying like a baby. Just...wailing. And when my mom offered to take her from the cop who found her, she wanted me instead." He finally faced me, his blue eyes standing out even more than usual against his red, tear-stained face. "And I knew at that moment that I had to get back to her. At least while she was little. I had to do my best to keep her safe while I could." He cleared his throat and sat taller. "So as soon as I got back to Colorado, I prayed hard, pulled some strings, sent in my request to get transferred here."

I put my empty popcorn bowl down and stretched. "I thought you don't get to pick where you move in the military."

He snorted. "You don't. Usually. And even with friends in the right places like mine, it's really hard. Thank God I got it, because it would have been really easy for them to say no."

"That's why you didn't want me to stay with Jade." It was all making sense now. And totally not in the way I'd expected.

He gave me a sheepish grin. "And again, I'm sorry about that. I just didn't feel like I could—"

"I get it." I elbowed his arm. "You don't have to explain."

"Hey."

I turned again, this time to see him giving me a genuine smile. It was gentle and yet, unflinching in its intensity. So much intensity. "Thanks again for having us over. We really needed this."

"And you're sure you're okay?" I sipped at my hard lemonade and tried to ignore the weird fluttering in my stomach. Shut up, Jessie. Stop looking at him like that.

"Well, it's not like I'm jumping for joy. But...I think maybe I knew it was coming. Like I've been in mourning since I left Colorado. And now I just feel...peace. I've been in limbo so long, I guess, always waiting for her, never knowing when she would actually come. Now I can get on with my life. I feel lighter if that makes sense."

"It does." I took a handful of patriotic popcorn and ate it slowly, one piece at a time. "You can be a pain in the rear end, Derrick Allen, but you deserve to be happy."

"With sentiments like that, how are you still single?"

I threw my head back and laughed, and so did he. When we had quieted, though, he was still looking at me.

"I mean it. You're a professional. You're obviously a people person. You're..." He paused. "Well, all I can guess is that something must be horrendously wrong with you for you to still be single."

"What were you going to say?" I gave him a dangerous look. "Annoying? Persistent? Frust—"

"Well, I was going to say pretty, but if you prefer the others, they work just as well."

For one of the first times in my life, I didn't know what to say. Annoying as it was, I was just as flustered as the first time he'd called me pretty at the equine center. So I folded my arms and sat back to watch Jade giggle as she chased my dad with another sparkler as my mother tried to stop her.

"Well," he put his hands behind his head, "we've already established that you're disgustingly ugly. But there's got to be something else." He sat back and studied me in a way that was slightly unnerving. "And I'm betting it's your fault."

I kept my eyes on Jade.

"I'm right, aren't I?" His eyes went wide. "Well, what is it?"

"I'm not telling you. You called me ugly."

"And pretty. I also called you pretty. So hand it up."

"Ask her about her rules," my mom called from the end of the drive.

"Mom!" I shouted. How had she heard that?

"Ask her—" My mom's voice quivered with excitement. "No, wait. Even better. I'll get them."

"Mom, what are you doing?" I watched in horror as my mother ran into the house and came back thirty seconds later with my newest planner.

"That's mine!" I made a grab for it, but my mother tossed it to Derrick, who caught it with ease.

"Look at the third page, ," my mother said as she went back out to Jade, her eyes sparkling mischievously. "It's titled *Dating Rules*."

I made a grab for the paper once more, but he swatted me away and turned to the page my mother had directed. I sat back and pulled my feet up on the seat, where I hid my face in my legs.

"Wow. Ouch." He let out a whistle. "No wonder you're single. One, no airmen. Two, must be gainfully employed. Three, must have a useful skillset. Four, has to make the first move. Five, must be a Christian. Six, must want kids. And there's eighteen of these?"

"They're not in any particular order," I mumbled. "Just wrote them as they came to me."

He held my planner up and waved it in my face. "If this is what you're waiting for, then this," he said, pointing to Jade, "is the closest your parents will ever be to grandparents."

"That's not true. Men like this exist."

"I'll give them visitation rights if you'd like." He grinned at me. "They can be honorary grandparents whenever they want."

"Give me that." I made a grab for the planner. And missed.

"Okay," he said, "some of those I get. I mean, I don't think it's ridiculous that he be the one to ask you out. Christian is good. Having a stable job is good. Not having a DUI record is good, too." He lifted his hands. "But come on. 'Must tolerate Jane Austen audiobooks. Must exercise at least four times a week on principle. Must be clean-shaven." He shook his head. "Jessie, these are ridiculous."

"You didn't ask about the first one." I snatched it back and hugged it to my chest.

"No airmen." He folded his arms. "You got something against the Air Force?"

"No." I hugged my planner to my chest. "It's military in general. I just said airmen because that's the kind of people I have to fend off around here."

He started to answer then froze, and an evil grin came to his face. "Is this rule because of me? Do I have some sort of charm that put my rule right at the top?"

"No." I stuck my tongue out. "That one was there way before you."

"So I trust there's an actual reason for it?"

I raised my chin. "Yes. There actually is."

He started to shake his head when he went still as a dead man. Then he moaned and leaned back, scrunching his eyes shut.

"What is it?" I asked, hoping he hadn't gotten food poisoning from our beer or popcorn. He looked nearly sick.

"I forgot." He peeked out from beneath his hand. "Please don't kill me, but—"

"Oh no."

"I have a squadron picnic at the end of the month. And I want to take Jade. But there's a pond I'm not comfortable with her around, and I won't be able to give her my full attention—"

I smacked my forehead. "Oh, Derrick."

"I mean," he melted into his chair until he was more lying than sitting, "you can say no, of course. It's your prerogative to kick a man while he's down..."

"Do you know you're horrible?" I crossed my arms. "Fine. Fine. Just...only because Amy broke up with you. Not because it's an actual date." I glared. "I should make you buy me a new book for this, you know."

His pouty lip immediately morphed into a guilty smile. "You're the best, Jessie."

I just took another long sip of my hard lemonade. Yep. This summer just got more and more interesting by the minute.

2 5

WHAT I WANTED

JESSIE

July flew by, during which we were in the car more than we were at the house, and when we were home, we were busy practicing Jade's song. She struggled with enunciation and rhythm, and more than once, she wanted to quit, but I was seeing too much progress to let her. Essentially, we were busy all the time. We practiced so much that pretty soon, the show tune we'd picked was stuck in my head nonstop.

But I was okay with that. Between Jade's lessons and therapy sessions, the contest was hot underway. Now that Amy was gone, something inside Derrick seemed to have been set free. He laughed more, teased more, and played a lot more pranks. And though I spent most of my time retorting and scolding and fending him off, it was impossible not to enjoy myself. I couldn't remember the last time I'd gone so many places just for fun.

We visited the children's science museum, the presidential library, and the submarine, just to name a few. Every day was something new. Jade was rather smug once she realized what we were doing, and she used that to her advantage, making us beg and plead for her approval, and more than once, she finagled new crayons or lemonade or souvenir stickers out of us, using our zeal to win as motivation.

As the weeks passed, however, it became apparent that the golden ticket that would determine the winner would be awarded to whoever figured out what Jade meant by "chocolate".

Not long after our frozen yogurt venture at the mall, Jade had begun asking for "chocolate". But whenever we got her dark chocolate chips (in my attempt to make her dessert somewhat healthy) or even the Hershey's bar Derrick bought her, her answer was always the same.

"No. The right chocolate." She would pout, crossing her little arms with as much disgust as a six-year-old could possibly muster.

In vain we tried. We visited the North Little Rock mall, the downtown mall, the outlet mall candy store, the gas station near her house. And every time we offered her a new source of chocolatey goodness, she would huff and shake her head. Derrick and I would exchange a look, and whoever had suggested the most recent attempt would sigh while the other breathed a sigh of relief. This went on until Tuesday morning of the third week of July when Derrick came dancing in from the casita.

"Should I be worried?" I stepped back as he slid into the booth with his toasted waffles. Still dancing in place as he cut them, he gave me a wicked grin.

"I think I can safely say that I will be winning this contest. So if you had plans for that day out, forget it."

I put down the juice pitcher I was holding. "No way."

He shoved a bit of waffle in his mouth and wriggled his eyebrows at me. "Hey, I forgot the whipped cream. Can you get it out for me?"

"Not until you tell me where you found out."

He shrugged, still chewing. "Fine then. Guess I don't need the sugar. I'll be getting it after all when we get chocolate today anyway." He nudged Jade, who was staring at her cereal. At first, she'd been all excited every time we told her we were going for chocolate. But too many dashed hopes had given her a chip on the shoulder. Sometimes I could have sworn that kid was seventeen rather than going on seven.

After breakfast was cleaned up, we piled into the truck for speech therapy, during which he spent most of the time making fun of me while I ignored him and read my Beauty and the Beast book.

"You're reading that again?"

I kept my eyes on the page. "I don't remember that being any of your business."

"I just don't see what the draw is, reading the same thing on repeat."

"If you must know, I'm planning a unit study on fairy tales for next year. I'm pulling out some of my favorite parts so the kids and I can have book talks."

"That's not a kid's book."

I put the book down to glare at him. "And where did you get your education degree? Because I don't remember that being in your resume."

His eyes were bright. "I'm self-taught."

I shook my head and went back to my book, to which he chuckled. "You can hide all you want. Doesn't change the fact that I'm going to win."

He did win. An hour later, to be exact. Jade's squeal of joy when we walked up to a small glass storefront was more than enough to prove that. I sighed as we went inside, Jade racing ahead of us.

I would never admit it to Derrick, but as soon as we walked in, the smell alone was enough to convince me that Jade was right to be this devoted. And if that hadn't done the trick, the lines of chocolate bites and truffles laid out on the counter behind the glass would have done it. There was a table on the left with a dried up pod and several bowls of what looked like dark brown chopped wood pieces behind four piles of chocolate bars, which were covered with gold foil and wrapped in blue paper.

"Well, hello there. Welcome to Izard Chocolate."

We looked up to see a young man with bright red hair and an equally bright beard emerge from the back of the shop.

"I'm Nathaniel." He looked down at Jade. "I remember you. Did you like your truffles last time you were here?"

I looked at Derrick, who was giving me the smuggest smile I'd ever seen. *Game over*, he mouthed. I shook my head and looked back on Nathaniel and Jade. But before I could wallow in my misery too long, my phone buzzed. It was a message from Sam.

You busy?

Your timing is impeccable, I wrote back. *What's up?*

. . .

I'm trying to get out of a family function tonight. Want to meet up at the bookstore? I can prep you for the first semester of your master's. I kept all my syllabi. There was a pause followed by, *You have been studying, haven't you?*

I wanted to bang my head against the wall. When was the last time I'd cracked open the book he'd given me? A week ago? Maybe two? Better to skip that part.

The bookstore sounds great, I responded. *The one on McCain? What time?*

His reply was fast. *Five-thirty. We can get coffee and something sugary if you're tired. My treat for dragging you out after a full day of work.*

"Jessie," Derrick called from the glass window, where he and Jade were sampling truffles, "Get off your phone and come taste defeat."

I rolled my eyes and typed back.

Five-thirty is perfect. I'll be there.

~

Eventually, we dragged Jade from the shop, though it wasn't without a few tears and multiple bars of chocolate for the family to share. I left with more truffles than I cared to admit. I swore that they were to share with my family, but I think Derrick knew better. And to his credit, he didn't say a thing.

When Mrs. Allen finally came home, I didn't waste time with long goodbyes. Jade was busy decorating her tutu for the choir tryout with fake jewels and glue, and for some reason, though I couldn't really say why, I wasn't able to look Derrick in the eye.

Not that it really mattered, I scolded myself as I got into the car. It wasn't his business who I dated. And this wasn't a date. It was two colleagues going out to coffee to discuss education. Who was Derrick anyway to know or not know what I did with my time off? It's not like he'd even asked anyway.

On my drive over to the bookstore, I was able to use the radio to get my mind on other things. But as soon as I stepped into the bookstore and saw Sam standing at the edge of the cafe, I couldn't kick the butterflies to the curb.

He was wearing a gray t-shirt, jean shorts, and flip-flops. His thin-rimmed glasses were on as he read the back cover of a book on the stand near the cafe's entrance. Interesting. A whole year of teaching next door to him, and I never knew he was farsighted. He really was cute. What would it be like if he did ask me out? Was this a man I could picture myself spending forever with?

He turned and faced me as I walked toward him. "Hey, there you are. Did you bring the book?"

I held up the canvas bag I'd grabbed from home on the way to the store. "Sure thing. But I'm starving."

We ordered our food and went to sit at the table he'd claimed toward the back. And though I was happy to be getting the help, my heart sank when I saw the pile of textbooks waiting for us. Weird. A month ago, I would have been giddy at such a sight.

"So how do you like the first book?" He nodded at my canvas bag as we sat down.

"It's thorough," I said, taking a big bite of my spinach and artichoke quiche.

"It is," he said, a half-smile on his face as I tried to keep mine on my food. "And exactly how far along are you?"

Crap. This was the one question I'd been hoping he wouldn't ask.

"Thirty percent," I mumbled as I took another bite.

"What was that?"

I sighed. "Thirty percent."

He blinked. "But you've had it for weeks."

"I know, I know," I groaned. "And I'm sorry. But this last few weeks—"

"Don't worry about it," he laughed. "You're working a full-time job, and that's tiring."

I nodded. Thank goodness he understood. Or thought he did, at least. Because I'd spent far more nights on the couch with my phone, looking for new places to take Jade than I had studying like I was supposed to.

"I also brought my syllabi." He wiped his mouth on his napkin and reached into the briefcase he'd brought along. "So we can look at some of the instructors you'll have."

"How do you know which ones I'll have?" I asked, taking a bite of my quiche.

"Everyone has these instructors during the first or second semester." He pushed his glasses higher on his nose. "Moss teaches one of the cornerstone classes, and she holds a lot of power in the college. So if you do well in her class and you get her to like you, you'll be set for most of your program."

And so we began. And didn't stop for an hour and a half. I couldn't help being impressed. Not only had he brought his textbooks, but he'd made a list of his instructors and notes about all of them, who wanted work turned in early, who wanted everything in pen rather than pencil, and the one guy who forgot what he assigned his students every single week.

"Please don't take this the wrong way." I leaned back in my chair and surveyed the piles of books and paper surrounding us. "But I have to ask."

"Okay?" He took a sip from what must have been cold coffee by now.

I folded my arms and studied him. "Why are you doing all this? Because I mean, this," I gestured to the piles, "is a lot of work."

"Well, like I said, I've been trying to get out of a family function." He rubbed the back of his neck. "And yes, it might make me a terrible person, but my sister's co-ed baby shower just wasn't something I've been terribly motivated to attend."

I laughed. "Granted, but still, this must have taken a ton of time." I held my breath, Madison's warnings about Sam's feelings circling in my head. If he really liked me, I was giving him the chance of a lifetime to tell me now. All he had to do was admit it, and he would no longer be breaking rule number four.

And if he was no longer breaking rule number four and actually admitted that he wanted to pursue something with me, maybe I could get Jade's infuriating brother out of my head because I would have someone else there instead.

He took a moment to answer, each second making my heart beat slightly faster. Finally, he clasped his hands and leaned forward.

"You…" He took a deep breath. "You are so talented. And I mean that. So talented that in my five years of teaching I don't think I've seen a teacher with as much potential and passion as you. You're patient and sweet, but you know how to take control of a classroom. You encourage the kids who are ready for more, while not leaving the others behind. And…I just think it would be cheating a whole lot of kids and a whole lot of your fellow teachers if I didn't help you reach your highest goals. And if earning this degree is what you need to become a better teacher, then I'm going to help you do exactly that."

"Oh." I sat back, a blush heating my cheeks. It wasn't the declaration of love I'm sure Madison would have wanted, but it was something to think about, at least. "Well…thanks."

"Let's finish this thing, huh?" He smiled, pushed his glasses back up his nose, and pulled out yet another syllabus.

An involuntary sigh escaped, but I covered it with a yawn. He was right. This degree was what I wanted.

It really was.

26

NOT A DATE

JESSIE

"**A**re you sure this isn't a date?" My mom gave me her best mom look as I held another shirt up in the mirror before tossing it on the bed.

"I told you. It's purely business. And me feeling slightly sorry for the guy whose fiancée dumped him because his little sister has special needs." I sighed and went back to my closet to dig into it once again.

"You know…" my mom said slowly. "You don't have to abide by all your rules all the time."

I stopped my perusing to look at her. "What do you mean?"

"I mean, you made those dating rules yourself. And while most of them are good…they're not the Ten Commandments. The only one enforcing them is you, you know."

"You know, you and Dad were the ones who drilled a bunch of those rules—"

"Honey, that was in high school. You're twenty-three now. Grown up enough to start basing your choices on maturity. In fact, what if…" She frowned thoughtfully at my desk.

I paused and turned around. "Uh-oh. I know that tone. What if what?"

"What if," she said slowly, "instead of getting rid of all your rules, you…what if you amended some?"

"Amended?"

She nodded. "Let's look at these and see how many you really need."

She went over and dug the planner out from where I had most recently tried to hide it to prevent talks just like these.

"Mom—"

"'Christian man who attends a similar church to mine.'" She nodded. "Definitely a good rule. Let's see what else we can keep. 'Great with kids.' 'Values my education degree.' 'Has a stable job.' 'Has a retirement account in place before the age of thirty.' See, these are all fine, but...oh, Jessie." She held it up and frowned at me. "'Hates the local football team.' Really? You live in Arkansas, girl. Odds are no one here hates them as much as you do. If you want this in a man, you'd better move to Alabama."

I rolled my eyes, but she had a point. Even the military guys here liked the the local college team. "Fine. We can scratch that one off."

"'Must make the first move.' 'Doesn't have a beard.'" She closed her eyes briefly and shook her head. "Whatever."

"Mom." I sighed. "I have to go in like three minutes. What's your point?"

"I just think," she picked up a pen and pointed to the first line, "that this one...well, maybe you should rethink it."

I pretended to study the pile of clothes already on my bed. But inside, I was panicking. Could I rethink that one? Did I want to? Because if I did, everything would change.

I grabbed one of the blouses I'd discarded and held it up again. It was white with little red and green cherries all over it, puffy at the top with a waist made with smocking that went all the way around. It was flirty but conservatively so, which was the vibe I wanted. At least, I hoped it was. This wasn't a date, but I didn't want to embarrass myself or Derrick by looking like a kindergarten teacher at his picnic.

"Those are cute together." My mom nodded at the shirt and dark jeans I'd paired it with. Then she cracked a smile. "Derrick should like it."

"I need to get dressed. Maybe we can talk about this later?"

"What about the rule?"

I huffed. "Fine. I'll think about it. Happy?"

"Yes." My mom snickered as she closed the door behind her. "Enjoy your date."

"Not a date!" I called after her. But I didn't have time to sit and stew. Throwing the blouse and jeans on, I ran to the bathroom and did the best makeup job I could before the doorbell rang. My mom answered, and I could hear a familiar voice answer.

Wow. Derrick was here. Not just in his truck, but on my front porch. He never rang when he came to pick me up. He just texted me that he was in the front drive, which was fine, as I'd always assumed it was because he didn't want to leave Jade in the car. My heart thumped a little unevenly. Why change things up now?

"Jessie, he's here," my mom called from down the hall.

"Coming." I snapped the lid back on my lip gloss, gave my face and hair a once over in the mirror, then took a deep breath as I grabbed my purse.

My stupid heart tripped on itself again as I reached the entry. I hadn't seen him in his full uniform since our fateful introduction, just the light brown shirts Jade called, "sand". He was fit without the uniform, keeping a tall, lean build with just enough muscles to fill his t-shirts out nicely and make women do a double-take (though I suspected he would have liked to bulk up more, judging by all the protein shakes I found lying around the house). But now I could see that his boots added several inches to his height, and the way he carried himself was different, like he was all about business. The snarky boyishness that was usually in the corner of his grin and the cocky tilt of his head were gone. And for the first time since meeting him, as he turned to look at me and his blue eyes met mine, I realized that he looked not like Jade's annoying big brother...but like a man.

He watched me with a strange expression as he filled the doorway in his camouflage pants and jacket, and I had to take extra care to avert my eyes so he wouldn't catch me gawking. Then I'd never hear the end of it.

"Ready to go?" he asked, holding open the door. "Jade's in the car, and I've got the AC running."

"Yep." I kissed my mom on the cheek and ignored her smug look as I made my way out to the truck. My door was already open, and Jade was in the back, oblivious to the world as she read what looked like a new book on geodes.

Derrick closed my door then got in and revved the truck up.

"Thanks again for coming to this," he said as we left the drive. "It's going to be a lot more enjoyable without a million questions about Amy."

"What will we tell them if they ask?" I pictured Amy in my head, and it wasn't without some sourness that I recalled her striking blue eyes, just as bright as Derrick's, and curly dark hair and perfect, unblemished skin. Like Snow White, if Snow White had been slightly tanned with the body of a triathlete. If his coworkers had seen her or her picture, no one would be able to mistake me for her. But we weren't dating, and I wasn't jealous, so it didn't really matter anyway. "I mean," I added with a shrug, "not that I care. They'll probably just be wondering where you got the blond, short-haired gnome and wonder where your forest elf went."

Derrick's laughter exploded through the quiet car. "You," he said, giving me another glance, "do not look like a gnome."

Was that a compliment?

Not that I cared.

"Speaking of clothes," I nodded at him, "I thought you didn't have to work tonight."

He grimaced. "Well, I'm filling in today for someone who got hurt this morning. They called me right before we left. I barely had time to change into my uniform."

A strange silence settled over the car. And though I scrolled through my inbox, I found myself more and more unsettled by the man sitting beside me. Which was stupid. This was Derrick, the guy who tormented me for half of our relationship and spent the other half playing pranks and begging me to help him avoid his boss.

So why did I feel like I was really meeting him for the first time? And why did it suddenly feel like maybe...maybe it was time to rethink the rules after all?

27

I DON'T MIND

DERRICK

Jessie was oddly silent as we drove up to the base gate. There had been times where I would have given my left foot to shut her up when we first met, but I found now that I didn't know what to do with the silence. Every so often, out of the corner of her eye, she'd sneak a glance at me before her eyes darted back down to her phone.

It had to be the uniform. Women were weird about uniforms. It was just something I wore every day. It had function and utility. Once I'd accidentally terrified a group of kids in a gas station, who I quickly realized were from another country. But Jessie didn't look terrified. She looked...curious. And though that would have concerned me two months ago, now I couldn't help but wonder if I liked it.

It was hard not to keep looking at her, too. She was dressed up more than usual today, wearing fitted dark jeans, and a blouse that was the kind that sat just on the edges of her shoulders, revealing her graceful neck and the sharp angles of her collarbone. Her blond hair was curled, rather than up in its usual ponytail, and she was wearing makeup. And every time she glanced up at me from below those long lashes, I had to remind myself to focus on the road.

"If anyone asks," I said, remembering the question I hadn't answered, "we can tell them you're a friend, and you're helping me with Jade this summer."

"And if they don't ask?"

Her question caught me off-guard for several reasons. First of all, she seemed fine with the statement that we were friends. A month ago, she would have nailed me for saying she was anything but Jade's teacher. This was progress, I supposed, that she let it slide now. And yet...friends. Not that we weren't. It just didn't quite fit what we were.

What were we anyway? A team, yes. Jade's sidekicks? That fit, too. But everything I could think of involved Jade. And I couldn't help but wonder about how if Jade were removed from the picture, we would have nothing left to tie us together. And it dawned on me that I didn't like that. After the summer we'd had, life without Jessie would have a gaping hole.

"And?" she asked, looking slightly bemused.

"Oh." I shook myself. "Sorry. Well, if they don't ask, we'll just let them think what they want." If they wanted to think the beautiful woman at my side was my girl, that was fine by me.

"I hate to ask this," I said, "but I don't know how long I'll be at work after this. Hopefully, it'll be less than an hour. If that's the case, you and Jade can come hang out at the barbeque. She's got a few extra toys in her backpack for if that happens. But if you really want to leave, maybe you could take Jade home in my truck? My mom could drive you home when you get back to the house."

She turned to gape at me. "You'd let me drive your truck?"

I cringed. "I'm honestly reconsidering this very instant."

She swatted me.

"But if you're determined to go home..." I shrugged. "Can't have your boyfriend thinking you're being held hostage."

"My...Oh geez. Sam is not my boyfriend." Something in her voice colored just slightly, and I grinned. I knew it was true, but for some reason, it felt good to have her say so.

After we got Jessie's pass from the visitor's center, we went through the gate, and I proceeded to give her a tour from the truck as we drove past the various parts of the base.

"This is the main road that almost everything for civilians lies on."

"What's that?" She pointed to the walking trail that wound in and out of and around a bunch of stationary planes, which all stood on their concrete beds around the flagpole in the center of the green.

"We call plane displays like that museums. They're really just old planes set up where people can see, but we're the military, so everything needs an important name." I pointed across the street. "Here's one of the two gas stations. This one stays open longer than the other one, which we'll see in a minute. There's the library and the base pool."

"It's busy."

"It's summer. Oh, and there's the chapel. That's where I went until we started going to your church. And there's the clinic on that side and the BX and commissary up ahead on the other."

"The commissary is the grocery store, right?" she asked.

"Right. And the BX is like our Walmart, but without taxes."

"Are those military houses?" She pointed to the other side of the street. "They're nicer than I thought they'd be."

I snorted. "Yeah, because those belong to the officers and senior NCOs."

"NCO?"

"Non-commissioned officer. Basically, higher-ranked enlisted people. They get the new ones. The old homes with all the problems are in the back, where you can't see."

"Where are the planes?" she asked, looking through the window like it was magical and everything might disappear.

"On the other side of all those trees. You can't see it from here, but I'll take you by the runway when we're done if you want. That's where I work, actually."

"It's like its own small city," she said, her eyes wide.

"It has to be," I said. "If something happened, like an emergency, everyone on base would need a way to keep functioning so we could do our jobs and help everyone else." I waved at the world around us. "And this is it."

She nodded and went back to staring, but as we neared the park, I found myself praying.

I also wondered if any of this would change her mind?

We passed the second gas station and turned onto a road that led to a small park with a large pond and a dozen picnic tables set up beside several large park grills. I found a parking space and pulled in.

"I'm sorry to ask this," I said, as I hopped out. "But I'm not supposed to carry Jade's backpack in uniform…or any backpack that's not regulation. If I get Jade, can you get it for me, and then I'll find a place to put it once we have our seats?"

I expected her to tease me about stupid military protocol because the rule really did seem stupid. But to my surprise, she only nodded and slipped the backpack on without a word.

As we made our way from the truck to the picnic area, where three guys were already grilling, and the rest created a sea of camouflage uniforms, sprinkled with civilian clothes from the spouses and kids, my heart clenched a little. It felt good to all walk up together. Almost like…

Nope. I wasn't going to think it. Best to not even let my mind wander in that direction, because either my own heart or Jessie would make me pay for it later, should she ever find out. But still…

"Allen." Sergeant Barnes greeted us as we neared the picnic tables, which were already nearly full. He was in civies, which I hoped meant he wouldn't follow me back to the office after the picnic to question me about Jessie.

"Sir." I shook his hand.

"And this is Jade." He smiled at my sister. "And," he looked up at Jessie, and I could see the confusion on his face.

"Jessie." Jessie reached out to shake his hand. For being so against dating anyone in the military, she seemed really comfortable around all these airmen. Then I remembered, she probably worked with half their kids. "We met at the mall," she said with a smile.

"Oh, that's right! Well, we're glad you're here today." He pointed to the line behind the grills. "Burgers and hotdogs are there. Dessert's on that table, and drinks are in the cooler there." Then he spotted someone behind me and waved. But as he passed me to greet whoever he'd seen, he grabbed my arm and whispered in my ear.

"That's not Miss Colorado, is it?"

I shook my head. "No, sir."

He gave me a long, thoughtful look before nodding slightly. "All right," he said and then moved on. I wasn't sure what that meant, but at least he wasn't pressing it here.

As we got our food, I felt like I could jump up and down. I'd passed the Barnes test, more or less, and now I just got time to hang out with my buddies and Jade and Jessie.

Jessie continued to amaze me as we moved in and out of the crowd. She was polite and easy with everyone, which was interesting, considering the impression I'd gotten that she was somewhat of an introvert. She didn't look tired at all, though, after I'd introduced her to the twelfth person who asked.

"Hey," she said, brushing her bangs out of her face and probably having no idea how incredibly attractive it was. "Jade keeps eyeing the pond, so I'm going to be proactive and take her to the swings. Sound good?"

"Sure." I smiled and watched as she led Jade over to where the other children and their parents were playing by now.

"Looks good on her," Hernandez said when Jessie was out of earshot.

"What does?" I pretended to mess with my phone.

"She fits right in. Look, she's already talking with the moms."

I looked up to see that sure enough, Jessie already had Jade on a swing and was laughing at something the woman beside her had said. And my friend was right. It did look good.

"This is the one you hired, right? The one you're going to the ball with?"

"Would you keep it down?" I glanced over my shoulder. "Barnes already approves." Well, kind of. "I don't really want to explain to him any more than I already have."

"Look, dude. All I'm saying is that she doesn't look hired. She looks happy." He bumped my shoulder. "And she seems to really care for Jade."

"She does." Jessie might curse me up one side and down the other one day, but I would never question her attachment to my sister.

"And Amy didn't." He shook his head. "Look, I just don't get it. Why aren't you going for her?"

"One problem." I gave him a wry smile. "She doesn't date airmen."

"What?"

"I'm serious. She has this whole list of rules about things that disqualify guys from being datable. And dating airmen is number one."

"But…" He frowned. "Why?"

"She's working on her master's degree, or is about to anyway, and she says she doesn't have time to move away anytime soon. She has to finish this degree."

Hernandez shook his head. "That sucks."

"Yeah, well, I get the feeling it has something to do with her family, too. She's crazy devoted to her parents, particularly her mom. And leaving has her terrified."

"Sorry, man." He picked up his empty paper plate. "Too bad there's not a way to change her mind." He paused and squinted up into the sky, which had grown dirty as the wind had begun to whip up around us. "Can you believe this weather? It was supposed to be nice today." As he spoke, the plate which he'd been holding was sucked from his hand.

As he ran to chase down his runaway plate, Jade's backpack beside me buzzed. I unzipped it and pulled out Jessie's phone. Even as I picked it up, I'd hoped it was her mom, but when I saw the screen, my heart sank for some reason.

It was him again. Sam Newman. This time, he was asking her how her day was going, and it looked as though he'd sent an image.

A strange sensation boiled in the pit of my stomach as I put the phone back. She might not be convinced, but that man was trying to get her attention, and he was trying hard. Not that I could blame him. It was probably a good thing she didn't make it a habit of dating airmen. A number of the single guys kept sending her glances, particularly after they'd ascertained that we weren't officially an item.

And what was there not to be attracted to? Hernandez had been right. She looked perfectly at ease as she took Jade over to the swings, talking with the other moms...the moms. She wasn't a mom yet, so she couldn't be one of them. But the sight suited her, especially with the breeze blowing her curls all around her face. And I liked that just a little too much. Warning bells were already going off in my head, and the whispers in my head that I was just getting over Amy. It was far too fast to let myself fall for someone else, particularly someone who had sworn not to date someone like me.

"Excuse me."

Everyone quieted and turned to see the squadron commander standing at the edge of the crowd holding a speakerphone.

"I hate to do this, but we're going to have to break it up early. We've just been put under a severe thunderstorm watch, and with the looks of those clouds over there," he pointed, "I'd like to send people home before driving conditions get dangerous."

We all turned to look where he was pointing. Sure enough, deep gray and blue clouds were piling up to our west. As if answering him, thunder rumbled in the distance.

"I need everyone to gather their things and head home. If you're going back to the flightline, make sure you've got a SIP room nearby."

Thankfully, my room had a Shelter in Place room in the building. But as Jessie returned with Jade, and I began to pack everything up, Barnes met me at the table.

"Don't worry about coming in this afternoon," he said. "I'll take care of it."

"Are you sure?" I asked, not sure whether I should be happy or suspicious.

"Yeah, get these ladies home. I'll see you Sunday night."

"Thank you, sir." I took Jade's hand as Jessie hefted on the backpack. As we made our way back to the car, Hernandez's girlfriend, who had arrived late, waved from a few cars down.

"Hey, Allen."

I waved. "Hey, there."

"It's so good to meet you in person," she called, pushing her dark hair from her face. "You have a lovely family."

"Thanks," I called back.

And then I realized what I had just said. And from the startled look on Jessie's face, she had heard, too. Mumbling something about getting out of here, I buckled Jade in and got inside. Jessie did, too. I pulled out of the lot and turned back onto Arnold Drive, and for a long time, we didn't speak. Rain started to pound the roof of the car, and lightning really began to crackle in earnest, but none of it could compare to the fear I felt inside.

Had I just ruined whatever it was that I had with Jessie? I didn't mean to. It had been a quick exchange, and I hadn't really been thinking when I'd said it. It just all seemed so natural. Way more than what I would have expected after knowing her for two months. But no matter how I tried to view it, there was only really one truth.

If I had a family, this would be exactly the way I wanted it to be.

We didn't speak until I pulled onto the freeway.

"So…" I finally ventured, daring a meek look. "I'm sorry about that."

"About what?" She looked up, eyes far too wide to be oblivious.

"Back at the picnic, when Hernandez's girlfriend said we were a family. I didn't mean—"

"Derrick." To my surprise, she smiled. "It's all right."

I blinked at her. "Really?"

"Yeah." She smiled again. "I don't mind."

As we turned continued through the pouring rain, I made a daring promise to myself that I would probably regret later. Sam Newman was breaking Rule Number Four. And if he could break the rules and still try to catch her attention, then so could I.

In fact, that was exactly what I was going to do.

28

MY LIFE

JESSIE

About five minutes from my house, my phone began to buzz with severe thunderstorm warnings as the sky really let loose. Rain hammered the car and smeared the windshield until it was hard to one car length in front of us. Thunder crackled on every side, ear-splitting in its proximity. Jade whimpered from the back seat, and I turned to reassure her while Derrick focused on the road. But even as I passed words of comfort, I found myself praying continually. There weren't any tornado warnings out yet, just the same watches as there had been earlier. But that didn't mean one couldn't drop any minute.

Breathing was finally possible again when we pulled into my parents' front drive. I began to open the door to race for the front porch, but a streak of lightning had me slamming the door shut with a squeal as I jumped back into my seat.

"I would wait a minute if I were you." Derrick peered into the dark sky.

"Ya think?" I laughed, hugging myself and shivering at how close that one had been. We waited in silence for a moment before he spoke again.

"Not to change the subject," he said, just a bit too casually. "But I've been thinking about that list you have." He turned off the engine and turned to face me, the sound of rain nearly deafening.

"Not you, too."

He ignored the comment. "Have you ever actually been on a date?"

"Of course. I've been on lots of dates." I didn't add that most of them had been coerced and with Madison. He didn't need to know that.

"What about kisses?" His eyes gleamed. "Have you ever had one of those?"

"That's not any of your business." My cheeks burned.

"Which means no." He snickered. "Okay, fine. But what about a real relationship? Because I can't see how anyone could possibly measure up to all these." He pulled his phone out and tapped it a few times before squinting at the screen.

"You took a picture of my list?" I grabbed for his phone, but he just held it away.

"Like this one. Number twelve." He continued to squint at the picture. "Must be willing to spend money annually on family pictures. What's that supposed to mean?"

"I don't want a miser that won't let me record our family history. Now delete that." But before I could get anything else, Jade announced that she had to go to the bathroom.

"I'm going to take care of this," I said, peering up at the sky, which had lightened slightly. "But you'd better have that thing deleted by the time I get back. And no posting it to social media or anything. I will have your head."

"Duly noted." He waved but didn't look up from his phone.

Thankfully, the lightning had abated by the time I had to get Jade out of the car seat. I ran her inside the house and let her use the bathroom there. As I was waiting, I dug into my purse to find my phone, only to realize that I must have left it on the front seat. As soon as she was done, I hurried us back as fast as I could, but not fast enough. And just as I'd expected, Derrick had my phone, and the slight upturn of his mouth promised trouble.

"Give that back." I held my hand out. To my surprise, he did as I asked, but the smile didn't leave his face as I scrolled to see what he'd gotten into.

"You read my messages with Sam? What is wrong with you?"

"He texted you, by the way. I heard the phone buzzing and wondered if it was your mom, so I picked it up."

"And you read my texts?" I paused. "Wait. How do you know my password?"

He just gave me a sly grin. "It's not like you hide your screen whenever you unlock, and your password's only four characters."

I gaped at him.

"Anyhow," Derrick shrugged, "I almost feel sorry for the poor guy." He linked his fingers behind his head and leaned back. "According to your list, he seems, from what I gather, to be the perfect man." He nodded at my phone. "But from what I can see, you've done nothing but push him away since he first met you."

I shoved the phone back into my purse indignantly. "You're unbelievable."

"But seriously." He sat forward and leaned toward me, his blue eyes locking onto mine. "What is wrong with him? Because you obviously haven't taken the bait from the most perfect man in the world."

I snorted. "Sam's nice, but he's not perfect. And he doesn't keep all the rules. Not yet, at least."

"And which one is this poor sucker guilty of breaking?"

"Number four." I skimmed the text messages to make sure Derrick hadn't answered back for me.

"Number four." Derrick pulled out his phone again. "Has to make the first move."

"Asking five times in a month if he can borrow a whiteboard marker isn't making a move," I said as I turned around to check on Jade. Nor, I added in my head, was meeting at the bookstore to "study". But I wasn't going to say that part out loud.

"Ouch." Derrick laughed. "Harsh much?"

I shrugged. "My life. My list."

At this, he laughed. "Granted."

I stepped back, thankful the rain had stopped. "And here I was, thinking you were all mature in your uniform."

"Shows how much you know about me." His eyes glinted as I closed the door. He pulled the truck forward about a foot then rolled the window down. "See you at church."

29

GO FOR IT

DERRICK

"Turn here. No…Okay. I guess you should go to the next one and try again." I glanced up from my phone. "Hernandez, are you even listening?"

"What?" My friend shook himself and turned so fast we nearly hit another car.

"Dude! Do I need to drive?"

"Oh, no. Sorry." He sat up straighter. "I'm just a little distracted, that's all."

"Yeah, no kidding." I looked back down at my phone. "Okay, turn left in two lights. Then you'll make an immediate right."

"Why don't you let the GPS just tell us?" He grimaced. "And why'd Massy have to move across town?"

"Because you quit listening to the GPS ten minutes ago." I shook my head. "And because he says the rent's going to be cheaper. So," I gave my friend another skeptical glance, "what's going on, man?"

"It's my girlfriend. She turned twenty-six two weeks ago, and suddenly I'm hearing nothing but wedding bells and realtor open houses and babies." He wiped his forehead. "So many babies. She talks about nothing else."

"Why don't you marry her?" I pointed to the stop sign. "You seemed happy enough to have her on your arm yesterday at the picnic. Oh, turn left here."

"I'm not ready to get married!" Hernandez's laugh was slightly hysterical. "We've only been dating six months."

"There. It's the third house on the right." As soon as Hernandez had pulled in front of the house, I hopped out and began untying the load from the truck's bed.

Hernandez joined me. As we carried the table up to the front door of a small house with blue siding, he muttered the whole time about how cheap Massy, our coworker who owned this place, was. "The least he could have done was buy us pizza. We're helping him move after all."

"Give the guy a break. His wife's pregnant with twins." I dusted my hands after we put the first load down. "They're actually at a doctor's appointment right now. That's why he gave me the key." We went back out to get the chairs. "Besides, it's a small table, and there are a whopping two chairs.

"And then the rest of his living room," Hernandez grumbled. "But speaking of couples and kids," he said, grabbing one of them, "for someone who doesn't date airmen, you and Jessie looked pretty cozy the other day."

I put the chair down. "You know we didn't even touch."

"Maybe cozy's not the right word. I guess what I'm trying to say is that if I didn't know better, I would have thought you two were happily married, and a few years down the marriage road." He shrugged. "Too bad she doesn't date airmen. You guys make a good team."

Why did that make my heart skip just a little?

"Actually," I said slowly, "now that you bring it up...I've been thinking about that."

He grunted as he moved his chair through the doorway. "How so?"

"I'm going to do it."

He frowned at me. "Do what?"

"I'm going to go for it." I took a deep breath. "I want to make her mine."

Hernandez leaned against the chair right there in the entryway. "Are you nuts? The girl actually has a rule that she doesn't date people like you. And you want to *marry* her?"

I picked up his chair and carried it to the table with mine. "Hey, one thing at a time." I paused. "But yeah, that's pretty much it."

"Wow. Just...wow." Hernandez shook his head as I locked up.

"You're either really dense or I'm going to have to hail you as the best that's ever been."

"Well, you won't have to wait too long to find out." I grinned. "I'm starting next Saturday." I clapped him on the shoulder then I locked the door behind us. "And since we have three more deliveries to make today, you're going to help me dream up a fairy-tale obsessed, twenty-three-year-old, obsessive-compulsive woman's dream day."

"Oh, joy." Hernandez shut the truck door a little harder than necessary. "Just when I thought this day couldn't get any better."

"Aw, cheer up." I put my seatbelt on. "If you're really that upset, I'll buy you a smoothie."

"It had better be chocolate," Hernandez grumbled as we peeled out into the street. No matter how much he grumbled, though, I couldn't help but smile.

30

DUES

DERRICK

E xactly one week later, Jade and I pulled up Jessie's drive, and my breathing was slightly erratic in a way it hadn't been since I'd first asked Amy out for a drink. But then again, this was different, too. Amy had been all smooth words and allure. Actually... now that I thought about it, how had I not seen that when we first met? She'd been looking to catch someone when I showed up at that bar with my friends, someone who would fit into her life exactly the way she wanted them to be. But Jessie...

Dating Amy had been like a constant tango. Every move had to be perfectly calculated and executed, and not a hair could be out of place. It was thrilling, I couldn't deny that. And there was always that hint of danger that made the whole thing feel like an adventure. When I was with Jessie, though, I felt like we were taking a long, warm, spring day hike. There was nothing pretentious, nothing for show. Rather, we were a team, and we knew we wanted the same thing. She was steady and strong, and she was constantly looking ahead to spot any danger to her fellow travelers. And that was the kind of partner I wanted at my side.

If only I could convince her to conquer new mountains with me.

I rang the doorbell and waited, glancing back every few seconds at Jade, who was strapped into the truck with the air conditioner on behind me. Mr. Nickleby answered this time.

"Derrick." He reached out to shake my hand. "What brings you by today?"

"Oh," I grinned, "your daughter and I made a bet, and I won. So I'm coming to collect."

"Collect?" He pushed the glasses up on his nose.

"She has to let me pick what we're going to do for a whole day."

He snickered. "She's going to love that." Then he turned and called down the hall. "Jess, Derrick's here."

"I'm coming!" She ran up to the door, still pinning her hair into place. Today she wore a white skirt with little pink flowers and a pink blouse. Instead of her usual sneakers, she was wearing little white shoes that looked like the slippers the princesses wore in all those movies Jade made me watch. Her green eyes were bright, and if I wasn't mistaken, she looked slightly flushed.

I had to take another long breath.

"Where all are you going today?" Mr. Nickleby was still watching me, but his brows were slightly furrowed this time.

I pointed back at the truck. "Well, we're starting with a few of Jade's favorite things, and we'll see from there."

At the mention of Jade, his expression relaxed. "Have fun, Jess. Let me know when you're coming home so we know what to do with your dinner."

"All right, Dad." She kissed him on the cheek and followed me out to the truck. I opened the door, and she hopped inside. Well, as well as one can hop in a skirt. Not that I minded. This girl had the prettiest legs I'd ever seen. I'd have to make sure I didn't catch myself staring at them like I had before on accident.

"When you said you won," she turned and gave me a sour look, "I didn't think you'd need to claim your victory quite so soon."

I laughed as I put the truck in drive. "You should know me better than that by now, Jessie Nickleby."

"Nickleby mad," Jade chirped from the back seat.

"You're just as guilty as him, girlie." Jade looked over her shoulder. "I was sure you'd like the diamond mine the best."

In the rearview mirror, I could see Jade's sly little smile, but she didn't look up from her book.

"So." Jessie grimaced. "Where are we going first? A monster truck rally? Some nasty, stinky gym?"

"Close." I turned the music up and gunned the engine. She just rolled her eyes and shook her head, but a small smile played on the corner of her lips. And I smiled, too. Today was a good day. And I prayed that by the end, it would be even better.

I was rewarded for my prayers when we parallel parked downtown.

She looked at me like I was drunk. "We're going to Dugan's Pub?"

"Would you just wait and see?" I pulled Jade from her car seat. She sighed but to her credit, quit guessing until we had walked about three blocks and turned twice. Finally, we were across the street from a wide brick structure with a curved silver roof. And I was rewarded for my scheming when she looked genuinely surprised.

"The farmer's market?"

"Jade likes it." I stooped down and hefted my sister onto my shoulders as we crossed the final street. "And since it's not absolutely boiling out today, I thought we'd start here."

The pleasure in her face was impossible to miss as we made our way through the market. We browsed charm bracelet stalls, bought a box of blueberries to snack on, and I stopped to sample some flavored beef jerky. Though browsing wasn't my preferred form of shopping, doing it with Jade and Jessie was fun. That feeling I'd gotten back at the picnic intensified as I watched them explore a hat display together, and my chest tightened.

How do I convince her that this is how it could be? I prayed. *Let her see that she doesn't have to be afraid.*

I ended up buying a bag of beef jerky. I felt kind of guilty spending twenty bucks on beef jerky, but it was amazing, and sharing might win me back some points with my dad. Then I turned to look for the girls.

"Oh, Jade!" Jessie's voice rose above the general din of the covered structure. "Isn't this lovely?"

They were still in the hat display, and I found them both trying on the same hat. Well, Jade's version was much smaller, but the hats were identical. They were giggling in front of a mirror while the woman running the stall was spouting to Jessie all the wonders of homemade hats. And while I didn't care a bushel what was in my hats, the girls were really a pretty sight. Jade had a light in her eyes I didn't often see, and Jessie was all rosy cheeks and sparkling green eyes.

"Let's get them," I said.

Jessie quit giggling with Jade, and her mouth fell open a little. "But you don't even know how much they are."

"My day," I reminded her as I pulled out my credit card and handed it to the woman. "I get to pick."

Jessie blushed even harder as the woman ran the card through her little phone extension and handed me the phone to sign. I had to keep myself from cringing at the total, but even as I signed, I knew it was worth every penny. If I wanted any chance at keeping Jessie, I would have to change some of my ways.

"All right. We need a picture with you two and these ridiculous hats." I pulled the girls out and posed them in front of the river. Jessie gave me a funny look but smiled for the camera. For once, Jade smiled when asked, and as soon as I looked at the picture again, I decided it was going to be my phone's background image until I died.

Jessie never took her eyes off me as we rejoined the throng of market-goers.

"You're spending an awful lot of money for someone who's supposed to be saving every penny he gets to travel one day."

"You forget. Amy's gone, so I can do what I want."

She didn't argue, but the look she gave me told me that she wasn't convinced. But that was okay. If I had to spend my entire travel savings to convince her, I would.

We ended up getting several jars of berry preserves, a homemade lavender candle that Jessie seemed almost as attached to as she had been to the hat, and smoothies because the day was getting hotter. And every time I made a purchase or insisted I pay, she gave me that same calculating look. But as she didn't actually object, I hoped that was a good thing.

My theory was tested when we crossed the street again. Instead of going back to the car, I led us into the old triangle skyscraper on the corner with a sign that said, "River Market Books and Gifts".

"I love this place!" Jessie squealed and immediately ran to the elevator, dragging Jade along behind her. Then we spent an hour in the children's book section, where Jessie found eleven picture books, among which were two different versions of Beauty and the Beast, and five minutes in the classical literature section, in which she found an old copy of Pride and Prejudice. She probably would have stayed all day if I hadn't dragged her out, promising her that the next thing would be just as good.

"I doubt it." She pursed her lips as the man behind the counter bagged up the books. "The library's used bookstore is pretty hard to beat." She met my eyes. "And I'm still waiting for that underground fight club to make an appearance."

"Well, what do you know?" I grabbed the bags and pulled the girls back out to the sidewalk. "We're doing that next."

"And we're taking Jade?" Jessie glanced up at our little charge.

"Hey, it's not like I'm taking her to some abandoned mine." I gave her an evil grin as she stuck her tongue out at me.

Nope. This was nothing like hanging out with Amy.

Our next venture had cost a pretty penny. But I would have paid more than twice as much to see the look on her face when we pulled into the parking lot.

"No." She looked at me like she'd seen a ghost. "You didn't."

"Well," I closed my door and went to open hers. She'd been so awestruck she'd forgotten to even open it, which gave me the chance to play the gentleman. "Last I checked, this is where the fight club is supposed to be." She glared at me through slitted eyes, and I laughed. "But if something else is being shown, I guess we can stick around."

"But this…this is the event arena" She got out of the truck slowly, her eyes focused on the giant canvas sign hanging over the entrance in the distance.

"And?" I asked.

"Beauty and the Beast is here right now." She turned to look at me. "But these tickets are impossible to get."

"Just call me your fairy godmother."

"Wrong fairy tale."

"Does it matter?" I held out my hand. It was a gamble. But whether it was because she needed help walking, due to her shock, or because she simply wasn't paying attention, she took it, and I was rewarded with the soft warmth of her skin on mine. And it was like a shot of an energy drink straight to my veins. Bolstered with this new confidence, I led us through the Blue Parking Lot and into the crowd that was slowly moving toward the six sets of double doors at the front of the building.

I was personally not a huge fan of people in costumes skipping around on a stage and singing at random points in the story. But Jessie was glued to the show. Jade was interested at first but fell asleep somewhere between the dinner scene and the wolf scene, which was probably for the best. If we'd watched that, she would have forced me to pretend to be a wolf for the next month.

Feeling unusually bold, I waved down one of the workers selling those plastic roses edged with rainbow fiber optics. And for a moment...just a moment, when I quietly handed it to Jessie, the look in her eyes, one of fear and wonder and something else I couldn't name, made me wonder if maybe...maybe I could really could change her mind.

She was silent on the ride home, aside from a few comments about the show. But the way her face glowed and the far-off look in her eyes kept me from being too nervous. It also gave me the courage to take the next step when we got back to my house.

Jessie started to get out, but I locked the doors as I pulled my phone out and hit the call button.

"Dad?" I asked quietly, as Jade was still asleep. "Can you come out and get Jade?"

"You can just drop me off at my house," Jessie whispered, seeming to finally snap out of her daze. "That way she can just get her afternoon nap in the car."

I just shook my head as my dad came out and walked toward us. "Don't worry about it. Dad's got her. Besides, we're not done."

Her eyebrows shot up. "We're not?" She looked back at Jade in confusion. "But you're dropping her off."

I allowed myself a slight smile. "Wasn't our bet for all day?"

She opened her mouth, but nothing came out as she frowned. "I...I guess so."

"Good." I grinned outright. "Because I'm not done having fun."

She folded her arms and sat back to stare at me. "There is no way this morning and afternoon made up your ideal day."

By this time, my dad had Jade out of her car seat and the door shut, so I let out a loud laugh. "I think I'm the one who gets to decide what I do and don't enjoy." I leaned forward slightly. "So you game for some more?"

She studied me for a long moment, and an icy fear crept into my veins that she might actually say no. But then she smiled slightly. "Fine. Where to next?"

SO MUCH

JESSIE

I did my best to keep a neutral expression as we drove back across the river, but my heart was pounding in my chest. Today had been...well, a dream. It was exactly my idea of a perfect day. Derrick had planned it better than if I had won. But the obvious question was one that rang in my head until I nearly had a headache.

Why was he doing all this? Had my mom told him I was rethinking the rule about airmen?

There had been a moment in that dark arena during the show when I could have sworn he'd looked at me like...like he wanted me. Me, with all my obsessive habits and Scroogish scrimping and self-imposed rules. My natural lack of style. (My mother had forced me to go shopping when she heard about the picnic, and I'd come home with far more clothes than I would ever be able to wear.) My obsession with children and my parents and fairy tales.

But that, I'd argued with myself for the remainder of the show and the entire trip back to his house, was impossible. It was too soon for him to be over Amy and looking at anyone else like that. And yet, that look he'd given me was one I'd never seen on his face when he talked about Amy.

I was fast in danger of following him around like a puppy, and that made my entire brain scream at me that I was out of control and needed to take it back. I'd nearly ended our time there in the truck. To keep us both safe. The invitation, however, was too enticing after what he'd planned for that morning. And so I'd said yes. And now we were hurtling south on the 440 going who knew where at seventy miles per hour with The Scorpions blasting on the radio and a very handsome man sitting in the seat across from mine.

No one, not even me on my most curmudgeonist day, could deny he was handsome. He wasn't in his uniform, but instead of his usual snarky cartoon t-shirt, he was wearing a dark blue Polo shirt and khaki cargo shorts. He hadn't shaved that morning, leaving just enough shadow to make him look very...manly. And responsible. Like a really hot, responsible man. Like he could easily be a dad or husband driving a family to dinner or church or a wife on a date.

My heart tripped over itself as I recalled the way it had felt again in the farmer's market. We'd felt like a family. And as much as the part of my brain that clutched the rules to its chest screamed at me to collect my senses, I'd been unable to ignore that feeling. And a longing had planted itself in me that I'd never known before, especially when he'd taken my hand in the arena parking lot. Sure, I'd always wanted a family of my own. And the perfectionist in me that had pushed me through college and now toward my master's had always said later. We'll find that later. But I wanted it now.

I wanted this now.

And that terrified me more than Derrick's strange behavior.

We finally pulled up in front of an outdoor shopping mall. Derrick, all the gentleman, got my door open before I'd pulled all my stuff out of Jade's backpack.

"Thanks." I got out and stood awkwardly next to him, not sure what to do as he closed the door and locked the car.

"So...what are we doing?" I asked, hoping I didn't sound as dorky as I felt.

"I decided I felt like a little window shopping and then some dinner." He paused. "And then some sight-seeing."

"Okay." I held my hands up and let them fall to my sides again. Wow. As if he had needed more reminders that I was not the smooth, sexy lady he'd left behind in Colorado. But he didn't seem to mind. Instead, he smiled and held his hand out toward the crosswalk.

"Shall we?"

At first, I was just as nervous as I'd been in the car. But Derrick made it easy to relax. We went in and out of shops, and he spent most of the time making fun of expensive accessories and clothes. I could see the manager in one of the stores giving us dirty looks, which made me giggle nervously and only encouraged him more. Then he launched into a diatribe about how bad the acting was in the show, which, of course, brought out the fight in me, which in turn, chased away the rest of my nerves. Arguing with Derrick was easy. I knew how to do that.

But as we passed a jewelry store on the corner, I saw the most beautiful thing I had ever seen in the entire world.

"What?" he asked as I stood there, hands pressed against my heart. Then he looked at what I was staring at. "Oh, boy."

"It's the Beauty and the Beast rose," I whispered as if that explained it. But it was truly breathtaking. The rose itself was made of rose gold with a red ruby that glittered in the center. The leaves curled out to where they met the gold ring itself.

"That's your dream ring?" he asked, an amused smile on his face.

"It's incredible," I whispered. Then I remembered who I was talking to and laughed. "I'm afraid to know the price, though. It's why I never go in places like this. But it's just so pretty to look at."

He looked back at the ring, but instead of making fun of it the way he'd made fun of the shoes I'd liked at the last store, he just said, "Huh."

Eventually, I dragged myself away from the display window and we went to dinner.

"Have you ever been here?" he asked as he led us toward a little Euro bistro with an outdoor eating area visible over a short wall. A live band played catchy jazz songs, and the smell of breadsticks filled the air.

"No, but it looks good," I said as I followed him inside. There was a waiting area in the lobby. I stood in line to check in as Derrick went to get us menus to look at.

"Are you sure you want to eat here?" I glanced at him over my menu. "You've spent a lot of money today."

"Jessie!"

I looked up to see Madison and Sam and a few second grade teachers already standing at the front desk. Madison ran over to hug me, and Sam followed. But he looked far less thrilled, and judging by the way Derrick was returning the look, the feeling was mutual.

"What are you doing here with him?" Madison turned around so

Derrick couldn't see her face. "I called to see if you wanted to join us tonight, but you never returned my call."

"I'm sorry, I've been busy all day." I glanced over her shoulder at Sam and Derrick, who were still sizing each other up. "Derrick won that bet I told you about, so he's been picking what we do all day."

"And you're *here*?" She looked at me in disbelief. "I would have thought you guys were going to a fight club or something."

I was about to answer her when Sam stepped toward us.

"Sam," I said, pasting a smile on my face. "This is Derrick, Jade's older brother. Derrick, this is Sam Newman, one of my neighbor teachers."

Sam's face tightened slightly, and Derrick looked just a tad smugger.

"Sam, party of four and Derrick, party of two," the waitress called, and I let out a deep breath as I started to follow her away from the awkwardness.

Derrick, however, shocked me by raising his hand. "Excuse me," he called politely. "If you have a big booth, we'd love to sit with them."

I looked at him incredulously, as did Sam, but the waitress went back and looked at her little blueprint of the seats before nodding. "I think we can squeeze you all in. Follow me."

This evening was turning out weirder than I could have imagined it. And yet, I obediently followed and slid into the outdoor booth then waited as everyone else crowded in, too. And who else could I be doomed to sit between but Derrick and Sam?

I was suddenly all too glad of the menu as I held it up like a wall to keep me safe from the rest of the table. Madison kept sending me frantic looks, but it wasn't like I could tell her or even text her anything. Not with Sam and Derrick sitting right next to me.

"So, you're Jade's brother," Sam said. "I hear you're also engaged. Congratulations."

I started scanning the wine section.

"Nope." Derrick grinned and put his hands behind his head, elbows angled out comfortably. "Single as they come."

Sam's face darkened slightly.

"What schedule do they have you on right now? I can't guess that's easy, taking care of your sister and working full-time."

Oh, Sam. Just stop. Please. For all our sakes.

"It's actually not bad. I work night shift right now, which means I get home in time to spend time with Jade and Jessie. Then when my parents get back from work, I sleep until it's time to leave again."

"That doesn't seem like a lot of sleep," Sam said.

Derrick shrugged. "Six or seven hours a night, and sometimes a nap in-between. It's not ideal but doable. And I wouldn't give up these days for anything."

I waved the waitress down. "We're ready to order now."

The waitress took our orders and brought our drinks, but much to my chagrin, the men started right where they'd left off as soon as she was gone.

"So you and Jessie have had quite a bit of time this summer to get to know each other," Sam said a little too casually. Where was he going with this?

Derrick nodded. "We have."

"Has she shown you her list?" Sam paused. "The dating one?"

I wanted to sink into the bench and just melt into the aquifer beneath it. Or any underground river that was willing to take me away.

"What do you guys want to drink?" Madison asked in a loud voice. "I want something with salt on the rim."

"She has." The smile didn't move from Derrick's face. "It's quite a list. No airmen. No huge debt, no smoking." His eyes glinted dangerously. "Not making a move."

Sam's face reddened as Derrick stood and went over to talk to the band's pianist, and Sam took a fierce bite from a breadstick. While Derrick was up, my phone buzzed. I looked down to see a text from Madison.

You have some splaining to do.

I groaned quietly as Derrick walked back. But instead of sitting down, he held his hand out to me.

"Wanna dance?"

Did I? Yes, actually. Yes, I did. I wanted this handsome man to take me dancing. For once, I wanted to have fun…and maybe even flirt a little. I wanted to chuck that rule about airmen right out the window.

Also, I desperately needed to get away from that table.

I could feel Sam's eyes burning a hole in my back as I took Derrick's outstretched hand. I was doing it. I was going to dance with Derrick Allen. But as I stood, I heard Sam's voice.

"What are you doing?"

Guilt flooded me, but before I could answer, Derrick leaned forward and winked.

"Making a move." Then he pulled me toward the little space that had been cleared right in front of the band, where he put one hand on the small of my back and took my hand with the other.

If my mind hadn't already been spinning in circles, it was going into overdrive now. I had to take back some control of the scene.

"That was—"

"Smooth?" He wriggled his eyebrows.

"Unnecessary. This isn't a war."

"Really?" He stared down at me, and I did my best not to be captured by those startling eyes. "Are you sure about that?"

"Not that it matters." I tossed my bangs out of my face. "Neither of you qualify anyway." Light. Keep it light.

"And yet, here you are." A small smile played on his lips. "And you haven't objected yet."

"Maybe I'm just trying to have an adventure," I said breathlessly. "You know, you're not as awful as you used to be."

His grin widened. "I try." Then he leaned down until his breath was hot on my ear. "And just think," he whispered, "if you were still following all those rules, you'd probably be at home right now, studying."

He was right. That would be exactly what I would be doing. Because if I was honest, I wasn't following the rules today either. But as the world continued to twirl around us, and his hand stayed warm and firm on my back, I couldn't help wondering. How many days like this had I missed because of those rules? How many more would I sacrifice?

As always, however, my inner pragmatist couldn't be silent.

And what will you do when he has to leave and he takes your heart with him?

"You know what?" Derrick glanced over my shoulder at what was probably an irate Sam. I felt bad for leaving him like that, but not bad enough to stop. "Let's order our food to go. There's something I want you to see."

I nearly said no, but the unsated hunger in his eyes kept my mouth shut.

"Do you trust me?" he whispered again.

Did I trust him? I trusted him not to drive me off into a ditch every day as he insisted on chauffeuring us around. And I knew him well enough to trust him not to do anything villainous or dastardly when we were alone. But did I trust him with my heart? Because I was rather sure that was exactly what he was going to ask for. And when all this was said and done, and I was in my right mind again and not thinking under the influence of his gaze or his arms, what would I think of such trust then?

"Take a chance," he murmured. "Before you say no, just see what one night of adventure can bring."

Slowly, I nodded and let him lead me from the dance floor. And this time, he didn't let go of my hand.

~

"You wouldn't let me eat for this?" I clutched my to-go box as he pulled into a dark parking lot beside the river. "You know, if this were a story, this would be a 'The Big Dam Bridge would be the perfect place to get rid of a body' kind of story." I cringed even as I said it. Somebody had gotten a kick out of naming this thing.

"Don't be getting any ideas, Miss Hangry." Derrick got out, holding his own to-go box. Once the car doors were shut, he pulled two long bags from the trunk and locked the car and reached out his hand. I knew it wasn't a good idea, but I slid mine into his anyway. I'd already gone past nine at night without my dinner, and I was in one of the best places in the city to die quietly, had he been a villain of sorts. I might as well let him hold my hand.

We made our way up the bridge, styrofoam food boxes in hand. I'd driven over this bridge a million times. In fact, we'd been on it today on our way to dinner. But now we took the sidewalk that was part of a long trail used for hiking and biking. Derrick stopped us at the very top. The sounds of water passing through the dam beneath our feet was a bit alarming at first, but after half a minute of listening, it was actually quite soothing.

But the sight was what took my breath away.

The bridge, which was aglow with white and blue and purple lights, lit the night air like magic from runaway fairies. When I turned around to see why Derrick was so quiet, I found two folding chairs set out, and him in one of them.

"Have a seat?" He patted the empty chair beside his.

I grinned and sat.

"Gladly." I took the plastic fork he offered me and dug into my chicken piadini. I couldn't remember the last time I'd been so hungry. For several minutes, we simply sat there, eating, and my muscles began to relax as the warmth of the food filled my belly. Likewise, Derrick just ate his dinner, too, like it was any other day, rather than the most romantic day I could have imagined in my entire life.

"Sam wasn't happy when we left," I finally said. Then I eyed him. "You did that on purpose, didn't you?"

The glint in his eyes was answer enough. But what he said took me by surprise.

"Why do you have those rules anyway?" He shrugged as he folded another piece of his pita bread. "I mean, I'm fine with you using them as an excuse not to date pocket-protector Teacher Man—"

"Sam does not wear pocket protectors."

"But," he held up his hands, "I'm curious as to why you came up with them in the first place."

I sighed, tucking a curl behind my ear. Was I ready to tell him this? Then again, we were so far in now, what did it matter? "My dad took a job here the month before I started my freshman year of high school. While we were getting all settled, just before the school year started, my mom was diagnosed with breast cancer."

My throat tightened as I remembered. "I started high school with a mom in chemo, and my dad working every extra hour he could squeeze in to help make up for the medical costs." I shrugged. "Having a mom in that kind of position changes how you see things, I guess. I decided during my freshman year that I was going to work hard enough to get all the scholarships I could so my parents wouldn't have to pay for college and could focus on medical costs instead. And as soon as I was in college, I decided to get a master's so I would be indispensable to whoever wrote my paychecks."

Derrick's chewing slowed, and since my eyes had adjusted to the low light, I could see him frowning thoughtfully. "But your mom got better, didn't she?"

"She did. But it was a long fight, and we nearly lost her several times. Then it came back last year." I shivered, despite the warm, humid air. "She's technically in remission, but she still has to go back for checkups quite a bit."

"And that scares you." It wasn't a question.

I drew in a shaky breath and twirled the food around with my fork. "The rules are my anchor. I made them up so I could confidently start a relationship that would be stable, should I ever actually find one I could start. That way, if something happens, and my dad loses his insurance or something like that, I can not only pay for my mom's treatments, but I can take care of both my parents, and I'd be sure to have a guy who would support me in that." I paused. "It's why I have to get this degree." My food was getting cold, and it didn't taste nearly as good as it did when we started eating.

"But..." Derrick looked out over the river. "Is that what they want you to do?"

"Does it matter?" I stabbed the chicken.

A few minutes of silence passed before he spoke again.

"You know," he leaned back in his chair and folded his hands behind his head. "When my dad had his latest heart episode, it terrified me. I'd just moved out here, and now I had to make sure that I was Jade's legal guardian. My parents didn't ask me to take that responsibility, but I knew that Jade needed me."

"Were they always like this?" I asked, glad to have the conversation off of me. "So busy, I mean."

"Actually, they were really involved when I was little. My dad coached my baseball team, and my mom came to all our games and practices. Then their business took off about the time I turned eleven or twelve. And as soon as we had money, they suddenly got everything they wanted."

"But not what you wanted."

He gave me a sad smile. "I got extracurricular lessons galore and trips to the Bahamas and exposure to all sorts of culture they thought I'd been deprived of before we could afford it." He looked down at his styrofoam box, which was empty now. "When Jade came along, it was a real shock.

They thought they were done having kids since they hadn't been able to have any more after I was born. But by then, they were so set in their fast-paced, workaholic lifestyles that they just couldn't give it up."

"So you know how hard it is," I leaned forward, "to be what others don't think you need to be."

"I do." He leaned forward, too. "And I think there has to be a way for you to live your life while helping them the way they need."

I gave him a wry smile. "You mean have my cake and eat it, too." I laughed a little. "You sound like my mother."

Instead of answering, he stood and took the box from my hands and laid it on the ground before pulling me to my feet. My breath hitched as he kept my left hand in his and pulled me close with his right.

"Your mother," he said in a low, gravelly voice, "is a smart woman. You should listen to her."

"My mother doesn't know what is good for her." I fought to keep my voice even as the heat from his body reached mine as we stood just inches apart. Being this close to him was messing with my focus.

"Neither do you."

I made a face at him, but his grip on mine only tightened, and the intensity in his eyes didn't diminish.

"Tell me," he breathed in my ear. My knees nearly gave out. "What would you do now if your mother had never gotten cancer and was perfectly healthy?"

"I don't know." I really didn't. I was too mesmerized by being this close to him.

"Use your imagination."

"Well," I swallowed, "I...I suppose it sounds glorious and frightening at the same time." And it did. All the possibilities. My safety net of excuses gone.

He smiled. "That sounds a lot like a fairy tale. But come on." His voice grew deeper once more. "What keeps you from living life as it is now? Instead of living life five or eight years in the past? What are you so afraid of?"

"In truth?" I whispered. The possibilities were endless. Losing my mom. Losing my dad. Losing my dad's insurance to pay for my mom's treatments. My dad working too hard. Failing at teaching. Not making it through the master's degree.

Falling for a man I knew I shouldn't have.

"So much," I whispered again.

He closed the last few inches between us until I was pressed against his chest. And as if that weren't enough of a shock, he touched his lips to my temple. I closed my eyes as he placed a gentle kiss on my skin. I wanted to fly and melt at the same time, though I'd be happy if walking were still an option after he released me.

I'd never been kissed, but if it was anything as nice as this, I might just pass out when I got my first real kiss. The most romantic gesture I'd ever seen on the big screen had been in the movie when the beast had touched Belle's hair. But in this moment in time, Beauty and the Beast had nothing on Derrick.

"Aren't you afraid you'll never live?" he whispered. I stared at him, unable to move or even speak. He just gave me a small smile, folded up the chairs, threw the boxes away in a nearby trash can, and held out his hand before leading me back to the car.

We didn't speak the whole ride back. But just before I got out of the car, something inside me, something crazy and foolish, decided to carry this whole charade one step further.

"You asked me once if I have an outlet or something."

He cocked his head. "I did?"

I nodded. "You said I was way too put together to be normal."

"I'm still under that impression, but try me."

"When I'm mad, I write letters."

"Letters?" He made a face. "By hand?"

"Yep." I stared out at the stars. "I even have a special pen reserved just for the occasion."

"But like…do you write them all the time?"

I tossed my hair out of my face. "Whenever I'm mad. It keeps me focused and out of trouble until I calm down."

He scoffed. "Like you would ever get into trouble."

I raised an eyebrow. "You've known me for how long now, and you doubt the poor choices made by my temper?"

His eyes twinkled. "Did you ever write me one?"

"If I did, I wouldn't tell. I don't actually send them. No, wait. That's not true. I sent one in sixth grade to the boy who had made fun of my hair. My mom nearly died of embarrassment."

"You are something else, Jessie Nickleby." He laughed and shook his head as I got out of the car.

"Hey, Derrick?"

"Yeah?"

I paused and laid my hands on the edge of the window, which was rolled all the way down. "Thanks. For everything tonight."

He gave me a funny smile. "I told you I wasn't all a beast."

"I'm glad."

He paused before putting the car into drive. "Me, too." And then he was gone.

DECISIONS

JESSIE

Just as Derrick had promised when we made the deal, a car full of women showed up on my front drive the next afternoon. I waved goodbye to my dad, grabbed my purse, and went out to join them. Before I could get in, a woman with thick, brown hair and a bright red shirt stepped out of the driver's seat and grinned.

"Jessie, right? I don't know if you remember, but I'm Kim. We met briefly at the picnic."

"That's right." I smiled shyly and gestured to the car. "Where do you want me to sit?"

"We saved the passenger seat for you. Hop on in."

"Thanks." I slid in and put my purse in my lap, where I could clutch it and hopefully, release all the tension that was squeezing my body to death. I was fairly comfortable with meeting strangers, but going shopping to spend lots of someone else's money on an expensive dress and probably equally expensive shoes was a new one for me. I turned tentatively to wave at the three women in the backseat.

"Thanks so much for taking me," I said to Kim as she buckled up again. "I've been to my fair share of staff meetings and dinners at my school, but never anything as fancy as a ball."

"Oh, we're happy to have you." Kim shifted gears, and the car, which was probably older than mine, started to move. As she did, she sent a conspiratorial glance at the backseat, and the women all grinned back. "I don't know if you remember, but my husband works with Allen at their shop. And that's Maria on the left side, Liz in the middle, and Tori on the right."

"Do your husbands all work in the shop as well?" I asked.

Maria nodded. She had long, dark, wavy hair and big brown eyes. "Yes, but our husbands are currently on the dayshift. They switch around every so often."

"Except mine. He's on swing," said Tori, a thin, petite woman with blond hair cut in a bob. She looked like she could have stepped out of a department store magazine. Everything about her looked more put together than I had felt in my entire life.

Liz made a face. "Swing is the worst. When Tom had swing, nobody ever got any sleep in our house." The other women all nodded in agreement.

"So," I said, squeezing my purse handles. "What are we doing today?"

Maria answered. "Well, considering how all of us but Tori have kids, and how little we generally get out of the house without them, we're going to be thorough in our search for dresses, shoes, and accessories." She winked at me. "And possibly frozen yogurt."

The drive was a lively one. The women, who I gathered hadn't seen each other in a while, seemed to have plenty of news to catch up on with each other. I listened in eagerly as I tried to make sense of what life in the military really did entail because I couldn't help wondering how close it could really be to my own.

Maria's husband, I learned, had been in the Air Force longer than any of the other spouses. According to Kim, he would be ready to retire in about six years, though she swore the Air Force might have to chase them out if they really want to get rid of him.

"Not my Todd." Maria shook her head. "He's determined that this stint will be his last one." She shrugged. "Though he said that about the last one, as well."

"What's a stint?" I asked.

"It's the number of years the service members sign the contract for to serve with the military," said Liz. "In the Air Force, at least in our husbands' fields, the usual contracts right now are being given out for 3 to 5 years."

"But it can be longer or shorter," Maria chimed in. "It just depends on what he agrees to and what the military needs."

"Right," Liz said, "and at the end of one stint, the service member and the military have to decide whether or not that person should keep serving or separate."

"It used to be," Tori said with a sniff, "that when you re-signed, a lot of guys would get a bonus." For some reason, the rest of the car seemed to think this was uproariously funny.

The conversation continued along that vein until we parked in front of a large storefront that said *Special Occasion Gowns* on the front. The windows were full of manikins dressed in elegant gowns of every color and design, and I felt dual waves of dread and unspeakable joy at the thought of trying all the dresses on. Never in my life, had I dreamed I would get to go to a ball of my own. I just hoped Derrick's wallet was up to it.

As we entered the shop, I was greeted with ten times as many dresses as there were even in the storefront.

"How do you even know where to start?" I felt the color draining from my face as I imagined showing up for the ball in something that embarrassed both Derrick and myself.

Kim laughed and took my arm and dragged me over to the section that was filled with all sorts of dresses, all in blue. "Don't overthink it."

"There are three rules to follow at any military ball." Tori stuck her head out from behind a rack. "Number one, don't look like a slut. Two, don't look like a peacock. And three," she held up three fingers, "wear something you can stand to keep on for at least three hours."

Kim laughed and rolled her eyes. "Thank you, Tori, for putting that so delicately." Then she turned to me. "What Tori means to say is that you never want to be the one wearing the scantily clad dress that makes all the men and women turn their heads."

"And then go home and talk to each other about it," Maria added.

"It's also best," Kim continued, "not to have a dress that's so over-the-top that people need sunglasses when they walk up to greet you."

I laughed. "Is that really even a thing?"

All three women nodded, and sure enough, Tori held up a dress that was covered from head to toe in sequins and rhinestones.

"And finally," Kim handed me a blue dress with delicate white lace edging the bodice and shoulders, "even though we will be sitting when we eat, you'll have to do a lot of standing before and after the meal, not to mention the dancing that comes after. So you want to make sure whatever you pick isn't so uncomfortable that you go insane while you wait for the whole thing to be over."

I cast a doubtful look at the pile of dresses Kim had already handed me. Three of the six were navy blue of varying shades, one was a soft pink, and the other two were different shades of green. And they all looked very, very expensive.

"So what else should I know beforehand?" I asked, taking yet another blue dress from Kim.

And so began my Air Force protocol and etiquette education. Teaching so many Air Force kids had at least brought me an awareness of the kind of order and organization I ought to expect. But none of the things my students had told me even came near to preparing me for the number of rules I should expect at the ball. Soup, for example, was to be ladled in the direction opposite me at the table, not in. Bread should be broken off one piece at a time, each piece getting its own little bit of butter rather than buttering the entire thing at once and taking a bite out of the bread itself. When the airmen saluted, I was to stand with my hands to my sides, unless, of course, the national anthem was being sung. In that case, I should put my hand over my heart. Thankfully, I didn't need to know the ranks or titles for the gentlemen and ladies that Derrick was sure to introduce me to. Sir and ma'am would do just fine.

"At least gloves went out of style about 15 years ago," Liz said, making a face.

"Gloves?" I asked.

Tori nodded. "Oh yes. Until recently, all women at the balls were expected to wear long white gloves, the kind that go up nearly to your elbows." She sighed a little. "I actually kind of liked the gloves."

"Well, then," Maria snickered, "you can have them."

After half an hour more of searching, I began to doubt that we would ever actually buy any dresses. But eventually, the time came where the ladies decided we all had enough dresses to try on, so we proceeded to the fitting rooms.

It was there that I realized why we had come in such a group. Just like the dresses at high school prom, these were nearly impossible to get into and out of without help. We all took turns zipping and snapping each other up and tying ribbons wherever they needed to be tied. And though the thought of what such dresses might cost still made me nervous, I began to feel the rush of the thrill when I stepped out onto the podium surrounded by mirrors and saw the first dress Kim had chosen for me.

It was navy blue, which had disappointed me at first, as at least half the dresses we had brought back with us seem to be that color. But the bodice was cut in a gently sloping V so it covered my chest in all the right places but left the collarbone and shoulders exposed with beaded spaghetti straps holding it in place. A thick band of silky material was wrapped around the waist with little white pearls sewn into clusters of stars, and the skirt was nothing short of a perfect swath of floor-length perfection that swished and swayed gracefully whenever I moved.

"What do you think?"

I turned to see Kim, Maria, and Tori watching me as Liz ran up to adjust the bottom of the skirt. I turned back to the mirror to revel in the fairy tale that had just become mine.

"It's perfect," I breathed. Maybe I wasn't about to embark upon a quest to an old, haunted castle or to search for my missing aged father, but I, Jessie Nickleby, was going to a ball.

Tori picked up the next dress in my stack and held it up. "This purple one is nice, too. Why don't you try it on next?"

I shook my head, unable to take my eyes from the elegant gathering of my skirt. "I want this one."

Kim gave a satisfied smile. "All right, then this one it is."

Only two of the other women found their ideal dresses. Tori, who I was beginning to think never had to ponder money or maybe she just chose not to, and Liz, who was quite satisfied with her clearance rack find. Maria decided to ask a neighbor if they could trade again this year with some of their old dresses, and Kim said she already had hers picked.

When I got up to the register, I had a minor heart attack when the dress was rung up.

"A hundred and thirty bucks?" I gasped, turning to Kim in a panic. "Derrick is paying for this. I can't ask that from him."

"You just need to relax." Kim took the dress from my hands and put it back on the counter and nodded at the employee. "I've already spoken to Derrick, and he knows full well what he's paying for." She checked her phone. "Shoes are next and then accessories."

"Is there anywhere a little less expensive that we could go to look for them?" I whispered, glancing at the man who was ringing up the dress. I had peeked at the shoes earlier, and though their price tag wasn't hidden like the one inside the dress, they were nearly just as expensive. I hadn't even bothered looking at the jewelry or handbags.

Kim winked at me. "I know just the place."

~

I left the store with my purchase feeling gleeful and more than a little fazed at the number on the receipt. Kim announced that the other women had to go home, as our dress shopping had taken longer than we had expected, but she and I were going to continue the date alone. We dropped off the other women at Maria's house and made our way back toward town.

"So," Kim said, "what did you think of them?" She smiled a little. "Tori's mouth didn't turn you off?"

I laughed. Tori, it turned out, had the mouth of a sailor. I heard more curses in the changing room than I had heard in a long time. "You forget," I said, "I teach for a living. We may have to watch our tongues around the short people, but as soon as the students are gone, teachers can have mouths that rival any practiced swear master." Maybe not quite as much as Tori, but almost.

"Just wait until you hear Tori and her husband together. You may need bandages for your ears."

"Truly, though." I looked earnestly at Kim. "I really do like them. They're frank. They don't mince words, but you know they mean what they're saying."

"Military life doesn't have time for pretenders." She sighed. "Unfortunately, our brusque nature often gets the better of us, and often we forget to speak what we think *kindly*. But like you, I'd rather someone say what they mean to my face than scurry around behind my back."

"I wonder why the military attracts that kind of personality," I mused, picking at the edge of my bag. "It's interesting they would all seem to congregate there."

"The military doesn't have time for foolishness. You have to get to the point or people die in war." She shrugged. "That mindset seems to carry over to families as well. Not that I mind."

I shifted in my seat. "I do have a question though."

"Sure thing, but give me just a second. You got your ID?"

I realized that instead of heading into Jacksonville, we were turning an exit sooner.

"We're going to base?" I asked.

"They have the best thrift store around. Since you're not keen on spending all of Derrick's money on shoes, which I must congratulate you for, we're going to go see what accessories we can scrounge up at the thrift shop. Then we'll finish with shoes at the mall and get something to eat."

We had to stop to get me another pass. This seemed like it took forever, but Kim didn't seem to mind.

"So what was your question?"

"Oh, yes. Liz said something about everyone getting a new squadron next year." I paused. "What did she mean?"

For the first time, Kim looked grim. "The men's squadron is closing next year."

"What does that mean?"

"Each branch of the military has its own name for different groups of people with different numbers in them. One of the larger groups in the Air Force is called a squadron. It has lots of smaller units where different people work. And theirs is going to be closing probably sometime next summer or spring."

I swallowed. "What does that mean for them?"

"It means that they'll all be transferred to other squadrons."

"Does that mean they'll stay here?"

"Some of them will." Kim tilted her head thoughtfully. When she spoke again, her words were slow. "And some of them will be transferred to other bases."

My stupid heart was racing faster than I was giving it permission to. It needed to stop that. "But why?"

Kim just shrugged. "Missions change. What was needed ten or fifteen or even fifty years ago might not be what we need now. It's better to dissolve the group in question and send the members places where they can better serve what the military needs."

"Do you think you'll go somewhere else? Or do you think you'll stay here?"

Kim gave me a look that told me she knew the question I wasn't asking.

"No one knows yet. Over the next six months, they'll start to slowly parse out the airmen one at a time to this other squadron or to that other squadron, to this base or to another base. Only God knows where any of us will end up."

Although the air conditioning in her car was on full blast to combat the summer heat, I felt as though all the oxygen had been sucked out of the cabin, and I was suddenly sweltering. Gone. In less than a year, Derrick could be gone. And even if they kept him this time, I had no guarantee that he would stay for any other set length of time. The Air Force owned him before anyone else did, and it didn't matter how much I cared or didn't care for him, he could still be gone at the drop of a hat. And if I did what he had hinted at, leaving my family and my job and my plans and my future for the sake of marriage, I would be gone, too.

"How do you do it?" I asked, sounding like I had just choked on a grape. "Start over and over again with new schools and new jobs and new friends and new lives on someone else's whim?"

Kim put the car in park and we hurried inside the mall away from the heat. "Let's get something cold before we shop accessories," she said, waving me toward the food court. We got iced coffee and found a table to rest at as we recovered from the heat. Once we were all settled, she took a long sip of her drink and gave a little laugh as she put it down on the table.

"I've got three kids, and uprooting them is never easy." She leaned forward a little. "And people can tell you all they want that it gets easier to say goodbye with time, but in my experience, it only gets harder."

"Then why do you do it?" I whispered. "The goodbyes to all the people you love and…and to the men when they deploy?"

"First of all," she said, "we don't have it nearly as bad as the Marines and their families. You want to talk separation? Try an eighteen-month deployment."

I shuddered. That didn't even seem humane.

"I mean, of course you've always got outliers. I knew an airman once who was deployed twenty-four months. But those guys are few and far between." She stirred her drink with her straw. "But more importantly, I fell in love with my husband in high school. And when he decided to join, I had to make a choice. Did I stay with what was safe and what I knew? Or did I leave to face the world with him?"

"How did you choose?" I asked, staring into the depths of my sad, empty cup.

"I decided I didn't want to wonder *what if* for the rest of my life. So I chose adventure."

"And you've never regretted it?"

She leaned back and gave a rueful laugh. "Don't get me wrong. It's hard. Leaving, church shopping, new friends, old friends, insurance, job instability for me, changing addresses and voting registration and driver licenses. Continually finding new sports teams for the kids. It's tough on everyone. And it hurts every time." She studied me. "What's wrong?"

I frowned. "I don't mean to sound rude at all. Because I completely respect your choice. I just...I can't understand why anyone would willingly sign up for that."

"Someone has to."

I looked at her.

"Do we leave our boys alone because they want to serve? They're doing the mission no one else will. And if we don't stand by their sides, we're leaving a gaping hole in their mission by tearing gaping holes in their hearts. Because they have enough to worry about without worrying whether or not we're going to be faithful while they're gone."

She stood up and chucked her empty cup in a trash bin. "Come on. Let's go find us some accessories." I followed her, but before we left the food court, she stopped and turned to me.

"Before you start thinking we're always miserable and lonely, though, you should know that military families never say goodbye."

"You don't?"

She smiled. "We say 'see you later'. Because we know that the love stays strong even after we begin a new adventure."

"But..." I said slowly. "What about your family? All those years you miss that you can't make up." No amount of optimism posters could make up for that, and I knew it.

"That's true. But if we hide forever because we're afraid, we can also miss out on a life of adventure with the love of our lives." She took my hands and sighed. "This kind of decision is one only you can make. Just...don't lead him on. He'll never move forward with his life if he thinks he'll be a part of yours. And Derrick is too good a man to treat that way."

I nodded, but my thoughts were only spinning faster. Before I could get lost in them completely, though, she broke into a grin. "Now, come up. I saw a pair of earrings last week that I think would look magical with your dress." And she dragged me off before I could think to ask anything else.

33

DARE

DERRICK

A ugust seventh was a day I'd dreaded for the first half of the summer and longed for during the second half. But it was finally here, and the day of the ball arrived. I checked my cuffs again before getting out of the truck and walking up to her door. For the first time, I didn't have Jade in the backseat. It was just me picking up Jessie for possibly what might be the most romantic night of our lives.

Or the biggest mistake anyone in the history of love had ever made.

It was funny, I'd always obsessed properly over my uniform, just the way they'd taught us to in basic training. I'd used a ruler to measure the folds, checked the order of my ribbons five times, and polished my shoes until I could see my reflection in them. I'd worn the uniform plenty of times for formal occasions like this, and it was always to impress whatever NCO or officer might be doing an inspection while he was out. But never had I cared so much about what someone thought I looked like in it as I did now.

I rang the doorbell and took a calming breath as I waited for an answer. No more than five seconds later, it was opened by Mrs. Allen. She put her hands over her mouth and did a few little jumps and a squeal before shooing me in and running down the hallway.

"Derrick." Jessie's dad was sitting in the living room with a beer and the paper. But when I walked in, he stood to shake my hand. "You look good."

"Thank you, sir." I held my hat and had to remind myself not to squeeze wrinkles into it. "How..." I lowered my voice. "How's she doing tonight?"

"I've never seen her such a nervous wreck." He smiled as though this pleased him. "Which is good. It means she likes you."

"Hopefully, that's enough." I put my cover in my pocket before I squeezed it into one of those folded snowflakes.

"You know you have my full support with whatever you're going to ask her tonight, provided I don't need to bring a shotgun to the party." His eyes twinkled. "But take it easy on her. She wants to believe it's possible, but she's a bit like a rabbit."

Before I could ask him for any tips, we heard the sound of clicking in the hall. And what I saw left me breathless.

She looked like a Victorian princess, in that long, flowing blue dress and her hair up in pretty ringlets, a few falling delicately on her face. Her hair looked as though sapphires were scattered in it, though, knowing Jessie's monetary sensibilities, they were probably just really good fakes. A similarly elegant bracelet dotted with blue stones hung from her wrist with a matching necklace across her chest, and her face practically glowed with her rosy cheeks and brilliant, emerald eyes.

The dress itself was far less revealing than the one Amy had worn to the ball last year. But it showed off her petite form just as nicely, maybe even better. The angles of the dress pointed the eyes down and then back up again to her lovely face.

"Jessie." My stupid voice cracked like a teenager's, and Mrs. Nickleby turned away to hide a grin, rather poorly, I might add. "You look magnificent." It was a dumb thing to say, but it was the only actual word that coherently formed in my mind when I needed it.

It must not have been too awful, though, because she gave me a shy smile. "Thank you."

We stood that way for a moment until I realized how awkward I was making it by waiting. So I turned back to Mr. Nickleby "Oh, um, I'm not sure what time they'll release us. I'm guessing around eleven-thirty."

"Wait!" Jessie's mother ran to the kitchen and returned, stopping so fast she nearly crashed into her husband. "I need a picture!"

"Mom," Jessie said, but her mother ignored her and waited until we were smiling and close enough for her satisfaction. And though I followed Jessie's example and released her immediately following the picture, I prayed such photographs would eventually become so commonplace that she wouldn't even spare a second thought if I touched her on the arm or back or waist. But for now, I only shook her father's hand again and thanked her mother for letting me borrow her before opening the door and following her to the truck.

She waited as I opened the truck door and helped her up, and her mother, who had followed us out, handed up her purse. As soon as the door was closed, I went around to my side, but my mind was still stuck on the way my skin felt, burning pleasantly from the places she had touched it. Which was ridiculous, since we'd touched each other a million times while passing off a sleeping Jade or trading the backpack or bumping into each other in the entryway at my house. But tonight was different. Every touch, every glance was electric. Even being in the same car together felt strange. And I prayed that was a good thing.

"I don't know what the ladies told you," I said as we pulled out. "But tonight's going to have lots of ceremony. It might seem a little outdated...or a lot outdated at first. But there's significance in everything. And when you're done, it's all kind of cool."

"They told me." She smiled. "Kim let me borrow her copy of the handbook for Air Force wives."

I let out a laugh. "And you actually read it?" Talk about the driest read of all time.

"Actually, it was really interesting. I'm looking forward to seeing the Missing Man table." She paused, and her cheeks brightened slightly. "I mean, I don't want it to have to be there, but the ceremony itself seemed really—"

"I get it." I nodded. "The gravity of it all is really...it means something."

"Exactly. A lot of that stuff doesn't happen in public anymore, and I'm looking forward to being a part of it."

My heart leaped a little as we got on the highway, and I had to remind myself to stay at a sane speed. The evening still had a long way to go. But its beginning was already more promising than I'd dared to hope. Maybe Jessie wasn't so out of reach after all.

34

THE MISSING MAN

JESSIE

This was ridiculous. Derrick was the same guy I drove in this same truck with day in and day out as we squabbled over what was best for Jade and where to eat lunch. He was the guy who had tossed his flipflop at me when I refused to go swimming because of the approaching thunderstorm. He was the same one I'd wanted to strangle for the first month of the summer.

But good grief, he was hot. His stiff, fitted jacket accentuated the contrast between his trim waist and his broad shoulders. When I'd come down the hall to greet him, I'd had to work unbelievably hard not to stop right at the mouth of the hallway and gawk like a fangirl. His shiny black shoes clicked when he walked, and though he always carried himself well, he stood erect and alert now as though he commanded the scene. All signs of the boy were gone, and he looked every inch a man, the kind that might grin at you and wink from a World War II postcard. And when he put that hat on to walk me out to the car, it about did me in.

How had I missed how freaking attractive this man was? Only as I continued to shoot him sideways glances did I remember how handsome I'd thought he was on our first meeting.

"What's so funny?" he asked.

"Oh," I smiled at my lap and shook my head. "I was just thinking about the first time we met."

"I'm a little afraid to know. I was in full jerk mode that day."

I chuckled. "Actually, I thought you were pretty cute." I met his eyes. "Until you opened your mouth."

He threw his head back and laughed, and suddenly, the truck cab seemed to have enough air in it to breathe again.

"What are those little rectangular decorations?" I asked.

"Which ones?"

"On your chest." On the chest I had the stupid, sudden desire to touch again, like when I'd leaned against him on the bridge.

He kept his eyes on the road. "Those are my ribbons. If you're part of a group that does something good or is in a certain conflict or you do something your superiors take notice of, you get a ribbon."

"Oh. That's neat." Yep. This man could be on the front of a historical romance cover, and I'd probably buy every copy on the shelf.

The parking lot was crowded when we got to a building Derrick called "the club". And though it was probably ridiculous, I felt absolutely giddy as he came around to help me down from the truck in my heels. The costume jewelry Kim had convinced me to buy made me feel like a princess as it sparkled in the light of the sunset, and the swish of the long gown against my legs made me stand taller beside him. And as he took my arm on his, which was the appropriate way in the military, apparently, to hold hands in uniform, I felt more confident and more terrified than I ever had in my life. It was hard not to feel proud on his arm, and yet, we were essentially walking into a lion's den, at least, based on all my reading. So many people to see and judge whether or not what I did was proper.

When we entered the building, however, beneath the large concrete overhang that looked like a spaceship docking, I immediately relaxed. There were scores of people already inside. And instead of generals and colonels waiting to inspect us, as I'd feared there would be, men and women in uniform and their significant others lazily wandered the bar area as they snacked on hors d'oeuvres and sipped wine and fancy drinks.

A photographer stood in front of a backdrop and snapped pictures of couples. Two men and one woman smiled in greeting as we made our way inside.

"Allen." A tall man in uniform with dark graying hair and about four times as many ribbons as Derrick had, shook Derrick's hand. He looked vaguely familiar, but I couldn't place him. The silver nameplate on his chest said Coleman. "It's good to see you. And who is this lovely lady?"

"Thank you, sir. This is Jessie Nickleby."

"Nickleby." He squinted at me. "That name sounds familiar."

"I...I teach at Hogs Elementary out of the Harris Road exit," I said.

His eyes lit up. "That's where I've seen you before. My daughter is going into fourth grade there. She had Mr. Isaacs last year."

I grinned, but this time, it wasn't hard. "Mr. Isaacs is fantastic."

"He is. What grade do you teach?"

After a little more chit chat, we bid the man farewell, and I leaned over. "Who was that?"

"The base commander, Colonel Coleman."

"Oh." Butterflies erupted in my stomach again. "Did I do all right?"

His arm squeezed mine a little tighter. "You knocked it out of the park."

I wished I could bottle up the way he was looking at me right now, blue eyes full of wonder and awe, though I had no clue what for. They softened as they moved to my lips.

"Thanks again for coming," he murmured.

"Thanks for bringing me." I looked down. "And for all this, of course."

"Jessie, if you'd wanted to wear the moon, all you had to do was ask."

I was saved from having to reply to such a heartstopping answer when it was announced that the ball would be starting soon in another room. We made our way with the crowd to the back of the building through two open doors to a much larger room with a wooden dance floor and a stage behind it, the kind of room that would host a wedding. Another row of who I guessed to be very important people awaited us. Derrick led me through that line as well, introducing me to everyone in turn and shaking hands. When we finished the line, I was relieved to recognize a few faces like Kim, Maria, and Liz in the crowd. We didn't have time to chat, but I was glad to see them nonetheless. By the time we found our seats, I felt as though I were walking through clouds. Clouds I couldn't remember the name or rank of, but important clouds nonetheless.

Soon the ceremony began with an address from Colonel Coleman and a prayer from the chaplain. The Missing Man Table ceremony made me glad my mascara was waterproof.

And as different speakers came and said the kind of things you might expect to hear in a movie before a battle, I began to feel wistful. This was only for tonight, I'd promised myself. I wasn't ready to make the kind of commitment I feared Derrick wanted, and this had been a business deal after all. After my talk with Kim and the others, I had been sure military life wasn't for me. At least, not yet. I wasn't ready to make that kind of choice.

But this…being a part of something bigger than myself, being a support to the ones who had sworn to serve others with their life…I wanted that. I wanted to be a part of it, too. And yet, as strongly as I felt the pull toward duty when I saw the table, there was another part of me that wanted to run as far as I could as fast as I could. Because every man that should have been at that table had been someone's son. Father. Brother. Best friend.

Someone's heart and soul had never come home.

Without speaking, Derrick silently handed me a handkerchief as the tears rolled down my face. I took it with a weak smile. Best to let him think I was just crying for the missing man. It was probably best he didn't know I was crying for the one standing beside me as well.

Eventually, dinner was served, and I got control of myself again. In fact, I even had fun. While it was rather typical catered food, marinated chicken and mushrooms drizzled with gravy with herbed potatoes and asparagus on the side, the conversation with a few of Derrick's friends was lively.

Derrick put his napkin on the table and stood. And before I could register what he was up to, he was holding his hand out.

"May I have this dance?"

My mind scrambled for something, anything to say. Here I was in the middle of one of my fairy tales, and all I could do was nod and let him lead me out to the floor. All the witty comebacks and snarky comments I usually reserved just for him flew out the door as he pulled me close and put his hand on the small of my back. The smell of his cologne enveloped me, and the way he wrapped his left hand around mine made me feel as though a wave of peace had washed over me. And I never wanted to come back up for air.

If only I could stay here in this moment, swaying back and forth with my head against his chest, lost in the rhythm, safe from the world and all it had to offer.

"Thank you."

I looked up to find him staring down at me, and I was captured by his gaze.

"For coming," he said softly, brushing the back of his hand across my cheek.

"Why?" I whispered.

"Why what?"

"Why are you so determined to keep me around?" I nodded at the rest of the dancers. "You could have invited about any girl, and she would have said yes. Why me?"

The corner of his mouth turned up as he cupped my jaw in his hand. "Because you," he whispered back, "are smart. And kind. And you strive to fill the needs around you. You face challenges head-on, and you're the strongest woman I've ever met." He bent until our foreheads were touching. "You are worth waiting for."

He reached into his pocket, but before I could see what he was pulling out, one of the women beside us lost her balance when the heel of her shoe broke off. She stumbled into him, and whatever he'd been holding bounced onto the floor. A hush settled over those around us when it stopped moving enough to see that it was a little blue velvet box. During its bouncing, the box had snapped open. And inside, winking at me in the low lights, sat the rose ring from the shop window.

I seemed incapable of doing anything but staring, open-mouthed, at the ring, but Derrick, smooth as always, leaned over and swiped up the box. Then, ignoring the onlookers and the excited whispers, he took my hand and led me outside.

The air was surprisingly chilly for a late summer night, but for once, I welcomed it. The evening…it had been so magical. But with the cool air came the stark reminder of what my ever-sensical mind had been trying to warn me of since the table ceremony. And before I could get control of myself like any sane person, I burst into tears.

"Jessie!" Derrick was at my side, wiping the tears from my face, his eyes wide. "Before you say anything, just know that I didn't mean—"

"No," I sobbed. "Derrick, that's the problem."

He stared at me.

"It's perfect," I whispered tearfully, waving my hand back at the building. "All of it. It's all perfect, like a dream, and that's the problem."

He frowned down at the little box in his hand. "I don't understand."

"I mean, this is everything I ever could have dreamed of. Here and now. But Derrick, this isn't real life."

"I still don't follow."

"What I mean is that tonight…it's beautiful. And romantic. And perfect. And you…gosh, you look like you belong on some vintage poster."

"And that's…bad?"

"No! You're not letting me finish! What I mean is what next? This… tonight. It's all just a lie to dress up the truth about this kind of life."

He gave a harsh laugh. "And what exactly are we lying about?"

"This life! You're always leaving and changing work schedules, and the government owns you before your own family does. And people… people die."

"I still don't see the lie. This is the military. Yeah, the life is hard. No one ever said it wasn't. That was kind of the point of the empty table."

"But it tries to paint a picture. All these beautiful people and smiling faces. But no one mentions the constant moving and uprooting the kids and giving birth away from your family and maybe your spouse, and when your husband deploys even though you're already stationed in Europe, and then you die. And I'm left with the kids alone across the ocean from my family." I sobbed even harder, but the words wouldn't quit spilling out. "The military can try to paint and polish life up all it wants, but none of that's in the manual."

"Jessie…" He huffed then groaned. "My job isn't technically that dangerous. Not nearly as bad as others, at least. When I'm gone, I'll be fixing planes, not rushing into enemy—"

"But you can't guarantee that!"

"Look." He stepped closer, and the light in his eyes was no longer gentle. "This job is a part of who I am. It has to be. When you put on the uniform and swear to serve the Commander and Chief with your life, it becomes a part of you, whether you like it or not." His voice softened slightly. "But you're only looking at the hard parts. There's so much good, too! I'm going to take you all over the world to all those places you're constantly reading to Jade about. You said you wanted an adventure. Well, I can give you one. I can give you more adventures than you can count."

I tried to think of something to say, but the part of my brain that should have come up with more words felt broken. Unfortunately, he seemed to take this as encouragement to go on.

"Is this life easy? No. You have to be a strong person to live it. But that's why I want you. You're strong and smart, and you make life beautiful." He reached up and brushed a lock of hair out of my eyes. And it felt so good it hurt. "Come with me," he whispered again. "Be my partner in crime. We'll see the world and set it on fire as we go."

For one moment, I was sure I could. Because I wanted this. In fact, I wanted more than this. I wanted to wake up beside him in the morning. I did want to see the world, and I wanted him to kiss me silly every night while we did it. I wanted to carry his children and to grow old and gray together. Because there would never be anyone like Derrick Allen.

But as I thought about growing old and gray, my mind drifted back to the empty chair at the Table of the Missing Man. My parents' faces. The faces of our children when I had to tell them Daddy wouldn't be coming home.

"I'm not ready," I whispered.

"What?"

"I said...I said I'm not ready."

He ran a hand down the front of his face and took a step back. "Jessie..."

"And that's another thing. I don't understand the hurry! We only met two months ago. Why can't we just take this slow and—"

"The hurry is that I'm deploying in a week."

I fell back a step. "Derrick..."

"There was an emergency vacancy, and I'm needed to fill in."

"Why didn't you tell me?" I felt like I was grasping at the ocean, trying to hold it back with my hands.

"I only found out last week. I was hoping to get through tonight before having to break the news to you." He swallowed and looked down. "We could be an amazing team. And after last week, I thought you thought that, too."

I did. I really did.

"Why not for once in your life take a chance?" He took a step closer, then one more. The way his eyes seemed to reach my soul nearly undid me. "Please, just—"

"I'm sorry, Derrick." Tears rolled down my cheeks, but this time, I didn't bother to wipe them away. "I just can't."

MISTAKES

JESSIE

The drive home was the most miserable I'd ever endured, even worse than the time I'd purposefully broken curfew with one of my friends on a dare when I was fourteen, and my dad had come to fetch me. Derrick looked more like a military statue than ever, his jaw hard and resolute. And it broke something inside me to know that it was me he was angry with.

We didn't speak a single word until he pulled up in front of my house. Even after he put the car into park, we sat there for several minutes in complete silence. He didn't even turn the music on.

This was why I didn't go out with airmen.

"Derrick, can't we—"

"You know why you'll never be like those characters in your books, Jessie?"

I winced when he said my name like that.

"Because," he continued, his eyes cold and hard as they turned to meet mine, "you're too much of a coward to step into the unknown. Because for once in your life, you might not be in control. And one of these days, you'll come to the realization that no matter where you are and who you're with, you don't control a freaking thing."

I grabbed my handbag and threw his door open, glad when it slammed shut harder than necessary. Then without looking back, I unlocked the front door, fumbling the key several times before turning the handle and falling inside and sliding down against it.

My perfect fairy tale had turned into a horror story.

∼

"Jessie?"

My mom poked her head into my room as I ran to my desk and yanked on the handle so hard the drawer fell out. I snatched a pen from my pencil cup, knocking that over, too. But just as I began to scratch away at the first piece of stationery I could find, her cool hands gently pried the pen from my grasp and pulled my hands over to her lap. I didn't even bother to get up off the floor, but let my head fall into her lap and wailed like one of my six-year-old students. She stroked my hair as I drenched her bathrobe.

How had this happened? Tonight was supposed to be a fairy tale. My knight had shown up in dress blues, and he'd ridden away with me on his fiery red horse. Then he'd done the most idiotic thing on the face of the planet. Then he'd stabbed me in a way not even my best friend knew how to do.

"What happened?" she asked when I'd finally quieted enough to hear myself think again.

"He asked me to marry him," I whispered.

She blinked at me. "And that's a bad thing?"

"Right before telling me he's deploying." I swiped at the tears that seemed determined to stick to my face.

"Well." My mother sighed. "This sounds like a long story. And pajamas make everything better."

There was sense to this suggestion, and my feet were killing me in the heels, so I changed while my mother went out to the kitchen to make me some chai tea. Ten minutes later, we were on the bed again, her sitting on the foot with me curled up at the top, clutching my tea mug like a lifeline. And I told her everything. Well, except his parting words. They hurt too much to repeat.

"Jess." My mom fingered the rim of her cup. "I know this was prob-ably...sudden for you."

"Probably?"

She chuckled. "What I'm getting at, though, is that you seemed happy with him. I've never seen you so excited to go out and try new things. No one's ever been able to pull you away from your studies long enough to get you to stop and smell the clover."

I stared into the depths of my mug. Not her, too.

"And I just can't help wondering…why are you so determined to stay here? To stay alone?"

"Do you want me to leave?"

"Don't even go there, Jessie. You know we don't. But don't tell me you're staying here just for your degree. You can get one of those anywhere. You used to talk about seeing the world or even just other parts of our own country. You've never been to Nashville, and we live five hours away." She reached out and tugged gently on my pajama leg. "What happened to that girl who wanted to see and do it all?"

"That was before my mom got cancer," I whispered into my tea.

"Jessie Nickleby!"

I looked up, surprised by the sudden anger in her voice.

"Now you listen to me because I'm only going to say this once. Don't you dare waste your life because you're afraid I'll lose mine."

"But—"

"I did not give birth to you so you could sit around and spend your life worrying about me. You have a good man who makes you happy and loves the Lord and genuinely cares for you. I've seen it in his eyes, all those weeks at church. When you're around, he can barely take his eyes off you."

"Bet he's not doing that now," I muttered.

"And why not?"

I took a deep breath and told her the last thing he'd told me.

"Stupid boy." My mother closed her eyes and inhaled deeply through her nose. "I don't know if I've ever met two people more suited to each other and so inept at showing it." She rubbed her face and huffed as I swallowed and tried not to show how much that smarted.

"Look," she said, taking my hand. "I know he moved fast. Even for… normal people, two months is fast. But people say stupid things when they're hurting. Why don't you talk to him? Ask him to slow things down. Use this deployment to get to know each other—"

"No."

"Excuse me?"

I shook my head. "I'm not going to go begging." I stood and went to my desk to begin picking up my mess. As I did, the table of the missing man flashed across my mind. I would not be an orphan and the woman whose man went missing as well. "There's a reason I don't date airmen."

"Are your plans really so important that you're going to put them ahead of love?"

I froze. "I nearly lost you," I said slowly. "And I couldn't take it if I lost him, too."

My mom looked as though she wanted to argue more, but after a long moment just shook her head and went to the door.

"I think you're making a big mistake," she said before stepping out.

Maybe. But as much as I loved Derrick now, I was saving myself from making an even bigger one. If I stopped right here and didn't fall any harder, the knife of loss couldn't be buried any deeper into my heart than it already was.

ALL I NEED

DERRICK

I stared blankly at the checklist for the millionth time that weekend. We were leaving a day earlier than had been planned, but that wasn't really a shock. It was a rare thing for deployments to go exactly as planned. It had been six days since the disastrous proposal, and I was more than ready to be gone.

She'd been like a dream. Or rather, like a fairy tale princess. And for one shining moment, I'd been her Prince Charming. But the moment that stupid ring had fallen from my pocket, the look on her face had told me all I needed to know.

Still, I pleaded my case. Begged her. Prayed as I groveled that she would say yes. But fear had won out. And if her mind hadn't been made up by the time I dropped her off, the cruel words I'd left her with would have done the trick.

It was my own fault, really. I knew better than to assume she would say yes. Good gosh, I'd barely gotten her to go out on one date, and even that was under the guise of a day out with Jade, based on a bet. What had possessed me to think she would be ready for me to waltz in and steal her away?

I rubbed my face and looked back down at the half-packed bag open on the bed in front of me. I knew exactly what had possessed me to think that. It had been the way her eyes had lit up while we'd danced in front of Teacher-What's-His-Face back at the bistro. And the way she'd nearly burst into tears when we pulled into the event arena parking lot. Or the way her breath had hitched up on the bridge when I kissed her temple.

The way she leaned into me during our dance at the ball, when for one beautiful second, everything had been right.

My reverie was broken by the sound of a tap-tap-tapping on glass. I went to the window and looked out, but nothing was there. Not that I could have seen it well anyway. It was eleven p.m., and the wind was blowing branches against my window. I went back to packing.

Well, what had she expected anyway? She knew I was the kind of guy to play for keeps. Everything had been right. It really had. She loved Jade nearly as much as I did, and I knew there wouldn't have been any surprises one day if Jade needed to come live with us. She would have been a great mother. And from our chats, I knew she wanted at least three, whereas Amy hadn't been sure she wanted more than even one. Everything had been perfect, but she was just too scared to see it. Refused to see it.

Anger heated my limbs as I opened the fridge door just to slam it shut again. It didn't make sense. I'd been with Amy a lot longer, and our breakup hadn't affected me like this. I hadn't felt increasing volumes of anger, frustration, and if I was honest, searing, hot pain, cycling through me on repeat. Really, we known each other for less than two months. I should probably be thanking her for saving me from a life-time of regret for marrying someone I barely even knew.

The tapping started again. This time, I threw open the sliding glass door and scowled down at my little sister. "Jade! You are absolutely never to be out here alone. You know that." I glanced at the pool, sending up a thousand prayers that she hadn't decided to take herself swimming. There was a gate around the pool, of course, but that didn't really make me feel a whole lot better. "It is two o'clock on a Thursday morning. What on earth are you doing up?

She just shrugged and walked past me into the casita.

"Nickleby gone," she said, climbing onto my bed and turning on the TV. "I'm bored." Apparently, she didn't care what time of night it was.

I stared at her for a moment before shaking my head and following her. I grabbed her up and plopped her in my lap as the melodious sounds of a talking sponge filled my little apartment.

She pointed at my uniform, which I'd hung on a bookshelf the night of the ball, barely coherent enough not to rumple it. "Nickleby's dress pretty?"

I worked to keep my voice even. Of course Jade would be interested. She loved rocks and sugar, but her third love in this world was princesses. And I wouldn't gain anything by refusing to tell her about Jessie's dress. I wasn't that immature.

"It was blue, kid." And fit her like graceful waves unfurling on the shore.

"You eat cupcakes?" She turned to study me with such a quizzical eye that I couldn't help laughing.

"Nah, no cupcakes." I ruffled her hair. "But there was cake. And it looked pretty good." Not that I'd gotten to eat any.

Still, she turned back to the TV, seeming satisfied for the moment. And as she snuggled in closer, I hugged her to my chest and closed my eyes. Soon she began to drift off, her eyes drooping and no longer attached to the TV screen. A few more minutes, and she was snoring. I should put her to bed. I needed to go to bed. We were deploying in less than twenty-four hours, and I'd had trouble sleeping since the ball, and not for a lack of trying. But I was sure going to miss this. I could afford five more minutes of holding her close.

A peace came over me as I listened to her steady breathing. Not a happy peace, per se, but one of resolution. Jessie could do as she pleased. If she didn't want to be my wife, I could live with that. Because for now, one woman in my life was more than enough. And I was going to do my darnedest to take care of her.

THAT, TOO

JESSIE

I put my pen down and closed my eyes, breathing deeply of the scent of work. Glue. Paint. Paper. Crayons. This was where I was meant to be. Not sitting at home, worrying about the fate of my fiancé, who would have been arriving at his place of deployment any day. Because he wasn't my fiancé, and I wasn't waiting for him to come home.

I opened my eyes and looked around my classroom. After a final week with Jade, which, thankfully, had been free of Derrick, I was back at school. This had relieved me more than I could say. According to his mother, who seemed to have no idea of what had transpired between us, he had actually insisted on sleeping properly for once and preparing for deployment. Every morning, I'd held my breath as I turned the corner onto their street, praying he wouldn't be home, and every evening, praying he wouldn't emerge from his casita until I was gone.

The days had seemed oddly empty without him. But I'd taken several deep breaths and told Jade it was for the best anyway. She was going back to her usual therapy schedule for the school year, and I used the extra time to work with her to prepare her for our first week back as well as her choir tryout. All the extra time we'd previously spent dragging Jade around, I used to prepare for my own return to the classroom.

Going. If I just kept going, I was able to keep the pain emanating from the hole in my heart from growing too sharp. And between the staff meetings, lesson planning, classroom prepping, and last-minute supply shopping, there was more than enough to keep me busy. I also had the paperwork for my master's degree to finish. But for some reason, even though it was staring at me from my desktop, I couldn't get myself to get past typing my name at the top. It was like lifting my fingers to press the keys was more than my mind could sort out. Like it just couldn't handle adding one more thing.

I'd been around Derrick far too long. He was rubbing off on me.

"Jessie?"

I turned in my swivel chair to see Sam standing in the doorway. I smiled. "What's up?"

He rubbed his neck and looked up at the ceiling, his light blue button-up shirt and slacks looking freshly pressed and clean as always. Nothing like the sweaty, frizzy mess I felt like. "Look," he said with a slight grimace, "I've been thinking about what that guy said."

"That guy?"

"The airman. Jade's older brother?"

"Oh. Okay. And what did he say?"

"He mentioned something about making a move. And I realized that while he was breaking your rules, so was I."

I stared. "What do you mean?" It was easier to play stupid than to try to figure out what the men were up to in their games anymore.

"I never made a move. I mean, I tried to. I tried to find excuses to spend more time with you, but he was right. I never actually asked you out or told you how I feel."

I sighed. "Sam—"

"Just hear me out. I know you're not over him yet…"

Was my personal life on display for everyone these days?

"…not wanting to go too fast for you. I just…so I was hoping we could go out and get drinks. Just you and me."

I studied him as he bit his lip, studying me back. Did I want to go out with Sam Newman? No, not really. What I really wanted was a handsome airman who took me to balls and brought me out to sightsee on bridges that were lit up in the night. If I was honest, I wanted Derrick. Badly.

But Derrick was gone, literally and figuratively, and after our parting words, I had little doubt we would never talk again if it was possible. And the more I thought about it, the more it made sense. I didn't have to fall head over heels for Sam Newman. Getting out, though, might feel good. A much-needed distraction from the circles that had been looping in my head. Who knew? Sam fit the list now. He checked every little box on my list neatly and even threw a few more into the loop I hadn't required. Not only did he respect what I did and support my future plans, but he already had his master's degree, and he was working on his doctorate. He was good, and he was safe.

"Fine," I said, chuckling a little. "Just promise me two things."

His face was already too bright for my taste, but he restrained himself quickly and nodded. "Sure. What are they?"

I gave him a wry smile. "First of all, don't propose to me on said date?"

He gave me a funny look, but to his credit, he didn't laugh.

"Sure thing. Is that a new rule now? No proposing on the first date?"

"From now on it is. And second?"

He stared at me. "Yes?"

I took a deep breath. Was I ready to do this? No. I wasn't. But that was exactly why I was asking.

"I like you, Sam. And I want to try. I really do."

He beamed, and I held up a finger. "But I need some time."

His face fell slightly. "Oh. Okay, um. How much?"

"October." I smiled. "Give me time to bury myself in work and the kids and to not...to not think about this summer quite so much. And once my mind is clearer, you and I can give this a go."

The shine had left his eyes, but he nodded. "I understand." Then his smile widened slightly once more. "And don't forget to finish the paperwork for the college. The world awaits the debut of Jessie Nickleby, speech therapist of the year."

I grabbed a stapler and stack of "Welcome back" posters. "Yeah. That, too."

ANOTHER CUP

JESSIE

I played with my coffee cup, tracing the geometric patterns in the coffee sleeve as I waited at an outdoor table connected to the little coffee house Sam and I were supposed to meet at. It was cool, and the leaves were lovely shades of orange, red, yellow, and brown. A month and a half had passed, and now that the newness of school was wearing off, it was the night of my first date with Sam.

And I was optimistic. Because no matter how many clean-shaven men in uniform had passed through my classroom doors, dropping their kids off and picking them up, I wasn't thinking about airmen. And when Jade's new nanny brought her to school for the first time, I was too busy getting to know her to think about how much her big brother probably hated the situation. I wasn't thinking about how much fun it would have been to wear that sparkly rose ring and to know that every time I looked at it, it was kind of like looking at him.

No, I was thinking about how this might be a new beginning. And even if it didn't work out with Sam, it was a new start for me.

My musings were interrupted by the buzz of my phone. I found a text from Mrs. Allen, and my heart sank like a rock.

Jade's nanny says Jade had her tryout for that choir today.

. . .

Shoot. Oh, shoot, shoot, shoot, shoot. I laid my head on the table in shame. Jade's big tryout. I'd talked to the mother in charge of the tryouts and convinced her to give Jade a chance, picked Jade's song, worked with her all summer, and built her hopes up. And I hadn't even remembered to be there.

I slowly lifted my head again and glared at my coffee as someone stopped beside me and turned around.

"Jessie?"

"Kim!" I stood and reached out for a hug, hoping desperately that Derrick's friend didn't hate me now. "How are you doing?"

She pointed back at the parking lot. "Doing well, thanks. Dropping off one kiddo to soccer while the other one finishes piano, and I figured I'd rather wait here than the car." She nodded at the empty seat across from me. "Waiting for someone?"

"Yes. I mean, no. I mean, I'm early, so I figured I'd do the same thing as you."

"Mind if I sit?"

"Go right ahead." I hoped my apprehension wasn't visible. If there was anything I didn't want to talk about it was our mutual acquaintance and the only reason we knew each other in the first place.

She excused herself to order coffee. When she had it, she returned and sat her purse on the ground. Then she studied me.

"I know it's probably the last thing you want to talk about."

I inwardly cringed.

"But I have to know. What happened?"

I stared morosely at the little hole in the lid of my cup.

"I mean," she went on, "Derrick didn't say much. Just told the guys at work that it didn't work out. But after talking to both of you, I know it had to be more than that."

"The simple answer?" I gave her a sad smile. "Too many variables."

"How so?"

"It's like we were talking about." I went back to tracing patterns on the coffee sleeve. "My parents' health. Derrick's safety." I paused. "And after what happened with him and Amy, even if I had said yes, I'm not sure he'd even want me after he got back. He could easily find someone else while he was gone." Oh, yes. My mind had been busy churning up excuses since my talk with my mother. And I had a million, each with its own boatload of sense.

That was, until I said it out loud just now.

"I just...I need more stability than that." I shook my head. "And I don't think I could stand it," my voice caught on the last word, "if something happened. I just don't see how love is possible with all the things—"

"Now, hold on there." She leaned forward, her dark eyes sharp. "I've been married to an airman for fifteen years now, and if there's one thing I can tell you, it's that love is only ever possible because you decide it's possible."

I stared back, gripping my cup with both hands.

"We have wills for a reason," she continued, leaning back, her eyes no less brilliant. "And if I'm not mistaken, you have a pretty strong one. If we love someone, we can't just rely on the ebb and flow of attraction and romance to carry our love along. We've got to decide whether we're going to love them or not. Through thick and thin, we stand by their side. And sometimes, it's not because we want to be there. It's because we made the decision, and we're going to honor our word and stick to it."

I shook my head. "But what if we choose wrong?"

"Well, that's a chance you'll take no matter who you choose. But when you do decide to love someone, you have to be the one to choose it. And stick to it." She shrugged and took a sip of her coffee. "Now, I'll be the first to admit that loving a military man is hard. In fact, it's really hard, especially when he's exhausted from prepping to leave, and you and the kids are emotionally drained, and you're both on your last straw." She chuckled. "Believe me. It's hard." Then she looked at me. "But that's where the real stuff begins. Jessie, if you want something worth waiting for, you have to get creative. You have to be willing to give God back the man He gave you. But again, it's not really all that different from any other Joe Blow next door. Just as deployed husbands can get shot or hit with some sort of explosive device..."

I flinched.

"...the guy next door could step off a curb and get hit by a car. Or get some sort of cancer or disease."

Did she have to hit home so hard?

"And you won't be able to do a thing about any of it." She took another sip of her coffee. "You like to be in control of things, don't you?"

I laughed ruefully. "Unfortunately, I do."

"See? We're never really in charge of anything when you think about it. An asteroid could hit us now where we sit. The military doesn't change that. It just makes the truth painfully obvious."

I held my hand up. "But what about here? I've got so many responsibilities. It feels wrong to just...abandon them all."

The corner of her mouth twitched. "And isn't it possible God has other responsibilities planned for you somewhere else, too?" She glanced at her watch. "I've got to go. My daughter's lesson will be over soon." She laid her hand on my arm. "And I promise, I'm not trying to make this decision for you. I just...I think you deserve to know the truth before you throw away this opportunity forever."

And there I sat, even more confused than before. The only thing that could wake me from my trance was the buzz of my phone, Mrs. Allen's name flashing across the screen. Sighing, I braced myself for the worst, which I fully deserved, as I opened the text. But where I had expected a tongue lashing of sorts, I couldn't have been more surprised.

She'll tell you Monday when she gets to school, but I was so excited I had to tell you now. The choir director loved her. She even agreed to let Jade memorize the songs instead of reading them. She said if she passed someone up who was as good at memorizing as Jade with such a sweet smile, she'd better quit her job now.

This text was followed quickly by another.

I can't thank you enough, Jessie. You've done more for my family than I can say. This is just another way to build Jade's confidence, and if it hadn't been for you and your hard work, I never even would have considered it. So...thank you.

I stared at the text, trying to decide how to respond. But the longer I thought about it, the more it hit me. Sure, I'd worked with Jade. But I'd gotten busy with school. Honestly, it had been almost two weeks since

Jade and I had practiced. Sure, maybe I'd talked to the top parent about giving Jade an alternative way to join. That was my job, though, to find ways for my students to participate in the world using their personal strengths. Whatever Jade had done to get on that choir had been her doing. Not mine.

"Jessie?"

I stood and forced myself to smile at the sound of Sam's voice. He was all grins as he came and sat down across from me.

As always, he was smartly dressed, a perfect blend of muted style and practicality. His hair was slightly rumpled, and his glasses were oddly endearing, and as he swam regularly, his form wasn't anything to sneeze at. In fact, if I looked around now, I'd probably find a few women glancing his way a second time.

"Hey, I was thinking Tex Mex, but this'll work, too." He grinned. "Can I get you a coffee?"

I forced a smile and held up my empty cup. "No, thanks. I've already had one."

Sam got himself a drink and then came to join me.

"I have to say," he blushed slightly, "I've been pretty excited about tonight. I should have done this a long time ago."

"I'm excited, too." I tried to take a swig of coffee, only to remember that I was out. Dang it. I should have gotten another one. "I'm in the need of a little fun."

"Yeah, you've buried yourself in projects since the start of school. I'm not surprised you need a break. Especially with all that studying and degree paperwork, too."

"Mm. Yeah, that was kind of intentional." I wished greatly I had the courage to tell the truth. Yes, I'd been buried in projects. Because projects meant keeping my mind on my own world and away from the one across the sea.

He looked away. "That makes sense." A long moment passed before he spoke again, and I couldn't help thinking that he was hearing the double-meaning behind my words.

"So," he finally said, taking a long sip and leaning back. "How is your mom?"

Ah, a safer topic of discussion. "She's doing well, thanks. We're not out of the woods yet, but the recent tests have all been good."

"Glad to hear it." He poured a packet of sugar in his coffee. I'd never understood that. It wasn't like you could actually taste the sugar by itself. Cream was needed for true enjoyment. "What about your paper-work? Are you all set to start classes in the spring?" His eyes were bright, and he leaned forward slightly.

I twirled my empty cup in circles on the table. "Actually, I've been meaning to talk to you about that."

"Oh?"

"I…" I cleared my throat. "I don't think I'm going to pursue my master's right now."

He blinked at me. "You mean…you're quitting?"

I laughed nervously. "I don't know if you can count it as quitting if I never actually started."

"I just…I know you wanted this so much. Are you sure about this?"

I nodded slowly. "I love what I do. And…I mean, you have your master's, and you're still teaching general ed."

"Well, yeah, but I plan on transferring to something else once I have my Ph.D." He took a deep breath and blew it out slowly. "Is teaching just burning you out?"

"No, it's nothing like that. I just…" I sat up straighter. "I'm tired of living like I'm the one making the world go round. I want to teach children, and I love the ones I have, but I can't help wondering how much I might have missed while working so hard for this next degree that I'm realizing I don't even want." As I spoke, I thought back to Mrs. Allen's text. Jade had gotten into the choir on her own, but last summer, I was convinced she wouldn't be able to do any of it without me. What else might I have been wrong about?

"Okay, well…" He scratched his head. "I mean, if that's what you really want…"

I smiled. "It really is."

"Well, good for you then." He nodded. "You deserve to be happy, Jessie. Whatever you do."

"Thanks." I took a deep breath. "Hey, I'm going to go get another drink. You want one?"

He stood. "Let me get it. What do you want?"

By the time he got back with our drinks, he looked a lot less worried, and that made me feel better. As for dates, this one had had an interesting beginning. And I wasn't exactly sure how I felt about that.

"Now that you have all this free time," he said as he handed me my drink, "what do you think you'll do with it?"

I took a long sip of my caffeinated pumpkin goodness and thought for a moment. "My mom always said we're made to serve in ways that bring us joy. I think maybe I'd like to find those ways without trying so hard to plan them."

"Well, then," he said, raising his cup, "to new horizons."

I met his toast. *And finding,* I added in my head, *where those horizons are meant to be.*

LIVE

DERRICK

I smiled as my sister's face flashed on the screen. I could tell she was trying to poke the buttons on the phone by the way her brows were furrowed. Hopefully, she wouldn't hang up on me. Getting video chats connected was hard enough here. I'd only successfully gotten three through in the three months I'd been deployed, and I would need to be heading to work soon.

"Jade," I called softly, trying not to wake the sleeping guy across the room, "what are you doing with Mom's phone?"

"Bored," Jade replied, as though this should be obvious.

"Girlie, you just had a birthday. You shouldn't be bored with the millions of presents people sent you." And millions was hardly an understatement. From the pictures Mom had sent me, our extended family, particularly on my dad's side, had sent Jade a pile of gifts that nearly made the dining room table beneath it invisible.

"Everyone's gone."

"Everyone is not gone," Mom's voice came over the phone as her face appeared behind Jade's. "And you're not supposed to have this until your homework is done."

Jade rolled her eyes and handed the phone to my mom, and I couldn't help chuckling. "Did she turn seven or seventeen?"

"This attitude is partly your fault, you know." My mom gave me the evil eye. "She got used to having someone to play with twenty-four seven this summer, and now she thinks she's desolate if no one is there to entertain her at the drop of a hat."

"She's probably lonely." I shifted on my cot. "At least I could go play with the neighborhood kids when I was her age."

"She's got school, therapy, choir, and Sunday school, so she's not abandoned completely."

"You're still taking her to church?" I sat up straighter. "That's awesome." My heart leaped as I inwardly rejoiced for my family. Was it possible my parents weren't doing the easy thing for once?

Of course, with the thought of church came other thoughts, thoughts about the pixie-like creature who sang on the worship team. But no, Jade had nothing to do with that. She was going to Sunday school, and I would simply be grateful for that.

"But we're not here to talk about Jade's playdate schedule," Mom said, rousing me from my thoughts. "I want to hear about you. How is it over there?"

"It's cold, actually." I laughed softly. "You wouldn't think so with me being in the desert and all."

"Are you warm enough?"

I shrugged and looked at my surroundings. "I'm currently in a real building, so I can't complain too much." I glanced at my watch. "Unfortunately, I've got to go soon. I've got work starting in about half an hour."

My mom was strangely silent for a moment, long enough for me to wonder if she'd heard me.

"Mom?"

"I'm here. I'm sorry, I was just thinking…" She sighed. "Dad isn't here right now, but he and I were talking the other day, and we…Well, we just want you to know we're proud of you."

I stared at my phone screen. Had I heard that right, or was the phone freezing up again and garbling all the words?

"I know we haven't said it enough," she said, looking down. "And I know we haven't shown it. It's just that I never pictured my sweet baby boy in camouflage with a gun."

I looked down at my uniform and brushed away a few crumbs from breakfast. "I usually carry a wrench instead of a gun, if that makes you feel better."

"But you were right," she continued as if I hadn't spoken. "We never stopped to ask what you wanted. And if this...if this makes you happy, then I want you to know that we support you."

My throat was suddenly too thick to swallow, so the best I could do to nod. All my life, I'd been waiting to hear that. And now that it was mine, I wasn't sure what to even do with it.

"Have you talked to Jessie lately?" she asked half a minute later, after a long stretch of silence. Her voice sounded hopeful, which was odd, considering I hadn't actually told them about me and Jessie, aside from the one night we'd shared on the bridge.

"Nah." I forced a smile. "We're not actually together. Plus, one of my buddies said he saw her out the other day with one of the guy teachers from her school at some restaurant."

"Oh. That's too bad." Then she brightened up again. "You should see some of the things she's doing with the kids at school. They're all going to be in a talent show, and Jade's choir is performing!"

"Is she Thing One in a skit like I was in second grade?"

Mom laughed. "She's going to be the fairy with the other girls. You should just see her, prancing around the house in her tutu and cowgirl boots."

I laughed. "Well, good for her."

"Jessie even made her choir try out for the part before she gave it to them." My mom looked smug. "Jade was a little miffed, but in the end, she and her choir did great." Then she paused. "Are you sure you don't want to chat with Jessie sometime? Even if it was just to catch up? I could let her know what time of day you're—"

"I'm sorry, Mom, but I need to get ready for work."

Her face fell, but she gave me a tight smile. "All right then. Take care of yourself, son. I mean it."

"I plan to, Mom. Love you. Tell Dad I love him, too."

As soon as the connection went dead, I closed my eyes and took a deep breath, trying to ignore the familiar ache in my chest. The separation had been good for me. It forced me to think about work stuff that was in no way related to Jessie. We didn't even wear our dress blues over here, so I didn't have to think about the ball or the way she'd felt pressed against me in the dance, or how bright her eyes had been when she'd seen me in my uniform, like I was the only man in the world. Out here, I didn't have to think about that at all. In fact, if I lost focus, I could make a mistake on the job and get someone killed, and that wasn't an option. So focus was the best cure for all my ails.

But there were days, particularly slower ones, like today, when she was much harder to chase from my mind. Still, the deployment was only halfway over. By the time I got back, it would be March, and that would double the time I had to get her out of my mind before being in the same city again with her. Only this time, I wouldn't fall prey to her charms. Because even if she refused to live her life, I would absolutely live mine.

40

ALL I ASK

DERRICK

I blinked in the light of the rising sun as I stepped off the plane and started my descent down the fold-up stairs that led us to the runway.

I couldn't see my parents' faces or my sister's in the throng of family and friends who had come to welcome us home. Six months away, and somehow, it felt like I'd never left.

Unfortunately, that also meant that as soon as the warm, wet air that smelled like clover and sweet grass hit my face, I was also bombarded with a million memories that came springing back like a Jack in the Box that just wouldn't close.

The deployment, while not what I would call fun and games, had been mostly uneventful. We'd had a few brushes with danger, but nothing to get over-excited about. The best part, however, had been my state of mind. I was focused on work, and when time allowed it, the long-distance college classes I'd started up again. A certain woman had been on my mind less and less, and by the end of the six-month tour, I was sure I was ready to face Little Rock again without her. But this sudden feeling of deja vu was so bad that when I finally found my family, despite knowing she wouldn't be with them, I was surprised to find only three people instead of four.

Good grief, the woman had only been in my life for two months. It wasn't possible for her to have taken this much of my attention and expectations, especially after I'd been deployed for three times that amount of time. It was early March, and time to be looking away from the past and to new adventures.

There was a short ceremony where we stood at attention while one of the commanders read out what I'm sure was a nicely thought out speech. All I wanted to do, though, was take Jade in my arms and hold that baby girl close.

Eventually, I got my wish, and we were released. Jade acted cool as a cucumber, which didn't surprise me in the least bit. She'd punished me before when I'd gone to other states for training. Usually, I had to buy my way back into her graces, and though she acted disdainful about the whole thing, I knew she enjoyed every minute of it.

My parents, however, took me by complete surprise. They were wearing red, white, and blue t-shirts, and had even made a WELCOME HOME banner by hand.

"You're home!" My mother clutched me, sobbing. "My baby is home!"

My dad cleared his throat about a dozen times and shook my hand four more times. Jade handed me a smoothie and managed to look completely bored while I smothered her in hugs and kisses, but I didn't miss the wry little smile as I finally put her back down.

After I got my bags, and we finally made our way to the car, I decided that no matter how sleep-deprived and time-confused I felt, this was going to be a new start. If only I could change the feeling that there was a hole in our party that just couldn't be filled.

∾

My mom turned around in her seat as we left the fast-food drive-through.

"You sure that's what you wanted?"

I raised my chicken sandwich in the air. "I've been dreaming of this for the last six months. If I died now, I could rest in peace."

"Derrick, that's not even funny." She grimaced.

"I'm alive," I winked at Jade, "so it is."

When we got home, my dad grabbed my bags before I could get to them and dragged them out to my casita. I went to the kitchen with my mom and Jade.

In spite of myself, I'd missed this kitchen a lot when I was gone. The memories with Jade from the summer before were some of my most precious. At least, that's what I'd told myself. But when I stepped inside, I was reminded once more that I would never again wake up and find Jessie standing in here, pouring Jade's cereal with new insults ready to throw my way.

Because Jessie was gone. And my stupid mouth had made sure she wouldn't want to come back.

Not that I'd forgiven her yet. Far from it. I still couldn't for the life of me understand why she would let herself (and me) get so deep and then run the other way as if she'd been taken by surprise. Okay, maybe it was a little faster than most courtships. But with the deployment looming, I didn't have much time. I'd really thought that after all that time we'd spent together, she'd have the courage to jump. And I'd been sure that if I waited, without a ring, she'd find a way to talk herself out of it while I was gone. And I didn't know if I could take that.

I wandered around the kitchen and rummaged through the cabinets. Jackpot. Mom had stocked the kitchen with all my favorite cereals. She really had forgiven me for joining the Air Force. And, it seemed, for losing Amy.

"Mine."

I looked down to see Jade pointing up at the cabinet.

"I want mine."

"A please wouldn't kill you, kid." I pulled down the cereal and began to pour her a bowl until she whacked my leg.

"Mine. I do it."

I wanted to tell her to lose the attitude, but my curiosity won out when I realized she was actually reaching for the box. I handed it to her and watched as she poured her own bowl of cereal and topped it off with about a cup too much milk.

"How long has she been doing that?" I asked my mom as she walked in, yawning.

"Oh, since about a month after you left. Jessie wasn't here, of course, but she and I had a talk about how she thought Jade was ready. And I didn't think so at first, but lo and behold, she was right."

I just let her talk, pouring my cereal, in spite of the fact that I'd just had a chicken sandwich, and pretending this was all fantastic. I hadn't told my parents about the proposal in hopes they could celebrate with me after instead of asking a million questions before. But for once, my mom didn't seem fooled. I could see it in the way she pursed her lips now as she studied me.

"I know things didn't work out between you two the way you wanted," she said in a soft voice, "so I'm really hesitant to ask this."

I paused mid-chew and regarded her warily. "Go on."

"Jade's choir is performing tonight, the one we told you she tried out for last fall. Anyhow, they're in the school talent show, and…" She sighed. "Jade is really hoping you'll come."

I stared at her for a moment before letting out a strange bark of a laugh. "Never did I think I'd see the day when you had to beg me to come to something for Jade."

"No, you're right. And I hate that you're right because it took you coming and leaving before we understood so much of what you were trying to tell us."

I folded my arms. "You do?"

She nodded. "We got rid of Jade's nanny. Now it's just us." She gave me a sad smile. "I'm trying. I really am. It's not easy, but…just please don't make me tell your sister that you won't come see her sing. It'll break her heart."

I took a deep breath. The talent show wasn't the issue. The issue was what neither of us had said aloud. If the talent show was at the school, Jessie was sure to be there and from what my mother had said before, was definitely involved. And if Jessie was involved, there was a ridiculously good chance I would have to see her face-to-face during some point that night.

I glanced over at Jade where she sat now, crunching away at her cereal. Her eyes were welded to me, and I couldn't help cracking a smile.

"Of course, I'll go, Geode."

There was no way I was missing my little sister's talent show for sleep…or to avoid the woman I'd thought I loved. Jessie would just have to accept that I was coming, and that would be the end of that.

Before we could say anything else, though, the doorbell buzzed.

"I'll get it." I put my empty bowl in the sink and went to the front door. When I saw who it was, I nearly dropped my coffee.

"Hi, Derrick." Amy tucked a dark lock of hair behind her ear. "It's good to see you."

～

I glanced back to make sure no one had heard me, then closed the door and moved out onto the porch for some privacy. Then I turned to the woman who, at one point, had been my future.

"What...um." I scrunched my eyes closed and rubbed them. I needed about three days of sleep and a fourteen-hour mental time adjustment to deal with this kind of stuff. When I opened my eyes again, she was still there, all five feet and eight inches of her, dark hair up in a pony-tail, smeared mascara beneath her eyes, and dressed in a t-shirt and jeans.

When was the last time I'd seen her in anything but work clothes? This was the Amy I had come to know and love. Before she was the high powered attorney and constantly wore pantsuits. Back when she was just...Amy.

She turned her face down to the ground, though I saw her continue to sneak glances up at me as she spoke, her blue eyes bewitching beneath those long lashes. "I called your mom and asked when you were getting home," she said. Then she took a deep breath. "And I had to come."

"Okay?" It probably wasn't the politest way to talk to someone who had just flown halfway across the country for me, but I wasn't in a particularly gracious mood when it came to women I wasn't related to at that moment.

She sighed. "I don't know how to say this. I've been trying for months, and you'd think being a lawyer would give me words..." She chuckled dryly. "But it doesn't."

"Amy, you're not—"

"I miss you, Derrick. Giving you up was stupid, and I was being petty. And if I'm honest, I was more than a little jealous. I was just sure Jade's nanny was doing her best to seduce you, and you were going right along with it. And Jade was just your excuse."

"Shows you how much you really know about me now, doesn't it?"

"Would you just listen?" She huffed. "After you were gone, I realized my world felt really empty without you. I missed calling and texting you first thing in the morning. All those bridal magazines my mom had bought for me seemed to mock me from my coffee table. I nearly bought a ticket to go see you back in September, but your mom said you were deploying, and I was too late."

I rubbed my eyes and slid down into one of my mom's cushy white porch chairs. "Amy, I appreciate the thought, but I don't see what any of this changes. We just want different things."

"I've been thinking about that," she said softly. "And I...I'm ready to make some changes."

"How so?"

This time, she didn't look away. "I know you love your sister. And the more I think about it, the more I want to love her, too. You were right. She deserves that." She took a deep, shuddery breath. "And if you'd just give us one more chance, I think life could be even more than we wanted it to be. Imagine it. The three of us, going on adventures, hiking." She paused. "I'd even quit my job. We could get married quietly if you want. No big celebration or expensive cake. Just us and our closest family and friends. I just...I want to be with you. And why it took you flying halfway across the world for me to see that, I'll never know. But I do know that I was wrong, and there's little more to tell." She put her hands in her pockets and shrugged. "So...what do you say?"

I swallowed and ran my hand through my hair. This was it. I was being offered everything I'd ever dreamed about since I was old enough to want a family of my own. A beautiful, supportive wife. The ability to take care of my sister, should the need arise. She was even offering to forego the ridiculously expensive ceremony she'd gone on about for months and just settle for...me. It was everything I'd ever wanted.

But as I tried to imagine us walking the Grand Canyon trails with Jade or going shopping or spending a day at the farmer's market, it wasn't Amy's face I saw in my imagination, with her dark hair and alluring eyes. Instead, I saw a little pixie face framed by short golden-brown hair, her hands enveloping smaller ones as she coached Jade on how to lift her feet the right way when climbing steps. And no matter how hard I tried to see Amy, all I saw was Jessie.

But at the memory of her pixie face, my heart hardened. You know what? If I was going to have to face her tonight, where she was probably dating that stupid teacher, then I wasn't going to leave myself vulnerable.

"Derrick?" Amy's voice wavered.

If only closing that painful chapter could close on all the rest. But it didn't. Because Jessie had dug her grips into my heart better than eagle talons on prey, and it would take an act of God to get them out. And I couldn't do a stinking thing about it. Except maybe protect myself tonight.

"Look…" I scratched my neck. "I'm going to my sister's talent show tonight, and I just got home from deployment, like fifteen minutes ago. I need to sleep today, but maybe tonight you could come. Then we can talk about this again in the morning."

She reached up on her toes and kissed my cheek. "Thank you, Derrick. That's all I ask."

41

I SEE

DERRICK

My dockers and polo shirt had never felt so hot or itchy as they did that night when we walked into the school along with the throng of other parents and grandparents. Posters made out of butcher paper in primary colors hung on all the walls like advertisements for trailers might hang in a movie theater. Children in costumes were everywhere, and parents stopped for pictures next to the posters, cooing and praising as their cameras and phones clicked and flashed.

Jade was chill as ever. She watched the exciting scene with a condescending gaze, regarding one boy dressed up as a pirate who was in tears with a rather disdainful eye. We'd practiced her song at home a million times that day, and this seemed to have given her a sense of superiority which I might have laughed at, had she not been there to see.

But it wasn't the stuffy air or the pressing crowd or even Jade's part that made me jumpy. It was the face I dreaded but was sure to see. Because this was Jessie's life. And unless she'd come down with a last-minute case of the plague, she was sure to be here tonight, front and center.

At least I had Amy.

"Hold on, hold on!" Amy stopped us. Then she grabbed Jade by the shoulder and dragged her over to the wall to stand beside a butcher paper cut-out of a ballerina. "Let me take your picture, sweetie!"

Jade scowled and marched back over to me, where she turned to glower up at me.

"Amy," I said, trying to keep my voice down. The last thing I wanted to do was have Jessie see me trying to rein in my ex-fiancée because she was going to drive my sister insane. Not that I should care what Jessie thought of it all. But the whole thing was...well, a little embarrassing.

"Jade doesn't like to be touched until she knows you," I tried to explain as Amy muttered at her camera.

"But we know each other, don't we, sweetie?" Her voice was loud and her words slow.

"Amy, you haven't seen her in over a year. And she can hear you just fine."

"I'll take Jade to her classroom," my mother said, stepping quickly between us. "You three go find seats in the cafeteria."

My dad kissed Jade and wished her luck and then we turned to do as we were told. I hadn't known it was possible, but without Jade, I felt even more exposed. At least with her along, I could divert the attention. If Jessie and I had been forced to talk, we would have at least had a subject on which to focus. But now it was just me.

"Should've gotten here sooner," my dad said as we entered the cafeteria. Sure enough, the place was already crawling with people. It was hard to find even four seats together, but we did eventually find a space right up in the far front corner.

"This is so cute!" Amy exclaimed, taking pictures of everything. "No wonder Jade loves it here so much." Did she always yell everything she said? I searched my memories for how loudly she'd talked before we broke up.

My mom slipped in a few minutes later.

"Look at her." She laughed as she held up her phone to show us the pictures she'd taken. "We got the costume to the room in one piece. She's still got her tutu and leotard on, and she had the wand when I left at least. But she refused to take off the boots. Jessie finally said it wasn't worth the fight and to let her wear them."

My dad let out an uncharacteristic chuckle. "She must be excited. I can even see her dimple."

I watched them for a moment, trying to remember the last time they'd made such a fuss over my sister. Honestly, I couldn't remember, all except for her birthday parties and surgery days. This was nice. *Please let it last*, I prayed.

"She's absolutely precious." Amy beamed. "I can't wait to see what she can do."

The lights dimmed just then, thankfully, and my mom stuck her phone in her purse as music played over the speakers, which were conveniently three feet from our chairs. It didn't stop until a man in a suit walked out onto the stage and began to talk about how someone years ago had thought up this talent show as a way to raise money for the school, and how it was a yearly tradition now, and how hard the kids had worked, and droned on and on until I was sure this evening couldn't possibly get any longer. Then I saw a movement to my right and caught sight of that Newman guy. And he was talking to Jessie, but his eyes kept darting back to me and Amy.

I had been wrong. This evening could get far longer than I'd ever dreamed.

~

The show was about an hour long as student after student came up onto the stage and danced or did magic tricks or sang loud, more than slightly off-key songs to the speaker that must have been built to break people's eardrums. Jessie didn't seem to mind the noise, though. In fact, she seemed to thrive on it. She fairly danced in the corners of the stage, ushering children on and off with seamless ease. And there was Sam Newman, standing at her elbow the entire time, pointing to her clipboard and constantly making her nod with whatever he was whispering.

My stomach churned, and in an effort to not stare at them, I turned the screen light all the way down on my phone and started to play some mindless game with fruit and bubbles until my mom nudged me…hard, and gave me a dirty look, the same one she'd given me back when I was twelve and had threatened to bring a toad to church to play with during the sermon.

Rolling my eyes, I put the phone down. I was twenty-five, and that look still wasn't completely ineffective.

Eventually, Jade did make it to the stage with her choir, and I could honestly say I enjoyed her part. That is, until I realized Jessie was

262 | BRITTANY FICHTER

watching, spellbound, from the floor in front of the stage. If I'd really tried, I could have touched her. But I didn't. Because at least some of my pride was still intact. That, and Amy had my other arm in a vice grip.

About three years later, the show was done, and we were free to find our kids and get them home. Jade was easy to pick out in her sparkly pink cowgirl boots and tutu. I swept her up and gave her a big kiss on the cheek.

"I'm proud of you Geode. That was fantastic."

"I'm a star," she said with a smug little smile.

I laughed. "Yeah, I guess you are."

"You were brilliant!" Amy squealed, throwing her arms around Jade and squeezing her in a hug that would have made my arms hurt.

Jade looked at me like someone was going to die. Before I could intervene, though, someone called her name.

"Jade," a grating, familiar voice called from behind us. "You forgot your wand."

Gritting my teeth, I turned to find Sam Newman following us. He was holding Jade's little pink wand. She snatched it up and regarded it happily.

"Thank you," my mom gushed. "She would have made us pay if we'd gotten home without it." She stuck her hand out. "I'm Jade's mom."

"Sam Newman." He shook her hand. "I'm not Jade's teacher, obviously, but I teach in the classroom next door."

He then shook my dad's hand as well, which, unfortunately, brought him then to me.

"Sam," I said, keeping my arms firmly around Jade while giving him the barest of nods I could manage.

"Derrick." He returned the nod and folded his arms. We watched one another for a moment.

"You two know each other?" My mom turned to me, slightly uneasy.

"We've met," I said.

"I haven't." Amy came forward. "I'm Amy, Derrick's fiancée."

"Ex-fiancée." I gave her a look, but she ignored it.

"Well, that's great. Hey, I hear you just got back from deployment," Sam said, a benign smile suddenly gracing his thin face as he pushed his glasses up higher on his nose. "Congratulations."

"Thanks." What was he up to?

"Have you seen Jessie since you got back?" The words were polite enough, but his eyes were bright.

"Nope."

"That's too bad. I mean," he turned to my mom, "she's just been so busy. We were having coffee the other day, and she told me she doesn't know if she'll want to run the show next year."

I swallowed the curse I wanted desperately to fling at the man. So she'd done it after all. After turning me down, she'd said yes to him. And for some reason, this felt worse than her first rejection. The world spun slightly, and I had to breathe deeply to stay standing.

"Ow." Jade shoved one of my hands off her arm. "Too hard."

"Well," my mom said, sending me an uneasy glance, "tell her to let us know if she needs anything. She's done so much for Jade that we're happy to help her in whatever way we can."

"Thank you so much." Sam stared into her eyes as though she'd offered him a kidney replacement instead of asking him to deliver a message to another teacher. "That means a lot to me, and I know it will mean a lot to her." His eyes flicked over to mine, and the hint of a smile played on his lips. "She's a special person." Then he turned back to Amy. "And it's fantastic to meet you. I hear Derrick here has good taste in women."

I'd heard enough. My parents could catch up when they felt like it. I turned and strode toward the car. Amy trailed along behind me, trying to keep up.

"Derrick? Why are we going so fast? I wanted a picture of your sister."

But just as I walked out the door, I nearly collided with someone who was coming in.

"I'm so sorry…"

Whatever I'd been about to say died when I saw who I was talking to. Because staring back at me was the biggest pair of sparkling green eyes I'd ever seen.

"Derrick."

Why did it make my chest get all tight when she said my name like that?

"Um." Her eyes glanced down at the ground, then back up to mine. "Hi."

"Hi."

There was a long stretch of silence. And so much I wanted to say. I wanted to scream that the pathetic excuse for a man who was standing inside, still talking to my parents, was the wrong man for her. I wanted to shout about how I could see it again, that she was a self-fulfilling prophecy, working herself to death for a few moments of 'one day'. I was also dangerously close to letting myself stare at the shape of her jaw, and admire how the weak outdoor light cast pretty shadows across her face, when Amy spoke, snapping me out of my reverie.

"Hi, I'm Amy." Amy offered Jessie her hand, but the sticky, coy voice she'd used all evening was gone. Her lawyer voice was back.

I couldn't tell for sure in the evening light, but Jessie looked as though she'd grown paler. Finally, though, she seemed to recover herself.

"It's good to meet you, Amy." Her eyes found mine, and they were accusing. "I've heard so much about you."

"Good things, I hope." Amy's smile was smug.

Instead of responding, though, Jessie just hefted the box on her hip and looked back at me.

"It's probably good to be home." She nodded at Jade, and her smile grew slightly genuine. "She's been talking about you an awful lot." Then her smile faltered slightly, and she gave me a quick once-over. "I'm... I'm glad you got back safely. I've been praying for you."

"Thanks." I couldn't help feeling at least a little satisfied at this. She might be Newman's girlfriend, but I was in her prayers. I was nearly tempted to go back and tell him just to see the look on his face. "Um... how's your mom?"

"What happened to your mom?" Amy cooed.

"She's good. Everything seems to be normal for now." She paused and looked down at the box she was holding. When she looked up again, all traces of her smile were gone.

"Derrick." She stepped closer, edging Amy out with her shoulder. "I've been thinking," she said in a low voice, "and I wanted to tell you that—"

The door opened, and my parents spilled out, followed by Newman.

"Jessie," he motioned behind him with his thumb, "Silvia Wickeroot has been looking everywhere for you."

She looked back and forth between us several times before sighing.

She turned to go, but without thinking, my hand shot out, and I gently grabbed her wrist.

"Just tell me," I said softly. "Really quick."

Amy shook her head and tugged on my other arm. "If you need to go, Jessie, don't let us hold you up."

"Jess," Newman said loudly, "you really need to handle this. Wickeroot's on the warpath."

"Yeah, um. I'm sorry," Jessie said quietly, pulling away and heading for Newman, who still stood in the door. "I've got to take this."

My throat thickened. "Of course you do."

It was a stupid thing to say, and I could see the hurt register in her face as I turned away. But that was the problem, wasn't it? I seemed to have a GPS for women who were more married to their other priorities than they could ever be to me.

"Derrick—" Amy began, but I shook my head.

"Let's get Jade in the car."

She studied me for a moment before nodding. "Okay."

As soon as we were in the car, Jade buckled in and waiting for my parents, she turned to me. The sweet innocence was gone, and in its place was the sharp look of a woman on a mission.

"That was Jade's teacher, wasn't it?"

"Yep." I stared out at the trees as the wind blew them hard against one another.

"She was also her nanny last summer, wasn't she?"

"Yep."

She took a big breath. "But she's not just a nanny…is she?"

I didn't answer. Instead, I started the ignition.

"I see." She pursed her lips. We didn't utter another word the rest of the drive home.

42

FIGHT

DERRICK

"Allen."

I looked up from the list I was supposed to be checking off. There were more Air Force-required errands to run after a deployment, it seemed, than before. Not that I was in a hurry to go home. Amy was still there, waiting on my decision. And though I knew what I wanted to do, for some reason, I hesitated. Maybe it was because I really just didn't want to do this. Or maybe it was because I was terrified of being left alone after successfully chasing every love interest out of my life for the last twelve months. Either way, I had little desire to run home anytime soon.

Sergeant Barnes was standing at the door of his office. "When you're done, I'd like to see you for a minute."

"Sir?" I came to stand in his doorway, and he waved me in.

"Sit."

I obeyed and did my best not to look as nervous as I suddenly felt. Had he found out about my deal with Jessie? While I'd not technically broken any rules, it would look less than honest if he found out I'd made the deal with her because of him. And though the old man was the last person I wanted playing Cupid in my life, I liked him as a boss, and the last thing I wanted was a reason for him to mistrust me.

He sat on the edge of his desk and folded his arms and stared at me for a moment. "How are you doing?" he finally asked.

"Well enough, sir."

He studied me, his dark eyes sharp. "I didn't notice Miss Nickleby at your return last week."

I looked down at my hands. "You were there?"

"I was meeting another friend of mine who was coming back, too. And you didn't seem like you were expecting her either."

I swallowed. If he was trying to set me up with his daughter again... Well, what if he was? Maybe I should go out with her. Maybe I'd find someone who wasn't married to their life already, too much so to buy into mine.

"Jessie and I are done." I tried to force my voice to stay calm.

"What happened?"

And so, throwing caution to the wind, I told him. He was a surprisingly good listener for one who liked to talk so much. And the more I spoke, the more at ease I felt, though I couldn't say why. Seeing it from a thousand-foot view, rather than having the events right under my nose made them look...well, not different. It still hurt like a dang knife. But better, all the same. Though I couldn't say why. Maybe just because I was telling someone. For the first time, I wasn't the only one hashing this out on my own, trying to figure out where we went wrong.

"I just...I don't understand." I looked up at him. "She seemed like she was okay with everything, coming out of her cocoon. And then she put the brakes on and took off running in the other direction as fast as she could."

"And you're sure she's with this Newman guy?" he asked.

I nodded. "Hernandez said he saw them out at a restaurant back after I left. And when I went to the school, he said they were an item, and she didn't give me any reason to think otherwise."

"But you didn't ask her?"

I opened my mouth then paused. "No. I guess I didn't."

He smiled just a little and sat slightly taller. "I see." Then he turned and looked at the motivational poster on his wall, though I was pretty sure it wasn't the brightly colored inspirational tree he was thinking about.

"You know," he finally said. "This life has a way of sucking the dreams right out of our wives."

I frowned. "Sir?"

"They get dragged all over the country...or the world even, for us. Their jobs are disrupted. They don't get hired because the employers know they've got them for two, maybe four years at best. While we're focused on our changing schedules and the needs of the mission, their emotional and physical needs are often the first things to get overlooked. And they don't say much because they don't want to distract us from the mission. But as we move out onto the flightline, they move farther and farther from the world they thought this would be."

I wanted to speak, but no words would come. I knew a lot of this, of course. In theory. Military divorces were higher than they were in the civilian world, or so I'd heard in some statistic. But I'd never heard it put this way.

"My wife nearly hit a breaking point five years after we were married." He gazed down at the woman in the silver picture frame on his desk. "Nearly cost me my marriage until I realized what she was missing thanks to this life."

"I...I don't understand, sir. If that's the way of the military life, should I just give up now?"

His eyes looked like they were about to pop. "Give up? Allen, are you listening to me? You've got to fight, boy! But you can't just stop once the ring is on her finger. You've got to keep fighting. In war and out, you have to fight for your marriage. You have to prove to that woman, even when you're spent and torn, that you still want her. That she's worth fighting for. And if that means roses when money's tight, you find some cheap roses and skip out on your bar time with the boys that week. Or pick wildflowers on the way home. If it means therapy, you go to therapy."

"But if she's dating—"

"If she's dating him, you'd better make your move before he offers up his own ring." He shrugged. "If she's not, you still make your move."

"How?" I stared up at him, too scared to hope that he might be telling the truth. That there might still be a chance in this race for me not to come in last and limping. Then I gave a laugh that sounded slightly hysterical. "I've got my ex-fiancée at my house, waiting for an answer, and Jessie—"

"Hold on, do you love your ex-fiancée?"

I took a deep breath. Did I? Had I felt that same old flame I had a year ago?

"No, sir."

"Then get rid of her, and go after your true girl." He leaned forward.

"Convince her you'll do everything in your power to make her dreams come true. And then do it."

I sighed. "She wants a master's from UCA. She wants to be near her parents. Her mom has cancer. She wants to be at her church and school and everything else she loves here. I can't change any of that."

"I never said it would be easy. Sometimes you've just got to get creative." He looked back down at the picture. "They fall for the knight in dress blues, not understanding that the knight is at the behest of the king."

I traced the stitching on the edge of my sleeve.

"But what many don't understand," he continued, "is that happiness is possible for both of you if you trust God and serve one another before yourselves." He paused. "Don't tell HR I said that. My inspirational lectures aren't supposed to be too personal."

I grinned. "Wasn't planning on it."

A clap of thunder exploded outside, and Barnes got up to look through the blinds. "Didn't I hear you say earlier that you're supposed to get your sister from school today?"

"Yes, sir."

"Well, you'd better get going soon if that's the case," he said, frowning at the window. "Looks like it's going to get nasty outside real fast."

I was still chewing on his little speech when I got in the car and started home. I was so lost in my thoughts that several minutes passed before I realized that the sky had turned pea green. Hail started just as I made this discovery, and within thirty seconds, I knew I wouldn't make it home. My visibility was nearly zero, and it would be nothing for my truck to hit someone else who had stopped for the storm as well. By the time I reached a recognizable building, my heart was in my throat, and my breathing was accompanied by prayers as quick as the short bursts of breath I was taking in and out, like my lungs could no longer expand or contract the right way.

I needed to get to Jade's school. I was supposed to pick her up today, and I knew how much she hated storms. But I couldn't reach it. Not in this. I would have to wait until it passed, or I would never reach the school at all.

I parked the best I could in front of some random building and decided to make a run for it. I didn't want to face this storm unsheltered. Hail the size of marbles pelted my skin as I slammed the truck door shut and ran toward the building, slipping twice along the way. Just as I was pulling the door open, a bolt of lightning struck something on the other side of the street. I stumbled inside, but before I could get my bearings, a woman grabbed me by the shoulder and hauled me to my feet.

"Come on!" she shouted over the thunder. "In here!"

I followed her, still somewhat disoriented, into the Shelter In Place room. Seven other people were already inside, staring at the walls and the ceiling uneasily.

"Everyone," the woman ordered as she closed the door, "get down on the floor and put your hands on your head! Why are you all staring like that's going to help? Come on, people, we trained for this!"

I did as she said, not needing a reminder, feeling sick to my stomach as I pictured Jade, screaming in terror as the rumbling of a train sounded through the air. But as the lightning grew faster and louder, all I could do was pray.

43

WARNING

JESSIE

"**A**nd what makes a square different from—" I paused my lesson to glance at my phone. It hadn't stopped buzzing for the last five minutes. And no matter how much I ignored it, it continued to go off again and again and again.

"A square," I said again, trying to find my train of thought as I flipped the phone around to see the screen. "What makes it different from all the other shapes? What properties are unique to the square? Take half a minute and think about it before I call on someone to answer." While they worked, I glanced down at my phone.

Another tornado watch. That was at least the fifth one today. This time I slipped the phone into my pocket so I could feel the buzz in case we had an actual warning. My phone's weather apps were usually about thirty seconds ahead of the emergency sirens outside.

"Okay, I'm going to choose—"

Before I could finish, a knock sounded on the door, followed by one of the office staff coming in.

"Hi, Mrs. Juniper," I said, nodding at the class to repeat my greeting.

"Hello, Miss Nickleby." She smiled her sweet cherubim smile and nodded at the class. "I'm supposed to take these ones for just a few minutes while you talk to Mr. Matthew in his office."

That was strange, being summoned to the principal's office during the school day. Instead of giving air to my grievances, though, I simply nodded at the class and handed Mrs. Juniper the clipboard I was holding.

"I want you to each tell your seat partner what you think makes squares unique." I pointed to the sheet and mouthed to the secretary, *triangles next*, before leaving the room and making my way down the hall.

I walked quickly, my shoes making sharp clicks that echoed down the corridor as I made my way to the office, which was located in the middle of the building, near the entrance. Though I doubted I'd done anything too terrible, I couldn't help feeling a bit like a naughty kindergartener who had been sent to the principal for breaking some cardinal rule. Only, I didn't know which one it was.

"Jessie." My principal, Conner Matthews, stood and greeted me as I entered his little office. Then he shut the door. "Please sit." He indicated to one of the two worn armchairs in front of his desk.

I saw and did my best to not seem overly anxious. "So," I said with the best smile I could muster, "how can I help you?"

He smiled. "I've got a conference call in ten minutes, but before I have to go, I wanted to congratulate you on the talent show last night. It was magnificent."

"Thank you, sir."

"I also wanted to ask you about your contract." There it was. I should have known. When I didn't answer immediately, he spoke again. "We love having you here. I was just wondering if you're going to sign again."

I gave him a guilty smile. I'd been ignoring the emails, and so he'd called me here. Of course I wanted to teach again. Didn't I?

Every time I'd considered signing that contract, my brain had screamed for me to do it. Do something. Do anything. But what was there to do? Sign or don't sign? Go crawling back to him? Beg him to reconsider? Maybe, if I thought it might change his mind. But the space between us might as well have been dark matter, judging by the way he'd looked at me last night. I'd hurt him. And he had hurt me. My heart felt like it had been hurled against the concrete and stomped on. And I still didn't have a clue as to what I would do even if we hadn't stabbed each other in the back.

So why was I hesitating? It wasn't like I would be getting married and moving any time soon.

"Jessie?" he began.

The buzzing in my phone started again, but this time, it also let out a startling wail that made both of us jump. We leaned toward the window, and he yanked the shade up.

My heart dropped into my stomach. The sky was a sickly yellow-green, and hail was beginning to pelt the window. The pellets were small, but they were also coming fast. And hard. And then the window cracked. I jumped away and then remembered the buzz in my pocket. Pulling it out, I saw the most terrifying words in the world flash across the screen.

TORNADO WARNING FOR PULASKI COUNTY

I was off like a bullet to my class. Out of his room, through the office, and down the hallway. Throwing open the door, I bolted in to find my students staring at me wide-eyed from the carpet.

"Everyone," I gasped, hating how the air had suddenly grown warm, and my skin felt clammy. We were inside, and the air conditioning was running, but I wished I could wipe away the filmy feeling that had settled on my skin. "I want you to line up in order of your numbers at the door."

Mrs. Juniper frowned. "Is everything—"

Interrupting her was the wail of the tornado siren just outside the window. Two of my students began to cry.

"Now, everyone!" I called. "Just like we practiced!"

"But I'm afraid of tornados!" Julieta also began to cry, refusing to budge as Manuel opened the door and held it for the others.

"We'll be safer in the hall!" I herded them toward the door. "Just go! This is exactly what we've practiced for!" I grabbed the whistle and emergency clipboard from the teacher's supply wardrobe on the way out. Then I stood at the door, relieving Manuel of his duty, counting heads as fast as I could.

"Twenty-one, twenty-two…" I paused. Someone was missing. Who was missing? I ran through my roll sheet again and compared it to the children sitting against the wall, the ones the office staff were ordering and pleading with to crouch into little balls and cover their heads with their hands.

Jade. I was missing Jade.

Darting back in the classroom, it took me three seconds that might as well have been three years to locate her, hiding beneath her favorite computer, curled up in a beanbag.

"Come on, Jade! We don't have time for this! We'll be safer in the hall!" I ran over and had started to pull her out from beneath the desk when something crashed through the window. Glass sprayed the room, and I stumbled. The wind roared outside, and rain began to soak the room. I felt something sharp slide across my arm, but I didn't stop to look. Snatching Jade up, thanking the Lord she was tiny, I turned and ran back to the hall, shutting the door behind us until I heard the click. Then I put Jade down, who looked ready to bolt again, and I laid myself on top of her. The last thing we needed was for her to run.

Chugging sounded through the walls and distant windows, which were thankfully far down the hall, away from us. Why did they even bother adding windows to schools in tornado country, I couldn't help wondering even as the chugging grew louder. It sounded like a train was right outside the building. I looked over my shoulder and shouted for several of the curious ones to keep their heads down and covered. Remorse and shame filled me as I wished I could cover them all. Jade was a must because she liked to run when she was frightened, as she had in the classroom. But the others were just as little and vulnerable as she was.

Only when I looked down again did I realize I was bleeding. The chugging grew louder as I tried to squeeze my arm to stop the flow with my other hand while leaning over Jade.

God, help us! Ear-splitting thunder rocked the world. And the sound of breaking glass served as the amen to my prayer.

44

THEM

DERRICK

We waited until the sirens and our phone apps had stopped screaming before we ventured out of the SIP room.

I was in the housing office for the base neighborhood, I'd been told while sheltering with the staff and a few of the local residents. This was good, as I'd nearly made it to the Harris Road exit, which put me less than a mile from Jade's school. But that mile felt like a million the moment we stepped outside.

The sun was out again, making the rain-soaked world sparkle and shine, which was odd, considering the wake of destruction all around us. Trees had been uprooted and tossed like sticks. They seemed to cover everything, from the parking lot to the public pool behind the housing office to the roads. Or rather, what you could see of the roads.

The silence was nearly deafening, punctured only by the sirens in the distance. And even though the wind had died down to what was no more than a gentle breeze, debris still fluttered down, as though the clouds had released little bits of wood and metal, rather than water, from the sky.

"How did we survive that?" one of the men whispered to his coworker. She could only shake her head, her mouth still open.

"It didn't hit the building," a woman said, turning to examine the brick structure. Tiles were missing from the roof, and one of the windows had been punched out, but just as she'd said, the building had been spared.

But the gate hadn't. Mechanically, I said a prayer for whoever had been manning the Harris Road gate. The guard box, thankfully, was still in one piece, but the gate itself was gone. Ripped clean off its hinges.

Then it hit me.

The tornado had taken out the gate because the tornado had ripped right up the road. The same road Jade's school lay on. Something clicked on inside me.

"Check the guard box!" I shouted, pointing at the guard's booth by the nonexistent gate as I broke into a run.

"Where are you going?" one of the women shouted.

But I didn't answer. It was obvious from the condition of the road that I wouldn't be able to drive. Trees from both sides of the road covered it, and even if they hadn't, debris of every kind filled in the spaces. And since I couldn't drive, the only thing left to do was run.

The closer I got to the school, the harder I pushed. The debris began to resemble things that were eerily familiar. A pink backpack. Lunchboxes. Small plastic chairs and even tables were strewn out on the asphalt.

Please, was the only prayer I could get out, pushing myself even harder. *Please let them be all right.*

Them. The prayer was supposed to be her. At least, that's what I had meant it to be. But with each passing second, as mental images of all the possible horrors awaiting me continued to plant themselves in my mind, I knew it was them.

It would always be them.

Because Jessie wasn't just Jade's teacher, the way I'd been trying to treat her in my thoughts. She wasn't an old flame. She wasn't even the cute girl on whom I had a crush.

She was the woman I wanted to marry. Present tense. The one I wanted to come home to and sleep beside at night. I wanted to fight and make up with her over stupid things like facing the toilet paper the wrong way and getting mud in my truck. I wanted her to have my children and to be the one who listened when work was hard. I wanted her.

I crested the hill and nearly dropped to my knees there.

The school had been hit head-on.

The front was all smashed in, and so was the back. Cars were flipped and turned in the parking lot, and a few were on their sides and roofs across the street.

No, Lord. Oh please, no. Please, please, no. I slowed at the edge of the lot, not sure how to proceed.

Or how to go on. Because if Jade and Jessie were gone…

The faint sound of crying reached me just as I stumbled closer. My heart picked up speed with my feet as I began to run again. And just as I reached the lawn, a side door that I hadn't seen opened. And a relief that nearly broke me flooded my senses as the principal, who I recognized from Jessie's talent show, began leading children out in two straight lines.

He saw me and gestured wildly. "Help us get them out!"

I was already running toward them, my training kicking into gear. "Jade and Jessie?" I asked breathlessly as I reached them.

He nodded behind him. "At the far end of the building. But their door isn't working, so we have to get everyone out this way."

I wanted nothing more than to dart down the hall at top speed and fetch them. But he was right. The school was already in shambles. It would be safer to get everyone out in an orderly fashion.

"Do you need me to call—" I started.

He shook his head. "Call's already been made." He pointed out to the far corner of the parking lot. "Let's get them started over there. The teachers will keep them organized. Once the hall is clear, I'll need your help with first aid."

I thanked God that the Air Force required emergency training once a year. And though it killed me not to rush straight in to look for the two people I loved most in the world, I knew I would have to be patient.

Loved.

It was the first time I'd really thought of it this way. I'd been sure I loved Jessie back when I proposed to her. And I did. But whatever it was I had then was different from what I was feeling now. That affection had been as sweet and innocent as Jessie was. But this devotion I felt inside now was as passionate and ardent as the sun. It had survived a six-month deployment, Sam Newman, Amy's return, and a tornado. I'd been kidding myself when I thought I could just give her up and move back to Amy. Jessie was in my heart, and she was there to stay. And no amount of my pig-headedness could change that. I just desperately hoped now that she would be in the shape to receive that kind of love. Because if something had happened...

Focus. I had to focus.

Five minutes later, most of the inner hall, which had been miraculously spared, was cleared. My uneasiness grew again, however, when I realized that the last class I helped to lead out to the parking lot was Jade's, but they emerged with neither Jade nor Jessie. Then a familiar scream echoed from down the hall.

Blowing by the principal, I sprinted toward the sound. Several people were lying in the hall, other staff members kneeling at their sides, but I headed straight for the sound.

Relief brought tears to my eyes as I saw Jade standing near the broken door. Aside from a few cuts, there was no blood. I scooped her up and squeezed her to my chest. She fought me until she realized who it was. Then she clung to me and screamed harder.

"She won't come with us," one of the other teachers said...Madison, I think. Her hair was wet and wind-whipped, but she looked like she would be okay as well. Then she looked pointedly at the ground, and I followed her gaze.

Jessie lay on the ground. Her eyes were fluttering, and there was a small puddle of blood under her arm.

"What happened?" I asked, putting Jade down and kneeling at her side. Jade continued to cry, but she stopped screaming at least. "Jessie." I raised my voice. "Jess, can you hear me?"

For a moment, I thought she might focus on me, but her eyes didn't focus as she moaned.

"I think it's from the blood loss." Madison's voice shook. "She had the cut when she came back from getting Jade. She didn't even notice it at first, I just saw it because I glanced up when she slammed the door shut." She broke into sobs. "She should have wrapped something around it, but it all went so fast, and the winds hit, and—"

I didn't hear the rest of what she said as I unlaced my left boot. Grabbing the knife out of my pocket, I cut part of the lace off and wrapped it around her arm as quickly as I could. It wasn't the most beautiful tourniquet in the world, but it should stop the majority of the blood loss.

"We need to get her out of here," the principal said, coming to stand behind me. "I'm not sure how long the building will hold."

I frowned. It would be best not to move her until the paramedics arrived, but he was right. The building was already groaning as it was. Gently, so gently, I picked her up, and we began the long trek down the darkened hall, small beams of sunlight filtering in through the holes in the roof. Jade followed, much to my relief, letting Madison take her by the hand this time. I hugged Jessie as tightly as I dared to my chest, thankful for the warmth still emanating from her. In spite of the rain and wind, she still smelled familiar and reminded me of home.

"Hang on, baby," I whispered into her hair, my throat threatening to close on the words as I spoke them. "I'm going to get you out of here." Despite my rush, I couldn't help but press one small kiss against her temple. It would probably be the last time I could ever pretend she was mine.

A medical helicopter arrived as we made our way out to her class. Teachers shooed their children away from the small space someone had cleared as it landed. Jessie was in the worst condition, so I was waved forward. I went as fast as I could without bouncing her too hard, praying every step of the way.

"Are you her husband?" the medic asked as I approached.

I shook my head and desperately wished I could even say I was her boyfriend. "I'm a friend!" I shouted over the roar of the rotors.

"You'll have to stay here then!" he shouted back as he reached for her.

Handing Jessie's limp, pale body over to someone else to care for was the hardest thing I'd ever done. "Take care of her!" I called.

He gave me a terse nod and turned to tend to Jessie. A lump the size of a baseball sat in my throat as I stepped back to watch the helicopter lift into the air once more.

When they were gone, I felt someone take my hand. Looking down, I found Jade, who was watching the helicopter as well. For the first time, I really looked at her. I'd glanced, of course, as soon as I'd seen her, but her angry screams had been enough to convince me she was probably doing fine. But now, I could see that not only was she fine, there was barely a scratch on her, which was more than I could say for some of the other kids.

"She's fine."

I looked up to see Madison, who I now recalled was Jessie's best friend.

"Jessie was on top of her the whole time." Her voice caught. "Even when she had to hold her arm because it really started to bleed, Jessie held onto Jade for dear life."

I knelt down to my little sister and took her face in my hands. She wore a solemn expression, her dark eyes looking back into mine. And all I could do was to clutch her to my chest and cry.

I'd worried once that Jessie might not take care of her the way she needed to be cared for. And now Jessie was in the fight of her life because she had. And I couldn't be at her side because I'd been too pig-headed to wait.

DERRICK, YOU PIG-FACED JERK...

DERRICK

As soon as I'd gathered my senses and done my best to help with the other injuries, none of which were as bad as Jessie's, I called Jessie's mom to tell her what had happened. What might have been a decidedly awkward conversation, considering how Jessie and I had left off, was short and full of stress on both sides. That was the last I expected to hear from Mrs. Nickleby.

We were recalled soon after that, with Sergeant Barnes sending out the message that those who could come were needed to return to the base to help with cleanup and emergency services. But since I had my sister, he sent me home instead.

"You're home!" my mother cried as soon as we opened the door. It was strange walking in the house. After seeing so much destruction, my parents' neighborhood was untouched. But I couldn't dwell on that very long. I was exhausted, despite sleeping most of the day yesterday between returning from deployment and going to the show, but there was one last stop I had to make. And it was out on the front porch.

"Your mom said you wanted to see me?" Amy pushed a strand of hair out of her face as she settled into one of the white porch chairs.

"Yeah." I couldn't bring myself to sit, so I settled for leaning against one of the porch posts. "Look, I appreciate you coming out here and trying to make things right."

"Uh-oh." She was smiling, but I could tell it wasn't real. "This doesn't sound like a let's-give-this-another-try speech."

I shook my head. "I need to be honest with you. And truth be told..."

"It's her, isn't it?" Amy's voice was sharp and tight, and her smile disappeared. "The nanny."

"Amy, you..." How did I say this without being cruel? And yet, what could I do to signal to this woman that we really were through? "You have different desires and needs than I can offer. And this summer showed me that I do, too."

"You don't know that," she whimpered.

"I know that last night was torture for you and Jade. Do you really want to do that every single day?"

She'd opened her mouth as if to argue, but then she shut it again. Finally, her shoulders drooped. "I suppose not." When she spoke again, her voice was soft. "You left because you wanted something I can't give you. And from what I gather, now it seems she's left you for the same reason. I saw the way you were looking at her last night, and it was clear that the ball was in her park." She stood. "I hope you can do better than I did." Then she turned and walked away.

∼

Amy was right. Jessie had left me, in a way. But I couldn't rid myself of the need to know how she was doing. Unfortunately, the base called me back that evening to help with rescue efforts, so I had to wait until I was done the next day before I could try again. So as soon as they let us go, I mustered my courage and texted Jessie's mom again.

I know I'm probably the last person Jessie wants to hear from, but I just wanted to make sure she's okay.

Honestly, I didn't even think I'd hear back from her. And yet, not a minute later, my phone buzzed.

She's had several transfusions, but the doctor says she should be fine. It's going to take a while, though. They want to make sure she doesn't develop an infection, and she lost a lot of blood.

I paused before responding, wondering how much Mrs. Nickleby must hate me by now. Jessie was steady enough that I knew she didn't give her heart away easily. Even if she didn't consider herself in love, I couldn't imagine her parents would be big fans of mine, particularly if she'd shared my parting sentiments that night of the ball. Five minutes later, I got the gumption to text again.

Thanks, Mrs. Nickleby.

Did I dare ask for her room number? I wanted to…needed to. Even if I hadn't been crazy in love with her, she'd saved my sister's life. That warranted a visit, didn't it? Before I could type back my bold request, another message from Mrs. Nickleby made my phone ding.

She's in room 401. Visiting hours are between four and eight. And she's allergic to baby's breath.

I laughed.

Yes, ma'am.

Maybe I wouldn't have to fight my way into that room after all.

～

I arrived the next day, at six-thirty, roses in hand sans baby's breath. (I'd had to ask the florist what baby's breath even was.) Her mother was in the waiting room and saw me first. She ran toward me, arms open wide. The moment I hugged her back, she was in tears, crying into my shoulder as Jessie's father, who was sitting behind her, gave me a more than slightly disapproving stare. I didn't take offense, though. I'd earned it, and I knew that.

"I'm so glad you're here." She pulled back and looked at me. "Did you just come from work?"

I looked down at my uniform. "Unfortunately, yes. I wanted to be here earlier, but they've had us working overtime with storm rescues and clean up and such."

She nodded and wiped her eyes. "I'm just glad you came." She pulled me toward the hall that led away from the waiting room. "She's asleep," she sniffed. "They think it's going to take weeks for her to recover completely. If someone hadn't put that tourniquet on, they said she probably wouldn't have made it." This brought on a whole new bout of tears, but I didn't say anything because I wasn't too far behind it myself.

The room was dark when I entered, curtains drawn and lights off.

"She's had trouble sleeping, so they're trying to help by keeping it dark," Jessie's mother whispered as we stood at the foot of the bed.

"I won't wake her," I whispered back. I just wanted to look at her. I needed to see the steady rise and fall of her chest and the color in her cheeks. I desperately wanted to touch her, but—

"Here."

I turned to see Mrs. Nickleby handing me a manila folder. Raising my eyebrows in question, I took it.

"I don't know if Jessie ever told you," she looked at her daughter tenderly, "but when she's mad at people, she writes them letters and doesn't send them."

"She mentioned it once."

She nodded at the folder. "Those are for you."

I pulled the first one out of the folder and read the greeting.

Derrick, you pig-faced jerk...

"Well, that's a promising start," I said in a low voice.

She pointed to the date, which was written neatly in the corner. The date itself had been smudged out by a water stain, but the beginning at least read back in May.

"Read the starting dates of each. Then keep reading." She paused and sent Jessie one more look of longing.

"What am I looking for?"

She tilted her head, and for a moment, I could have sworn it was Jessie looking at me twenty years down the road. "I told you you were good for her." And then she left.

I moved closer to sit in the chair beside the bed. My promise not to wake her had been made with good intentions, but I was unable to stop myself from running the backs of my fingers over the side of her face. Then I looked back down at the first letter in a stack that was surprisingly thick.

The first letter was dated for the week we'd first met. Apparently, I'd been getting under her skin for longer than I remembered. I touched her cheek one more time before settling in for a nice, long read.

What started as a humorous trip down Memory Lane, however, quickly became something else altogether. There were fewer letters during our truce, usually only when I'd done something to really annoy her. But the one that made me stop and reread it, however, was the one she wrote the week after the ball.

Derrick,

I'm not going to say dear because I'm angry with you. So angry I can't even think straight.

I knew this was going to happen. The moment I laid eyes on you, I knew you were trouble. Probably the kind of guy to go around making women fall in love with him just for the sport, I told myself. And every time you had her, you would move on to the next challenge. You were hot, and you knew it, and you exploited that fact. Men like you were the exact reason I don't date airmen.

Until I got to know you and realized that's not you at all. You don't swing wildly from woman to woman. You're worse.

You lower defenses and take out the artillery. Then, when it's all clear, you attack. You go for the throat, and you don't take no for an answer. I tried to say no to you. I really did. But you were hopeful in a way no man has ever been about me. And you somehow knew exactly what would unlock my defenses. And I loved and hated you for it. Why did you want me? Why did you need to unlock the sacred places of my heart? It was like walking toward a cliff. I knew better. And I kept trying to change paths. But for every step I took in another direction, you lured me two steps closer.

And you know what's sickening? I let you. Because that stupid voice of hope in my heart said maybe this one would be different. Maybe there would be a way to make this work. I wanted it to work. I had no idea how it would happen, but there was something in your smile and promises and words that made me see that maybe we could have something different from what I'd had planned.

Then you raised me up and dashed me against the rocks because you couldn't have your own way. At least I found out before it was too late.

Ouch. I put the letter down and looked at Jessie again, guilt washing over me like it hadn't in weeks, or maybe even months. Did I even want to finish these letters? I sighed and held up the next one. It was dated for the next day.

You're leaving today. That's what your mom says. Well, I hope you find every-thing you were looking for in this blasted career.

I want to be angry with you. And I am. But I also can't help feeling like a huge chunk of my heart is gone, and I've lost a piece of me that I'm not sure will heal. How did you do that, sliding your way inside and taking part of my me with you? I want you so much it hurts. It's weird going places in my car instead of your infernal truck, and Jade asks for you constantly.

I'm still angry with you, but I'll pray for you nonetheless. Jade needs you, no matter what kind of jerk you are to people your age. Stay safe, and don't do anything stupid.

I moved to the next letter, afraid to see where the spark of hope in my chest was leading me but unable to stop.

So today was Jade's first day back to school. You would have been so proud of her. I know we're not speaking, and I'm still not speaking to you, but I wanted to tell you this anyway. One of the new boys decided to pick on her by tossing crayons at her. I was impressed first, by her ability to ignore him. I was across the room dealing with another behavior issue, so my response time was slower than I would have liked. But he got his just desserts.

They were playing ball at recess, and to my surprise, Jade wanted to play. Now, the game was soccer, but Jade didn't hesitate. She picked the ball up in her hands, and from three feet away, nailed the kid, point-blank in the face.

"Jade!" I called as I ran over to check the boy's nose. "This is soccer! You have to use your feet!"

Jade looked at me for a moment before getting that smug little smile she has and said, "Oops." Then she shrugged and turned away.

The teacher side of me had to make her apologize. I'm required to for my job. But inside, I was cheering her on. That girl isn't going to lie down and take crap from anyone.

Anyhow, I'm still not talking to you. But I thought you should know. I was proud of her. And I knew you would be, too.

As the dates changed, the anger began to dissipate, and I found myself filled with more than a little awe. She'd written to me, and nearly every day at that. Gone were the threats and rants, and instead, they were filled with all the little random things we used to talk about. She told me all about her class and how Jade was progressing, and eventually more about herself.

Okay, if I'm being honest, I've tried for the life of me to picture what our kids would have looked like. I keep trying to see them with green eyes, but all three have blue. I think the girl would have hair like mine, and one of the boys would have your color. Maybe we'd get a ginger in the mix. That would be fun. I've always wanted a red-haired kid.

If I'm still being honest, I have to tell you, this school year is dragging on. That's not supposed to happen, as this is only my second year. I can't be getting tired of it already.

Maybe, though, it has more to do with the fact that you're not here. I didn't realize how much I've isolated myself until you were gone. And now that you're not here, I'm missing it. I miss laughing with you. Arguing with you, if you can believe that.

Final confession, it's like you opened up my heart and plucked out every romantic movie I've ever watched and cried through. And as much as it pains me to say it, I'm beginning to see that you were right. I want a lot of things in life, and as of now, I'm the reason they're not here. I'm the one who wrote the list of rules, and it was my decision to work myself to death through high school and college. And now that I'm here in adulthood where I always wanted to be, it's not enough. Not that God hasn't given me enough. More that...I've been keeping it out. Because I'm terrified to let anything new in. It's so easy to feel like if I can just keep everything planned and plotted, everything will turn out fine.

What do I really want? If I'm being unrealistic here, and completely impractical...I want to marry you. I want you to carry me over the threshold all old fashioned-like. You could tuck me into bed beside you every night. We could squabble to our heart's content until we're old and gray and arguing over which kind of bran cereal is best. I want to stay in Jade's life and watch her grow and mature and discover where she's meant to be in this crazy world. I want to have your babies and raise them beside you. I want to follow you around and have my adventure. And if God decides to cut it short and leave me alone...

Well, you'll have been worth it. I'd rather live a little of my life with you than none of it at all.

I want you, Derrick. Every inch of the godly, infuriating, dutiful man you are.

But my mom's still sick. And there's nothing I can do about that. I used to know where I was in this world and exactly what purpose I served. I was a daughter and a teacher. I sang in the choir, and everything was right. But you've fractured my worldview, and I can't see straight anymore. And as much as I want all this, none of it changes the vast number of variables in military life. That's a risk I just don't think I can take.

Not that it matters. You're fun and adventurous, and I'm a frightened coward. You probably won't want me anymore when you see just how much of the world there is to offer outside Little Rock. And that breaks my heart more than anything else.

I wiped my tears on my sleeve and for a long time, just watched her. She moaned a little sometimes and turned over in the hospital bed several times. After an hour and a half, visiting hours were up, and I made my way back out to the waiting room. Her mother went up to me and pulled me into a hug. I hadn't known I needed one until she did, but as soon as I was in her arms, I cried like a little boy. Finally, she pulled back.

"I know it's hard to understand," she said, sniffling along with me. "Think, though, about your devotion to Jade, and you'll get a glimpse at the way Jessie is determined to take care of me." She laughed, more a sob than a chuckle. "The only difference is that I'm a fully-capable adult with a fully-capable husband, and Jade is not. But even if you could leave her with someone else who you knew was fully capable...would you?"

That question haunted me the rest of the way home. Because I didn't even have to think about it to know the answer.

46

I KNOW

JESSIE

"You feeling okay?"

My mom's voice snapped me out of my reverie.

"I'm sorry, what?" I blinked a few times. For a moment, I'd forgotten that the TV was on or even that I was curled up in my favorite blanket or that I'd been home from the hospital for three days.

She sat down beside me and sipped her tea. "You've been quiet since you've gotten home from the hospital."

"I'm still pretty tired, I guess."

"The doctor said it would be another day or so before that went away." She studied me again, and when she spoke, her voice was lower. "Would it also have anything to do with a certain someone not coming to visit again?"

I tried to smile and shrug it off. "I don't know about that. I guess my brain just isn't up to stuff right now."

"You know what Madison told me?" She continued as if I hadn't spoken at all. "She said that Derrick was the one who made the tourniquet for your arm. And the doctor said if you hadn't had that tourniquet, you probably would have died. The glass was too close to your artery to have survived without it." Her voice dropped nearly to a whisper. "He saved your life, Jessie."

My throat felt too thick and dry to answer. Everything from the tornado was hazy. I remembered grabbing Jade from my classroom and the window blowing out. There had been pain in my arm and blood on my hand. And the train. I would never forget the sound of the train, like it was chugging away over our heads. But sometime during those few minutes in the hall, the world began to tilt, and my vision began to spot. Familiar voices had drifted in and out, and I remember nearly waking when I realized one of the voices was his. And for just a moment, I'd been encompassed by the feeling of security and warmth, like someone was holding me close.

My mom swore he'd come to see me and had even waited with me while I slept. When I woke up and really came to for the first time, there were even pink roses in my room. But that had been the day after the tornado, when I was still sleeping most of the day away, and I hadn't seen him in the week-and-a-half since. Not even a text.

And I think that hurt the worst, knowing he'd been so close, only to retreat again. He was just doing the honorable thing, I was sure. He'd run to the school to check on Jade, and I had just happened to be there. Derrick was the kind of guy who wouldn't leave anyone in peril.

But there had been a kiss somewhere in there…I was sure of it. Then nothing.

"Is your soup all right?" My mom nodded at the bowl in my lap.

I looked down at it. "It's fine." Truth be told, the chicken chunks tasted a lot drier than I had hoped when my mom had ladled it out for me, but I got the feeling that the chicken itself was fine. It was me who had changed.

Two days later, I was cleared to drive. The area up north by the base and school was pretty torn up still, but I was desperate to go somewhere. Between all the visitors and calls to the house phone to ask how I was, I needed to hear myself think. I couldn't bear to tell one more person that I was fine when I wasn't. Because even though my body was mostly healed, my heart felt like it was slowly splitting in two.

Something had to give.

After driving what felt like random circles around town, I finally realized where my wandering had taken me. I parked the car and got out. After a moment of searching for the perfect spot, I lay down on the grassy slope, and I closed my eyes. It was peaceful here, like there had never been a tornado in all the world. The birds sang, and even with my eyes closed, the yellow-green of the afternoon sun-lit leaves filtered through my lids.

What was I supposed to do? I couldn't stay, and I couldn't go. I was stuck. And it already felt like my life had been that way forever.

The roar of an engine interrupted my reverie. I opened my eyes to see a big red truck parked beside my old beat-up car, which had miraculously somehow survived in the school parking lot.

"Your mom said you were gone, but I thought I might find you here."

I sat up, afraid to believe my eyes. "You did?"

He came to sit beside me on the little grassy knoll. Then he looked up at the church. "I'm still amazed this place wasn't even touched."

I nodded, feeling a little dazed. "Yeah. Um, the weather guy said it bounced in a few places before settling in a steady path." I looked up at the white steeple as well. "I guess this was one of them."

We were silent for a few minutes. I couldn't move, but my mind felt like a tornado had ripped around inside my head as well. Every hair on my body seemed to be standing on end, as though lightning was in the air. I felt like a magnetic force was compelling me to sit closer, to touch him to make sure he was real. But I kept my hands to myself.

"Sorry I took so long to stop by again," he said eventually. "They had us working from sunup to sundown cleaning the damage on the base and doing rescues on and off. A bunch of us volunteered to do more, too."

"That's nice of you." I nodded, as though this were an everyday occurrence. But inside, it only added to my trepidation.

More silence. Say something. I needed to say something. This silence held too much...

Too much what? Truth? How much more could the truth hurt?

"I always thought I'd get married here," I finally said.

He looked up, as though I'd pulled him from some reverie of his own.

I nodded at the church. "From the first day we visited, I looked around this place and knew I wanted to get married right here." I plucked a dandelion and studied it as I pulled all the little petals out. "Thought I'd baptize my babies here. Volunteer here. Move through life here. All right here."

"And what about when it changed?" He asked, his blue eyes searching mine. Oh, how I'd missed those eyes.

"Changed?" I echoed.

"You know," he said slowly, leaning back on his hands, "in all the places I've been, change follows you. Even if you stay in the same place forever, everything around you moves."

"I know." My voice was barely a breath. Everything had been perfect. Then he had come and changed it all.

There was another silence. He seemed unsure of what to do with his hands because he opened and closed them again, as though grasping for something I couldn't see.

"I'm moving to Texas in three months," he finally said.

And there it was. The words I'd been waiting for. The ones I knew would one day change the course of my life.

"I can't..." My voice warbled, and it was a moment before I could speak again. He wasn't inviting me to go with him. Just telling me. So did that mean this was goodbye?

"You can't what?" His voice was unusually low and his jaw tight.

"I've tried to imagine life as it should be. Life here forever, living out my fate as I always imagined it." I shook my head and laughed as tears began to spill down my cheeks. Finally, I got the courage to look him in the eyes. "But I can't."

His eyes widened, so I plunged in before I lost my nerve. I'd already turned this man down...and quite rudely at that. It was a wonder he was listening to me at all.

"I can't see myself anywhere else or with anyone else." I reached up gingerly to touch his cheek. "Derrick, I've lived six months without you, and I never want to do it again." I paused. "At least, not without knowing I'm yours, and that no distance is going to change that."

Before I knew what was happening, his hands were on my face, and he was kissing me with a heat that dove into my chest and twirled around my heart. When he pulled away, it was only to rest his forehead against mine.

"Do you know what it felt like," he was breathing in short, ragged gasps, "running up to that school and thinking you and Jade were gone?" His voice broke, and his shoulders shook. Almost in a daze, I put my hands on them. At my touch, he cried even harder.

"I thought..." he choked. "I thought my life was over the moment I saw that building." He looked back up at me, his eyes searching mine, desperate and fierce as his hands traced every angle of my face.

"I thought you were done with me," I whispered. "After you left. After you left, and when Amy came back—"

"Jessie." He sat up. "I have done nothing but regret those things I said to you since the moment they left my mouth. I'm ashamed of the way I treated you and pushed you away. I was just so afraid to lose you." He shook his head. "But I was afraid that the moment I left, Newman or some other schmuck was going to make a move, and you'd come to your senses and marry one of them."

"I tried." I gave another strangled laugh. "But I couldn't even make it through the first date with him before I knew it wasn't going to work."

"Why?" he breathed.

I smiled tremulously. "He wasn't you."

He reached behind him and pulled a familiar blue box from his pocket. And when he opened it, that familiar red rose glistened up at me in the afternoon sun.

"Marry me," he whispered, "and I will make sure you can fly back here whenever your little heart desires. You can see your mother every weekend if that's what you want."

I opened my mouth, but he held his hand up.

"Please hear me out. Look, I have five years left in the military. But if those five years pass and you want me out, just say the word, and we'll never move again. If you want to finish your degree, all you have to do is sign up, and I'll make sure we can afford it. Just…don't make me leave you behind again without knowing you'll be there when I return. Because I don't think I can handle that."

"What about all your travel plans?" I pressed down the corner of his jacket collar and gave him a teasing smile. "All that money saved up to travel."

He shook his head, still holding the ring box between us. "Having you by my side will be the best adventure I could ever have."

I wanted so much to speak. Every word, though, seemed to be stuck in my chest as I tried to take it all in. His look of hope began to look strained as I struggled to find the right words.

"Please say something," he whispered with a nervous smile. "Because if you don't, I'm going to have to resort to singing like the beast. And though I've seen the movie, I can guarantee you that it won't sound anything like that."

"Why?" I whispered. "Why are you so determined to have me?" I thought back to all those horrible things I'd said about and to him, and how cantankerous I'd been on purpose. The way I'd refused him at the ball. All the awful names I'd called him in the letters stashed in my desk drawer.

He got up on his knees and leaned toward me. "I have never," he said, taking a lock of my hair between his fingers, "met anyone like you. I tease you about all your self-assigned duty, but the truth is that you're determined to love those that others won't. You love my sister like she was your own, and you nearly died proving it. You stoop to lift up the weak without a thought for yourself. And I can't think of a better person to have by my side as I face this crazy world."

"Are you proposing again Derrick Allen?" I asked.

"Are you accepting this time, Miss Nickleby?"

I laughed and nodded, tears rolling down my face again as he slid the rose gold ring onto my hand. It fit like it had been made for me.

"What do you think?" he asked, watching me with an intensity that reminded me of a tiger I'd once seen at the zoo.

"It's perfect," I whispered. Then I closed my eyes and shook my head. It was all too much. Too perfect, like the ending of a storybook.

"What's wrong?" he asked, looking slightly alarmed.

"I didn't mean to hurt you the first time." I bit my lip. "I didn't want to. I mean, I wanted to say yes! I really did. I just…I was so afraid…"

"I know."

I looked at him. "You do?"

The corner of his mouth quirked up. "You said so in your letters. Lots."

I felt the blood drain from my face. "How did you get my—"

He grinned wickedly. "Your mother gave them to me."

"Oh no." I lay back in the grass and covered my face with my hands. "She did not."

"She did."

I felt the sudden change in the air. It prickled with electricity, like someone was very near. When I peeked through my fingers, I found him leaning over me, his face inches from mine, one arm on each side of my head.

"I also know," he said, bending until his lips were brushing my ear, and his body was only inches above mine, "that at one point at least, you wanted to have my babies."

Was it possible for one's blush to get stuck forever? Because I thought mine might.

He skimmed his nose down my cheek. "You know that can be arranged."

I should say something. I knew I should. But it was difficult to think with him so close. Deliciously difficult. "You know," I giggled breathlessly, "the pastor's office is just across the parking lot. And he has a window."

"Fantastic." His breath was on my cheek now. "We can just ask him to marry us here and now." He wriggled his eyebrows. "Then we can get started on those babies."

I laughed as he gathered me up in his arms and pulled me tightly against his chest.

"You know what, Derrick Allen?"

"What?"

"I think that's a fantastic idea."

47

THE LONG HAUL

JESSIE

W e did not ask the pastor to marry us then and there. Largely because I still wanted my fairy tale wedding, and also because our mothers would have killed us. Instead, we settled for the week after school got out, two days before Derrick was scheduled to PCS.

Though I'd dreaded the thought of leaving in all my imaginings and dreams, the day I turned in my resignation, I realized I didn't feel a lick of remorse.

"Is this what I think it is?" Mr. Matthews asked when I handed him the folder in his makeshift office. Well, everything was makeshift. After the school was demolished, the district had sent out a bunch of portable classrooms to finish the year in.

"It is." I smiled.

He studied me for a moment before nodding. "Good for you."

I laughed. "I honestly thought I'd feel a lot worse about this than I do."

"I'm not sure if I should take that as a compliment or not, but I'll just chalk it up to your happiness."

"And that," I grinned, "is exactly it."

He tilted his head. "What about your degree?"

I fingered the hem of my sleeve. "I never actually applied. I mean, I was accepted, but that was the farthest I could get myself to go." I shrugged. "I guess I needed a chance to just live for a little while. You know?"

He looked at my resignation letter and smiled. "I actually do."

My mom and Derrick's mom became inseparable overnight. They were slightly put out with me for having purchased a wedding dress on my own years before…the one frivolous purchase I'd made in college without telling a soul. That is, until they saw it for themselves. Princess cut with a gold tint and light pink roses embroidered into the sheer lace that lay atop layers and layers of golden-white tulle that floated centimeters above the ground. Layered silk hung off each shoulder, and the bodice sparkled with crystals. It was like every book and movie I'd ever read sewn into one.

Madison was the one part of my life that marred my shining bliss. She and I hadn't spoken much since I'd turned Sam down. After a year of being nearly inseparable, I had no idea who to make my brides-maids. And once again, I was reminded of just how much I'd cut myself off from other people since I'd begun teaching.

One afternoon, just a few days after getting engaged to Derrick, however, someone knocked on my door. I nearly fell over when Madison was the one standing there. She shifted from one foot to the other and clutched at her purse strap.

"Jessie—"

"Madison—"

I did my best to smile. "You go first."

She took a deep breath, and her eyes never left the floor. "I…I'm here to say sorry. I've been cold and distant, and I kept thinking I knew what was best for you."

Enough to ignore me for six months? I wanted to ask. Instead, I just nodded. "You did sometimes. A lot of times, actually."

She shook her head. "Nothing that deserved the treatment I gave you. I guess…I suppose I was jealous."

I blinked. "Jealous?"

"You had a whole list of guys you wouldn't go out with, and Sam was waiting there in the wings. And you know my track record with men. And I just…I wanted us to go on being what we were forever. But you refusing him meant things were going to change. And I didn't want change." A tear ran down her face. "I know I can act like I've got it all

MY LITTLE ROCK AIRMAN | 303

together a lot, but I really don't. You two were my steady rocks. Without you, I guess I didn't know quite where I belonged in the world anymore. That made me angry, and I took it out on you. And by the time I realized how awful I'd been, too much time had passed to make it up to you." She drew in a shuddery breath. "But the tornado was what really opened my eyes." She shrugged. "Since then, I've been trying to get my courage up to apologize to you, but it's taken this long, and I nearly didn't come today—"

I pulled her into a hug. "I miss you," I whispered.

"You're not mad?" She sniffled.

I probably should be. I should be furious. But I couldn't be. My life was falling into place, and all I was missing was my friend.

"What can I do to make it up to you?" she whimpered.

"Just be happy for me," I whispered.

She gave a choking laugh. "I can do that." Her eyes brightened slightly. "As long as I get to be your maid of honor."

Once Madison was taken care of, packing up was the next hardest thing. Putting twenty-four years of memories into boxes as my mother sobbed happily wasn't exactly my idea of the best day ever, but Dad put on a good face, and then we all went out for boba after, which cheered Mom immensely.

The whole time, she kept repeating, "I've always wanted you to be happy. And now you're all grown up, and it's here." Then she'd burst into sobs again as my dad and I exchanged looks.

There were times, especially as I tried to finish the year with my kids in a portable with very few teaching supplies, that I never thought the wedding would arrive. But Derrick kept me upbeat and laughing with awful pranks and his terrible teasing as the day drew near. And eventually, it arrived.

Waking up the morning of my wedding was somewhat like a dream. For just a second, I was still in my room in my bed, and it was just another Saturday. Then I blinked as the morning light spilled through my blinds, and I knew. This would be the last morning I'd wake up alone. Because this was the day I'd no longer be my own.

Our pastor's wife oversaw all the details with a finesse I was sure most professional wedding planners wouldn't have attained. And in no time at all, I was standing in the lobby for what would be my last time in a long while. My gown made me feel even more a princess than I remembered from the gown shop, and the little gold silken slippers beneath made me feel a lot less likely to fall than the heels the shop lady had recommended.

Jade, who stood in front of me, sported her own little princess dress. Derrick's mother had asked a seamstress to make one that complemented mine, and she couldn't have been prouder. All by herself, she went on her cue and dropped rose petals all the way up the aisle. She had that determined look that said she wasn't stopping for anyone. Which made it all the funnier when she paused in front of Derrick and curtsied before continuing her petal work all the way to her seat.

Madison and my other bridesmaids made their way up the aisle, as did our grandparents, the ring bearer, and parents, minus my dad.

Then it was my turn.

I gripped my dad's arm as the doors opened to the sanctuary. We'd practiced yesterday, of course, but this...

This was like something out of a movie. Garlands of ribbon and flowers hung from vaulted ceilings. The windows all had flowers as well, as did the pews. The music began, and though I knew it wasn't Pachelbel's Canon, as I despised that song, I suddenly forgot what song was even playing. Because at the end of the aisle, just before the pastor, stood Derrick.

His hair was freshly cut with sharp new angles, and he stood tall in his dress blues. He was every part the American warrior any girl might dream about. He was also my protector. And my friend. I felt my breath leave me as I watched him watching me, those blue eyes drawing me in like the flashes of a lighthouse, beckoning me home. And if I'd felt any nervousness or had second thoughts about leaving all I knew behind, they went up in smoke as I floated toward him.

He had been right. Change came whether I wanted it to or not. And my home was no longer with my parents or in Little Rock. It wasn't Phoenix or anywhere else I'd ever laid my head. Home was with Derrick, and where he went, I would go. Where he stayed, I'd stay. And if the military sent him somewhere I couldn't be, my heart would go with him to the ends of the earth, as would my love and my prayers.

Our pastor smiled at us, his eyes warm and very possibly glistening slightly. "Good afternoon, everyone," he said, gesturing for the audience to be seated. "Thank you for joining us as witnesses to the union of this woman and this man. May what God makes one, no man ever seek to part."

No, I thought as I gazed into his face. This was for the long haul. And I couldn't wait to start.

48

HAPPILY EVER AFTER

EPILOGUE

"Texas is a weird state." I stared at the map as we hit a pothole. "On one side, it's all short trees and green fields, and on the other, it's red dirt and…" I looked up. "More red dirt."

"Well, I hope this little addition of red doesn't dampen your spirits." Derrick brought the truck to a stop. I groaned as I stuffed my phone in my purse and turned to look at the house. But when I saw it, my disgust fled and my heart fluttered.

The house was old, made in a sixties style, a one-story red-brick building with a slightly slanted roof. Its shutters and door were painted light blue, and the garden in the front below the main front window was bare except for a skinny rose bush. But the grass was neatly trimmed, the shutters were painted to match the door, and there was a sweet little window that would be perfect for a Christmas tree. The siding above the brick was clean and white, and the way the sun was coming through the back window I could just barely make out through the front window made me want to curl up in its rays with a warm book. Something inside me warmed the moment I took it all in. I couldn't say exactly how, but somehow, I knew.

"This is it," I said, staring with love at the little L-shaped house.

Derrick laughed. "We haven't even been inside. And you've said that about the last two houses they've shown us."

But I was already out of the car, unable to look away. "This is it. I know it."

Derrick shook his head and turned off the engine. But when he caught up to me, he intertwined his fingers with mine and dug into his pocket for the key the base housing office had loaned us with his other hand, and my heart jumped even more. This was going to be our house.

The inside wasn't grand. The countertops were linoleum rather than marble, and the kitchen floor, also linoleum, had several stains on it. There was carpet instead of hardwood, half-closets in the bedrooms instead of whole, and it was easy to see where holes in the wall from picture frames hung by former renters had been painted over. But just as with the outside, there was a hominess to it that even Derrick couldn't deny. From the big windows, which would be perfect to show-case a Christmas tree next winter, to the cozy little rooms, everything was perfect for us. And for one of the first times in my life, I was completely at peace.

"You sure you're okay with this?"

I turned to see Derrick studying me.

"What do you mean?"

"Well," he scratched his neck, "this isn't exactly the ritz. Especially after the house your parents have." He shook his head. "I guess I'm just not convinced you're ready to move just yet."

I smiled and ran my hands up his chest. "Does that help?"

He kissed the top of my head. "Maybe a little."

I sighed and leaned back to look at him without letting go. "Leaving my parents was one of the hardest things I've ever done. Just like leaving Jade was hard for you. And if I'm honest, I'm going to worry about my mother until the day she dies, just like you're going to worry about Jade. But this…" I paused and looked around. "Abilene is where we're supposed to be. God put us here. And where He puts us is where I want to be. And I can't really say what it is about this house that tells me, but this is it. This is where we belong."

He quirked an eyebrow. "Even if that means waiting five years to move back?"

I shrugged. "You never know. If the adventures are good enough, I may ask for more."

Before I knew what he was doing, Derrick had grabbed my waist, lifted me off the carpet, and sat me up on the kitchen counter. His lips were hot on mine as his hands explored my back and then slid back down my waist.

"You know," he said into the kiss, not opening his eyes, "this place actually is the perfect size. More than enough room to make some of those babies you were talking about."

"A perfect place," I whispered, "to begin our happily ever after."

And that's just what we did.

Dear Reader,
Thank you for reading My Little Rock Airman.
If you'd like more of Jessie and Derrick, visit BrittanyFichterFiction.com. *By joining my email list, you'll get free access to:*

An exclusive secret chapter from My Little Rock Airman

You'll get secret chapters, sneak peeks at books before they're published, chances at giveaways, and much more.

Sign me up!

Also, if you liked the book, it would be a huge help to me if you could leave an honest review on Amazon or Goodreads so others can find my work, which in turn, helps me to keep writing.

<u>Coming soon…</u>

My Carolina Airman (My Air Force Fairy Tale Book #2)

"This was a magic I'd long forgotten existed."

ALSO BY BRITTANY FICHTER

COMING SOON IN THE MY AIR FORCE FAIRY TALE SERIES...
My Carolina Airman
My Las Vegas Airman

∼

The Classical Kingdoms Collection
Before Beauty: A Retelling of Beauty and the Beast
Blinding Beauty: A Retelling of The Princess and the Glass Hill
Beauty Beheld: A Retelling of Hansel and Gretel
Girl in the Red Hood: A Retelling of Little Red Riding Hood
Silent Mermaid: A Retelling of The Little Mermaid
Cinders, Stars, and Glass Slippers: A Retelling of Cinderella
A Curse of Gems: A Retelling of Toads and Diamonds

∼

The Classical Kingdoms Collection Novellas
The Green-Eyed Prince: A Retelling of the Frog Prince

∼

The Autumn Fairy Trilogy
The Autumn Fairy
The Autumn Fairy of Ages
The Last Autumn Fairy

∼

Historical Fantasy Romance

Clara's Soldier: A Retelling of The Nutcracker

~

The Entwined Tales

1. A Goose Girl: A Retelling of The Goose Girl - KM Shea

2. An Unnatural Beanstalk: A Retelling of Jack and the Beanstalk - Brittany Fichter

3. A Bear's Bride: A Retelling of East of the Sun, West of the Moon - Shari L. Tapscott

4. A Beautiful Curse: A Retelling of The Frog Bride - Kenley Davidson

5. A Little Mermaid: A Retelling of The Little Mermaid - Aya Ling

6. An Inconvenient Princess: A Retelling of Rapunzel - Melanie Cellier

ABOUT THE AUTHOR

Brittany lives with her Prince Charming, their little fairy, and their little prince in a ~~sparkling~~ (decently clean) castle in whatever kingdom the Air Force has most recently placed them. When she's not writing, Brittany can be found enjoying her family (including their spoiled black Labrador), doing chores (she would rather be writing), going to church, belting Disney songs, exercising, or decorating cakes.

Facebook: Facebook.com/BFichterFiction
Subscribe: BrittanyFichterFiction.com
Email: BrittanyFichterFiction@gmail.com
Instagram: @BrittanyFichterFiction
Twitter: @BFichterFiction

My Other Blogs:

BrittanyFichterWrites.com

MY LITTLE ROCK AIRMAN

My Little Rock Airman / Brittany Fichter. -- 1st ed.

Cover Art and Design by Daniel Perlstein

Edited by Kimberly Kessler

Made in the USA
Monee, IL
22 January 2020

20632913R00187